T0204297

GLASS SOULS

Maurizio de Giovanni

GLASS SOULS
MOTHS FOR COMMISSARIO RICCIARDI

Translated from the Italian
by Antony Shugaar

Europa
editions

Europa Editions
214 West 29th Street
New York, N.Y. 10001
www.europaeditions.com
info@europaeditions.com

Copyright © 2015 Maurizio de Giovanni
This edition published in arrangement
with The Italian Literary Agency and book@ literary agency
First Publication 2017 by Europa Editions

Translation by Antony Shugaar
Original title: *Anime di vetro. Falene per il commissario Ricciardi*
Translation copyright © 2017 by Europa Editions

Library of Congress Cataloging in Publication Data is available
ISBN 978-1-60945-409-8

de Giovanni, Maurizio
Glass Souls

Book design by Emanuele Ragnisco
www.mekkanografici.com

Cover photo by Massimiliano Ghionna

Prepress by Grafica Punto Print – Rome

Printed in the USA

To Mamma Edda, for her song and for all the songs.
To Patrizia, enchantment within enchantment.

GLASS SOULS

T he young man narrows his eyes in order to accustom them to the room's dim light. The blazing afternoon sun stretches its fingers through the slats of the tightly fastened shutters, and dust dances in the light. The woman of indeterminate age who ushered him in now slips silently away, closing the door behind her with a faint click.

The young man stands there. He can just make out the outlines of the furniture, piles of books, and a shapeless mass, perhaps an armchair, from which comes the sound of labored breathing. He waits. He shifts the weight of his body from one foot to the other. Maybe the man's asleep, he thinks to himself; the woman didn't say a word. I wonder who she is: a housekeeper. His daughter. Some relative.

He makes up his mind to venture a greeting and says buongiorno, in a faint voice.

Welcome, says the armchair. Open the window, if you please.

The voice is scratchy, the words slurred. He must have been sleeping, thinks the young man, feeling he's been rude. Forgive me, he murmurs, you'd asked me to come at three and I . . .

I know that, says the armchair, brusquely. Open the window, just one side though. If you please.

Taking care where he sets his feet out of fear he might knock something over or step on something, the young man makes his way to the window and opens one shutter. The light comes flooding in, a powerful glare that makes him blink. He takes a quick glance out at the stunning panorama, though it impresses him *less than it did before, when he sat on the low wall outside for a full hour, waiting for the appointed time. The sea stretches out, glittering, before him, and the island seems close enough to reach out and grab.*

He turns around. The light washes over a dusty bookcase packed to bursting with volumes, phonograph records, knick-knacks, and objects of all shapes and sizes. The room isn't particularly large, or perhaps it just looks smaller because of the immense number of things in it. The young man's eyes wander the room curiously. Now the armchair, set off to one side, just out of the shafts of light angling in through the window, reveals its guest.

I know what you're looking for, says the old man. It's right behind you.

The young man turns around and sees it; or perhaps we should say, he sees the case containing it. He steps aside, moving away from it as if driven by an impulse of respect and shyness. The old man laughs softly.

Bring it here, he says. And come over here and sit by me.

As he says it, he clears a bundle of papers off a low stool, a foot or two away from the armchair. By now his eyes are used to the light, and the young man recognizes the musical staffs, the notes that run the width of the paper. Outside, a dove coos insistently for a couple of seconds, and then flies away.

You play the mandolin very well, says the old man. You're good. Really good.

The young man is tempted to ask how the old man knows that and where he heard him play. But the old man hadn't asked him a question, and the young man has learned to answer only when he is asked.

The old man goes on: I came once to hear you play. I'd been told about you, and when you asked to meet with me, I became even more curious. You're good. And you have a nice voice, too.

He sits without speaking for a while, and the young man

finally can't resist: did you really come to hear me play? Then why didn't you let me know you were there? I . . . it would have been an enormous honor. It was, certainly, an enormous honor. I'd have . . . well, I'd have welcomed you in the manner you deserve.

Once again, the old man laughs softly. That's exactly why I didn't let anyone know. I wanted to hear you the way you are. I wanted to hear what you know how to do. Give it to me.

The old man takes the case in his hands. He can't play, thinks the young man. His hands are gnarled and twisted with arthritis, and if I'm not mistaken they're shaking. He's an old man. I was wrong to come, there's nothing he can give me. An old man.

You must be thinking that I'm an old man, says the old man. Nothing but a poor old man. And you look at my hands, all twisted. They're shaking. And you're probably thinking: how on earth can he even play?

No, no, says the young man, how can you say such a thing? You . . . your name is a legend, for all of us. I'd never dare.

The old man nods.

It's true, I'm old. And I wouldn't be able to play, if you only used your hands to play. Not the way you do, when you play with just your hands.

There's a certain harshness in the old man's voice. Like an accusation. And yet there's been no change in his tone, which remains flat and low. A shiver runs through the young man, who asks: Why do you say that? What do you mean?

The old man doesn't answer right away. He looks at the light pouring in through the window: from where he's sitting he can't see the water, nothing but a patch of sky with a cloud that's half white and half pink in the slanting beams of the setting sun.

I mean that there's more than just one way of playing. There are plenty of ways. You play the mandolin well and you have a fine voice, you don't hit wrong tones and you even have nice finger technique. That's a good foundation.

Foundation for what? the young man would like to ask. But he restrains himself. There's something about that old man that keeps him from speaking. He thinks confusedly to himself that he ought to be asking questions, expressing opinions. I'm the one who asked to see him, after all. He must think I'm a fool, he tells himself.

He clears his throat. I, in other words, didn't come here for . . . yes, the mandolin is fine. But I'd also like . . . I know that I'm good. That is, people tell me so, they come to hear me play. But I think, I think that there ought to be something more, no? I have a teacher, I still study, I've already graduated, but I know that I need to keep studying. And that's why I've come to see you.

The old man coughs into a handkerchief, a thick, rheumy cough. He reaches a hand out toward the side table, and the young man leaps to his feet and gets him a glass half full of water. The old man drinks, thanks him with a nod of his head, and puts the handkerchief away in one of the pockets of his smoking jacket. For the first time, the young man catches a conscious whiff of the smell of old age that fills the room: a pungent aftersmell underlying the old paper, the dust, and the years.

The old man uses his thumbs to snap open the latches on the case. Ever since he asked the young man to hand it to him, he's been holding the case in his lap as if it were a baby.

The sound is perfectly synchronized, as if those two latches were just a single latch. A sharp snap, a gunshot.

The deformed, hooklike hands pull the small, fat-bellied musical instrument out of the case. The young man greedily eyes the gentle curves of the body, the neck inlaid with mother-of-pearl and ivory, the four pairs of strings. He realizes that he's been holding his breath and he exhales, rather loudly. He's in the presence of a legend.

The old man shifts forward in the armchair, slightly bending one leg and carefully setting the case down on the floor. His trembling fingers run the length of the instrument until they reach the pegs. The young man realizes, to his enchantment, that the old man is adjusting the tension of the strings by memory, without listening to the sound. Impossible, he thinks. That's impossible.

The old man looks up at the young man. Now his face is perfectly lit and the young man can see the web of deep creases, the complexion as dark as leather, the sparse white hair, too long, and the thin lips. The eyes, whitened with cataracts and yet still curious, intense.

In his right hand a pick has appeared. The young man wonders where that popped out from, because he never saw him extract it from the case or from his pockets: maybe, he thinks to himself, it was stuck between the strings. The old man strums a harmonious chord, proving that, incredibly enough, he has perfectly tuned the instrument. The deep sound hovers and throbs in the air for several seconds.

The young man tries to break the inexplicable tension that has seized hold of him. He says: Maestro, I wanted to ask you if you'd give me a few lessons. I know that you don't give lessons to anyone, that you say there is no one deserving of . . . That no one knows anymore what it means to really play the instrument. But I, I'm really in love with this music, and I'd like . . . I want to learn. I'm not looking for success, you saw for yourself, you've been told that lots of people come to hear me play. People are satisfied with how I play. But it's me that . . . I'm not satisfied, Maestro. I study and study, I play and I play, but I'm never happy with what comes out. I want to learn, really learn, Maestro. I'm begging you.

The old man has dropped his gaze to the array of wood and strings that he holds in his hands. He caresses that object, as if the young man's words were nothing but the sound of the wind coming through the window and rattling the sheets of paper on the desk.

A story, says the old man.

What? asks the young man, caught off guard.

A story. Every song is a story.

The young man decides that the old man hasn't heard a word he said and is simply following his own line of thought. He's an old man, after all. A poor senile old man. He can't teach me anything, I'm just wasting my time here. He is sorely tempted to get up and walk out of that grim old antiques shop.

Just as he's about to get to his feet, the old man plays.

It's the introduction to a very famous song, one of the songs that he, the young man, plays every night to the impassioned applause of his audience; the same chords, the same tempo. And yet the young man feels as if he's hearing it for the first time. The old man's hands, those shaky, deformed claws, have turned into the wings of birds, running up and down the mandolin's short neck, as light as air, as intense as water.

At the end of the introduction, the old man stops, and looks up, into the young man's face.

You play very well. But you're not satisfied, and you're right not to be, because you're far away, very far from the place you want to reach. Because you sing, but you don't tell a story.

What do you mean, Maestro? The lyrics? Do I need to improve my delivery, should I . . .

The old man laughs, and it sounds like sandpaper against wood.

No, not just the lyrics. The instrument, you see it? It tells the story, and it must say what the words to the song say. It's not there as accompaniment, the instrument: it needs to tell the story too. It has its own words, it comments on everything you say, it underlines it.

And it sings on its own.

The young man is afraid even to draw a breath, and his expression looks like a question mark. The old man laughs again.

Do you know "Palomma 'e notte"? Do you really know what the song says?

The song that he plays every night, the applause, the dissatisfaction deep within.

Maybe I don't, Maestro. Maybe I don't know at all.

The old man nods. Bravo. Bravo. That's the way you ought to be: humble. You're a part of the instrument, just like the strings, just like the spruce wood the body is made of. Maybe I don't know, he said. Did you hear him?

He's talking to his instrument, thinks the young man. What am I doing here? Then he remembers about the introduction, and decides to sit still on that stool.

The old man talks as if he's telling a fairy tale to a child.

He is forty-five years old, and she is twenty-six. She writes him a letter, she tells him that she's in love with him, head over heels in love. He doesn't know what to do: she is beautiful, she is tall. Lovely. He likes her very much. But he feels like an old man. He thinks: this isn't what's best for her, this love. "I" am not what's best for her.

He tells her these things, but she insists: what's best for me is my decision. If you don't want me, you just need to tell me: I don't want you. But he does want her, he very much wants her indeed; so he can't tell her that, in all good conscience. He thinks it over: what should he do? It's evening and he's at the window, and a gust of sweet, warm wind is coming in just like now, and a palummella, a moth, approaches, drawn by the flame of his sleepless candle.

That's what a song is good for. A song tells a story. A song enters into a story and changes it. He writes a poem, goes to a friend of his who's a musician. And that is how he tells her.

The old man drops his gaze, caresses the instrument.

And he sings, with a young man's voice. The young man thinks, as he listens: no, not a young man's voice, a man's voice. The voice of a forty-five-year-old man, speaking to a young woman.

Tiene mente 'sta palomma,
comme ggira, comm'avota,
comme torna n'ata vota
'sta ceroggena a tentà!

Palumme', chist'è nu lume,
nun è rosa o giesummino,
e tu a fforza ccà vvicino
te vuo' mettere a vulà!

Vattenn' 'a lloco!
Vattenne, pazzarella!
Va', palummella, e torna,
e torna a 'st'aria
accussí fresca e bella!
'O bbí ca i' pure
mm'abbaglio chianu chiano,
e ca mm'abbrucio 'a mano
pe' te ne vulè caccià?

(Watch this moth,
the way it spins, the way it flutters,
the way it turns once again
to venture close to this candle!

Little butterfly, this is fire,
not a rose or a jasmine
and you insist on flying
so very close to it!

Get out of here!
Get away, silly thing!
Go, little butterfly, and go back
go back into this air

so cool and clear!
You see that I, too,
am slowly being dazzled
and that I'm burning my hand
as I try to shoo you away?)

I

Sitting looking out at the September night, Ricciardi contemplated his new solitude.

This solitude was a different companion from the solitude he had always known. The solitude that had gone before was his awareness that he existed along a borderline; a place of madness and despair, filled with screams of the dying and the living, screams that go on echoing, but only to his unfortunate senses. The solitude that he had known from his earliest childhood was a subtle, all-pervading malaise, a reminder of sorrow that continually surfaced to break the skin of an existence that had no way of being normal.

Through the half-open window came a breath of wind that tossed the curtains in the darkness. Far away, but enhanced by the silence, a voice was singing who knew what song, carrying all the way to his ear incomprehensible sounds that distance stripped of any harmony. September. The memory of warmth, the promise of coolness. Windows open, windows closed.

And yet, thought Ricciardi, this new companion, compared to the old one, is like the sea compared to a lake.

These days, he no longer slept more than a few hours every night. He, who had always found in deep, untroubled sleep his refuge and comfort from the muted cries that echoed in his head as he walked through the dead and the living, cries that maliciously and insistently befuddled his senses. He, who had never taken more than a few minutes to fall asleep, turning off all sensory perceptions as if he'd flipped a switch in search of peace, at least during the nighttime.

With his eyes wide open, staring at the ceiling, he hoped that he was just caught in some nightmare, that he still had a chance to awaken into that world that might have once been hellish, but which he now understood could become a far more horrible inferno than it had ever been before.

Rosa.

Rosa as she smiles at him while singing an incomprehensible lullaby, in a dialect so old that it's long since been forgotten.

Rosa as she checks his temperature by pressing her lips to his forehead, and then hurries off to make him an infusion of wood sorrel, chervil, and lettuce that is far worse than any sore throat.

Rosa as she moves around the house muttering under her breath, until you don't even hear her anymore because she turns into an agreeable background noise.

Rosa as she keeps shaking salt into the water she washes the linen in, to make sure it doesn't freeze stiff when she hangs it out to dry, pretending she doesn't know perfectly well that here in the city the temperature never drops below freezing, even in the middle of winter.

Rosa as she begs him, enjoins him, supplicates and threatens him to find a woman who can take care of him once she's no longer around to do so.

Ricciardi was now discovering, to his immense regret, that he had never believed her. He had never really been able to imagine that his *tata*, the only real flesh-and-blood and blankets-and-food mother that he'd ever had, would actually leave this life on a July night, during that same summer that now seemed to gasp along, determined not to die the way it normally did every year in September.

Why didn't you ever tell me that you really would be gone someday? Why didn't you make me understand that all those threats concealed some deeper malaise, something that went much deeper than the petty, pointless aches and pains you complained about from dawn to dusk, though you did it so that you would be told: No, you weren't old at all.

And I can't even see you, now, sitting on the bed beside me. Obsessively repeating your message of farewell, like so many other dead souls I meet on the street, in the parks, in rooms, and in alleys, screaming and whispering the half thoughts that death had interrupted, singing their song of sorrow. An immense chorus for just one solitary spectator: my madness.

You just left us, and that was that.

The wound torn open in his life by Rosa's death, Ricciardi thought, would never heal. It would leave an unmended scar, ready to bleed again every time that a word, a sound, or a glance brought back his childhood and youth to the eyes of memory. A dull, pulsating grief, ready to renew itself over and over again. He understood only now, he who had become acquainted with suffering ever since he was a child, just how terrible it was to suffer a loss like that one.

He was helped a little by the presence of Rosa's niece Nelide, who so closely resembled her. Rosa had just had the time to prepare her; one last, extraordinary gift to soften a bit the pang of missing her. Sometimes, with a sidelong glance, when he was rather distracted, Ricciardi almost thought he could perceive the presence of his old *tata*, because of how strongly the young woman echoed Rosa's physical appearance and ways; and in fact everything at home remained unchanged, as if home economics were a single, well known piece of sheet music and Nelide were simply continuing to play the same tune.

But there was more, Ricciardi reflected as he watched the September night slide toward dawn. Now he was alone. Even in his most absurd dreams, the ones he allowed himself in the most tightly closed room of his tormented soul.

Through the darkness, and without seeing it, his eyes wandered in search of the window in the palazzo across the alley.

That window was only a few yards away, and half a floor down. The window opened into a kitchen, as far as he could tell; a large kitchen where a sizable family gathered to eat and where, after washing up, a tall, bespectacled young woman with an enchanting smile that flowered when least expected would sit and embroider, left-handed.

He had watched for months and months those slow, methodical motions; season after season, through the rain that pounded on the windowpanes, in the baking summer nights, the movement of that hand, the tilt of that head, the gleam of light on those lenses had entranced and captivated him. Certain he was unseen, in the shelter of darkness, he had fallen in love with the life he knew he could never hope to have. And he had gradually identified with that serene and sweet-natured young woman the absurd hope of his own happiness.

The green shoot of that dream had slowly sunk roots.

Who knows, perhaps someday he'd find the strength to share his terrible condition of mental illness. Or perhaps love, and the need to take care of someone, would muffle the howls of the dead that he met on every street corner. And the desert in which he forced himself to live might stop being an unappealable sentence.

Rosa's impending death had driven him to commit a desperate act. He had gone to see Enrica, who had run away in search of some sense of equilibrium outside of that impossible love story. He had been able to track her down because Enrica's father, encouraged by the love he felt for his daughter to break the bonds of privacy that his own upbringing and personality imposed upon him, had finally told him where she was and what she felt in her heart.

But now the night had progressed to that instant of absolute hovering suspension that comes just before the light. This was the moment when Ricciardi, wide-awake and tormented, knew that he would have to face up, defenseless, to his own loneliness. The moment in which he would have to level with himself. Through the window came that faraway song, made clearer by the wind that tugged its sound along. He was able to make out a few words, it was a man's voice: in dialect, but comprehensible. *Get out of here! Get away, silly thing! Go, little butterfly, and go back go back into this air so cool and clear!*

He had managed to find Enrica. He had seen her in the moonlight, beneath the stars. He had glimpsed her, dressed in white, lovelier and happier than he remembered her. If she had been alone, he would have told her that Rosa was at death's door. He'd have told her how sorry he was, for everything. And that he wished he could find a common acquaintance to introduce them properly. And write her ever more impassioned letters, and request of her father the honor and permission to take her to the cinema, or out to dance. If only she'd been alone, he would have taken her hand and, perhaps with tears in his eyes, he could have told her about his perennial sorrow.

But she hadn't been alone.

Through the darkness, his ravenous green eyes had glimpsed a man's blond hair, broad shoulders, and chiseled profile as he'd leaned closer to her. For a kiss.

You see that I, too, am slowly being dazzled, said the distant song, *and that I'm burning my hand as I try to shoo you away?*

Alone, thought Ricciardi. Alone without so much as a crazy dream to keep me company. But at least you'll be happy, my love. You'll have a husband who'll love you completely, by the light of day, without visions of cadavers whispering mysterious words and vomiting blood out of their twisted mouths. And you'll have limpid, serene children, so different from what mine would have been like.

He realized that he was starting to be able to make out the shapes of things around him. The night had lost its battle.

Silently, he got to his feet, to face once again that cruel enemy that was life.

II

They're singing. What they have to sing about, I couldn't say. Maybe they just sing to keep from going crazy, and in so doing, they drive everyone else crazy.

And this air, the same air as outside. It seems impossible. I remember this weather, September, when we'd return from the holidays and Papa would console me because I wasn't going to see my pony, Bianchino, until we returned again next year. Damned Bianchino. Damn you, Bianchino, because you're the one who gave me my passion for horses.

Night, sweet air, and songs. Once those were enough to make me happy. No, that's not true, they weren't enough: I needed that gleeful anxiety, that instant of dolorous anticipation. Because that's what gambling is all about: the moment of anticipation. It's better than wine, better than opium, better than two whores at the same time. When four racehorses round the curve and come galloping down the straightaway, head to head, frothing at the mouth, foam on their coats. Or when the dice tumble irregularly, leaping and tilting: on one face is good fortune, on the other, catastrophe. When the roulette ball hops along, searching for the right number only to miss it by a hair and land in the wrong slot. When the dealer gives you a pair of cards and you lift a corner, your heart in your mouth.

Four paces by two, and how high can the ceiling be? Ten feet, if that. And this tiny window, with a wall right outside and a bit of sky without stars. Even the stars are ashamed to show their faces. Even they are afraid of losing their minds, if they look in here. And this guy sings and sings, and no one shouts for him to shut up.

My love, my love. My great, sweet love. Who knows if you're awake, right now. Who knows if you're thinking of me, if you even understand what I did for you. Who knows if the moon caresses your profile, if it laps at your skin.

I did wrong, and now I'm paying. That's how it works, right? I've paid every penny that I owed. Every time I lost, I paid. With money, real estate, fortunes. I paid servants, carriage, automobile. I paid respect, honor. I even paid my name. I caused suffering, and I'm causing it now, and I'll go on causing more. My mother died of shame. And yet I know that, if I had the opportunity, I'd stop again to watch the dice tumble, and I'd make a bet, and I'd win ten for every thousand I lost.

Night, September night. When will you be over? And when will that wretched man stop singing?

Bars. Bars on the window, bars at the door. Bars that let air through, but not people. Bars to keep freedom at a distance.

Sleep, that's what I ought to do. I should sleep without dreaming. If I'd had the strength, I'd have died then, when I understood there was no way back. Instead of causing death. Damn you, I hate you still. Even now, I'd still yearn to see you dead, another hundred times, and another hundred times I'd tell you that I thirsted to see you dead, you cowardly beast, you ill-born bastard risen up from the slime. But it would have been far better if I'd died in your place, and long before you.

Because people like me, you know, are unfit for life. We're people unprepared for utter ruin. Whereas you, cursed wretch, would have known very well how to move out of the mud from which you came, you who are the son and the grandson of no one, whereas I can count back ten generations prior to myself. And this night I see them all, my ancestors, who've been waiting for me, to tell me to my face what they think of me for selling their name. Tonight, when I have nothing to drink in this place, when I can't get myself drunk to get to sleep and stop thinking, or even just to stop having to listen to this cursed song.

I, Count Romualdo Palmieri di Roccaspina. I, who owned the lands of a king. I, who received an unbroken procession of visitors for three days when I was born, and more gifts of silver and gold than any prince, and now I've gambled it all away, right down to the last gram, without pity.

It would have been better if I'd died in that baby bunting. Died before you, you cursed shitty cowardly loan shark, you who have never tempted fate because instead you forced fate to do just as you pleased. And yet, even tonight, as this starless sky turns from black to milky white, before day dawns again upon my disgrace, I still can't wholeheartedly wish I had never met you.

God, when will this song come to an end? This love song that's devastating me.

The last night. She has decided that this is the last night she'll spend wide awake, awaiting the dawn. The last night, though she doesn't know why.

She's asked herself a thousand times, maybe ten thousand times, over the past three months. Why did he do it? What motive could he have had?

Fine, agreed, he's sick; he's unstable, unbalanced. She's spent dozens of nights wandering around in sordid alleys, searching for him at addresses scrawled on the backs of lottery tickets, with the ink blurred by tears and rain. Dozens of nights standing in the shadows, hiding from filthy, slobbery individuals, to make sure that he didn't meet his death with a knife in his belly, caught up in some drunken brawl. Terrible nights, which even now leave her with a trembling fit of fever and fear, though even those nights weren't as atrocious as these, with their torment and their doubt.

Because she knows that he is innocent.

She knows that that night he was asleep in his bed, in the other room, just a dozen feet away from her. The usual, restless sleep, besieged by ghosts and wine, tossing and turning in the throes of who knows what monsters generated by a guilty conscience and the fear of the sun he knew would rise tomorrow.

She knows that if blood was shed that night, it wasn't his hand that spilled it.

She knows that a man, however mad, however sick, however cowardly and false he might be, still isn't the devil in the flesh and cannot simultaneously be in two places at the same time.

And so she has decided that this is the last night she'll spend without taking concrete steps to discover the truth. To find out why he claimed to have done it.

She turns once again toward the half-open balcony door. The curtains are tossing to the last gust of night wind. By now, day is dawning.

She knows very well what she needs to do. She decided it days ago, weeks ago. It was just a matter of finding a bit of courage, and this last night without sleep brought it to her.

She clearly remembers the man's name. Odd, because she usually doesn't have much of a memory for names. And yet she remembers his name clearly, even though his face is bound up with another moment of fear and fury.

But in particular, what she remembers about that man is his gaze.

And the pity that she had read in the depths of those incredible green eyes.

III

Brigadier Raffaele Maione was worried.

The night before, in bed, when he had told his wife Lucia about it, she had smiled and replied, you're always worried. If you're not worried about money at the end of the month, you're worried about work. Or about this son, or that daughter, or about me. You worry incessantly, and when you're not worrying you start to fret about the fact that you're not worried about anything at all. That's your nature, it's the way you are.

In effect, the brigadier had to admit he had an apprehensive personality; though for that matter, he'd like to see how anyone in his place, with the dangers that his profession showed him on a daily basis and five children of various ages, plus Benedetta, who by now was more of a daughter than his other children, and who'd been living with them for nearly a year. The world wasn't a safe place, and this city was even less safe than the world at large.

There were times when he couldn't understand how she did it, Lucia, how she could remain so serene and unconcerned with the times they lived in, with the Fascists who never missed an opportunity to show that they were in command, knocking people over the head with billy clubs and delivering kicks with those horrible jackboots. And you'd think that the terrible loss they'd suffered when Luca, their firstborn, died would only have increased her fear. But instead she said to him, playfully mocking him, that they couldn't imprison their children after all, couldn't keep them from having friends. After all, she reminded him, the two of them had met in the streets, hadn't they?

Maione, though, just couldn't calm his nerves. If he cared for someone and he imagined that that someone was unwell or in danger, then he inevitably got upset and tried to do everything in his power to protect them. That was intrinsic to his nature as a man and as a father.

And now he was worried, very worried.

He was worried about Ricciardi.

At police headquarters, no one shared his anxiety, he knew. The commissario was disliked by his colleagues, and wasn't especially popular with his superior officers and his underlings either. Not because he was arrogant or a bully, nor inclined to insubordination or possessed of an outsized temper. He wasn't undisciplined, and he was anything but a lazy good-for-nothing; and yet there was something about his personality that made him everyone dislike him. Too shy and silent, never cheerful, never entirely open with others; in that backward, superstitious city, the idea had spread that he possessed something of an evil eye, and people avoided him like the plague.

His finer qualities, such as the ability to get to the crux of the most intricate cases, never missing a day of work, willingly taking on the most burdensome tasks, and never complaining about working the least appetizing shifts, rather than attracting the benevolence of others instead conferred a somewhat inhuman quality upon him that simply accentuated his distance from his colleagues. Only Maione was absolutely devoted to him, and with that devotion came an awkward, rough-hewn affection. Beneath that rough exterior and aside from those silences, the brigadier had always perceived in his superior a profound sensibility and the dull reflection of a constant, deeply human sorrow. It was Ricciardi who, sparing no effort and working as if it had been his own personal loss, had conducted the investigation into the murder of Maione's son Luca, and that was something the brigadier would never forget, even though he later realized that every single violent death was seen by the commissario as a personal, unerasable wound.

That was what he liked best about that skinny man, who wore no hat, who had green eyes: a silent humanity that had no need of the sobbing and shouting and overstated displays that were so much a part of the spirit and behavior of that city. Ricciardi knew how to suffer, and he directed the force of his suffering into stubborn, in-depth, relentless investigations that inevitably led him to crack murder cases; and this in the full knowledge and understanding, shared by Maione, that finding a murderer, unfortunately, never meant bringing the victim back to life.

But now there was no mistaking the fact that something inside the man had snapped. The death of Signora Rosa, the *tata* who had always been his entire family, constituted a devastating loss, and this, thought the brigadier, was all too understandable. No one grasped the proper weight of family in a man's life more than Maione did, even a man as closed and reserved as the commissario.

He had been at the man's side when it was necessary to take care of the formalities required for the transfer of Rosa's corpse to Fortino, the Cilento town where both the woman and Ricciardi himself had been born and raised, and he had accompanied him to the train in a strange, tiny procession made up of Rosa's niece, Nelide, who so resembled her aunt, Dr. Modo with his inseparable leashless dog that followed him like a shadow, and the dark silhouette of the widow Vezzi's car. He remembered that scalding hot day, with an infernal sun beating down mercilessly. The blistering air seemed to stand still, and it was hard to take so much as a breath.

Dr. Modo had told him that poor Rosa hadn't suffered, and that she had slid from sleep into death with serenity, watched over by Nelide who had never moved an inch from the old woman's bedside the whole time. The doctor was fascinated by the silent force of that solid and homely young woman. Her permanently furrowed brow and her large nose, jutting above the brown fuzz on her upper lip, combined with the fact that she only expressed herself in dry proverbs, uttered through clenched teeth, and yet she had displayed an absolute dedication that, upon the death of her aunt, had transferred itself wholeheartedly to Ricciardi.

The commissario too had been close to his old *tata* all through her last days, save for a brief absence the night of her death, and yet he had never neglected his professional duties. Maione had worked beside him to solve the case of the professor of medicine who'd fallen from the window of his office at the general hospital, and he had seen no slackening in the legendary close attention that Ricciardi always devoted to his investigations, even though there was no missing the immense burden that was crushing his heart.

When he had returned from Cilento with Nelide, in the face of the brigadier's polite questions he had replied curtly, saying that now Rosa rested in peace next to his own mother and everything had been taken care of; still, Maione sensed that something about him had changed.

He had always been a grim man, a man of few words, who only occasionally indulged in sudden, razor-sharp outbursts of irony. But now, in those eyes staring into empty space and that vacant expression, there was a new loneliness; a hopeless silence. Ricciardi gave him the shivers, since he'd returned to duty.

Nor was police work much help. Aside from the occasional theft, a few robberies with battery, and a brawl down at the harbor with a few men sent to the hospital, nothing significant had happened, and Maione hadn't been able to rely on a challenging investigation to distract the commissario.

The brigadier, in a somewhat confused manner, was worried about Ricciardi's mental health, and he even wondered whether he ought to be afraid of the commissario harming himself in some way. And so he took advantage of every excuse to go into his office: one time he'd bring him a cup of the terrible ersatz coffee that they made in the guardroom; another time he'd go to inform him about hallway gossip, which his superior officer commented upon with, at the very most, a distracted half smile.

Maione had noticed that Ricciardi never even went to eat a quick pastry at Gambrinus during the lunch break, as he'd used to do, and that in the evenings he lingered at headquarters to keep from having to go home. Now that's a bad sign, he'd told Lucia, that's a very bad sign. But she had reassured him. It's just a difficult moment. It'll pass. It always passes. His wife hadn't mentioned it, but just then the ghost of the two years of silence that had separated them after Luca's death had brushed past her face with its icy wings.

And that was why, the minute he set foot in police headquarters, Maione catapulted himself up the stairs: he wanted to make sure that the commissario was at his desk, safe and sound.

And he was surprised to see that, despite the early morning hour, there was already someone sitting on the bench in the hallway, waiting to be admitted.

IV

Ricciardi heard a knock at his office door. At that hour of the morning, it could be no one but Maione. He heaved a sigh and called out to come in.

Recently, the brigadier had become a little irritating. The excuses he invented to check whether the commissario was all right were clearly fatuous, and Ricciardi was less tolerant than usual. He understood that Maione was fond of him, and in his way he returned that feeling in full, but what he needed now was to be alone and think. And remember. Work didn't comfort him and the presence of other people, even those few people toward whom he felt friendship, was only a source of disturbance. He didn't know how to convey this feeling without being offensive, but if the brigadier kept it up, he was going to have to make himself clear well beyond the bounds of benevolence.

Maione entered, shutting the door behind him.

"Commissa', *buongiorno*. How do you feel this morning? You've had something to eat, haven't you?"

Ricciardi looked up from the report concerning a brawl that had broken out down at the harbor.

"Yes, Maione, don't worry. Nelide takes care of everything, this morning at five she already had breakfast ready for me. *Magnanno ven'a famme*, she said. Whatever that means."

Maione snickered, shaking his head.

"Folk wisdom, Commissa'. 'Eating will bring you hunger', or something along those lines. That young woman is fantastic."

Ricciardi nodded.

"Which means there's no reason to fret. My stomach is in good hands."

"Whatever you say, Commissa'. Anyway, you must have gotten here quite early indeed, because outside there's a person waiting who said she got here three quarters of an hour ago, but she's still waiting for you. Since it's eight o'clock now and you haven't seen her, that means you've been in the office since at least seven o'clock."

Ricciardi heaved an impatient sigh. "Excellent work, Raffaele. You could practically be a cop, at times. And just who would this person be?"

Maione threw his arms wide.

"A lady, Commissa'. She's wearing a veil and she wouldn't tell me her name. She insists she'll speak only to you. Should I show her in?"

Ricciardi shrugged his shoulders.

"What else are we going to do, keep her out there to take the place of the usher? Certainly, show her in."

Maione stepped out and came back in, leading the way for the lady with the veil. She was tall and slender and held a purse in her gloved hands. She was dressed in black and wore a light overcoat, well-made but short, out of keeping with the long dress, which looked slightly unfashionable.

She took a step forward, hesitantly, and then came to a halt, just inside the door.

Ricciardi rose to his feet, remaining at his desk. He gestured with one hand, pointing her to the chairs facing the other side of his desk.

"Please. Have a seat. You asked to see me, I am told."

His tone had been rather brusque: he didn't like people who covered their faces. The woman straightened her back and approached the desk, though without taking a seat. She turned her head ever so slightly toward Maione, who had remained off to one side, waiting to be dismissed. But Ricciardi was in no mood to take his guest's discreet hint that she'd rather speak alone.

"Brigadier Maione, whom you've already met, works with me on all my official business. You can speak freely in his presence."

There was a moment's hesitation. The woman wondered whether she shouldn't just turn and leave, then made up her mind and sat down. She put her purse in her lap and lifted the veil, finally showing her face.

Ricciardi was immediately certain that he'd seen her before. The refined features, with a tiny, turned-up nose and an upper lip ever so slightly lifted to reveal a gleaming white set of teeth. Fierce, elongated eyes, calm and decisive, with dense eyebrows. The odd and remarkable color of her irises, an intense blue verging on purple. Ricciardi guessed she might be in her early thirties, though the expression on her face bespoke a suffering that made her look older. Even though she was pale and without makeup, she was definitely quite pretty.

Because the visitor gave no sign of wanting to break the silence, Maione said: "Signora, this is, in fact, Commissario Ricciardi, whom you asked to see. And you would be?"

The woman replied without taking her eyes off the eyes of Ricciardi, who was still standing: "I am Bianca Palmieri di Roccaspina. The Contessa of Roccaspina."

Without meaning to, the commissario shot a glance at the worn gloves that were threadbare in spots and the satin handbag that was mended at the bottom. The dress and shoes were likewise in less than perfect condition. The contessa noticed his glance and compressed her lips, offended in spite of herself. In her violet eyes, there was a glint of fierce pride and melancholy.

Ricciardi sat down.

"Tell me, then, Contessa. To what do we owe the pleasure of your visit?"

Bianca whispered: "Don't you remember, Commissario? We have met before. It was two years ago."

Ricciardi furrowed his brow in an effort to bring up the circumstances in which they might have met, but nothing specific came to him. Suddenly, a gleam of recollection lit up his mind.

"Ah, certainly, now I recall. The Rummolo murder. The fortune-teller. I was in your home, for your husband. Is that right?"

"Of course, *'o Cecato*," Maione broke in. "The Blind Man. You went alone to interview the count, Commissa'. It was a Sunday, you remember? We turned the whole quarter inside out."

A blind man—an *assistito*, as those with supernatural powers to foretell the numbers that would be chosen in the lottery were called—had been murdered. The Count of Roccaspina had been the last person to visit the victim and was therefore among the prime suspects. But that time, as it turned out, the killing hadn't been a matter of money. It was a crime of passion. A case resolved in a hurry, that same day and right on the spot. If only they could all turn out like that, thought Ricciardi, and in his mind he saw once again a picture of the count as he'd seen him then, a man still in the prime of his life but devoured from within by the fever of gambling, his eyes reddened, disheveled, a walking stick to which he clung like a shipwrecked sailor on a wooden beam in the open seas. A threadbare, haggard figure, similar in a sense to that of the woman before him, but lacking her ferocity, lacking her pride.

The contessa nodded, calmly.

"Yes, Commissario. That's right. One of my noble consort's habitual companions, I'd have to guess. A grave loss for society, wouldn't you say? But he was promptly replaced, make no mistake: first there was a hunchback, then a woman with a limp. In fact, even before that, a little girl with smallpox. What an absurd city this is."

Her voice was nicely modulated, with no local accent of any kind, but there was no missing an undertone of anger, a festering malevolence. The encounter was gradually returning to Ricciardi's memory: the count hadn't been there, he had come in only later, and the woman had received the commissario in the largely bare living room of an aristocratic palazzo in unmistakable decline.

The dress, he noticed with a sense of baseless unease, looked like the same one she wore then.

"Now that we've recognized each other, Contessa, would you care to tell me what I can do for you?"

Bianca said nothing, continuing to hold Ricciardi's gaze. There weren't many capable of meeting the commissario's green eyes without faltering or dropping their gaze, but she seemed able to do so without difficulty.

She took off her hat slowly, using both her hands. Her hair, tucked up in a bun, was a vivid blonde, with coppery highlights. Her long, fair neck was ornamented only by a black satin ribbon fastened with a brooch that looked to be made of silver. She wore no earrings.

Maione coughed softly, in embarrassment.

"Commissa', if you don't mind, I'll go take a look at the officers' duty roster, that way we can get the day started."

"No, Maione," Ricciardi replied without looking at him. "You can go afterward. Right now, let's hear what the contessa has to tell us."

He didn't want to give the woman the satisfaction of a confidential interview. Many people in that city were of the opinion that an aristocratic title gave one the right to issue orders and expect them to be carried out without question, and that very opinion was reason enough for Ricciardi, born the Baron of Malomonte, to consider that no one enjoyed such a right.

The Contessa of Roccaspina clenched her jaw in a moment of well-concealed annoyance, then resigned herself.

"I'm here about my husband. He's been arrested."

Ricciardi arched his brows.

"Oh, really? And why is that? Something to do with gambling, I'd imagine."

Maione wondered what could be driving Ricciardi to such pointless rudeness. Still, the woman gave no sign of detecting the sarcasm. The tone of voice with which she replied was, at least to all appearances, perfectly austere.

"No. It's murder."

The word landed in the room like a stone tossed into a pond. There was a moment's silence, then Ricciardi's tone of voice became decidedly more courteous.

"I'm sorry to hear that, Contessa. But you must have been directed to the wrong office, I'm not working on any case that . . . "

The woman lifted one gloved hand, interrupting him.

"It's not a recent case. My husband was arrested at the beginning of June. More than three months ago."

Ricciardi exchanged a glance with Maione, who shrugged his shoulders.

"Contessa, I think this is more of a matter for lawyers than for the police, now that so much time has gone by. The investigation . . . "

Bianca smiled sorrowfully and shook her head.

"There really wasn't any investigation to speak of, Commissario. My husband was arrested immediately, even though he wasn't found on the scene of the murder."

"But that can't be, Contessa! There's always an investigation, I'm sure that . . . "

"I'm telling you, there was no investigation. For the simple reason that my husband confessed that he had done it."

V

Livia leaned forward and told Arturo, her chauffeur, to pull over and she'd get out at the corner. She felt like taking a walk. It was such a beautiful day.

The driver hesitated and feebly protested, which only made the woman laugh. She was greatly amused to see how the inhabitants of that city had a perception of it that clashed so sharply with the reality. To hear Arturo and her housekeeper Clara tell it, she ought to go nowhere without an armed bodyguard for fear of the evildoers, thieves, cutpurses, and cutthroats who were bound to attack her along the way, even in broad daylight and on heavily trafficked streets like this one.

In fact, she'd rarely felt as safe as she did there. Certainly, people were a little nosy and never left you to mind your own business, but they were likeable, affectionate, and it was impossible to feel lonely for even a second.

It meant a great deal to her, not to feel alone. In fact, loneliness had cruelly branded her life for so many years, while her husband was still alive. Indeed, especially while her husband was still alive: the great Arnaldo Vezzi, Il Duce's favorite tenor; the singer who had been called the Voice of God by a prominent American music critic, after a memorable concert in New York; the unfaithful swine, murdered in a dressing room at the Teatro San Carlo by a woman he had seduced and then abandoned.

And she'd been alone afterward, too, even though she was at the center of a Roman social life that she found fatuous and empty, until she had decided to follow her heart by moving to that strange, song-filled city that abounded in light and shadows.

She stopped for a moment, inhaling to fill her lungs with the sweet-smelling air that rose from the sea. By now, it was the last ten days of September, but the weather showed no sign of turning wet and chilly. Her mother, in a phone call, had told her that it was raining cats and dogs where she lived in the Marche. And the night before, watching a newsreel at the movies, she had seen a very recent Fascist demonstration in the capital, and had noticed that the ladies were all wearing overcoats. But down here, even in the early morning hours, the sunshine was warm and soothing, and you could rely upon it to bring pleasure as it caressed your skin.

By the side of the road, standing next to two bags full to bursting, was a young man hawking his wares to passersby and to the women who lived in the tall apartment houses: bunches of grapes, each individual grape gigantic. It's gold, not grapes, this is! he was shouting at the top of his lungs. Ooh, so lovely, solid gold, it's pure gold!

He was a stunningly handsome young man, and he might have just stepped out of a gouache painted fifty years earlier, the kind of canvases that Livia admired on the walls of the drawing rooms she sometimes frequented. His hair was curly and dark, his workshirt was unbuttoned, revealing a tanned and hairy chest, he wore a pair of knee breeches and went barefoot; his eyes gleamed with laughter, his voice was full and stentorian. From many balconies up above housemaids leaned over, going through the motions of folding linen in the sunshine, but actually gazing raptly down at him.

Livia came into his field of view just as he was raising high a bunch of the fruit toward the sun, to show off its hue. The young man cut short the gesture and the shout with which he was calling his wares, only to clutch his chest theatrically with one hand, pretending to be thunderstruck at the sight of such loveliness.

"Oh, sweet Mary, mother of God, Signo', are you real or am I dreaming? No, because if this is a dream, I never ever want to wake up again!"

In spite of herself, Livia smiled at how spontaneous the compliment had been. She was accustomed to attracting looks from men, but it was rare for anyone to give vent to such an instinctive outburst of gallantry.

"Wait, Signo', don't be in such a hurry. You shed such magnificent light that, with you here, my grapes look like molten gold. If you stay a while, I won't have to move to follow the sun this morning!"

A couple of passersby burst into laughter, and Livia joined in. She took a couple of coins from her change purse and extended them toward the young man, who in return pulled a sumptuous bunch of grapes out of the nearest bag.

"Signo', I implore you, take a taste: then your beauty will infuse all the rest of my grapes, and I'll sell them all in less than ten minutes, and I can go spend the rest of my day making love to my sweet Rosetta!"

An elderly man, just a few dozen feet away, put a monocle to his eye and upbraided the youth.

"Hey, youngster, go slow there with the impertinence! Signo', forgive him. You are no doubt from some other city and you can't be accustomed to our ways, but here the youngsters never seem to know when enough is enough."

But she was now laughing, and could hardly restrain her mirth. She took just one grape from the cluster that the young man was extending in her direction and popped it into her mouth with a bit of coquettishness; then she waved her gloved hand and continued on her way, well aware that she had more than a few pairs of eyes glued to her back. The grape vendor pretended to lose consciousness, slumping to the pavement, drawing peals of slightly envious laughter from his small audience of housemaids lining the railings of the balconies above, while the elderly censor, in memory of his long-lost youth, heaved a rapt sigh after Livia's sashaying hips.

After she turned the corner, the woman headed for a small café. Recently, the circumstances of her meetings with Falco had changed. Until three months ago, she had had to place a blank sheet of paper into an envelope and deliver it to a nondescript address not far from her home, to a stony-faced concierge who never uttered so much as a word; and within a few hours that man whose duty it was to protect her would materialize before her as if he had simply been waiting tirelessly for her summons. But now Livia was to leave a calling card at the cash register of that café, and the following morning she would go and sit at one of the tables, certain that a few minutes later she would see him.

She took a seat inside the café. Though the sun was already high in the sky and she could have comfortably sat outside, cirumstances recommended the greatest discretion. Before she had a chance to order, and without having heard the tiniest sound, she sensed the presence of Falco, standing behind her. She smiled and tilted her head toward the empty chair across the table.

The man took a seat, silent and anonymous as always. Livia studied him, attentively. Of average height, his thinning salt-and-pepper hair brushed back, a gray double-breasted suit and a hat of the same color, a light beige overcoat draped over his arm, two-toned shoes and white socks, a slender walking stick. He had a knack for becoming practically invisible, in all things identical to the dozens of financiers, professionals, and good-for-nothing time-wasters loitering in the sunny streets, in the tailor shops choosing a fabric for their shirts, outside of the theaters waiting for a matinée, or in the front halls of the expensive bordellos.

But Falco was quite another matter. Quite another matter indeed.

"*Buongiorno*, Signora. This morning you're even lovelier than usual, and you're usually stunning. To what do I owe the privilege of seeing you?"

Livia smiled, cheerlessly. Every time she saw him, something about Falco left her vaguely uneasy. Oh lord, he was always well behaved and gallant, to be sure; and she had discovered that he had an artistic and cultural sensibility of the highest order. Not long ago, when she had finally made up her mind to sing once again in public, she had glimpsed him, applauding in ravished delight, his face twisted with deep emotion: only to vanish seconds later so suddenly and completely that she was left wondering if she'd ever actually seen him.

What made her uneasy was the fact that Falco (and she didn't even know if that was his first name, his surname, or neither of the two) belonged to a government organization that had no public presence, that was, in fact, very, very secret. That he had been assigned to protect and assist her by someone quite high up, at the very apex of the party structure, because she was a personal friend of Il Duce's daughter. That the man carried out that task with excessive zeal, to the extent that she often thought she had caught sight of his silhouette on the street or in the theater or at the movies, to say nothing of the drawing rooms where the highly exclusive receptions that she often attended took place.

Still, she had to admit that the man had the gift of discretion, to say nothing of invisibility; no one ever seemed to notice him.

She waited until the waiter had taken their orders, then she said: "It's been a while since I last saw you, Falco. Or since I was last aware that I was seeing you, perhaps I ought to say. Evidently, I've been a good girl." The man flashed her a fleeting smile.

"Good, but not quite good enough, Signora. But then, you wouldn't be yourself and I wouldn't have the very welcome charge of keeping an eye on you, if you were too good of a girl. Still, as you know very well, we know how to keep to the shadows."

Livia's mouth tightened.

"If you ask me, you lay claim to a duty to which you have no right. I don't understand what it is you're supposed be protecting me from."

Falco turned to gaze across the street; a small crowd of barefoot *scugnizzi*, or street urchins, was laughing as they played at yanking the skirts of passing ladies, and then dodging the straight-armed slaps to the back of the head that ensued.

"Protect you from what, you ask. That question has every right to a thoroughgoing answer that not even I can give you, unfortunately. But first of all, from this city. Which is actually quite a dangerous place."

The woman heaved a sigh of annoyance.

"Don't tell me that you too are going to start telling me how dangerous this city is. Sometimes I think it's just an excuse for people to claim the right to stick their noses into other people's business. I've been here for a year now, and I don't think I've ever once been at risk of anything worse than a couple of wolf whistles as I walked by."

For a moment, Falco said nothing. Then, without taking his eyes off the *scugnizzi*, he said under his breath: "The day before yesterday you left the theater at 10:14 P.M. The car driven by your chauffeur was waiting for you, as usual, at the corner of Via Madonna delle Grazie, just a short distance from the theater's front doors, but you told Arturo that you preferred to walk, because it was such a beautiful evening."

Livia felt the usual lump in her throat from the oppressive nature of that surveillance.

"This show of confidential information tells me only that you tail me obsessively," she hissed. "It seems to me that the worst danger looming over me is you and your colleagues!"

As if he hadn't heard a word, Falco continued in the same tone of voice: "They started following you when they saw that you weren't going to ride in the car. There were two of them, we know them well. One of them comes up next to you with a knife, the other one grabs your purse and jewelry. They're very fast, but sometimes they like to have a little fun, so they take the ladies they rob into an atrium and take advantage of them: one claps his hand over the victim's mouth while the other one . . . the other one does what he's going to do. It wasn't my shift, or I would have stepped in sooner. My . . . my friends instead waited for them to make a move, to make sure they knew exactly what their intentions were. We aren't vigilantes."

Back out on the street, the *scugnizzi* scattered all at once like a flock of sparrows, heading in different directions. A moment later, two constables strolled into view, walking with their hands in their pockets and their ties loosened, chatting idly.

"Why should I believe you?" Livia murmured under her breath. "I didn't hear anything, no one approached me during my walk, and I arrived home safe and sound."

Falco's mouth twisted into a grimace.

"No one can make you believe me. All that matters to me is the knowledge that those two gentlemen are never going to bother you again, and that in all likelihood, when and if they ever recover, they are most likely going to find some other way of earning their living. But they're not the only ones, believe me. At least on this one point, believe me."

Livia shuddered and moderated her tone.

"I know that you do your duty, there can be no doubt about it. And I thank you."

Falco returned his attention to her and his eyes lit up for a moment. A shaft of sunlight came through the front door of the café and struck Livia's dress. He admired its extreme elegance. An electric blue skirt suit, clinging tight around her narrow waist, where a velvet belt ran, latticework gloves in the same shade, an apricot-colored blouse whose collar ended in a long scarf that rested softly on the jacket. A small satin hat, in the same shade of blue, was adorned by a large camellia that echoed the blouse.

The man thought about how enchanting she was, and how difficult it was to maintain the proper level of professional detachment required by his job. He nodded, pretending to have forgotten the attack of just moments ago.

"What can I do for you, Signora? Usually, when I receive your summons, it's a source of delight at the same time that it casts a shadow of concern. Is there something on your mind?"

Livia burst out laughing, attracting curious glances from a couple of matrons having tea a few tables over. She regained her composure and said: "I can just imagine your concern, Falco. It's true, I do have something in mind, and it's no easy thing for me to tell you what it is, it's a request that might strike you as . . . bizarre, perhaps. I've thought long and hard about whether it's right to trouble you. But you would be able to gather the information I need in a flash, while I, if I asked the people around me, housekeepers, concierges, and suppliers, would never really be confident of the result, and above all, it would take me too long. And it's a well-known fact that we women don't have much patience."

Falco nodded, gravely.

"I understand. And now my concern has grown, after hearing this preamble. But I have orders to work with you and help as much as I am able, as you known. Tell me more."

Livia sipped her coffee, as if searching for the right words. As she did, Falco savored the perfume wafting off her, a wild, pungent essence. He had looked into the matter and learned that she had it concocted for her by a perfumery in Rome, an exclusive arrangement. Money well spent, he thought to himself.

At last, the woman spoke.

"You know all about him. We've discussed this matter many times before, and you've never concealed that you don't care for my interest in him one bit. For official reasons, I'd have to imagine. But you also know that he is what convinced me to move to this city."

Falco said nothing, expressionless as a sphinx. Livia went on: "I know that he likes me. I know it. I can sense it. And believe me when I say that I can tell if a man likes me or not. Yet there's something that's keeping him from opening up, from coming to me. Something that's stopping him. Something. Or someone."

Falco tightened a muscle in his jaw, but betrayed no sign of knowledge. Livia continued.

"Last fall, as you may recall, he was in a car crash. He survived by some miracle. I rushed to be at his side, in the hospital, and I made sure that he was all right. I went back every day, and taking turns staying with him were his *tata*—the woman who died just recently—and Brigadier Maione. Only those two. But the first time, just as I arrived, there was another person waiting to learn of his condition. I only saw her that one time, she never showed up again. I only remembered about her later. She was next to Rosa, the *tata*, and on her face was an expression of absolute terror. She was praying, I believe."

Out in the street a vendor of *franfellicchi*, the bits of colorful, sugary cooked honey that children went wild about, strolled past. Without warning he started hawking his wares, splitting the air with his shouts: "*Cinche culure e cinche sapure, ccà stanno 'e franfellicche!* Five colors and five flavors, get your *franfellicchi!*" The women at the nearby table lurched in surprise, and then burst into laughter.

"I know exactly what she looks like," Livia resumed. "A tall young woman, with glasses. Dressed quite simply, I doubt she even wore makeup, but with delicate hands. Not a housemaid, in other words. Perhaps a young schoolteacher, or an office-worker. She clearly was on some terms of acquaintance with the *tata*. And she was certainly worried about losing him: then and there I assumed she was a relative, then I reconsidered. No spectacular beauty, not remarkable to look at, but the kind of woman men find reassuring. Quite young."

She had uttered that last word with reluctance, almost as if it had been a doleful confession.

"The kind that men fall in love with, you understand. Not the kind they want for a night of fun, or to show off at the theater or in high society. The kind that, in the end, they marry."

Falco wondered whether Livia was still speaking to him, or whether she were just thinking aloud. But the woman looked him square in the eye and whispered, with determination: "I want to know who that woman is. I want to know everything about her, where she lives, what she does. Whether he loves her, and if so, how and to what extent. Once he told me that his heart was pledged. Is that young woman the pledge he had in mind?"

Falco opened his mouth and then, abruptly, shut it again. He looked away, in embarrassment.

"Signora, I don't know whether . . . in other words, and surely you understand, this is a matter that lies outside my professional duties. Gathering information about questions of the heart does not lie within my purview in your regards."

Livia laughed, mockingly.

"Are you quite certain? After all, Falco, everything that concerns me has to do with questions of the heart, and you know that very well. The matter isn't complicated: either you accept the task of obtaining this information for me, or you'll never see me again except from the shadows where you lurk.

And in that domain as well, I'll make life very, very difficult for you. Are we clear?"

Falco hardened his gaze.

"Are you threatening me, Signora? I doubt you're in any condition to do so."

Livia took a deep breath. Maybe she had overstepped her bounds, and now she realized it. "You're quite right. But in a strange sense, I feel that you and I are becoming friends. Or something like it. And when a person is in pain, or worried, then she should turn to her friends, don't you agree? So let me ask you as a friend: Can you help me? And, more importantly, are you willing to?"

Falco stared at her a little longer. Then he slowly nodded.

"Yes, Signora. I can do it and I will. But you must clearly understand that this will be something that remains outside of our professional relationship. This is a highly personal matter. You won't discuss it with anyone, especially not with . . . with your friends in Rome. This will be something that concerns us, and us alone. For once, I'm going to have to ask you to keep a secret."

Livia smiled at him, and she looked like a dark-eyed cat.

"I promise. It will be our secret."

VI

The woman's words had left Ricciardi and Maione speechless.

The two men gazed at each other, openmouthed, certain that the Contessa of Roccaspina must be joking: a murderer, self-confessed, already four months behind bars; what could he possibly want from them? Ricciardi, moreover, thought the whole thing seemed especially strange. A noblewoman he'd met once, a couple of years ago, during the course of a rapid investigation, and with whom he had exchanged a few hurried words at most. To call this a superficial acquaintanceship would be euphemistic. Admittedly, she had clearly fallen on hard times and had few resources, but could it really be that she had no one else to turn to?

Maione interrupted his train of thought by slapping himself on the forehead.

"Ah, of course, now I've got it! It's the murder of that guy, that lawyer in Santa Lucia, isn't that right? I remember, all the papers talked about it, it was quite the scandal. That was a case that idiot Cozzolino looked into, with Commissario De Blasio. And how they crowed about solving the case in a hurry, the two of them! As if a cop deserves special credit when someone comes in and says, I did it, I was the one, then anyone could pull it off . . . "

Suddenly realizing that he'd put his foot in it, the brigadier gave himself another slap, this time on the mouth.

"Oooh, *madonna*! Forgive me, Conte', I didn't mean to . . . "

Bianca smiled wearily.

"Don't think twice, Brigadier," she said without turning to look at Maione. "I think the same thing. The rapidity of my husband's confession was enough to put an immediate end to any investigation. The guilty party had been found right away, so why bother to go on looking?"

Ricciardi had no interest in playing word games.

"Signora, you'll excuse me I'm sure, but we don't have much time, and it's not professionally ethical to stand around denigrating the work of my colleagues. There was an investigation, it was concluded, and there's a prime suspect who, among other things, has made a full confession. I really don't understand . . . "

Bianca nodded sadly.

"You don't understand what I'm doing here. And I understand that. Maybe I don't understand myself, really."

She got up and put her hat on her head. She was clamping her lips together, as if trying to keep them from quavering.

"Still, please believe me when I tell you that I'm not one of these little ladies who go around denying reality just because it's different than the way they'd like it to be."

She turned and walked toward the door. When she had her hand on the doorknob, she turned and leveled her fierce eyes at Ricciardi's. He couldn't help but notice how pretty she was.

"You see, Commissario, it might not count for much, I'm sorry to say. But I know for certain that my husband is innocent. Still, no one will listen to me. Have a good day."

And with that, she turned and left.

Maione and Ricciardi exchanged a baffled glance, speechless for several seconds. Then the commissario briefly nodded his head in the direction of the door and the brigadier took off like a bloodhound. Less than a minute later, he came back in with the contessa.

Ricciardi stood up.

"Signora, you said that you're certain your husband committed no crime. Would you be so kind, if you please, as to tell us the source of this certainty?"

Bianca lifted her veil and looked calmly at Ricciardi.

"I never said that my husband hadn't committed crimes. He's a gambler, he's failed to pay both debts and taxes, and he has surely robbed and defrauded friends and relatives, to say nothing of me. He is a man with a number of bad habits and he seems incapable of shaking them. But he didn't murder Ludovico Piro that night."

Ricciardi leaned forward, placing both hands palm-down on the desktop.

"And how do you know that, if I may ask?"

"Simple. He was home. He was home, fast asleep, for a change."

Ricciardi shook his head.

"Contessa, forgive me, but I continue not to understand. Why didn't you just say so at the time?"

The feverish conversation had put a bit of color in Bianca's cheeks, and now she looked much younger.

"But I did say so. At first, very calmly, then sobbing, shouting, angrily, stubbornly, firmly, and even sweetly. But it was all no good, no one was willing to listen. Until, finally, here I am."

Maione shifted his considerable weight from one police-issue boot to the other.

"I think I remember something of the sort, the newspapers wrote about it. Commissa', we were already working on the case about the professor, at the polyclinic, and when you're in the middle of an investigation, you don't want to know about anything else, but the whole city was talking about it. You were the only one, Conte', who insisted it wasn't your husband, isn't that right?"

The woman nodded. She seemed exhausted.

"Yes. I was the only one. And I was also the only one who

could do so, since I alone knew where my husband had been that night."

Ricciardi broke in, flatly.

"Not you alone. According to what you say, your husband also knew that. And yet . . . "

"And yet he confessed," put in Bianca, beating him to it. "And he filled out that confession with numerous details. But the medical examiner said very clearly that Piro died during the night, and that night my husband was at home, dead drunk, in his bed. Still, yes, he confessed, and he hasn't retracted his statement yet, after more than three months behind bars."

"Why would he ever do such a thing, Contessa? Why would a man who, according to what you tell me, burns his candle at both ends, indulging freely in bad habits and pleasures, invent a story that might condemn him to spend the rest of his life in prison?"

They stood there, staring each other in the eye, the violet in the green without blinking, expressions cold and hard, resembling one another slightly without realizing it.

"I don't know," the woman murmured at last in an almost unintelligible voice. "I just don't know, dammit. I ask myself all the time, every hour, every minute, but I have no answer. Everyone thinks I've lost my mind. My family, my friends, and even his lawyer all think I'm crazy and do their best to talk me out of repeating this story, and instead to throw myself on the mercy of the court in the trial that's about to begin, which they expect will be short, with a predetermined verdict."

Ricciardi ran a hand over his forehead.

"Let's see if I've got this straight: the investigation is closed, there's a man who'll be facing trial soon, who's been in jail for some time, who has confessed and confirmed his confession, providing details and particulars on how the murder took place. Everyone is in agreement, including his lawyer, but you alone insist that things went differently. And in all these months, you've repeated your version of events to anyone who would listen, but no one believed you. Is that right?"

Bianca lifted her face, proudly.

"Yes, that's right. And one thing you've forgotten to say, Commissario, is that it's the truth. The truth, pure and simple."

"Can I ask why you chose to come to me?"

"Because when we first met you struck me as a person who digs deeper than mere surface appearances. Who has no prejudices and who doesn't fall back on the most convenient solutions. And also because I have no one else to turn to."

They remained silent for what seemed like an interminable amount of time. Bianca was clutching hard at the handle of her tattered handbag. Maione looked at his feet. Ricciardi listened to Rosa's voice as she told him, as a boy, to answer all requests for help he received in life. At least respond.

At last, he nodded.

"I'll ask around a little. But I'm not promising anything, let that be clear. Not a thing."

VII

E ver since she had returned home from the summer colony on Ischia at the end of August, Enrica Colombo had feared the arrival of only one moment: the preparations for bottling the tomatoes.

Because up till that moment, she had been fairly confident of her ability to sidestep the interrogation to which she was sure to be subjected by her mother and her sister Susanna, their efforts backed by that cursed flock of gossips, the neighbor women.

In time, she had become very skilled at pretending to be otherwise occupied and to dodging the interest of others, using as an excuse the countless petty activities of the day. Moreover, school would soon start up again and she needed to look after the summer projects that had been assigned to her younger siblings: inasmuch as she had a teaching certificate that responsibility fell to her, and it allowed her to sidestep the topic when it veered into dangerous territory, by pretending to have to break off the conversation because Luigino or Francesca had this composition to finish or that geometry problem to solve. It was all useful in her efforts to avoid the beady-eyed scrutiny of the women in her family, who were ravenously eager for news about Enrica's mysterious German suitor, a figure who was beginning to take on an absurdly mythological dimension.

She might even have been able to keep Manfred's existence a secret from almost everyone, had it not been for the methodical stream of letters that began to arrive, starting three days after her return home, every Monday, Wednesday, and Friday, at a precise rate of dispiriting regularity. Enrica found the perfect operation of the postal service to be quite irritating, and in her mind she silently cursed poor Signor Egidio, the middle-aged, flat-footed postman who delivered mail throughout the quarter.

Impossible, therefore, to keep her mother from intercepting them: the woman had a gift, a sixth sense that allowed her to predict in advance the little man's arrival, and to be waiting magically next to the wooden postboxes in the building's atrium, to take them in her own hands. Please, please, Signor Egidio, don't bother to put on your reading spectacles, I'll just rifle through your bag myself.

Nor had she felt up to the idea of writing Manfred and asking him to redirect his correspondence elsewhere, such as to her father's haberdashery, for example. It struck her as somehow excessively conniving, and it would give him an impression of her and her family that she found distasteful. Moreover, it was unnecessary for the moment, because her mother, with some considerable effort, seemed capable of resisting the temptation to open those ochre-yellow envelopes, with the address filled out in a strange, Gothic-style handwriting, and with the exotic return address neatly compiled on the back flap.

The ceremony that accompanied her mother's delivery was quite annoying. Maria Colombo would walk from one end of the apartment to the other, from the front door all the way to the room where Enrica sat waiting, like a ship sailing majestically across the bay, foghorns blasting, to the wharf where it would finally tie up, waving the envelope like a pennant fluttering in the breeze. Along the way, she collected a small following consisting of the housekeeper, her younger daughter with the toddler grandson in her arms, and the younger boys, until she finally fetched up in her room, extending the envelope to Enrica as if she were bestowing some honorary title. Then she would stand there, arms crossed and with an irksome little smile on her face, in the hope that Enrica might open and read it, ideally aloud, in the presence of the entire motley crew. Of course, Enrica had no intention of doing any such thing; she would tuck the letter away in the pocket of her dressing gown and calmly resume whatever she had been doing, humming a song and making a great show of her absolute lack of urgency to learn the news that had just arrived from the town of Prien, in Bavaria, as was clearly written on the back flap.

When her audience finally resigned itself and went back to its proper pursuits, Enrica would withdraw to her bedroom and begin reading. Manfred wrote better Italian than he spoke, unhindered by the harsh pronunciation and the overemphatic consonants; his lengthy stays on the island of Ischia and a heartfelt fondness for a culture so abounding in art and beauty had led him to read and study extensively, and he seemed happy to be able to carry on a correspondence in that language. With an affectionate tone, in his frequent but not overlong missives he told her about the profound changes in his everyday life.

The National Socialist Party had won the federal elections. For Manfred, an activist from the earliest days, this outcome had opened an array of important opportunities. He aspired to a position in the rebuilt armed forces, the Reichswehr, or else in the diplomatic corps where Hitler would soon start making changes. He was attracted by the clear ideas and the desire to redeem the country's national pride that emerged from the heartfelt and frequent speeches that the party leader often delivered in public, and which he himself often attended, as an army major. When he wasn't writing about that, he'd tell her about life in the lakeshore town where he lived, a place full of flowers, often battered by sudden downpours: solitary bicycle outings, calisthenics, lunches with his elderly parents. And he'd also express his desire to see her again, of course, to reestablish the magic of their early meetings.

Whenever those very regular lines took her back to her memories of certain moments, Enrica would feel a struggle in her heart that was starting to become very familiar to her. A mixture of unease, guilt, excitement, pleasure, and a subtle sorrow: like an elaborate, complex cake whose individual ingredients you can try to guess, but which still has a strange and mysterious flavor, so different from the sum of its parts.

What did Enrica really want? She couldn't lie to herself. She had liked being embraced by those strong and solid hands, savoring the taste of those lips in the moonlight, in the seething perfume of that summer filled with sea breezes and dreams. But if she thought about her life, if she imagined herself turning to look at her man while she walked with him on the street, or worrying about someone as she turned to look out a window and awaited his return, it wasn't Manfred that came to mind.

It was as if she were trapped in an ongoing struggle inside her own body. Her heart pounded every time she left her home, at the thought she might be confronted by those green eyes. And she had heard about the death of Rosa, a woman she had become very fond of and who had been her only bridge, her only link to the world of a strange and solitary man she had fallen deeply in love with. But by now she was certain of it: That man didn't want her. If he had wanted her, he would have reached out to her, and she would have made sure he had no trouble finding her. And so, it was now up to her to answer herself, reply to the crucial question: what did she want from life?

A family. Children. A home of her own. Someone to take care of, someone to take care of her. Nothing transcendental, nothing any different, really, from what, she had to imagine, were the desires of any young woman. Manfred with the confident smile and the strong hands, Manfred so full of certainties,

Manfred who had painted her portrait while she was taking the children to the beach, Manfred who was a widower and was thirty-eight years old and who therefore knew what it was a woman wants.

Manfred who would take her far away.

There was only one person at home who didn't question her about what her "German fiancé," as her brothers mockingly liked to call him, wrote her. A person who, in fact, put on a show of the utmost indifference to the matter in general, and who never asked her trick questions to try to get her to tip her hand. And yet, that person knew more about her than everyone else in her family put together.

Giulio Colombo, Enrica's father, would have had every right to delve into the matter of his daughter's inner turmoil. He knew about Ricciardi, and—through the lengthy letters that, all summer long, she had been sending him directly at the haberdashery that he ran—he had been able to keep track of the developments in her relationship with Manfred. Moreover, he knew the place in the young woman's heart that both one man and the other enjoyed. But precisely because of this knowledge, Giulio lacked the courage to ask her just what she meant to do, for the very simple reason that he had no idea what would be best for her.

I have a soul of glass, thought Enrica. Fragile and transparent, ready to be filled with something lovely and colorful, and ready to shatter into a thousand pieces. She felt as if anyone at all could easily see what was happening inside of her, and she felt ashamed, as if she'd committed many wrongs. That was the real reason she said nothing about Manfred to her mother or her sister: for fear that they might be capable of seeing clearly, though the transparent surface of her eyes, that she liked him, certainly, and a great deal, but that she wasn't in love with him. And she never would be, as long as she loved another man, who did not want her in return.

But the last letter changed everything. The last letter carried important news, momentous enough to put her on the horns of a dilemma.

With a certain sense of drama and with fatal timeliness, it had been delivered to her on that fateful day. The day that they were going to start bottling the tomato sauce.

That was the kind of undertaking that involved entire nuclear families: in the case of the Colombos, it also dragged in the two Signorinas Lapenna, a pair of old maids well along in years who lived next door; the Barbatos; a childless Jewish couple; and the Greco family, a young widowed mother with three small children that everyone did their best to help out.

The beer, wine, and soda pop bottles were collected and stored all year long, then painstakingly washed and dried, a task assigned to the younger girls and the little boys. The men were entrusted with the responsibility of finding, selecting, and buying the tomatoes from trusted peasants and farmers who could be relied upon for high quality. The transport of the crates of tomatoes was a job performed by laborers recruited in piazzas and on the street, and their arrival was greeted with jubilation by the children and gimlet-eyed wariness by the housekeepers, lest a certain amount of the product might "lose its way" in the process. They oversaw the "discard," as the task of choosing the usable tomatoes was known, with the elimination of the ones that were too soft or riddled with bruises, after which the select, chosen fruit was slow-cooked in a double boiler, and the stalks removed and carved out. This rather complicated part of the operation fell to the experienced hands of the mothers and the eldest daughters. Only after that was complete could they move on to the slow boil, the crushing, and the fine food mill, culminating in the decisive phase of canning proper.

Throughout the entire process of canning and bottling, which was going to provide for the occupants of that floor of the apartment building for the rest of the year—raw material for the production of superfine ragús and marvelous eggplant Parmesans—the women remained alone for hours with nothing to do but chatter, with no escape from the work at hand save for momentary restroom breaks.

Enrica felt like a defendant on trial, and what's more, one who was guilty and facing a teetering stack of damning evidence. She knew that she was bound to be subjected to a withering hail of questions, and she had always been completely incapable of lying. This time, she would have no chance of dodging the questioning the way she usually did, by remaining silent and merely smiling, only to escape until the next occasion.

For that matter, Manfred's latest letter had been quite different in tone from the others that preceded it. His usual account of events in Germany had been replaced by an unmistakable enthusiasm for what he clearly considered a major piece of news.

Standing in front of the mirror in her bedroom, while the court of women armed with wet rags and cork stoppers had already gathered in the apartment's vast kitchen and were waiting for her so they could begin the inquisition, she asked herself once again what it was she really wanted. She wondered whether she truly desired to leave that window closed, never again to feel those feverish, suffering eyes upon her, peering deep into her soul of glass.

She compressed her lips, tightly. She was determined not to cry. Manfred was coming, to the city she lived in, and he might be staying long enough to force her to deal with a potential future that she felt completely unprepared to take on. He asked her, in his letter, to arrange to invite him to dinner so that he could meet her family. He promised her promenades in the bright sunshine, arm in arm, and assured her that she would be at his side at receptions and dinners to which, as a member of the diplomatic corps of a great and allied nation—now even more closely allied than before—he was bound to be invited.

Manfred took it for granted that this would meet with her approval. He trusted that their kiss, stolen in the moonlight amidst the chirping of crickets, meant that they were all but engaged. Who could say whether Manfred's eyesight would be good enough to see deep into her soul of glass. And who know if that would be enough to spare her from from inflicting pain upon him. What's more, she felt unequal to the challenge of withstanding her mother's determination, and she felt sure that her mother would be wholeheartedly delighted to embrace the long-awaited husband-to-be of a daughter who gave her nothing but worry. And perhaps it really would be best for everyone.

Choking back her tears, Enrica went to crush tomatoes and bottle them.

Bottles made of glass. As was her soul.

VIII

After Bianca left the room, Maione said: "Commissa', if you ask me, you just took on quite a thankless job. You don't know anything about the details of what happened with her husband, because quite rightly you mind your own business and pay no attention to hallway gossip."

Ricciardi looked at him, perplexed.

"What do you mean?"

Maione shrugged his shoulders.

"And for that matter, you don't even read the papers. Well, let me bring you up-to-date. The Piro murder was quite the story, this summer. A case that involved high society, the wealthy and the aristocrats. You know that there's an ongoing war between the groups: there was a time when there was no difference, but now there are always more and more penniless noblemen than there are aristocrats getting rich. Do you follow me?"

Ricciardi made a face.

"More or less. But go on."

"Anyway, this Ludovico Piro was a lawyer, but to the best of my recollections, what he did was lend money to the nobility. He could be found in all the finest drawing rooms, everyone in the city knew him. Early one morning he was found dead in his office, stabbed in the throat or something like that. Our men were on the scene of the crime immediately, but before they so much as got a chance to start asking questions, the Count of Roccaspina shows up and says: it was me. And that was that."

"Yes, that's what the Contessa told us. But she is also certain that her husband never left their home the night of the murder."

Maione nodded.

"That's right. For days and days it was the talk of the town. The case involved prominent citizens and everybody had something to say about it. The Fascists took advantage of the opportunity to attack these decadent aristocrats, and the aristocrats retorted: You see what happens the minute you give moneylenders and loan sharks entry into our clubs? The count was in debt to the lawyer, he was a heavy gambler, cards, lottery, and the racetrack. You know the way it works, don't you? The heavier the losses, the greater the determination to win it back, and then the losses only grow. And so on and so forth. Then, of course, that opened the door to even worse, as is always the way."

Ricciardi got to his feet and strolled, hands in pockets, over to the window. Outside, the September day was bursting out in all its loveliness.

"Delicate material to handle, you say. I understand. Being able to pin the murder on the count was a convenient solution for everybody. Everyone in their proper role: the loan shark squeezing him dry, the count in despair, swept away by an outburst of rage and frustration. But convenient solutions often conceal other things. The contessa . . . A strange woman."

"Yes, she's an odd one," Maione admitted. "She seemed determined, and quite convinced. But no sign of grief."

Ricciardi turned to look at him.

"Exactly. No sign of grief. And yet, as his wife, she ought to have been heartbroken. We should have seen tears, imprecations. Instead she was perfectly calm, almost cold to her husband's plight."

"Then, in your opinion, why did she come here, Commissa'? What did she want from you?"

Ricciardi turned back to the window and looked out.

"That's what convinced me, you know. If she had come begging me to help, I wouldn't have had any reason to believe her story. Instead, she didn't even ask me to get her husband out of jail; she just told me the truth as she saw it. I think it's worth doing a little investigating, and for that matter I don't believe we have anything urgent on our plate right now."

Maione thought it over rapidly. This was exactly what Ricciardi needed. Something to sink his teeth into, a lead to follow. To keep from being held prisoner of his own personal hell.

"Nothing indeed, nothing at all, Commissa'. Just think, it turns out the Fascists were right after all, this has become a safe, quiet city."

Ricciardi swung around.

"No, Raffaele. It never has been, and it never will be. Who did you say it was that handled this case?"

It was to Commissario Paolo De Blasio's embarrassed surprise that he saw Ricciardi appear in the doorway of his office. Like practically everyone at police headquarters, he had only the rarest of interactions with that taciturn and vaguely sinister Cilento-born officer, and like nearly everyone else, he felt that he couldn't place his trust in a man with no known vices. He shared the general opinion that, with that face and those absurd eyes, Ricciardi even carried something of a hex about him, a whiff of Neapolitan *iella*, or evil eye, and so, like almost everyone, he did his best to steer clear of him.

Glancing around as if in search of someone's support, De Blasio invited Ricciardi in. De Blasio was overweight and nondescript, a man in his early fifties who showed considerable skill in threading his way through the twists and turns of the bureaucratic labyrinth and particularly well known for a pathological terror of getting into trouble. He had the short man's complex, and in fact that was the one topic that could truly get on his nerves, and so he remained perennially seated behind his desk, with a wooden dais beneath his feet and a couple of cushions on the seat of his office chair, raising him sufficiently to make it look as if he were of normal height. One of the favorite pastimes of personnel at police headquarters was to figure out ways of making the little man get down off his artificial pedestal for the sheer sadistic fun of embarrassing him. In fact, despite the substantial lifts he wore in his shoes, De Blasio inevitably found himself face-to-face with his interlocutor's belt buckle.

Ricciardi came straight to the point.

"De Blasio, you were in charge of the murder case involving a certain Piro last June, weren't you?"

De Blasio furrowed his brow in wary concern.

"Yes, that was my investigation, in fact. But in practical terms we didn't have to do a thing, the guilty party turned himself in immediately Count Romualdo di Roccaspina, as you may have read in the papers. But, please, take a seat."

Ricciardi remained standing in front of the desk, his hands in his pockets, eyes fixed on his interlocutor's face, who was now squirming on his double cushion.

"I don't read the papers, myself. I don't have the time. Tell me exactly what happened, if you please."

The man coughed, uneasily.

"Listen, what are you trying to say with this comment about the newspapers? What do you think, that while you're working we're taking it easy? Getting information is part of our job. And do you mind telling me the meaning of all these questions?"

"Each of us spends our time as we see best," Ricciardi replied tersely. "I'm investigating a case that might have some connections with the murder in question, nothing more. Certainly, if there are secrets I don't know about or confidential matters at stake, then I'm happy to work through official channels. If you prefer, I'm happy to have Garzo put in a request directly, or I can go to someone even higher up."

De Blasio jerked in his chair. If there was one thing that he did his level best to avoid, and with maniacal obsessiveness, it was any contact with his superior officers, and, specifically, with Garzo, the deputy police chief who was in charge of all investigative activity, a bureaucrat completely devoid of imagination, who never tired of nitpicking and fault-finding in all of the work done by his underlings.

De Blasio thought fast.

"Why of course, full collaboration among colleagues, I'd never act otherwise. The thing is I really can't tell you much, we went over and . . . "

Ricciardi stopped him with a wave of his hand.

"Hold on. Start from the very beginning, and don't leave out a thing. When did you get the call? And from who?"

De Blasio sighed in defeat. Now he had to get down off his chair and go in search of the report.

With a leap he landed on the floor, vanishing from sight behind the desk save for his neck and head, and then headed straight for a metal filing cabinet by the wall. He climbed onto a wooden step that had been specially placed next to the cabinet and pulled open the first drawer, muttering to himself.

"Now then, let's see . . . I keep everything in strict chronological order . . . lately it's not as if much has happened here in the city. Ah, here we are: you see, a thin file, practically speaking there's nothing here but the report on the crime scene and the confession itself."

He jumped down from the step and hastily clambered back onto the heavily padded armchair, where he clearly felt immediately much more at his ease.

"Well, then: the call came in early on the morning of Friday, the third of June. A phone call to the switchboard. I went out with Cozzolino and two police privates, Rinaldo and

Mascarone. That Mascarone is an idiot, he was a driver but he couldn't find his way to Santa Lucia; the few times that there was actually a car available, it took longer than just walking. In any case, you'll find everything right here: address, phone number . . . "

Ricciardi interrupted him.

"Who found the corpse? And who was home?"

De Blasio ran his finger over the page.

"Everything, you'll find everything in this report. I'm a real stickler, as you probably know. The corpse was in the office, the housekeeper found it when she brought him breakfast. She was terrified, absolutely terrified, she was babbling: it took us half an hour to get two words out of her, a young woman from the area around Avellino. The wife was still at home, a harridan who barely speaks, a cold one, like a slab of marble, and his son, a boy aged twelve. The daughter, sixteen, had already left for school, and learned what had happened to her father when her mother sent the chauffeur to pick her up."

"What was the position of the corpse?"

His colleague narrowed his eyes in concentration.

"Wait, aside from what is written in the report, I want to remember clearly. He was slumped over the desk, his head twisted to the left. There was blood on the desktop, but not really all that much. He was wearing a suit and tie, he either hadn't gone to bed at all or he'd gotten up very early; the autopsy report stated that death had taken place sometime between midnight and two in the morning."

"And the wife couldn't say whether or not he had gone to sleep?"

The little man shrugged his shoulders.

"I guess not, she said that she'd gone to sleep early, when her husband was still in his office, and since she slept soundly she hadn't heard anything. To tell you the truth, the impression I got was that this guy often didn't sleep with his wife. Their place is nice and big, they have plenty of money, and maybe the lawyer had a room of his own and the signora preferred to skip over that detail. In any case, the dead man was fully dressed, and there was a pile of promissory notes on the desk. I'd guess he was doing some accounting."

"Cause of death?"

"He had a nice big hole in his neck, on the right side, which you're not likely to strike unless you're left-handed. A long knife, or something of the sort. He must have died almost instantly, and since the wound perforated the larynx, he died in silence, too. End of conversation."

"Who did the autopsy?"

A little smile escaped De Blasio.

"Your friend, Dr. Modo. You are friends, aren't you?"

Ricciardi didn't dignify that question with an answer.

"Who did you interview?"

"The family members, the housekeeper. While we were still there, not even a couple of hours later, the murderer arrived and confessed."

"That is, he came there? The Count of Roccaspina?"

The little man nodded.

"That's right. He made a fine, unprompted statement, here in police headquarters where we brought him first thing. In the dead man's office he said nothing more than: It was me. Take me away. And that's what we did."

Ricciardi said nothing, and thought for a while. Then he asked: "Do you mind if I hold on to the reports for a while? I'd like to see if there are matches with what I'm working on now."

De Blasio put on a guarded expression.

"But what case are you working on, now? Sorry, but you know that Garzo insists on being kept apprised of all investigations, and when an official report leaves one office and enters another, there has to be a good reason. I wouldn't want to get in trouble."

Ricciardi gave a vague reply.

"References to dates and events, a couple of burglaries in that part of town. Maybe someone saw suspicious people entering or leaving a building at that time of night. Who knows, maybe something will emerge. I wouldn't want anyone to be able to say, at some later date, that due to a lack of collaboration between the two offices, the investigation was in some way hampered. Because, in that case, I'd be obliged to make mention of your refusal. I'd be forced to, in spite of my own best wishes."

De Blasio considered Ricciardi. That bastard with his reptilian eyes wouldn't hesitate to do it, he felt certain.

He hefted the file folder in his hands, sighed, and said: "All right. But let's be clear: I'm only letting you have it for this afternoon. Tomorrow morning I want it back, I don't like letting my reports out of my office. All right?"

Ricciardi had to lean over the desk to make up for the shortness of reach of his colleague's arms. He flashed him a grimace that distantly resembled a smile.

"All right."

IX

Ricciardi and Maione were skimming the reports, written in the classical language of the police bureaucracy, hunting for relevant details between the lines.

The brigadier, standing behind his superior's armchair, gave up.

"As far as I can see, they didn't do anything wrong, Commissa'. Okay, they might have wrapped up the investigation in a hurry, but the thing is that once someone's shown up who has means, motive, and opportunity and who can tell you in excruciating detail exactly what happened, what else were they supposed to do?"

Ricciardi tapped his finger on the sheet on which were written the justifications for closing the case.

"I'd even be willing to go along with you on that, but I don't see any conclusive confirming evidence. In practical terms, there was no interrogation of the alleged self-confessed killer, and no comparison of his statements with the objective documented evidence. They simply arrested the Count of Roccaspina and 'immediately transferred him to the judicial prison of Poggioreale, under the jurisdiction of the authority for public safety.' And with that, they put the matter out of their minds."

Maione shook his head.

"And, excuse me, but what else were they supposed to do, Commissa'? Just read what it says here: the count told them everything, right down to the smallest details. During the night, having had too much to drink and lost heavily at gambling, the idea occurred to him that he might go see Piro and talk him into giving him more time to repay one of his debts. The lawyer, who was a bit of a night owl, answered the door in person and invited him into his office. There they exchanged angry words, whereupon the count picked up an object from the lawyer's desk, he couldn't recall whether it was a pen or a paper knife, and stabbed him with it. Then he took fright, left the building, and went home. When he awakened, sobered up, he went to Piro's office to see whether by chance he'd dreamt the whole thing, and instead he found himself face-to-face with both the corpse and the police, in the persons of those outstanding specimens of official valor, De Blasio and my colleague, Cozzolino. At that point, he made a full confession, and the case was wrapped up. Do me a favor and tell me, what's wrong with that version?"

Ricciardi continued to read and reread the same pages.

"First of all, we don't have the murder weapon. The count doesn't remember what he used, that's true, but nothing was found in the office or in the front hall."

Maione threw his arms wide.

"But they asked him about it, don't you see? And the count answered that he can't remember, in fact; that maybe he threw it away along the way home."

"Well, then, the fact remains that we have no murder weapon. Then there's nothing about cross-referencing the timing. Where was the count coming from? What time did he leave his nocturnal company? And is it conceivable that no one thought to pay a call on the Piro household?"

The brigadier walked past the desk.

"Commissa', I can see that there are a few elements that look pretty wobbly and you know that I detest from the bottom of my heart both De Blasio and that overdressed fop, Cozzolino. But quite honestly, I don't know what else they were supposed to do in that situation. They were handed the solution to the case on a silver platter, so they took it. Simple as that."

Ricciardi thought it over, nodding. Then he got to his feet.

"True, but there's still a little legwork we can do, even at this late date. And if we're going to listen to what the contessa has to say, and it strikes me that that's what we've decided to do, we're going to have to get started somewhere. Let me ask you a favor, Raffaele. Since we have to give back these reports to that idiot De Blasio first thing tomorrow, copy them over for me from start to finish. In the meantime, I'll take a little stroll over to the Pellegrini hospital and find out if Bruno Modo remembers anything about the autopsy he did on Piro."

Maione turned disconsolately to look at the small stack of pages in the folder.

"*Mamma mia*, Commissa'. You know that's something I'm not much good at, writing: my fingers are just too big. Do you mind if I drag Antonelli, from the archives, into this? He really enjoys it, he says that he has beautiful handwriting, and that at school they always gave him gold stars."

Ricciardi produced the usual grimace that he called a smile.

"Do as you think best. But take care: extreme secrecy. I don't want to find Garzo sticking his nose into this, asking what we think we're up to. We've decided to reopen a closed case, remember that. Now, let's get to work. We'll talk later."

Walking up Via Toledo, as noon gave way to afternoon. Walking up the main street of the city, at the very time of day when people were returning home or going to work, or out looking for food, or just trying to get by. When everyone was out on the street, enjoying the air that flowed through it, the air between the scent of the sea, rising from below, and the sparkling aroma of the woods, wafting down from above, to be inhaled as if it were opium that could change your mood for the better for no good reason, and God only knew there was plenty of call for that.

Ricciardi walked the short distance to the hospital, savoring the momentary solitude that you can only enjoy in the midst of a busy crowd. He tried to keep his mind on this case that wasn't a case, this investigation that couldn't be an investigation. He wondered how and why he was even working on the matter at all, since he always saw work as a necessary factor, and dealt with the shadows of the human soul because he was obliged to, and never of his own free will.

He wasn't one of those guardians of law and order who make a sort of moral precept out of their pursuit of criminals. He realized that to the eyes of others, his colleagues on the police force and perhaps even the magistrates he worked with, it might look that way: the way he sank his teeth into his cases, the way he dedicated himself body and soul to solving them, never taking a break, never slackening his pursuit, did in fact seem as if he were on a mission, something that went well beyond mere professional dedication. For that matter, the fact that he had no social life, no woman in his life, no friends, parties, or receptions to attend, no clubs he belonged to: all this only confirmed the opinion that one might easily form of him.

But that's not the way it was, he thought to himself as he walked along, hugging the wall, skirting the mass of people that crowded the street. In reality, he detested the dark side of the human soul and was terrified at how well he was able to conceive of the variegated and ripe-smelling river of humanity that poured laughing, singing, shouting, and chatting through the streets and alleyways, creating the passions that would carry them to the shores of joy or, more likely, to utter ruin. He would gladly have avoided having anything to do with crime at all. He'd have given all he owned just to be a normal human being, with the single goal of starting a family and caring for it as best he could.

At the corner of the street, his eyes were met with a grotesque and terrible scene. A little flower girl was squatting on the ground, and in front of her sat a basket of violets, wild roses, and jonquils. Smiling, she was trying to attract the attention of the passersby with a singsong: *ciure, ciure delicate, evere addirose, ma vuje vulite bbene a quacchedune?* Delicate flowers, Ricciardi translated, and aromatic herbs. A gift for the one you love.

Right in front of the girl, less than a yard away, the commissario perceived the corpse of a middle-aged man. The dead man's eyes, his teeth gnashing in horrible pain all the while, stared unseeing straight into the little girl's eyes: the body had been sliced neatly in half by the trolley he'd jumped in front of, and he vanished from Ricciardi's sight right where his bloody pelvis ended, with white vertebrae and pink intenstines dangling out. The dead man's voice, perfectly audible to Ricciardi, at least as clear as the young girl's singsong cry, was cursing the poverty and despair that had led him to seek that atrocious demise.

He picked up his pace without responding to the flower girl's invitation, extracting a perfumed handkerchief from his pocket and pressing it to his mouth to stifle his sudden nausea.

That's the reason, he thought. That explains why I'm so devoted to my work, to what might seem like a pathological pleasure in muckraking, delving into the filth that men and women carry hidden away in the inmost rooms of their hearts. How can I do it, how could I ever hope to ignore all this pain? How could I escape it, how can I avoid it, if it hits me between the eyes at an ordinary street corner on this wonderful September afternoon?

He entered the cool shade of the Pellegrini hospital and was enveloped in a silence that seemed unreal, after the noise and clamor of the piazza that the hospital overlooked, where a bustling street market was always under way.

He knew the place well, and he quickly climbed the staircase that led up to Dr. Modo's ward.

X

The doctor emerged from the autopsy room, rubbing his hands on his lab coat.

"Oh, what a lovely surprise! It's our dear Ricciardi, deprived of his usual vaudeville sidekick, the famous Brigadier Maione. To what do I owe the honor? I don't recall having checked in any murdered guests, here at the hotel."

Despite his usual ostentatious display of sarcasm and irony, Ricciardi knew that if there was a man who fully empathized with the suffering he beheld from dawn to dusk of every working day, that man was Bruno Modo. The doctor ran his hand through his full head of thick white hair, scrutinizing the commissario over the lenses of his gold-rimmed spectacles.

"Well, let me take a look at you. You've lost a little weight, if I'm not mistaken? It seems to me that that sideboard of a girl who's come to take care of you has less authority than poor Rosa in terms of stuffing food into you."

The physician's eyes darted to the black band that Ricciardi wore on his arm, over his jacket. As the only person who was at all on close personal terms with the commissario, he was well aware of Ricciardi's strong bonds of affection with his *tata*. He had battled with all the weapons that science put at his disposal to save her, but in the end the cerebral hemorrhage had triumphed.

"What are you talking about? Nelide is worse than her aunt," Ricciardi replied. "She stands there like a bloody-minded gendarme and she won't clear the dishes from the table unless she can see clear through to the porcelain. She's been good, as far as that goes, it hardly seems that a thing has changed. Rosa was perfect in that, too. She taught her everything."

Modo, who remembered her perfectly, shook his head.

"She was extraordinary. An extraordinary woman. And what's more, she put up with you, which made her an authentic heroine. Come on, step outside with me so I can smoke a cigarette and get a breath of fresh air. I imagine it's a lovely day, though here in prison you'd never know it."

They walked out into the rear courtyard, where there was a large flowerbed with a couple of benches next to a centuries-old tree. The shade was pleasant. It seemed impossible to think that just a few yards away, on the other side of the enclosure wall, the city was still there, teeming like an anthill.

The minute they sat down, a little white dog with brown spots showed up, one ear drooping and one perked up high, his tail frantically fanning the air. The animal came up to the doctor, who roughly scratched his head, pulling a chunk of bread out of the pocket of his lab coat.

"Here you are, dog. How is your day going? Here, a little something for you to eat, that way you won't pester the people in the hospital kitchen. Do you think I don't know that you take up a position outside the kitchen door? And that those wretches who work there toss you all the scraps and leftovers?"

Ricciardi smiled briefly. He'd been a witness to the first meeting between the doctor and the dog, a year before or thereabouts, and it gave him pleasure to see how inseparable they still were.

"So you still haven't given him a proper name?"

Modo shrugged his shoulders.

"Why should I? It's not like there are any other dogs that live with me. No names and no leashes, my friend: the secret of relationships is freedom. But tell me, on the other hand, what brings you here? I don't believe for one second that you have been able to withstand the temptation to absorb a shred of my wisdom and profound culture."

Ricciardi reached out and distractedly patted the animal who, having recognized him, had placed a paw on his leg.

"Yes, in fact, I do need to ask you for some information. But you're going to have to stretch your memory, this case dates back several months."

Modo lit a cigarette, inhaling the smoke with gusto.

"That's no problem, I remember everything, I'm not an old man like you. It will be a pleasant variation on my everyday routine. Lately all that's come in here are suicides, dammit. Yesterday they brought me a man in two pieces, just think: he threw himself under a trolley car not a hundred yards away from here. What a depressing story."

Ricciardi saw before him the severed torso of the man murmuring imprecations at the unsuspecting flower girl.

"In the first few days of June, earlier this year, you performed an autopsy on a certain Ludovico Piro, a lawyer. Do you remember?"

Modo furrowed his brow.

"Certainly, I remember, I've already told you that of the two of us, the one who's going senile is you. And after all, how could I forget? A coming and going of carriages and chauffeur-driven automobiles: that man was in business with all the debauched good-for-nothings of the anemic aristocracy of this dying city. From my point of view, though, nothing special. Aside from the mortal wound, no other lesions."

Ricciardi nodded, and resumed stroking the dog's head.

"Yes, I read the report. But tell me something more about the cadaver. Are you sure that you remember clearly?"

The doctor exhaled a plume of smoke.

"Let me tell you in no uncertain terms that you are in the

presence of the clearest mind in this nation, and in fact I'm the only one who clearly sees the abyss toward which this country is barreling now that Germany, too, has chosen to allow itself to be governed by buffoons. Now then: the dead man was about fifty, and he wasn't in particularly good physical shape. The arteries, the lungs, the internal organs displayed the usual signs of wear and tear found among the people of that class. Still, barring complications, a couple of decades of life remained to him, if that other gentlemen hadn't decided otherwise."

"And were there any signs of a struggle? You know, flesh under fingernails, bruises . . . "

Modo shook his head.

"No, I told you, there were no other lesions. I went myself to take a look at the scene of the crime; a beautiful place in Santa Lucia, a splendid summer day, with the sea that practically seemed to come in through the window. Such a shame to die, in a place like that."

Ricciardi sat up more alertly.

"So you really did arrive while the dead body was still there? What position was it in? Did you see any details, did anything catch your eye?"

Modo looked at him curiously.

"Oh, *mamma mia*, what enthusiasm! Do you mind if I ask what's going on? Have you reopened the investigation? I thought that the murderer confessed. At least that's what I read in the papers."

The commissario vaguely waved his hand.

"No, no. On the contrary, I need this conversation to remain private. I'm reconstructing certain aspects at the request of . . . well, let's just say, privately. Well, are you going to tell me whether you remember anything?"

The doctor concentrated.

"Well, now, let's see. The cadaver was slumped over, on the

desktop. There were documents, promissory notes, contracts. There wasn't a great deal of blood, from which I deduced that the fatal blow hadn't severed any arteries, and in fact that's what I found during the autopsy."

"Besides that? Nothing else?"

"Nothing else. Just that one blow. As if he'd caught the victim off guard: boom, and then facedown on the desk. I remember that there was a bronze statuette on the desk, a little boy fishing, and it hadn't even been knocked over. An inkwell, full of ink. A letter tray containing letters and documents, still upright. And then him, as if he'd fallen asleep."

The dog curled up at Ricciardi's feet and fell into a light sleep, but one ear remained upright, ready to pick up any noise out of the ordinary.

"And you didn't have any further thoughts about this paper knife or pen that is thought to have been used to murder Piro?"

Modo shook his head.

"No, it was no paper knife. It was a clean wound, a hole at least seven inches deep, but there were no lateral cuts. Not a knife, or a paper knife either. A pen, yes, that could be, in fact, that seems quite likely. But dry, because there were no traces of ink on the flesh."

The commissario seemed to be observing with the greatest attention the dog's rhythmic breathing.

"Well then, how did he die?"

The doctor indicated a point beneath his right ear.

"The blow was delivered directly behind the mandible, on the right side, medially to the sternocleidomastoid. The sharp point, whether it was a pen or something else, entered obliquely, at roughly a sixty-degree angle, and penetrated the throat muscles until it hit the larynx, as I wrote in the autopsy report. The victim, in practical terms, was suffocated in his own blood in less than a minute's time."

Ricciardi was completely absorbed by the description.

"To the right. So a left-handed killer, then?"

Modo shrugged his shoulders.

"Not necessarily. To strike a blow, either hand will do, it's not a piece of precision work, after all. But whoever delivered that blow was certainly above the victim, the angle speaks clearly."

"And he never called for help."

"No, he didn't. He couldn't have, with the laceration of the cartilage. If he'd been able to, he would most likely have been heard, even at that time of night. It was hot out, and the window was open."

The commissario said nothing for a long while. Then he spoke: "The wife and children were sleeping only a few yards away. The window was open. Someone comes in in the middle of the night, argues, probably has a loud fight because otherwise it's unclear why he'd kill him, and then murders him. Then he turns and leaves, untroubled, opens the door again, walks downstairs, and exits the building. No one sees him. No one hears him."

Modo threw his arms wide.

"Or maybe someone does see him and decides to mind their own business, quite simply. Or maybe at that hour of the night, in a well-to-do neighborhood, everyone is asleep in spite of the heat. The fact remains that Count Whatsisname made a full confession, right? Why should he have done that, if he wasn't the murderer?"

Once again, silence. Then, in an undertone: "Right, why should he?"

The doctor stood up.

"I have to get back to my ward, I have an old man with a nasty case of pneumonia who I doubt is going to live to see tomorrow. Listen, Ricciardi, I've made an important decision that concerns you: one of these nights you're going to have to get over your proverbial stinginess and invest a little of your

substantial assets to take me out to dinner. There's a new trattoria that I'm told has such piss-poor wine that you can get
drunk on less than a liter of it. Agreed?"

Ricciardi protested weakly.

"Bruno, you know I don't like going out at night. It's been
a kind of tough period . . . "

Modo lifted his hand, brusquely.

"Maybe you didn't understand: this is your doctor's orders.
No excuses. I'm going to come pick you up at police headquarters the day after tomorrow at eight in the evening,
because I'm on duty tomorrow."

"Has anyone ever told you that your way of doing things is
reminiscent of the Fascists?"

The doctor burst into laughter, waking up the dog, who
leapt to his feet.

"Ah, you've found me out! In reality, I'm a spy appointed
by Il Duce personally to discover all those who would be willing to establish bonds of friendship with a dissident, and
arrange to send them into internal exile. Instead of me, a dozen
Blackshirts will come to get you, and they'll beat you bloody."

Ricciardi was resigned.

"Fine with me, better a dozen Blackshirts than an entire
evening spent listening to you rave on about politics."

When he left the courtyard, Modo was still laughing, and
the dog was happily wagging his tail.

XI

W hy had he decided to delve into that absurd story? Ricciardi couldn't help but ask himself.

By now it was late afternoon. From the dull grumblings of his stomach he realized that he had skipped lunch; that had happened many times in the past, but never once since he had returned from Cilento after Rosa's funeral. He stopped at the cart of a street vendor who was calling his wares in a stentorian voice, comparing his pizza to the most exquisite products of the finest pastry shops.

As he was rapidly gobbling his meal, bent forward to prevent olive oil and tomato sauce from dripping onto his trousers, the question kept whirring through his head: Why?

A closed case, an investigation without leads; the impossibility of surveying any of the evidence with his own eyes, no chance of picking up clues that might have eluded others, and, most important of all, of hearing the dead man's last scrap of thought, by means of that terrible, deranged faculty that the Deed endowed him with.

It was like looking for something in an empty dresser drawer.

And yet, he somehow felt that he had come back to life, as he focused on something other than his own anguish, this new loneliness. That was already a considerable step forward, he was forced to admit.

After gulping down the last bite and rewarding the vendor with an added tip, prompting the man to ask, with ill-concealed professional pride, whether that wasn't the best fried pizza in town, Ricciardi decided that he would spend his last remaining hour of daylight by visiting the home of the Contessa of Roccaspina. He remembered the place, and he had read the address in De Blasio's crime report.

Was it plausible that the count could have gone out and returned home without his wife's noticing? He wanted to look into that question and he also wanted to speak to the woman again to agree with her on their ensuing lines of attack. He knew that he would need to move cautiously, otherwise his superior officers would be sure to cut him off. Reopening a closed case was a mortal sin: in practical terms it amounted to an admission that the police had put an innocent man in jail, and while he might have confessed to the crime, it still constituted an error. The results would be to trigger an immediate reaction from Rome and an ensuing earthquake at police headquarters.

What's more, though it wasn't easy to admit it to himself, he wanted to see Bianca again. He wanted to understand why she was so adamant in her belief that the count was innocent. He sensed that neither love, conjugal loyalty, nor the bonds of marriage were what drove the woman's determination. Then what was behind it?

The street door was open, but there was no one guarding the entrance, and Ricciardi ventured into the courtyard. At the center of the courtyard, a large flowerbed displayed an untended tangle of vegetation surrounding a dizzyingly tall palm tree. There was no sign of carriages or automobiles: the garage was empty, save for a few crates stacked up in the shadows. The general impression was of a long-ago splendor that had now faded, a depressing abandonment.

He climbed the broad staircase to the second floor, where there was a single, large door made of dark hardwood.

A fairly elderly woman came to the door; she wore a stained apron and looked up at him with unmistakable mistrust. He asked to see the contessa and the old woman vanished into the interior without a word, leaving him to wait in the spacious, unadorned front hall.

Bianca arrived almost immediately. She wore no ornaments of any kind, and yet she somehow conveyed an impression of extreme elegance and refinement. She wore a navy blue dress with a small white pattern, simply cut, and her hair, with its coppery highlights, was pulled up in a bun and fastened with a brooch.

She gave Ricciardi a calm, level gaze.

"Commissario, what a surprise. I wasn't expecting visitors, forgive me if I'm less than presentable. Has something happened?"

He nodded his head ever so slightly.

"I hope you'll excuse me, Signora. I've been over to the hospital to see the doctor who performed the autopsy at the time of the murder, and I had a little chat with the colleague who opened and closed the investigation. I wanted to talk about the case with you, too, for a moment, if you can spare the time."

Bianca nodded.

"Why, of course. In fact, if anything, I should be thanking you for your prompt activity. Frankly, I was hardly expecting this much. Please, come this way and make yourself comfortable," she said as she led the way into a small sitting room near the front door.

Ricciardi recognized the same room where he'd been received at the time of the investigation into the murder of the self-proclaimed seer. The room emanated a general sensation of decrepitude, something that he had already noticed the last time, and which reminded him of a brief quarrel between the count and the contessa. The man, he remembered, had the wild-eyed expression of a wounded, cornered beast, while she had given him a vague sense of disquiet, the same feeling he was now experiencing in the presence of those calm, chilly eyes that somehow, at the same time, conveyed impassioned suffering; they displayed a fire that burned behind a thick slab of ice that was at once immobile and translucent.

Bianca pointed him to a small armchair facing a settee.

"Can I offer you a glass of rosolio liqueur? I'm afraid I don't have much else. As you may have noticed, we're a little short on domestic help and on provisions."

Ricciardi pretended not to understand the bitter irony.

"Nothing, thanks. I've just eaten."

"Then tell me, Commissario. Have you learned anything from these first contacts?"

Ricciardi pushed the hair off his forehead with a distracted sweep of his hand.

"I confess that I'm having a hard time getting a clear idea of what happened after the murder for which your husband was arrested. And in fact, the investigation might very well have been wound up in something of a hurry: reading between the lines of the police reports, there's no mistaking an evident sense of relief at his confession."

The shadow of a smile flashed rapidly across Bianca's lovely face.

"I have to say I am of the same opinion, Commissario. All the same, I can hardly blame your colleagues. Stumbling upon someone who conveniently ties it all up with a neat bow, and especially when it's a murder that brings a certain whiff of scandal with it, is too big a piece of luck to turn up your nose at."

Ricciardi agreed.

"You show a very balanced point of view, Signora. For my part, I have to admit that this case might bear a little more looking into. Luckily, the autopsy was performed by the finest medical professional we have in this city, which means we have some very solid information in that regard. Now, we just have to figure out . . . "

The last rays from the setting sun angled in through the window and played over the contessa's hair, extracting a reddish gleam. She suddenly looked like a girl pleased to have been given an unexpected gift, and the commissario felt a surge of tenderness caress his soul.

"Then you've decided to take on the case!" the woman exclaimed. "I sensed it, you know, when we first met, that you were a perceptive soul. Even then, it would have been easy to accuse Romualdo. It was the most obvious solution, and yet you didn't do it."

Ricciardi displayed caution.

"Let's be perfectly clear on this. I can dig into this case and try to find a little evidence that might have been overlooked due to the haste we were just talking about. But that doesn't mean that the larger picture, as it's currently configured, can be completely overturned."

"Of course not. But you see, Commissario, I know for sure that Romualdo never left home that night. And if Piro was murdered that same night, then I am completely certain it wasn't Romualdo who did it."

Ricciardi remained silent for a few seconds. Then he decided that the time had come to ask his question.

"Would you care to tell me how you can be so sure of that? Couldn't he have gotten out of bed while you were asleep, for instance? Couldn't he had returned home before you awakened?"

Bianca blushed violently and compressed her lips. Ricciardi noticed the sudden change of expression and was baffled. The woman got to her feet.

"All right then. After all, you could hardly form a worse impression. Please, come with me."

The commissario followed her through a long procession of rooms immersed in the partial darkness of closed shutters and curtains pulled tight. Barren rooms, with flaking walls and faded frescoes on the high ceilings, only infrequent pieces of furniture, and a layer of dust over everything, accentuating the image of dreary abandonment of a great home that had once enjoyed luxury but now maintained only the faintest of memories of it.

Bianca walked briskly, said not a word, and kept her eyes fixed straight ahead of her. It was a seething humiliation for her to have to display the squalor in which she lived to that man, and yet at the same time she felt an angry pride surging inside her. Conflicting sensations that she puzzled over. She'd never displayed so much of herself, and now she was doing it to save the man who had put her in that condition in the first place. Ironic, if you stopped to think.

She stopped when she came to a pair of doors, side by side. She heaved a deep breath, then turned to stare at Ricciardi.

"Listen carefully to what I have to say, Commissario. Romualdo and I have been married for ten years. We haven't had children, and our relationship has been deteriorating over the years. I imagine that's something that happens frequently in marriages, and usually people just conceal the fact behind a façade of respectability and fake affection. Unfortunately, I'm no good at pretending. And that is a very grave defect for someone born into my social world."

Ricciardi said nothing and, in his embarrassment, wondered to himself why she was confiding such things to him.

As if she had read his mind, Bianca added: "You must be wondering why I'm telling you all this. It gives me no pleasure, but I think it's necessary that you have a complete understanding of the situation if you are going to realize why I'm so sure of what I'm saying."

Ricciardi, for no good reason at all, thought of Enrica and Livia, but also of Rosa and Nelide. The warm, noisy, chaotic home of a large family, which he was able to intuit based only on two windows across the way and a smile; the rich and fashionable apartment with a hint of loneliness, a small house-hold run by two housekeepers and a scrubwoman, a place that was scented with lavender and redolent of cleanliness; the comfortable, safe, muffled and silent apartment that first an aunt and later her niece kept for him as if it were a temple. Each of those homes had taken on the personality of the women who lived in it, each of them resembled those who moved inside them. But this house remained completely unmarked. It was impossible, as he looked at the rooms, to sense the personality of whoever lived there.

"Signora, I'm not here to pay a call on you or to judge you or the life you lead. You contacted me for a reason, and that reason is why we're talking right now."

He had uttered those words to reassure the contessa, but he immediately realized how harsh and cold it had sounded, the way it had come out.

The woman seemed to ponder Ricciardi's words.

"I understand. And in fact the things that I've told you are crucial, in my opinion, to a fuller understanding of what actu-ally happened. My confidences concerning the state of my rela-tionship with my husband were a necessary premise upon which to explain to you, Commissario, that my husband and I haven't slept in the same room for years now."

Ricciardi was surprised.

"Then . . . how can you possibly be sure that he was home that night? I'm sorry, I don't understand."

"That's why I've brought you here. You see?" Bianca waved a hand toward one of the doors. "This is my bedroom, and this room next door is where my husband slept. They share a wall. A very thin wall. It was originally a single large bedroom. But that was long ago."

Bianca's voice betrayed no regrets. She was simply stating facts.

"And it's precisely because of how thin that wall is that I

can, or rather, I could know with absolute precision both when he came home and when he left. I'm a very light sleeper, and before falling asleep I always read for hours. That night he came home at nine and the next morning, he left at seven thirty."

Ricciardi was angry at himself. That woman was wasting his time.

"Signora, I frankly believe that it's quite impossible for you to be certain that your husband never left, if you were in a different room from him. You're basing your certainty on a mere impression, and I'm afraid that such a claim is far too vague to justify opening a case that has already been closed. Now I hope you'll excuse me, but I have to go."

Unexpectedly, Bianca smiled at him.

"That's what I expected. It's too convenient to have someone who simply confesses to a murder to just toss out the solution. Much less if the person calling this convenient solution into question is a woman, and a woman who no longer shares her husband's bed."

Continuing to hold Ricciardi with her gaze, Bianca reached out her hand to one of the two doors and opened it. The heavy door squealed pitiably, and when she shut it again, it echoed with a dull thud. Both of the sounds, even during the daytime, against the noises that came in from outside, were perfectly and irritatingly audible.

"Believe me, Commissario: I can tell you with absolute precision when this door is opened and when it is shut again. I told you that I'm a very light sleeper and that I wake up quite often during the night."

Ricciardi thought it over.

"Let's admit, for argument's sake, that you heard clearly and that your husband never left that night. Let's admit that he had some mysterious motive for confessing to a murder he didn't commit. Let's also admit that the autopsy is correct and that Piro actually was killed between midnight and two in the morning. How would your husband have known that there had been a murder? And why would a man so dedicated to living a life of pleasure have left home at such an early hour?"

Bianca never once took her eyes off of Ricciardi's.

"My husband was a gambler, Commissario. For the sake of this cursed vice, because of this disease, he ruined his life and mine. But that doesn't mean that he was a social butterfly or that he was out till all hours attending the theater and living the rake's life. When he ran out of money, and if no one would extend him credit, he came home and shut himself in this room. It was a common occurrence for him to come home early, and there were times when he didn't even go out at all. As for leaving home early in the morning, that had become a habit with him for the past few months. I have no idea where he went."

"And you never asked him?"

The contessa smiled sadly.

"Commissario, Romualdo and I never talked much. In fact, we almost never did. There were times when I couldn't believe I ever married him, and I can't even remember the last time we had a laugh together. He has . . . had his life and I did whatever I could to hold together the last few pieces of my own. We had nothing in common, and we hadn't in years."

Ricciardi recalled that, when he had come to the palazzo to interview the count, she had immediately told him that, if he was a creditor, she had no idea where her husband might be. In a flash he understood what kind of hell that woman's marriage had condemned her to.

"Signora, could I see your husband's bedroom?"

Bianca once again opened the door, and it produced the same unpleasant screech as before.

In the room, disorder reigned. Stacks of yellowed newspapers and magazines gathered dust. An old oversized armoire displayed, through a half-opened cabinet door, a few suits and an overcoat that had clearly been patched and mended. A ramshackle vanity table with a mirror dulled by the passage of the years, with a shaving bowl and all the attendant paraphernalia. A dresser drawer pulled open, with linen inside. A couple of down-at-the-heel pairs of shoes, an unmade bed.

Bianca had remained just beyond the threshold. Her eyes were avoiding the sight of that display.

"He never let us come in to clean the room, the housekeeper and me. It's all exactly as he left it, when he went to . . . That morning, in other words."

Ricciardi reviewed those ordinary everyday objects, trying to form an idea of the person who had inhabited that room. A man who had simply given up, abandoning all dignity: it looked like a stall or a garage inhabited by a vagabond. There was a smell of dust and a pungent whiff of something rancid, covered up by cheap perfume. He went over to the vanity table, hoping to find a few letters, some personal documents. There was nothing.

He looked up.

"Signora, there's something I need to ask you, a favor, and I apologize in advance for the intrusion. Would you mind very much if I entered your bedroom and asked you to open and shut your husband's door?"

Bianca's eyes delved into his soul, but Ricciardi withstood her piercing gaze.

In the end she stepped forward, opened the adjoining door, and gestured for the commissario to enter.

Ricciardi kept his eyes downcast, to make perfectly clear that he had not the slightest intention of breaking in on the contessa's personal privacy. All the same, he could not help but notice, out of the corner of his eye, a clean, tidy, sweet-smelling bedroom, with two adorable curtains and a book lying open on the side table.

Turning his back to the bed, he shut the door behind him.

A moment later, he heard Bianca opening and then shutting the door in the adjoining room. The woman had been right, that noise was more than enough to awaken anyone, unless they were an extremely heavy sleeper.

He walked out of the room with determination and spoke to the contessa.

"All right. All right. I'll go forward with this. But I'll need to meet your husband, and that will require me first to meet his lawyer. Could you arrange a meeting with him for me?"

"Why, certainly, Commissario. He's a dear friend of my family. Hopefully by tomorrow, if you like. Would you want me to go with you?"

"No, there's no need for that. In fact, without you there he may speak more freely. I'll wait for you to let me know the time and place of the appointment."

The woman nodded her head again.

"Tomorrow morning I'll send my housekeeper to police headquarters. And, commissario . . . "

"Yes?"

"*Grazie.* You are the first person who has listened to me since . . . since this thing happened. And I need to know. Absolutely need to."

Ricciardi waved his hand vaguely in the air.

"Don't thank me. I assure you that, at this particular moment, it's a great help for me to have something to focus on. One last question: is your husband left-handed?"

A stunned expression appeared on Bianca's face.

"No, Commissario. He uses his right hand. Why?"

Ricciardi shrugged his shoulders.

"You never know what evidence may turn out to be important in an investigation. Best to gather all the available evidence in the meantime."

When they were at the front door, the contessa turned to look at him.

She chose her words carefully and uttered them in a low voice.

"I need to break free of this thing, Commissario. And I won't be free until I know the reason why. You understand that, don't you?"

Ricciardi nodded and left, in a hurry.

XII

Major Manfred Kaspar von Brauchitsch raised his eyes to the sky and took in a deep breath of air.

His eyes and nose, involved in that operation, gave him surprising reports. The eyes saw no stars, in spite of the fact that it was evening, because of the nearby illumination cast by the street lamps along either side of the narrow street; the nose, instead of a whiff of the sweet-smelling air so characteristic of this phase of transition between summer and fall, brought him a gust of distinctive aroma, a blend of garlic, onion, and cooked greens that came from a small trattoria on the street corner. For that matter, his ears, if they had been questioned on the matter, would have confirmed that he was close to a place that offered dining, because they would have conveyed to him the sounds of music and drunken singing from the diners standing outside of the little restaurant, smoking and laughing.

The major shook his head in amusement, thinking for the hundredth time in two days just how different that strange, disorderly, carefree city was from his hometown of Prien. And yet, he thought, they were each part of the south. Bavaria and southern Italy, though they were both as different from each other as were Germany and this strong and hopeful nation he had come to visit.

How many things had happened since July, when he had come here for the thermal spa where he spent time every summer. And how many things were bound to happen still, in just a short time to come. Life can reserve enormous surprises, and it can pack together in just a few days events that are sufficient to change not one but two lives.

Manfred headed off, whistling a tune, and climbed Via dei Mille until he reached the Ascensione church, near the pensione where he was staying. If someone had told him, as recently as that spring, that his life would change so radically, he would have replied with a bitter laugh.

He thought back to himself, to the way he was just a few months ago. A wounded, anguished soldier, without prospects, whose heart had been chilled by loneliness and time, on the threshold of middle age. What's worse, a soldier in a country that was practically without an army, paying for a long-ago defeat, a decade and a half old, turned in upon itself with fear and uncertainty. A weary man of thirty-eight years, who had lost any hope of being able to fill the void left after the death of his wife, more than ten years ago; but he still wished for a family, children to whom he could bequeath the future he had dreamed of but which, for the moment, he had been unable to create.

Then, suddenly, two meetings had changed everything.

One of those meetings had been innocuous at first glance, a political speech delivered to an assembly by a little Austrian, an event he had attended at the urging of a fellow veteran who had heard the man speak. He had gone because he trusted his friend, a man motivated by sincere love of country who was every bit as heartbroken as was Manfred at the condition to which the enduring economic depression had reduced that country.

The little Austrian had a way of speaking that emptied your heart of all uncertainties and filled it with furious hope. He had a strong, decisive voice, that could also be sentimental and delicate. He dispensed dreams and concrete instructions on how to escape that terrible moment and reaffirm the role that Germany had always played, a role of leadership for the entire continent, first among nations. It was God who wanted this, the minuscule condottiere had said, and God's will always wins.

He hadn't been surprised to learn that the Austrian was a veteran of the Great War, just as he was. Only a soldier could know what words other soldiers needed to hear. At the end of the assembly they had met and had gone off to have a couple of beers together. He had had many opportunities to notice that those who spoke in public were often quite different in private, but such was not the case with Adolf. With less drama, but with the same degree of determination, he had repeated at the table in the smoky beer hall the concepts that he had expressed onstage, before the adoring audience of his followers. He had a gift, Adolf did, of entering into immediate empathy with those who listened to him, like some perfectly tuned instrument that suddenly insinuates itself into the melody being played by a small-town combo and magically transforms it into a great orchestra.

Manfred had joined first the movement and later the party with joy and conviction. He wasn't capable of doing things halfway. Either he was an activist or he limited himself to ignoring the topic. He wasn't cut out for the role of sympathizer.

He crossed paths with two young women who exchanged a few whispered comments and smiled brightly at him. He replied with a gallant bow, lifting his cap in greeting, but continued on his way without slowing even slightly, to the unmistakable disappointment of the two girls. He knew women liked him. His tall, athletic physique, his thick blond hair, his blue eyes, and, of course, his uniform unfailingly drew stares, and in the past he had taken advantage of the fact to strike up pleasurable and amusing affairs that never lasted long.

But now, he could no longer pursue those stares, because he was engaged.

To tell the truth, it wasn't official, at least not yet.

But he was going to be officially engaged very soon, he felt sure.

It was one of the two reasons he was now in that city. The other reason was far more confidential, and for two days it had kept him occupied at the German consulate without being able to inform Enrica that he had already arrived: she would be disappointed that he hadn't already rushed to be at her side.

Major von Brauchitsch had in fact been appointed cultural attaché to the diplomatic corps. It had all come to pass in early August, when he had gone to Berlin to see Hitler in person in order to congratulate him on his resounding victory in the federal elections. Hitler had given him a quick hug, and then he had locked arms with him and led him away from the festive group of veterans that surrounded him.

The conversation had been rapid and intense. Adolf had asked him whether he would be willing to reenlist, and he, of course, had expressed his enthusiastic willingness; the pain in his shoulder was diminishing, in part due to the assiduous treatment and the training to which he subjected himself, and he now felt ready. The other man, however, had explained that it wasn't military service in the field he was talking about, but another kind of military activity, one that was far more important to the German state.

Manfred had turned serious, had looked the little Austrian right in the eyes, and had recognized an exceedingly pure determination in him.

That man was going to make Germany great again. And he, Manfred, wanted to take part in that project. With all his strength, he wanted to.

Adolf had put him in touch with a commander of the German navy, and they had had a lengthy conversation. He had been chosen for his perfect service record, the commander had told him, because of the fact that he'd joined the movement in the earliest days, and because he spoke perfect Italian. Then he had explained that a campaign of information-gathering was under way, and that Italy was a friendly nation. It was the Party's intention, he went on, that Italy would and should become a model and an ally. It is from models that we learn, and in some cases there is knowledge that cannot be obtained easily and quickly through official channels, but that was exactly what Germany needed in order to grow quickly and once again take its place of leadership, as it ought to. In other words, he would need to go to places where there were military installations and take a discreet and well-trained look around. And report back in detail.

Manfred was no fool, and he had understood instantly: the commander, a young and ambitious officer who had immediately understood which way the wind was blowing, was asking him to work as a spy. But then, he wasn't a headstrong, starry-eyed raw recruit, he was a major in the cavalry of the Reichswehr, he had been in combat and he had killed men in the name of his country. He understood that there were many ways to serve the nation, and that every man was called upon to give his contribution according to what was asked of him. He thought it over quickly, and agreed without hesitation.

The weeks that followed were devoted to training. On the one hand, they had explained to him exactly what he ought to look for and what he was expected to find out, and on the other they had instructed him in the duties of a cultural attaché. Manfred had noticed with joy that among the cities that were crucial to the collection of information deemed useful to his country, there was the one that was of particular and personal interest to him, because in that city, Italy's most important port city, a city that lay quite close to his beloved Ischia, Enrica lived, his as yet unsuspecting fiancée.

There was nothing wrong with the Reich making use of him and him making use of the Reich.

It was a piece of good fortune that not far from the city itself, a campaign of archeological digs was under way, with the participation of a group of German scholars, and it was therefore quite plausible that the German scientific mission should benefit from reinforced assistance on the part of the consulate. Another cultural attaché was needed, and his arrival could hardly arouse any suspicions.

Just the month before, the German Reichsmarine had intensified its contacts with the Italian Regia Marina, or royal navy, and two high officers, Boehm and Ritter, had been invited as guests aboard the cruiser *Giovanni dalle Bande Nere*, on the occasion of the fleet's great naval maneuvers. It had been the first direct contact, and the two officers returned home greatly impressed by the efficiency of the Italian crew and, especially, by the modernity of the port facilities. Manfred's mission was to determine the scope of the resources that had been brought to bear in order to ready the overwhelming naval forces that had been deployed on that occasion.

Moreover, that city housed a military airfield; and the new German government was intensely interested in rebuilding an adequate air force, something that was unjustly forbidden by the other European nations in the aftermath of Germany's defeat. It would be necessary to gather information about this area of endeavor as well, and so a young pilot had been assigned to Manfred's entourage and placed under his command, in the bogus role of logistical cultural aide; this young man had arrived at the consulate that very afternoon. In other words, an intelligence team was being assembled, which testified to the importance that the German high command placed on that mission. The major was pleased and flattered.

But now that his work had been properly arranged, he could finally turn his mind to the second important reason he'd decided to accept that posting. A more personal reason.

Tomorrow, he thought to himself as he walked across the

little piazza that lay before the building housing the pensione where he was staying, he'd write a note to Enrica. He would tell her that he was in town and that he would be very happy if he could come to see her. He wanted to get to know the family that the young woman had told him so much about during those wonderful days in the sunshine of Ischia, those days when Manfred had painted her portrait while she, on the beach, tended to a noisy and colorful crowd of children. For her, he would bring his beaming smile, for her mother a bouquet of flowers, and for her father a pouch of tobacco and a Bavarian pipe that he had chosen in Prien.

He would let them get to know him and, in time, they'd come to love him. Without haste, with persistence and perseverance. He had chosen Enrica to become his wife and to give him the children that he desired. Germany and Italy, to be brought together in his life, for work and for love.

For no good reason he said hello to four men playing cards at a rickety table under the glare of a streetlight; one of the men responded with an awkward military salute while the three others laughed. And he also said a cheery hello to the proprietor of the pensione, a fat lady who stood drying her hands on a rag, enjoying the evening air.

He climbed the stairs whistling a happy tune and savoring in advance the sweet dreams that the crackling air of September was bound to bring him.

From the shadow of a front hall, a pair of eyes scrutinized him coldly.

XIII

Just as she was about to get into bed with a glass of warm milk and a book, Livia heard a discreet knocking at her bedroom door.

"Come in," she said.

The door opened a crack and Clara, her housekeeper, poked her head through. Her eyes were puffy with sleep, and she wore a housedress; her hair, which she wore tucked up during the day, tumbled loose over her shoulders. She had never known, Livia thought, how long Clara's hair was.

"Signo', please forgive me. We have . . . we have a visit from that gentleman, the one you know, the one who comes here every so often. The gentleman who says: 'The signora is expecting me, let her know that I'm here.' After all, he just showed up at the door, and . . . But if you wish, I'll inform him that you're sleeping, and that he should come back tomorrow."

Livia had already put on her housecoat and was just brushing her hair.

"*Grazie*, Clara. Tell him that I'm coming, and you can go to bed now."

The young woman was heistant; she didn't like leaving her mistress alone, at that time of night, with a man.

"Signo', what if you want to offer him something? I can wait for you in the kitchen, that way if you call for me, I'll hear you. It's very late, it's 11:30. Gentlemen don't go to a lady's home, at this hour."

When Livia entered the living room, Falco was, as was his

custom, standing by the window, hat in hand, his eyes trained down upon the now deserted street below. Despite the late hour, he looked as if he'd just left the barbershop: his thinning hair was neatly combed and there wasn't so much as a shadow of whiskers on his face. He emanated the usual faint odor of lavender.

Without turning around, when the woman entered the room, he said: "Not all nights are the same, Signora. In the summer, people tend to stay out in the streets, to escape the heat. Women in the *vicoli* put chairs outside and talk, and then they go to sleep while the others, men and children, get up because it's impossible to breathe in the ground-floor *bassi*. And people talk and talk. Every *vicolo* becomes a single big family. Everyone knows everything about everyone."

Livia lit a cigarette and puffed the smoke into the air, a little annoyed but, in spite of herself, worried as well.

"Falco, why at this time of night? Has something serious happened?"

The man went on, as if he'd never been interrupted.

"And in the winter, as you no doubt know, things aren't all that different. People light fires to warm themselves up, but in tiny spaces that's not a possibility, everybody would die. And so they start talking again, just like in summer, words pour out of mouths like smoke. The souls of the *vicoli* are glass, you can see right through them."

"Falco, I don't understand you. I . . . "

He swung around, finally turning his back to the window.

"But not in September. In September the doors can be left shut, and you can sleep without talking. To sleep, perchance to dream, as the poet says. But it is our good fortune that there are those who dream aloud. You requested that I bring you some information, Signora. And I have brought you that information."

Livia felt that she'd been put in an awkward situation,

though she had no good reason. The man's tone of voice, flat and unemotional, contrasted with the subtle sensibility of his words.

"But there was no need for all this haste. I'd have gladly seen you tomorrow, if only . . . "

"Let's just say that I'm accustomed to working speedily and conscientiously. The young woman that you saw on the occasion of the car crash in which . . . in which the person who is of interest to you was involved answers to the name of Colombo. Enrica Colombo. She lives on Via Santa Teresa, as does he. Two apartment houses side by side, with windows overlooking the same alley, Vicolo Materdei. She studied to be a schoolteacher, but she has not secured a position in a public school. Instead she tutors children who come to her home."

Livia's interest had exploded.

"What . . . what is she like? What does she do? Are they a couple? Are they engaged? Are they . . . "

Falco proceeded very calmly, as if he were reading a report.

"She lives with her parents and is the eldest of five children. She'll turn twenty-five in a month, on October 24th. Her younger sister, Susanna, the mother of a little boy, is married to a certain Marco Caruso, who is a party member with a reputation as a good and disciplined activist. Her father, Giulio Colombo, is the owner of a haberdashery that sells hats and gloves, a fairly well known establishment, toward the end of Via Toledo, not far from Piazza del Plebiscito; he sympathizes with the Italian Liberal Party, though he is not politically active."

Livia reacted with irritation.

"Falco, you're not answering me! Are they engaged?"

A strange, sad smile appeared on the man's face.

"No, Signora. They aren't. For a brief period, more or less around Easter, the young woman spent time with the late governess, Rosa Vaglio; and we believe that on a couple of occasions she went to see her at home, but always when you know who was away."

The woman fell silent, perplexed.

"But in that case . . . I don't understand, why was she at the hospital?"

Falco shrugged his shoulders.

"I didn't say that there were no feelings between the two of them. Perhaps they look at each other through the windows; after all his bedroom directly overlooks the kitchen and living room in her apartment. It is likely that they know each other, though no one has ever seen them together. We have . . . we have more than one source of information among the suppliers and residents of that neighborhood, and my men had done some serious investigations. We already possessed a fairly thoroughgoing report, so all I had to do was fill it out with the more recent information."

Livia stood there, openmouthed.

"What do you mean, you already had a report? Did you already have her under surveillance? And if so, why? What has she done?"

The man put on a harsh expression.

"Signora, I'm afraid I'm going to have to ask you never again to ask questions about our activity. These are things that do not concern you, and I'll remind you that at this instant I myself am violating a great many regulations concerning secrecy, just to do you a favor."

Livia blinked her eyelashes like a little girl who receives an unexpected scolding.

"Why . . . certainly, of course. In fact, I'm very grateful to you for your efforts. It's just that she strikes me as such a . . . such an ordinary, normal person. I couldn't have dreamed that she might have attracted your attention, that's all. Nothing more."

Falco seemed placated now.

"You know, at times it is not so much the individual person that matters, as much as that person's relationships. And that brings me to the real reason I've ventured to bother you so late at night. This summer, while she was teaching at a beachfront colony on the island of Ischia, Signorina Colombo made friends with a man. And for the past several days, this gentleman has been in town. He is a German soldier, actually, to be precise, an officer. Major Manfred von Brauchitsch."

Livia was confused, but also relieved.

"Well then? Can't a man pay a call on a lady friend, nowadays?"

"Of course he can, Signora. It's just that the officer in question has just taken up duties at the consulate as a cultural attaché. He clearly intends to remain here for a while, in other words. And I can't rule out that his friendship with the young lady might be part of his plans."

The woman didn't seem to grasp the point.

"And do you think I'm disappointed to hear that? I couldn't be more delighted, and I wish them both every happiness."

Falco dropped the irony and went on in a very serious tone of voice.

"Signora, this man is of the greatest possible interest to us. The greatest possible interest. We know that tomorrow he is going to call on Signorina Colombo, because he asked the porter at the consulate to give him directions to her address, and the porter is one of our men. He is staying in a pensione over by the Ascensione church. There is a matter of great importance at play, and it might affect a great many people. I must ask you to steer clear of anyone who has anything to do with him, at least for the next little while."

"What do you mean to say, Falco? Are you afraid that I may be running some risk? Is he ill-intentioned, or is . . . "

"No, no, absolutely not. No danger, lord, no. But we're keeping an eye on this person, and if your name were to surface in a report, that would constitute a short circuit in terms of our functions that would be . . . uncomfortable for you, you see."

"I don't understand, but I accept your advice. I sense, in some strange manner, that you really do have my welfare at heart. But this is about the young woman, isn't it? Not Ricciardi, I mean. You said that they don't socialize, that perhaps they are mere acquaintances and that in the circumstance of the car crash, this Enrica was there only to keep the *tata* company. And since I don't know this woman, nor am I interested in getting to know her, there's no cause for worry. Isn't that right?"

Falco nodded.

"Certainly. But if there were to be any contact between the young woman in question and your commissario, and then between your commissario and yourself, in that case you might find yourself in a problematic situation, which is something I'd like to spare you. That's all."

"Which is why you came to put me on guard. Don't worry, Falco, you've been perfectly clear. But if you're hoping that I'll stop seeing Ricciardi then I'm sorry, and I ought to let you know from this point forward, that I have every intention of seeing him, no matter what you might say. And spending more and more time with him. To keep him from seeing other women, among other things."

She'd uttered the last few words with a laugh, but Falco didn't see the humor.

"Signora, this matter is very, very serious indeed. Don't take lightly the advice I've given you. I beg you. It was the thought that your impulsive nature might have led you to speak with this young lady, and that you might happen to be with her at the very moment that von Brauchitsch was present as well, that led me to do what I would never have done otherwise, and that is, to come here at this hour of the night."

Livia smiled at him, touched.

"Don't worry, Falco. It's not my habit to stop my sentimental rival in the street, or go to her home. In my life, actually, far too often what's happened is the opposite."

Falco was visibly relieved by these reassurances. He headed for the door and Livia admired the elegance and aristocratic style with which he moved. Impulsively she asked him: "One more thing, Falco. How is it that you know so much about life in the city's *vicoli?*"

The man smiled.

"It's quite simple, Signora. I was born and grew up there. And I know that if there's one thing to look out for in this strange city, it's September nights. And the dreams that September nights bring. Good night, and once again, forgive me for this untimely visit. Which, by the way, as usual, and as you know full well, never took place."

XIV

September, September. September night.

Treacherous night, that presents itself hot from the day's sunshine, which still carries memories of summer and brings the many smells of freshly cut grass and burgeoning flowers, when all you have to do is leave the tiniest opening and the night will burrow in with its long, light, chilly fingers to brush you the wrong way, for a minuscule shiver of unease.

But by now your eyes are already drooping shut with exhaustion, and you can't seem to get up to close that window through which the usual notes of that melancholy song come drifting. And with those notes come the first hints of the cold, of the nights when that light breeze will be fully grown, and it will come blowing and shrieking down the empty street, rummaging through balconies and overturning wicker baskets and tossing leaves in whirlwinds, and the fear of outdoors will become the warmth of indoors, and comfort, beneath the covers, with the smell of wood burning in woodstoves tickling your nose.

But that is another time, another weather. That is November of the rains or January of the forgotten holidays, or the desperate tail end of the icy beast that refuses to die in mid-March. Not now.

Now it is September, and the perfumes win out over tomorrow and any terror. It is September, and it seems that the tenderness of this city on the sea, this city of the sky and the leafy branches that toss in the fragile air, will never end. It seems that the souls can remain glass, and display everything within them, and have no need of fear.

So it seems. Because September, at night, loves to shuffle the deck and urges you to pick a card. A card that it already knows full well.

So fall asleep peacefully, then. And dream to your heart's content.

Because you'll dream nothing of what you expect, while your hands reach out in your sleep to grab a blanket that can protect you from the sudden chill that will enter the room, treacherously, through the window you left open just a crack, exposing your soul.

Your soul of glass.

Ricciardi would have liked to dream of Rosa, but instead he dreamed of his mother.

At least in his sleep he would have liked once again to hear the old grouch complaining about her loneliness and her aches and pains, clumping around the apartment in her slippers as she prepared the terrible, enormous bowls of *pasta e fagioli* that she inflicted upon him at regular intervals.

And instead he found himself at the bedside of that minute, fragile woman, her thick black hair streaked with white, the wan face that had once been so full of delicate beauty and now, now that she was about to die, was nothing but flesh pulled taut over a skull with a pair of enormous, haunted green eyes staring out into the darkness.

His mother frightened him. He always dreamed of her the same way, dying and stunned, as if she were about to hurl herself into an abyss whose depth she couldn't begin to guess.

As always, he went over to the bed and stood there, motionless, waiting. She turned her head around to look at him, swiveling it without her body following the movement in the slightest.

In many dreams, which he remembered in the morning and which stayed with him for hours throughout the day, afflicting him with a sense of despairing helplessness, his mother started weeping slowly, silently, tears swollen with unknowable regrets. In other dreams, she gave him a horrible, toothless, demented, black smile that plunged him into an anguish he was unable to escape, even once he had awakened.

This time, though, his mother spoke.

In a dry, rasping voice, like the crackling of burning fire-wood, she said to him: Alone. Now you're alone. Did you believe that this moment would never come? Did you think you could hold out forever, wrapped in a cocoon?

He answered her, and his voice came out in a hush, in coun-tertime to his own breathing: What else could I have done? You know it, Mamma. You know the reason why. You gave me the reason why.

His mother laughed, her eyes wide open and motionless, with eyelashes that never blinked, enormous and green and fixed in his. And the laughter had the sound of the Count of Roccaspina's door as it slammed shut on hell with a bang. Yes, she said to him, I know. But what if I'd chosen to remain all alone? And what if I'd never wanted you or thought you or imagined you? Would you have preferred never even to exist? Never to have seen this girl through the window, never feel the touch of Rosa's rough hands?

Before he had a chance to answer, his mother was trans-formed into a woman with coppery hair and a long slender neck. In his dream, Bianca said to him: Help me. Help me.

Ricciardi shivered in the nighttime breeze that forced its way through the curtains, and piteously the dream faded away.

At a distance of a few yards and a million miles, Enrica would have liked to dream of Manfred, but instead dreamed of Rosa.

In one of her mother's women's magazines, she had read that you dream of whatever you've thought about most during your day. A part of your brain continues to think about it while you're asleep, transforming those thoughts into images. Simple.

In that case, she would ask herself when the next day dawned, as she tried to clear her soul and her heart, how could it be that a thought she'd never had in her consciousness had materialized so well and so clearly, in three dimensions and full color, as she was pulling the sheets up to her chin to escape the sudden chill of the night?

Signori', the *tata* had said to her, brushing her shoulder with one hand; Signori', don't be afraid. It's me. Rosa, she had replied, Rosa, how are you? The old woman had smiled at her: I'm fine, I'm just fine. My legs no longer hurt me, you see? And she'd tried out a clumsy dance step. Then she'd looked her in the eye, somewhat sternly: And you, Signori'? How are you? You don't look a bit well. You're not smiling. Do you remember what I told you about how you're supposed to cook? Do you remember?

Rosa, Enrica had muttered in her sleep, I can't cook the way you taught me. You know, some things have happened. There's Manfred, now. He's been writing me letters, you know. Nice long letters. And he dreams of a family, of children. So, after all, I can't cook the way you told me to.

The old woman had stroked her face: my daughter, my poor daughter. Only with your heart, that's the only way you can cook. Don't you know that? Only with your heart. You see? And she opened her smock, and through her blouse, her petticoat, and her flesh, Enrica saw her big red heart, beating regularly. If you don't have this, you can't hope to cook. You can fill all the bottles you want with tomato sauce, but you'll never know how to cook dishes. And you'll let him die of hunger, this poor . . . what's his name? Alfred? No, Enrica laughed, it's

Manfred. And I have a heart, you see? And she, too, displayed her breast. But underneath it was nothing. Nothing at all.

In her dream, Enrica was frightened to death. How could she live, without a heart? Rosa, Rosa, where is my heart? she screamed, and as she slept a faint lament passed her lips. Signori', don't be afraid, said the old woman, you have a heart. You just need to find it. And when you find it, take my advice, listen to it carefully. The way I did, my whole life.

Rosa didn't even mention him in the dream, and she herself certainly never said his name. But someone was watching them talk from the shadows. Enrica could feel Luigi Alfredo Ricciardi's green eyes on her, the man that she loved in her dreams but who she expelled from her soul during the daytime.

Or at least she tried to.

Livia would have liked to dream of Ricciardi, but instead the September breeze drew for her the face of Falco.

She dreamt she was following a man down the street who looked exactly like the commissario. It was difficult, he was walking quickly and she had to struggle with her high heels. She could hear her labored breathing, it was hot out and the street was crowded. Then she caught up with him, she put a hand on his shoulder, he turned around, and she found the indecipherable expression, the square jaw, and the faint smile of Falco before her eyes.

In her dream, she experienced a blistering disappointment, and she didn't conceal it. But the man didn't even seem to notice and he took her by the arm. He said to her: Livia, you have to understand, what I do is for your own good. She felt offended by his patronizing attitude, and replied: I'll decide for myself what's good for me.

And then, without warning, he kissed her. Just like that, on the street, in front of everyone. The passersby, however, looked firmly away, clearly frightened. Livia struggled to break loose, but the man's grip was strong and she couldn't get away. Anguish pressed down on her chest, and she woke up with a start with a crushing sense of uneasiness.

But she couldn't remember what she had dreamed.

Romualdo Palmieri di Roccaspina would have liked to dream of his beloved, but instead he dreamt of his wife.

It had never happened to him before, in all the time he'd been in prison. He had slept heavily, agitated, an oppressive and anguished slumber, only rarely lightened by a nice thought; but occasionally he had sensed that flesh under his hands, and he'd kissed a smile that opened his heart. That was enough to reinforce him in the belief that he had been right to do what he had done.

That night, though, there was the September air that felt like reshuffling the deck, and he found himself face-to-face with Bianca's stern expression.

She sat there rigidly, her eyes that absurd shade of periwinkle staring straight ahead, her hands crossed in her lap. She was sitting in his favorite armchair, one of the few sticks of furniture that his demon hadn't gambled away, a relic of a bygone time and of the man he ought to have been but never was.

Bianca, forgive me, he wished he could have said. But, as usual, he couldn't manage to speak to her, nor could he look her in the face. He could never tell her what he felt in his heart. He had done her too much harm, and who was right and who was wrong were both too clearly defined to open any discussion.

But this time the count found the strength in his dream to explode. The forgiveness that he'd never had the strength to ask of her became a burst of vomit, a succession of angry words with an infinite trail of rancor and resentment. He said to that pale, impassive face everything that he would never have had the courage to even think in his waking hours. He expressed the solitude of a man with many faults, but who had never tried to conceal his true nature; a man who could not and would not feel guilt over the children they'd never had; that it was she who had never understood him, with that demeanor of a Madonna being speared that had always made him feel inadequate.

That with her mere presence, that mute, distasteful presence, she had made the air unbreathable, had made it impossible to live in that home with her. That even with all his defects, his moral handicaps, he could still arouse a sweet sentiment and an attraction in someone wonderful, delightful, and splendid. A superior creature, enchanting and alluring.

That if he did have a fault, it was that he hadn't understood immediately that he couldn't remain close to her, his wife, for another second longer. And that it was a thousand times better to be there, in a filthy prison cell, with the prospect of never again seeing the outside world, than in the prison of conventional behavior and manners in which he'd been confined since his birth, a cell to which she, Bianca, had the key, but which she would never use to free him.

In his dream, he relished his malevolent venting, those words he spat out into his wife's face, finally free of the hypocritical curtain of her silent accusations and his sense of guilt.

But when he woke up, in a gray dawn, his face was flooded with tears.

Bianca would have preferred not to dream at all, but instead the treacherous air of that September night gave her a dream of Ricciardi.

She found him sitting right there, in her bedroom: the same room he had entered to listen to the sound of Romualdo's door closing. For much of the evening that had ensued, holding a book in her hands but without reading it, she had tried to understand something of the effect that it had had on her to see that man among her things, so deeply ensconced in her life.

She ought to have felt violated, she thought to herself. How dare that stranger, that unknown person? What was he doing there? How dare he lack respect to her like that? Was it perhaps her poverty, the misery of her surroundings, that had tempted him to presume so shamelessly?

Then she had been forced to admit that Ricciardi was there at her request. She had summoned him, asking him and even begging him to look into Romualdo's case. What might seem like an intrusion was actually only a way of testing whether she, Bianca, was a reliable witness or a silly little woman who lived on illusions.

It was this, she understood, that truly offended her. The thought that Ricciardi might consider her delusional, so deranged by her desire to see her husband found innocent that she might be willing to come up with a lie.

The commissario's eyes were completely uninterested in her personal privacy, that much was immediately clear to her. He only wanted to understand whether that sound could be clearly heard from her bedroom. And yet that wasn't what upset her. It wasn't because of that thought that now, as she tossed and turned uneasily in that September night, she dreamt she was looking at that same man, sitting in the chair in front of the vanity table, his legs crossed, his arms clasped in front of his face, and his eyes glittering in the dark, focused right on her.

Dreams, she would have told herself if she'd had the strength to be honest with herself, are shameless, my dear Bianca. Dreams have no decorum, they feel no need to remain confined within the bounds of custom. Dreams are alive and true and they sink their roots into your desires.

Bianca would have asked herself, if she'd had the nerve to look herself in the face in her waking hours, how long it had been since she'd made love. And how long it had been since she'd felt a man's hands on her body. And how long it had been since she'd felt the urgent need of it.

She would have asked herself how real was that image of icy confidence, good manners, and reserve that she projected of herslf. And whether she still remembered how much fun it was to laugh and breathe deep the perfume of flowers, and how good it was to kiss.

Because that is exactly what her dream meant, the dream that she wouldn't even remember the next day, except for a vague, inexplicable sense of disquiet that would stick with her for hours. The dream of two green eyes scrutinizing deep inside of her, brought by the sweet-smelling September air that came in through the cracked-open window.

Nothing could be better than the air of September, to tousle dreams and unsettle emotions. Nothing could be better than the air of September, to call into question all certainties.

Nothing could be better.

And nothing could be worse.

XV

When Maione appeared in the doorway of Ricciardi's office with the usual tray of ersatz coffee, the commissario was already reading the copies of the crime reports filled out in the brigadier's large, neat handwriting.

"Commissa', have you seen the work I did? And after all, I didn't feel it was right to drag Antonelli into it, after what you said, so I took care of it myself. You'll find word for word everything that was written in the file. That De Blasio is an idiot, but he takes care of details, which is our good luck."

Ricciardi nodded.

"Yes, it was all done impeccably. But it's evident that Roccaspina's confession interrupted all investigative activity. Now the problem is how to go about reconstructing, four months later, exactly what actually happened."

Maione set down the tray and tipped the Neapolitan double espresso pot, pouring a cupful of the boiling hot brew.

"Then let me understand something, Commissa'. Are we going to look into it anyway, this murder? Do we believe the contessa? I have to say you looked a little mistrustful to me, actually."

Ricciardi raised his eyes and looked at him.

"I went to her home. I checked out the plausibility of her claims and I took a look around. It's possible, indeed it's probable that what the contessa claims is true: if her husband had gone out, she would have heard him. What's more, the economic conditions of the Roccaspinas are truly desperate, they've even had to sell their furniture. And therefore I can't understand why the count would have murdered someone who could have helped him out by lending him more money."

Maione poured some ersatz coffee for himself, too, in a glass cup. The slightly chipped demitasse with a mismatched saucer was for the commissario.

"In his confession, Count Romualdo explains that he had requested certain extensions on his payments and that Piro had refused that request. De Blasio also noted that Piro's wife reported another argument that took place the day before, with shouting that could be heard outside of the study."

Ricciardi drank a sip and then grimaced in disgust.

"God, this ersatz coffee is disgusting. It just gets worse and worse, how can that be?"

Maione snickered.

"No, Commissa', it's not that it's worse, it's just that you forget. The memory tries to help the stomach and it immediately cancels the flavor. It's been proven. And just think that Mistrangelo, down at the complaints desk, is proud of the ersatz coffee that he makes. He says: Brigadie', this morning it's pure nectar! You'll see, the commissario is going to lick his chops!"

Ricciardi shook his head, disconsolately.

"I'm not sure I even know what chops are, and I'm certainly not going to lick them. In any case, coming back to us: we're going to have to work differently than we usually do, since we won't be able to rely on fresh evidence. And we'll have to work with discretion, because if anyone complains to our superiors, Garzo is going to tell us to stand down."

Maione lifted his cap to scratch his head, the way he did whenever he was feeling doubtful.

"That's true, he'll blow his top if he discovers that we're digging into an investigation that's already been declared closed. And we'll need to work very very carefully, because it's the world of high society and Garzo, as we know very well, aspires unsuccessfully to make friends with the powerful. For that matter, we're going to have to question at least someone, aren't we?"

Ricciardi stood up, setting the demitasse down on the tray with a sense of relief.

"In fact, this is going to be risky business. Therefore, you'll do me the favor of forgetting all about this matter, and let me take care of it on my own. There's no reason for both of us to run risks, and after all, you know that when it comes to me, Garzo is very cautious, while with you he can afford to play the tough guy."

Maione laughed.

"Commissa', you know very well that I only take orders from you if what you tell me to do concerns my job. Concerning my own free time, though, I'll do as I like. So forget about the idea of keeping me out of this thing, if you please. I intend to investigate right alongside of you, and since if I do it all on my own I'm as likely as not to screw things up, then you might as well go ahead and give me the necessary instructions."

Ricciardi thought it over, then sadly shook his head.

"You know, Maione, you're exactly like this ersatz coffee: terrible, but necessary. All right then, your help will be extremely useful to me. But let's make a deal. I'll deal with the aristocrats all on my own, that way no one can lodge any complaints about you. You can give me some help gathering the other information. All right?"

Maione threw his arms wide.

"Commissa', I can't make any promises. Let's just say that I'll follow your suggestions, but I'm going to have to keep an eye on you all the same, otherwise you're liable to get yourself into trouble. Well, what am I supposed to do then? What's our next move?"

Ricciardi tapped his finger on the copies of the police reports.

"Now then: I've already gone to see Modo, and he confirms everything written in these reports. The interesting thing is that the murder weapon cannot have been a knife, but must have been an object without a blade, such as a metal punch."

Maione looked as if were about to fall asleep, the way he always did when he was concentrating.

"But in his confession, the count said that he couldn't remember what he used to kill the lawyer, so it's entirely possible that he picked up, I don't know, a fountain pen with a golden nib like those people use, or else some pointy piece of bric-a-brac. I remember clearly, he said exactly that, right? I copied it last night."

"Yes, that's what he said. But here, in the list of objects found on the desk, there's no paper knife, but there are not one but two pens. I've never seen a paper knife without a blade."

Maione shrugged.

"All right then, Commissa'. The murder weapon can't be found. But that's not enough to solve the problem of the confession."

Ricciardi went on, pacing back and forth as he spoke.

"And then there's another thing that I can't quite figure out. The wound. The blow was struck to the right side of the victim's throat, and the count, as his wife confirmed, is right-handed."

Maione sat there like a Buddha, his hands clasped across his belly and his eyes half-closed. You would have expected him to begin snoring any minute now.

"In that case, standing face-to-face, the murderer would have had to use his left hand to strike the lawyer on the right. So? When you're angry, you don't stop to check which hand you're using. And to strike a blow, you don't need all that much precision, Commissa'. Maybe his right hand was busy holding something."

The role of devil's advocate always fell to Maione; when it came to the task of reconstructing what had happened, he was very skillful at dismantling theories, and Ricciardi was happy to give him full credit for that. A skill that had always proved very useful.

"Fair enough, but what are we going to say about the timing and the modality of the murder? No one saw a thing, no one heard a thing. It was hot out, the windows were open, and given the location, it's even possible there were people out and about. How can it be that there wasn't so much as a shred of an eyewitness?"

"Commissa', maybe there were witnesses, but there was no need to go out looking for them, because the guilty party turned himself in of his own volition. And after all, what difference does it make?"

"What do you mean?"

Maione explained.

"Someone had to have killed the lawyer, am I right? Let's just say that, as her ladyship the contessa says, her husband had nothing to do with it and for some reason of his own—and I'd certainly like to know what reason someone might have to want to spend the rest of his life in prison—he's chosen to accuse himself of the murder. Whoever it might be, whoever killed the man, we'd be presented with the same problems that we're facing if it was the count, no?"

"I understand what you're trying to say. But we aren't the count's lawyers, so that means we don't have to find a scapegoat in order to proclaim his innocence. We just have to understand what really happened, and that's all. Then, if it emerges that it really was the count and that her ladyship simply didn't hear him when he went out, in any case, we'll have done what we were supposed to do."

Maione hadn't moved a muscle.

"There's something else I wonder about, though," he murmured.

"Which is?"

The brigadier heaved a faint sigh.

"Someone comes to see me to ask for an extension on some payment. We quarrel, I raise my voice, people hear us. I refuse to give the extension. That same person comes back in the night, half-drunk and probably even more desperate than the day before. What new wrinkle could there be? Why would I let him in? And this time there's no argument, because no one heard a thing. For him to have an outburst of anger and kill me, I must have done something to make him mad, no? But no, nothing, absolute silence. And apparently, everything in the room was neat as a pin. That's the thing I find a little strange."

Ricciardi nodded in conviction.

"Exactly! And I'll tell you that it even strikes me as absurd, given the count's personality, which, as I recall from when I met him, is highly emotional in nature. In other words, it just doesn't add up."

Maione shook his head.

"No. Something doesn't add up. All right, then, Commissa', how do we proceed?"

"I'm just waiting for the contessa's housekeeper to come tell me when and where I can meet her husband's lawyer. He may have some more information, perhaps he can give us some details about what his client claims. You, in the meantime, do your best to gather some information about the count's life: if he had other relationships, what interactions he had with the victim . . . In other words, you're going to have to . . . "

Maione sighed again, a longer sigh this time.

"Yes, I know what I have to do. Take a long, steep walk up to San Nicola da Tolentino, hoping that no one sees me."

XVI

For the tenth time since he'd opened the shop that morning, swinging open the heavy wooden shutters, Cavalier Giulio Colombo peered toward the front door. He was expecting Enrica.

Work had never been a burden to him. A businessman, the son and grandson of businessmen, he knew very well that he had to conform to an ethics consisting of a few essential principles, and the first of those was absolute reliability. His clients, and especially the women who frequented his shop, needed to know that starting at a given hour, they could depend on his presence behind the walnut counter, at the center of the spacious interior surrounded by high shelves upon which the finest goods were displayed. Everything had to be neat and clean and sweet smelling, the interior had to give an impression of freshness, honesty, and prompt attention. He demanded of himself, and therefore by right also of those who worked with him, a courtesy shot through with good humor that must never falter or crack, even when it became necessary to serve Baroness Raspigliosi, the old harridan who would invariably force him to get down dozens of hats and pairs of gloves, only to murmur, in her voice rendered hoarse with tobacco smoke, and with her pestilential halitosis: Yes, thanks, I'll think it over.

This matter of deference and courtesy in the shop was an issue to which he gave his utmost attention, and it often turned into a source of contention with his son-in-law Marco, the husband of his second-born daughter Susanna. A reputable young man who'd been working with him for years, good-hearted, smiling, and tireless, but liable to argue. More than once he'd been forced to weigh in to prevent Marco from assuming an attitude with some of his more indecisive customers that might easily be interpreted as impatient. He had pointed it out to him and on a couple of occasions he had even been forced to upbraid him, though naturally in a whispered aside to keep from undermining the authority that, as a member of the family, Marco wielded over the other two salesclerks, young women. If he wished to inherit Giulio's position, Giulio had made it very clear, then he would have to learn to behave like a perfect gentleman. Otherwise, Giulio would be quite capable of making other arrangements.

There was no sign of Enrica. In the meanwhile, punctual as a tax bill and every bit as welcome, none other than Baroness Raspigliosi entered the shop, accompanied by her housemaid. This time, the housemaid was a heavyset, red-cheeked young woman, squeezed into a black-and-white smock that had undoubtedly been purchased for a person of much smaller size. Understandably. The baroness's servants all came with an unconscious sell-by date dictated by their threshold for abuse and mistreatment, a date that was proportional to their state of financial need.

Concealing a sigh, the cavalier smiled at the old hag.

"My dear Baroness, what a magnificent appearance you have this morning. How can we serve you?"

The magnificent appearance consisted of a faint but unmistakable black fuzz on a wrinkled face, a hooked nose upon which a hairy wart enjoyed pride of place, a chin that rivaled the aforementioned nose in its attempt to break free of the face, and a body that was substantially larger in width than in height.

The woman grunted.

"Gloves. Today I want to see a pair of gloves. What color do I want?"

It was one of the baroness's finest qualities. She would never say what she wanted, she always let you try to guess. Giulio took off his glasses and cleaned them with his handkerchief, putting on a show of calmly weighing his answer.

"Now then: we're heading into winter, so I wouldn't look at anything that's too light, but at the same time I wouldn't want to have you spend money on something you're not going to use for too long, after all, next year you might find yourself with a pair of gloves that have gone out of fashion. What do you think of these? They're genuine chamois leather, soft and warm but not heavy."

Raspigliosi emitted a sound that could have just as easily been a belch as a grunt of agreement.

"Mhm. This idiot of a housemaid is incapable of washing anything without ruining it, I ought to kick her out the door and down the stairs, only it breaks my heart because back home in her village they're all starving. So nothing very expensive, Cavalie'."

The young woman's cheeks turned even pinker. Giulio shot her a quick glance of understanding, which she ignored, continuing to stare vacantly straight ahead. Perhaps, Colombo mused, she was lucky and simply didn't understand.

As he was preparing to answer, shifting his attention to the merchandise, Enrica's tall figure appeared in the rectangle of the door.

Giulio Colombo had made his decision the night before. He'd thought it over for a long time, he'd never been someone who operated on impulse. Ever since his daughter had returned home from the summer colony, he'd never made the slightest reference to the letters they'd exchanged, the things that she had only been able to confide in him from a great distance, how she'd opened her heart to him. They truly resembled each other, he and Enrica.

Leaving aside their physical appearance—both tall, wearing

glasses for their nearsightedness, dark-complexioned with open, luminous smiles—they were also both shy and retiring, disinclined to express themselves outwardly. Only rarely had he seen his daughter cry, since even as a girl she was more mature and sensitive than the other little girls, at once commonsense and reflective. Father and daughter understood each other profoundly, with no need to talk. In fact, they intuited each other. All they needed was a gesture or a sigh, and their state of mind was mutual.

The other children resembled Maria, enthusiastic and strong-willed, always ready to weep or burst out laughing, always engaged in endless, loud arguments that only rarely came to any satisfactory conclusion. Not Enrica. Enrica smiled, said nothing, and did what she thought right to do. Not easy, or opportune: right. Even when it redounded to her own disadvantage. Even at the cost of her own unhappiness.

Knowing his daughter's state of mind because it was sure to be a mirror image of his own, he'd never subscribed to his wife's obsessive worries. At nearly twenty-five, Enrica was still alone, not married much less engaged, but Giulio felt certain that when the moment came, when she met the right person, that person would recognize her. And in the meantime, he would be there to protect her and love her, to smile at her silently as a proper papa should.

Then there had been the letters, with the revelation that his daughter had in fact met the right person. Only this person had not taken any of those traditional steps that one would have reasonably expected of him: there had been no invitation to go out with some discreet chaperone, no presentation at the family home, no engagement. He'd done nothing more than watch her from a distance in the dark, his cat eyes glittering in silence. Enrica, in keeping with her nature, had waited. Until she had come to the conclusion that actually that man didn't want her, at which point she had made up her mind to leave.

In her letters, Enrica, his small, fragile, determined Enrica, had confessed to him just how her heart was bleeding.

And in the face of that sorrow, Giulio had made a decision of which he never would have thought himself capable. He had approached the man. He had to understand. He had to check this out in person.

He and the man hadn't spoken much. The cavalier was an old-fashioned liberal, and he was aware that times were changing faster than he could possibly hope to keep up with. He didn't belong to the generation that would have no difficulties with approaching a young man and asking whether he was interested in the daughter who had fallen in love with him. But he was still a father, and he couldn't stand to watch his Enrica consume herself in pain without lifting a finger to help her.

In some strange way, he'd liked the man. He was quiet, he engaged in no pointless flattery, but you could see that he wasn't lying.

But Cavalier Colombo must have misjudged his daughter's state of mind, because without warning Enrica had suddenly begun limiting her letters to the ones she sent to their home address, in which she tersely informed them of her state of health and what she was doing with her time. Then she had started talking about the German.

She was cautious, brief, and rather remote; there was nothing in her accounts that betrayed any particular emotional engagement. But, Maria had decreed, if a young woman Enrica's age speaks of a man so often, then there must be something going on. For certain.

Giulio hadn't replied. Knowing her as he did, he doubted Enrica was capable of changing so suddenly the object of her interest. But if she wasn't talking to him, it meant that she didn't need him. And that was enough for him. For that matter, he thought, it wasn't necessarily the case that Maria was wrong, perhaps what his daughter needed most was to break free of an infatuation that no one else knew about but him, and establish a concrete relationship that would bring her happiness. Happiness: Giulio wanted nothing else for her.

And yet, there was something. Something that he'd sensed in a half sigh, in a gaze lost in the empty air for a fraction of a second, in the way she held her shoulders when she thought no one was looking.

There was something. And Giulio, the night before, had screwed up his courage.

He'd been surprised to learn that talking with Enrica was even harder for him than it had been to approach that man back in July. Back then he had been fighting against himself for the sake of his little girl's peace of mind, and he had easily won out against the natural shyness that was baked deep into his personality. Now, however, it seemed to him that he was forcing himself, practically, into her inner sanctum, her very right to privacy, and that he was trying to make her talk about something that could hurt her deeply. The thought that it was he, who loved her so tenderly, who was causing her this discomfort was practically intolerable.

And yet it had seemed necessary. Even the slightest possibility that she was about to make a choice she'd regret for the rest of her life justified his interference. He'd made up his mind and asked her to join him the next day at the shop. Talking to her at home was virtually unthinkable, with all those ravenous ears ready to pick off any and every variation in the domestic temperature.

But now that she was there before him, with that tranquil and good-tempered gaze of hers, he felt like a rude and high-handed gendarme about to grill an innocent suspect. He gestured to one of the salesgirls to come attend the Baroness Raspigliosi and listen to her lucubrations, and to the baroness he murmured his excuses, then moved off, followed by the old woman's malevolent curiosity. She would stomp off ungraciously, he knew, making no secret of her disappointment at having been abandoned just as she set into the two hours of examination, hemming and hawing, during which she'd study every item of haberdashery in the shop, only to decide, in the end, to purchase nothing, as was her custom; but his daughter's peace of mind was far more important than a pair of gloves.

He locked arms with Enrica and they headed off toward the Caffè Gambrinus.

XVII

The café was packed with people but the oldest waiter, who had known the Cavalier Colombo for years, immediately found him a table.

The gentle September air encouraged people to stay outside, so there were no tables free and people were even standing waiting, leaning against the low railing smoking and chatting or reading the morning paper. The piano room, on the other hand, was a little less crowded, and Giulio preferred to be out of the way of indiscreet eyes and ears anyway, when it was time to talk with Enrica.

The young woman hardly seemed to be wondering why her father had asked her to meet him. Actually, her heart was in complete tumult, because she had no idea what answer she would give when the inevitable questions arrived. She was inured to the interrogations of her mother, and had been since she was a little girl: she knew perfectly well how to steer the subject toward less treacherous terrain, and each time Maria's impetuosity ran helplessly up against the brick wall that Enrica was quite adept at erecting. But all her father needed to do was take one look into her eyes, so similar to his own that they seemed to reflect his thoughts. She had never been able to tell Giulio a lie. But then, he had never before asked her anything she was reluctant to tell him.

This was the first time.

The cavalier ordered an espresso for himself and a glass of rosolio liqueur for his daughter. Then he started to study her, without speaking.

Enrica shifted uneasily in her chair.

"Papa, I should apologize to you for the letters I sent you this summer."

Colombo was surprised.

"Apologize? But why? Were they not sincere, by any chance?"

"No, no, they were sincere, absolutely. It's just that . . . I had no right to burden you with my problems, that's all. There was nothing you could have done about it, and I was so selfish to confess it all to you from a distance, without looking you in the eye."

Giulio objected.

"You shouldn't say such a thing, even in jest. I'm your father. This is what fathers are supposed to do, carry whatever weight they can, to lighten the load on their children. But that's not why I wanted to see you."

Now it was Enrica's turn to be surprised.

"No? But then . . . "

"Listen to me, sweetheart. You mustn't . . . Your mother, you see, is only interested in your well-being. She's a woman who sometimes . . . doesn't look into the depths of things, that's true, but she adores you, and she'd throw herself into the flames for all of you, for her children."

Enrica's face lit up.

"Certainly, Papa, of course. It's just that sometimes she can be a little . . . overhasty. It seems as if she's trying to manipulate the lives of other people, and that's something I . . . "

" . . . you can't accept, of course, I understand. But as for your letters, you wrote what was in your heart. And when there's something in your heart, then you have to listen to it. You know that I never finished high school."

Enrica looked away for a moment.

"Yes, Papa. You had to work, because Grandpa had died."

"That's right, your grandfather had died. But I could have insisted on it, maybe I could have gone on working while I studied. Hard work never frightened me. And I was a good student. I would have studied philosophy, you know that I'm interested in everything that has to do with politics. Maybe I could have secured a position as a professor. I would have enjoyed that."

The young woman was astonished. It had never occurred to her that her father might have had aspirations to anything but running the family business.

"But . . . the store? I thought you really liked your work. That's what you always told us."

Giulio shook his head, with a hint of melancholy.

"No. Not all that much, to tell the truth. And it wasn't bringing in all that much money, actually, you know? Your grandfather never understood how to modernize, how to keep up with the times. We were practically bankrupt. I could just let the business go, my mother and my sister could have gotten by with the money from the sale of the store, money I would have gladly let them have, and they had a place to live. And I could have followed my dreams."

Enrica didn't know what to think.

"Then why didn't you do it? Why didn't you continue your studies?"

Her father sat raptly watching two children who were playing with a hoop in the street, outside the plate-glass window. He was reviewing his memories.

"Because I had met your mother and fallen in love with her. And she wouldn't have waited for me to complete my studies and find a job. She wanted to get married and she wanted to have children. You know what she's like."

The young woman felt a stab of pity to her heart.

"What a shame, Papa. How sad, having to give up your dreams for . . . "

Colombo suddenly turned and stared at her.

"No. No. The error, the shame, as you say, would have been

to give up what you have in your heart in the name of some other convenience. I long carried within me the doubt that I might have made a mistake; an oppressive doubt, massive as a mountain. Everything in me, my sentiments, my very nature, my pride made me hate this work, the duty to pretend courtesy and reverence to ignorant folk who have nothing but money. But do you know when that doubt dissolved into thin air? Do you know when I knew that I had been right?"

Enrica felt her eyes growing damp behind her lenses.

"No, Papa," she murmured, "when?"

Colombo's voice cracked ever so slightly. Outside, one of the boys tried to talk the other one into giving him the hoop.

"When you were born. When they brought me to you and put you in my arms. And every time I look at you, the way I'm looking at you now, every single time I look at you or your brothers and sister, I thank God I made the right choice. No philosophy, no classroom full of students, nothing could have given me more joy than what I'm feeling in this very instant."

Enrica would never have guessed how much love there was in the heart of that shy, quiet man, who could never express his affection more openly than a fleeting pat on her head. She struggled to choke back her tears, in silence.

When she felt the vise grip of emotion that encircled her throat begin to relax, she whispered: "But why are you telling me these things, Papa? Why?"

Giulio coughed softly in his turn, to dispel his own emotions.

"The reason I'm telling you this, my sweetheart, is that I don't want you to muffle the voice of your own heart. This German . . . this man you wrote us about. Your mother tells me that he may come to our home to ask my permission to see you. I want to know, I have to know what you desire. What you truly desire, I mean. If you need any help from me, have no fear. No one will be any the wiser. I don't look favorably on the policies of Germany, any more than I do where Italy is concerned, for that matter. I could easily justify a refusal of his request with your mother on that basis, and I'm certainly not happy at the idea that someday someone might take my little girl far away from me. If you wish, I could . . . "

Impulsively, Enrica laid her hand on Giulio's arm.

"Papa, please. Don't say another word. I know that I can count on you, we resemble each other so closely that there are times when I hear in your words the very echo of my own thoughts. But he, the man I wrote you about, doesn't want me. I've even been forward with him, and you know how far that is from my very nature. I made it perfectly clear to him how I feel, what I feel about him. He doesn't want me, otherwise he would have put himself forward. There's no timidity, there's no bashfulness that could justify his silence. While Manfred . . . he is a good, kind man, who has had a full life and understands the importance of sentiment. I feel that I could find a genuine equilibrium with him, true serenity. And I could make Mamma happy."

Giulio objected.

"There, you see? That's the last thing you should be worrying about. What any of us wants doesn't matter, the only thing that matters is what you want. It's your own life that you're talking about, don't you understand that? If you love another man, you can't even begin to imagine . . . "

Enrica interrupted him, her voice suddenly hard.

"Then I don't love him enough, Papa. I will never allow anyone to toy with my emotions. He knows, and I'm sure of that. He knows how I feel about him. If he hasn't reached out to me, it means he doesn't care for me. And that's that.

"There's one thing I know for sure. I want a husband in my life, a home, and children. I was born to be a mother, I feel it every time I tutor a child, every time I take my little nephew in my arms. And if the man I would have chosen, that I had chosen, doesn't want me, then I'll live my life all the same."

She had started to cry. The tears now flowed unhindered down her cheeks, dripping over her tightly clenched lips. Giulio felt his heart dissolve.

He leaned forward over the café table to wipe her face with his handkerchief.

"It's all right, Papa's sweetheart. Don't cry. It's all right. But remember this: as long as I'm around, you never have to do something you don't want to. If you did, then that would mean I've failed in my duties as a father. You should always and only do what you want. Do you promise me that?"

Enrica hesitated, then nodded her head yes, though she was incapable of speaking. They sat there, staring each other in the eyes, tenderness for tenderness, love for love.

Outside, one of the boys ran away with the hoop. And the other one chased him into the sunlight.

XVIII

The two little drowned boys were lying, gray, with their arms wrapped around each other, in the sunlight, just a few yards away from the entrance to the yacht club. Ricciardi stood motionless a short distance away, hands in his pockets, as he looked at them. He seemed to be looking out to sea, the water that stretched, placidly glittering, all the way to the horizon.

It always had a strange effect on him, going down to the sea. He was, after all, born and raised in the mountains of Cilento, and he'd grown up around pragmatic people accustomed to battling nature for a living. He was therefore unfailingly stunned by that expanse, always the same and always changing, in perennial movement but apparently motionless, an unsettling bridge to the rest of the unknown world, and itself unknown, both in its depths and on its surfaces. His introspective soul perceived its terrible beauty, and was caught in its meshes. But he couldn't become sufficiently comfortable with the sea to feel true affection for it, even after all these years.

Then, of course, there were the dead, he thought as he continued to stare at the two trembling cadavers locked in the embrace that had killed them. The dead, who dotted the coastline. The dead, fishermen in the winter and bathers and beachgoers in the summer, whose maleficent emotions were borne in to shore by the undertow, as if instead of dozens or hundreds of yards out they had died right there, on the rocks of the shoals. The dead, translucent and faded by rain or sunshine, who whispered their terrible refrains for an audience of just one spectator.

One of them was a little older, the other couldn't have been more than seven or eight. The littler one was bluish, his mouth half-open, out of which issued a bubble of white foam that looked like some horrible fungus, his eyes half-closed; and he kept murmuring: Come, come get me, I can't stay afloat. The other one, the hairs on his body standing straight up and goose bumps all over him, his eyes rolling up in their sockets and his lips and tongue dead black, kept repeating: Don't pull me down, stop pulling me down.

A day at the beach, Ricciardi thought sorrowfully. They look alike, they must have been brothers.

He thought of the father of those two children, wherever he might be right then, that is, of course, if the man hadn't already grieved himself to death. Whether the man might not still be awaiting him somewhere, dangling from a rope, or his back broken by a leap off a bridge. He wondered whether the man's heart had been crushed by regret for not having been there, on the beach, to save his sons.

He shook himself out of his reverie and went in, passing under the coquettish little arch in front of the yacht club. It seemed as if he'd entered another world. Around the perfectly designed and cared for flowerbeds elegant couples promenaded, in morning dress; gentlemen sat on the benches, white hats on their heads, their newspapers spread open for reading, and every so often they'd mop the perspiration from their brows with gleaming white handkerchiefs; waiters in livery moved discreetly from spot to spot, distributing cocktails and espressos.

Ricciardi felt out of place, and very happy to feel that way.

Less than an hour earlier, an officer had ushered the old woman who had first admitted him to the Roccaspina home into his office. Without a word, continuing to eye him with mistrust just as she had the first time they'd met, she had given him a folded note and then turned to go without so much as a goodbye. The note read, in a handsome flowing script: "Golden Oar Yacht Club. Counselor Attilio Moscato. Eleven o'clock." Not a word of greeting or regards, not a hint of explanation or accompaniment. Ricciardi smiled briefly. The contessa knew how to go straight to the point, whatever the circumstance.

He looked around and, even before he had a chance to wonder how he would be able to recognize the man he was looking for, his problem was solved by a gentleman in a panama hat and a white jacket who was waving a handkerchief in his direction from a table on the terrace, overlooking the sea. When he walked over to him, the man stood up and extended his hand.

"You must be Commissario Ricciardi. I'm Counselor Moscato, at your service. Attilio Moscato."

Ricciardi gripped the extended hand.

The lawyer was a man in his early forties, with fine facial features, white, regular teeth, and a carefully groomed little mustache. A red flower in his buttonhole and a gold chain leading to the watch in his waistcoat pocket completed the elegance of his attire. He pointed the commissario to a chair at his table, which was strategically located in the shade of the overhang. Just a few dozen yards offshore, a number of pleasure boats rode lazily at dockside, with sailors here and there carefully polishing their decks.

"Please, take a seat. In the mornings here, it's a race to grab tables in the shade, don't be surprised; it's a jungle. What can I get for you? An espresso, a bite to eat? Is it too early for a drop of liquor, what do you say?"

Ricciardi shook his head.

"An espresso would be perfect, thanks. And thank you as well for the time you're willing to give me."

The lawyer studied Ricciardi for a moment, as if trying to judge whether he might not be pulling his leg, then he decided that he wasn't and smiled as he gestured to a waiter. When the man came over, he ordered an espresso for his guest, and a *sfogliatella* pastry for himself.

"What can I tell you, the salt air always makes me a little peckish. Well then, so you've met Bianca. A remarkable woman, don't you think? Lovely, one of the prettiest in our circle. But also a bit sad, a touch serious. Not always an easy person to be around, in other words."

The commissario wasn't there to gossip, and he decided to make that clear.

"Counselor, I asked the contessa if she'd arrange for me to meet with you. As you are no doubt aware, she is convinced that her husband has been wrongly accused of Ludovico Piro's murder, that it wasn't him. The contessa declares that the count was at home all night, that he never left the building. What do you think of that?"

Moscato ran his eyes over the boats, continuing to sip the tea that he'd been drinking when Ricciardi first arrived.

"Bah, Commissa', what can I tell you: Bianca has maintained this version of the facts from the very outset, but in the face of a detailed confession that has never been retracted, without any factual contradictions, and expressed in full mental lucidity, there was nothing that could be done. And there's very little that can be done now. If you ask me, you're wasting your time."

Ricciardi wasn't willing to be given lessons on how best to employ his time.

"Still, I'd like to understand a little more about this case, even though the investigation, as you no doubt know, has been closed. Have you known the count long?"

"Why, certainly, since high school days. Who, if not a fond, close personal friend, would have taken on the burden of the defense with the certain prospect of having to eat the legal costs as well? I love him, that miserable wretch. And I care for Bianca, too, whom I've known since she was a young girl, because her mother and my mother played canasta together. But that doesn't mean that I believe in Romualdo's innocence myself."

"What kind of a person is he?"

"Eh, Romualdo . . . I actually ought to tell you what kind of a person he was, and who he's turned into since. He was a cheerful young man, bighearted, funny to be around: he was always laughing, always joking around. An important family, very important. An ancient family. His father was one of the most important figures of his generation. He had a future ahead of him, Romualdo did. He took his law degree just like me, but he never practiced: he was too busy gobbling up his entire fortune."

"Did he have any vices?"

"He didn't have 'any vices.' He only ever had one vice. Romualdo is a gambler. He's always been a gambler, but in the end it turned into an obsession. First it was the horses, then the lottery, and finally cards. Then all three put together. He ran through an immense fortune, believe me; and he dragged Bianca down into ruin with him, draining her fortune as well. A tragedy."

Ricciardi insisted.

"Nothing else? I don't know: luxury, women . . . "

A look of wonder appeared on Moscato's face.

"Women? Certainly not. He was practically engaged to Bianca as a boy, one of those things that, I'm not saying it was arranged by the families, but certainly encouraged, and for that matter, they were two very good names. Romualdo was a well-read, elegant young man, and you've seen her, when she was at all in a good mood, she was a ray of sunshine. No, it wasn't other women. Just that one demon. But that was more than enough, believe me. It devoured him, that demon. An inextingushable disease."

"And his relations with Piro? When did the two of them meet, and how?"

The lawyer heaved a lengthy sigh. An enormous seagull, perched on a mooring bollard, let out a brief cry.

"You see, Commissario, this is a very small world. Just a few dozen people, maybe a hundred in all. We all go to the same schools, we all frequent the same drawing rooms at the same time of day, we all attend the same theaters. It's as if the city were a train, and we populated a single car of that train without ever leaving it. Every so often it happens that there is a moment, perhaps certain years, when for various reasons the door to the compartment swings open, someone gets off, and someone else comes aboard."

He stopped as if he had said, with false nonchalance, something extremely important. He took a bite of his pastry, chewed, swallowed, and then cleaned off his mustache with a napkin. Ricciardi waited patiently for him to go on.

"Ludovico Piro was a social climber. A good-for-nothing who took advantage of those in this club who, for one reason or another, had slid into ruin, and believe me when I tell you that there are a great number of people here like that. You see them? Look at them carefully. They smile, they stroll to and fro, they dress to a fault, they vacation at the beach in winter and in the mountains in summer, but many of them haven't a penny to their names, and they simply don't know how to do without the style in which they have lived since they were born. Piro was a moneylender. He would get the money from various religious institutions that he administered, and with the interest that he demanded everyone made a profit, he more than anyone else. Romualdo, poor man, had fallen into his net and had no idea how to escape. And that's why he killed him."

"Then you're convinced it was him? That Roccaspina murdered Piro?"

Moscato looked at him, baffled.

"Commissario . . . why else would he have confessed?"

Ricciardi said nothing for quite a while, as he thought. Apparently, he was the only person Bianca had been able to convince.

Then he said: "Counselor, I'd like to meet with your client. I'd need to talk with him for a while, and most important of all, look him in the eyes. Do you think you can arrange that?"

Moscato appeared to be surprised by that request.

"Why . . . I imagine so. You could come in with me, maybe we could say that you're one of my assistants. I would guess that the fact that the investigation is closed prevents you from requesting a pass from police headquarters."

Ricciardi agreed.

"Certainly, that's right. All I need is to be in his presence, and I don't mind if you're there too. I just want to ask him a few questions, and check that off my list."

"All right. I was planning to go see him anyway, in part just to bring him a little comfort, poor man. Unfortunately, in terms of mounting an effective defense, there isn't a great deal to be done. If your client confesses, there's not much a poor lawyer has left in terms of legal maneuvering, don't you agree?"

Ricciardi stood up.

"I thank you, Counselor. If anything else occurs to you, please, let me know. Otherwise, if you'll allow me, I'll take care of matters. I believe that the contessa has every right to free herself of this doubt that has been tormenting her."

Moscato smiled sadly.

"There are times when having a doubt helps, Commissario. A person can stave off ideas that are difficult to accept. Who knows, maybe you won't be helping poor Bianca, if you rid her of her doubt. Have a good day."

And he returned his attention to the seagull perched motionless on the bollard.

Outside, in the sunlight, only the two drowned brothers remained, still embracing. Ricciardi heard them murmuring, but he didn't turn to look at them.

XIX

Just like every other blessed time, Maione began to curse Bambinella around the time he reached the next-to-last curve in the staircase that led to the apartment house on Via San Nicola da Tolentino.

He felt sure that that freak of nature had chosen to live at the top of such a steep climb for the single purpose of causing his death, without the use of weapons, but with the apparently normal cause of a simple heart attack; also because every time that he was obliged to go there, for a complex of absurd climatic circumstances, there was always also an infernal heat wave that combined sadistically with his heavy uniform to drench him head-to-foot in sweat.

There was also a further component to his unease, and it was purely psychological in nature. His labored breath, the abundant sweat, his trembling legs, the increasingly painful and slow climb up the steep incline were all factors that reminded him of his age, his obesity, and how little exercise he customarily got. Three things that quickly KO'd any flicker of a potential good mood.

That is why the Maione who prepared to scale the last flight of steps, the flight that led up to Bambinella's garret apartment, was as usual in a foul temper and disinclined to conversation. And it certainly did nothing to improve his mood that he had crossed paths with a young man descending that same staircase without looking where he was going, but instead inveighing loudly toward the upper stories behind him. The young man, who was whipping around the landing while curs-ing, ran headfirst into Maione, giving the brigadier a violent head-butt straight to the solar plexus, depriving him of the already scanty supply of oxygen remaining in his lungs.

Massaging his head and bending down to pick up his fallen cap, the young man spoke to the indistinct mass he'd just plowed into.

"Damn you, and damn your eyes! What the hell, why don't you look where you're going when you climb the stairs? I've got a good mind to get out my knife and . . . "

After regaining a minimum of heartbeat, Maione wearily extended a hand in the half-light and grabbed the youth by the neck, lifting him a good four inches off the ground. The young man, caught off guard, stared bug-eyed and realized that he was staring at a gigantic policeman who looked completely ready and willing to take his head off his shoulders in a single bite, and he began to whimper.

When Maione set him back on the ground, deciding, for the moment, to ignore his impulse to mete out summary jus-tice, the young man coughed in terror and started to babble.

"Oh, Brigadie', for-forgive me, I . . . And how could I pos-sibly know that I was going to come face-to-face with you of all people that . . . it's that stinking faggot who won't take cus-tomers anymore, and it took me so long to scrape together the money . . . but he wouldn't even open the door for me, and so . . . but don't you worry, he's bound to show you the proper respect, please, be my guest, go right ahead on up! You know the way, don't you?"

Maione, when confronted with the young man's unmistakable allusion, was sorely tempted to reverse on appeal the acquittal for the head-butt and transform it into an unequivocal death sen-tence, to be inflicted in the form of straight-armed smacks.

"Oh!" he wheezed. "How dare you? I'm not here for . . . I don't engage in any of that filth, is that clear?"

A look of disconcerted astonishment appeared on the young man's face.

"Ah, no? Then why are you here, if you don't mind my asking?"

For an instant the question caught the brigadier off guard.

"Why, me? Why, I . . . Why, what the hell is it to you, eh? I'm here on police work! Do you know that I can throw you in prison, directly?"

The young man snickered, in complicity.

"Sure, sure, you're here on police work . . . I know the kind of work you're talking about! And you're quite right, Brigadie', that Bambinella is unequaled on earth, when it comes to certain things. Which is why I was so upset when he wouldn't let me in! Tell the truth, for instance, when he starts to . . . "

Sadly for him, he was never able to complete the vivid description of his favorite specialty, because by this point Maione had recovered the strength necessary once again to lift the young man bodily and deliver a swift, sharp kick that launched him six feet through the air.

The kid hadn't hit the ground yet when, legs windmilling, he had already taken to his heels. But not before turning and yelling: "Have a good time, Brigadie'!"

When he reached Bambinella's front door, Maione was emitting a low growl, like a revved engine. He gave a couple of loud kicks to the door, which—unusually—was locked tight. From behind the door came the deep and modulated voice he knew all too well.

"Francu', you just have to accept it: I told you that I'm not taking in customers anymore, and that's that. You'd better go, or you'll soon regret it."

Maione roared.

"Bambine', open up immediately, otherwise I'll knock down the door and I'll drag you by your hair all the way to police headquarters, as God is my witness!"

The echo hadn't yet died out before the door flew open, revealing Bambinella who was the very picture of astonishment.

"O-o-oh, Brigadie', so it's you! Why, what a surprise! Excuse me, it's just that the kid who lives at the end of the alley and who usually alerts me is sick, and the one who was supposed to take his place is always late. Please be patient, and come on in! Why, what is it, are you angry? Now I'll fix you a cup of ersatz coffee that will set you up, and the way the coffee I make sets you up, there's nothing else that will set you up quite so good and solid."

Maione entered, mopping his brow.

"Bambine', let's not get started with the dirty puns, because today is the day I'm ready to throw you out the window, that way for once you'll understand just how long the climb is to get all the way up here. But do you mind telling me the reason for this locked door?"

The strange individual stepped into the cone of light pouring in through the window. The impression of a tall and slightly angular woman was canceled by details that had remained hidden in the shadows. Decidedly feminine features, like the large, liquid eyes, the carefully painted fingernails, and the black hair tied back into a flowing ponytail mixed in an unsettling way with the masculine traits, such as the halo of hairs on the arms and chest, partially hidden beneath the flowered nightgown, the shadow of whiskers on the face, and the broad, strong shoulders. The heavy makeup was a further source of bewilderment, as was the voice, low in tone but sweet and contrived. The feet, long and gnarly, were slipped into a pair of oriental-style slippers.

Maione looked the *femminiello* up and down, from head to feet and back again, and threw his arms wide.

"*Madonna*, Bambine', what a mess you are. And to think that that idiot of a young thug downstairs I gave a kick in the rear to was even sorry he hadn't been able to get in here."

Bambinella snickered.

"Eh, Brigadie', you always say the same things. As if we didn't all know that the world around there's a simple rule of the market: those who dismiss the quality of the product are secretly itching to buy. Ah, did you meet Francuccio? *Mamma mia*, how relentless he is! He really has fallen head over heels, poor boy. It was a good thing you gave him a good hard kick, I'd almost be tempted to hire you as a bouncer to keep people out of my house."

Maione grabbed a small Chinese chair and waved it in the air like a hammer.

"I'll break this over your head, don't you dare say such things! I'm not a bouncer, I'm a sweeper-up, I'll sweep you up and send you to prison! Just don't tempt me, or you'll see what the full service looks like, understood?"

Bambinella pretended to be worried about the chair.

"*Mamma mia*, be careful, Brigadie', these Chinese items aren't exactly cheap, you know. But what can I do about it, I just love those things! But instead of hitting me over the head with that chair, why don't you sit on it and give me a minute to make you a cup of ersatz coffee."

Maione thought carefully about whether he ought to carry out his threat to shatter the chair into a thousand pieces, as he stood balancing it in midair. Then he opted for the more peaceful solution and set it back down and took a seat. The groaning sound from the bamboo suggested that the chair itself might have had other preferences.

"All right, then, Bambine', are you going to explain what all this is about? Why did you lock the door and send the boy away? Is there some problem?"

The *femminiello*, as he continued to rummage around on his cheap stovetop, replied with a braying laugh that sounded like nothing so much as a donkey.

"No, no problem at all, Brigadie'. Quite the contrary,

something wonderful, for a change. Shall I put the sugar in myself?"

"Bambine', I asked you a question. What's going on?"

Bambinella handed Maione the demitasse and sat down coquettishly across from him, a broad smile on his face.

"Brigadie', I'm in love."

Maione sighed and ran a hand over his face.

"*Mamma mia*, just the thought of it is enough to turn my stomach. Anyway, what does that have to do with you locking your door? And above all, who's the lucky girl . . . I mean, boy?"

Bambinella blushed and cast a modest glance at the floor. He seemed like a parody of a schoolgirl being presented with a risqué joke.

He murmured: "No, you know how it is, Brigadie', it's just that a girl might not feel like doing certain things, let's say, on a professional basis. Forgive me, but I can't tell you the name, just this once, that's a piece of information I'm going to withhold. He came here on a bet—certain friends of his had told him that I'm famous because I know how to . . . "

Maione raised a hand, imperiously.

"For the love of all that's holy, Bambine': spare me the technical details. Go on."

" . . . and anyway, he came here. At first, I just thought he was some ordinary guy, all sorts of people come up here, you understand. But then, I realized that he has an . . . "

Maione moaned, and reached for the handgun in his holster. Bambinella decided to skip over the reasons for his sudden crush.

" . . . And I don't how it is or how it isn't, but this love affair sprang into being. What can I tell you, since that moment I have stopped being a working girl. Over the years I've managed to put a little something aside, nothing much to speak of, but after all a small nest egg, and you know I don't need much, once I've got some lipstick, some blush . . . It's just that there are a few who won't give up, and they come all the way up here any to see if I'm willing to take on a job or two."

The brigadier shook his head in amazement.

"Well, what am I supposed to say to you? If you're happy, then everyone's happy. At least this way I won't have to trouble my conscience every time over the fact that I'm not running you in. Does this mean you won't be able to procure information anymore?"

Bambinella laughed his usual donkey bray, fetchingly putting one hand over his mouth.

"Why no, Brigadie', what are you thinking? I get news for you from my friends, male and female, not from my customers. Don't worry about that. Speaking of which, what fair wind blows you in my direction today? I don't think anyone was murdered recently, at least not to the best of my knowledge. Or am I wrong?"

Maione shook his head.

"No, in fact, this isn't about a recent death. I'm interested in an old death. It dates back to June, to be exact: a lawyer from Santa Lucia who . . . "

The *femminiello* bounced happily up and down, clapping her hands as if she knew the answer to some parlor game.

"Ah, I know this one, I know this one! Piro was his name, am I right? Of course, everyone was talking about it this summer! But didn't they catch the murderer straightaway? In fact, I remember thinking, what good policemen these are, they barely begin the investigation and already they've figured out who it was . . . O-o-oh, *madonna santa*, Brigadie', forgive me . . . "

Maione had leapt to his feet and was glowering down at Bambinella.

"Look, I won't kill you for the idiotic things you've just said because I want to explain to you just how idiotic you are. And you're idiotic for two reasons. First. That moron De Blasio, the commissario who was in charge of this thing, didn't catch a blessed soul because the self-proclaimed criminal, Count Romualdo Palmieri di Roccaspina, turned himself in of his own free will. Second. Maybe it wasn't even him. So before you start flapping that open sewer of a mouth of yours, think twice, *capito?*"

Bambinella put both hands together in astonishment.

"Jesus, sweet Jesus, then it wasn't him? *Mamma mia*, what a hot piece of news!"

Maione immediately reversed course.

"That's not what I said. I said that it might not have been him. We need to investigate, and we're trying to figure out what happened on a top-secret basis, so don't let a word of this leak out. That's why I'm here. I need information about the victim and the alleged murderer. Anything you can find out: bad habits, personal relationships, secret debts, everything. And I need it fast."

Bambinella smiled.

"Of course I will, Brigadie', seeing that I'm not working for the reasons I explained to you earlier, I have more time on my hands. I'll take a walk up to Santa Lucia, I have a girlfriend there who keeps house in the same building as the dead man, she was the one who told me all about it. And then I want to ask someone I know whose brother runs a clandestine gambling den, oh lord, he's a fine young man, but his bad friends needed someone who had a place where they could gamble and he, who happens to own a basement space that . . . "

Maione emitted a snarl and Bambinella got her story back on track.

"In other words, I have a few contacts I can fall back on. Tomorrow during the day I hope to let you know something, Brigadie'. Maybe, if it's not too much of a bother, I'll send for you."

Maione nodded menacingly.

"You'd better. Remember that I can always still find a reason to arrest you, even if you've stopped being a working girl."

He turned to go, but the *femminiello* stopped him.

"Brigadie', forgive me, just in case anyone happens to ask why I let you in, since I'm turning away all my usual clients, do you mind just telling them that you came out here on a case? You understand, my sweetheart is terribly jealous and I wouldn't want him to . . . "

Slowly, Maione swiveled around, his jaw clenched and his eyes aflame.

"Don't worry. I'll say that I came out here to track down some facts, and in fact I tracked down the fact that you're a moron, an idiot, and a cretin; but that unfortunately none of these are actually crimes, and therefore I let you out on your own recognizance. Let me have the information I requested by tomorrow, otherwise I'll come back. And believe me, that's not in your best interest."

And he turned and left, walking stiffly but with his mind set at ease. At least the way back would be downhill.

XX

Since they arrived at the office at roughly the same time, Ricciardi and Maione briefed each other on their meetings and tried to establish a concerted line of action.

The commissario had no doubts about what the next step would be.

"We need to see the place where the murder happened. Otherwise we won't be able to form a clear idea of things."

Maione agreed.

"Yes, Commissa', that's true. But it's dangerous, and it's no simple matter. How are we going to explain our presence in the victim's home after the investigation has been completed and all we're waiting for is the trial? What if the family calls in to police headquarters, or speaks to someone important and asks why the police are still investigating?"

"That's true. But it's also true that if we fail to figure out how the murderer managed to enter and exit undisturbed in the middle of the night, with the arrangement of the rooms in that apartment, and why the family members heard nothing, unless we can see their faces and unless we hear what they remember, beyond what's written in the reports, we can't move forward."

The brigadier was very happy to rediscover in Ricciardi the motivations of days gone by. It was the first time since Rosa's death that he had heard him utter more than a few monosyllabic words of generic courtesy.

"We could do what we did with De Blasio, invent some case

that we're investigating in the surrounding neighborhood, that might have some connection with the murder."

"No. They wouldn't let us ask specific questions about the event and the days that preceded it. Don't forget that the family believes that the murderer is in prison, and that as far as they're concerned, the case is closed."

Ricciardi thought it over, pacing back and forth in the room.

"Sometimes the investigating magistrate will order a supplementary investigation if some detail in the accusatory charges is less than perfectly clear. We could pretend it was something of the sort. I could go on my own, that way no one would get you into trouble."

"Commissa'," Maione replied, "if they see you show up on your own, they wouldn't even let you in the door. They need to see someone in uniform, and you know that. So, either you find an extra and you dress him up, or else you take with you a trusted assistant, precise and intuitive, who, as usual, can solve the case for you while giving you all the credit. What do you say?"

The building where the Piro family lived was one of the most prestigious palazzi on one of the loveliest streets in the city. It was on the corner of the waterfront promenade, it was warmed by the sun on three sides, and its front entrance overlooked a quiet little *piazzetta*, complete with flowerbeds and benches.

Everything oozed wealth and comfort.

In the serene September afternoon, the clamor of the city seemed like a distant memory. The sea was preparing for the coming evening by donning a darker suit, a vivid blue that was reminiscent of the color of the paper in which sugar was sold, and the sky hosted a couple of innocent-looking clouds that helped to distinguish it from the mass of water beneath. In the

various parks, nursemaids and nannies in uniform promenaded with tall baby carriages and the occasional elderly gentleman with a monocle hobbled along with a cane, making a
great show of what might be wounds won in combat or simple
inflammations of the sciatic nerve.

How September resembles June, thought Ricciardi, the
only difference is in the outlook for the future. Probably, on
the day of the murder this is exactly what the neighborhood
had looked like. Maybe a little bit warmer, maybe with a few
more open windows.

An automobile went rattling past, with the chauffeur in livery sitting proudly at the wheel and a lady with an elegant cap
sitting in back. The noise had the general effect of an explosion
in the tranquility of the street, to such an extent that a couple
of women sitting talking on a bench shot the car a malevolent
glare. Impossible, thought Ricciardi. Impossible that no one
heard a thing.

The doorman didn't ask many questions. What had happened was grave and quite recent, and so, when he saw
Maione's uniform, he showed no suprise. He led them up to
the third floor, where they were met by an attractive housemaid in an apron and lace headpiece who ushered them into
an elegantly furnished waiting room. Ricciardi didn't leave his
calling card, well aware as he was that it was best to leave as
few traces as possible of this visit.

They looked around. The apartment was very elegant, with
an expensive wallpaper on the walls and a great deal of fine silver on the walnut furniture. The waiting room had two doors:
one was closed, the other led into a room with a window overlooking the sea.

After a few minutes a middle-aged woman entered the
room, dressed in black and wearing no makeup. Her face bore
the signs of suffering that, Ricciardi decided, must date back
several months, if not longer.

"*Buonasera*," she said in a low, firm voice. "I'm Costanza Piro. With whom do I have the pleasure?"

Ricciardi bowed his head ever so briefly.

"Commissario Ricciardi from police headquarters, Signora. I apologize for not having alerted you in advance of our visit. It's nothing more than a minor formality, and we hope not to take up much of your time."

Intentionally, he had refrained from introducing Maione in order to ensure that the woman couldn't bring up his name in case she grew suspicious and decided to make inquiries. The brigadier, slightly ill at ease, doffed his cap and murmured a greeting.

The woman looked them up and down, mistrustfully.

"I thought that the . . . whole matter was taken care of, after the arrest. What is it now?"

Ricciardi was ready for that question.

"Unfortunately the draft version of the police report is marred by a lack of details concerning certain areas, and in the trial phase such a lack could create a risk for the appeals process. No one wishes that to happen, especially since what happened is so crystal clear. Don't you agree?"

The woman's expression changed, taking on a new harshness.

"That's for sure. That damned murderer must pay and should remain in prison for the rest of his life. A prison that can be no worse than the one to which, by murdering my husband, he has sentenced the rest of us, who deeply loved him. Well?"

Maione ostentatiously pulled out a notebook and a pencil, licking the tip of it and preparing to jot down notes. Inwardly, Ricciardi approved of the pantomime.

"Can you take us to the place where the misfortune occurred?"

"It was no misfortune, Commissario," the woman replied tersely. "It was a murder. Please, come this way."

As they walked through the room from which they could just glimpse the sea, they headed into a charming little parlor with a sofa and two armchairs, and from there walked on through a dining room, until they fetched up against a closed door.

Costanza Piro opened the door and they found themselves in a small study shrouded in dim light, with a large elaborately carved mahogany desk. Behind the desk was a balcony shut off by a heavy curtain. When the woman pulled it aside and opened the window, a marvelous panorama of the bay appeared.

Ricciardi ran his gaze over the large bookshelf, over the massive tomes of law codes, over the two green leather arm-chairs and the coffee table in front of the sofa that backed up against the wall opposite to the balcony. He waited, but the image of the dead man didn't appear to him. It's been too long, he decided. In the cool air wafting up from the sea, he thought he could detect the usual sense of surprise and nostalgia, that mixture of the detached and the serene, the sorrowful memory that accompanied violent death like a stench that only he could perceive. But perhaps it was only his imagination.

He concentrated on the desk and the high-backed chair that stood behind it, where Piro must have been sitting. He tried to imagine him slumped over the mahogany desktop, his head lolling on the right cheek, one arm next to his body, the other dangling toward the floor.

The woman broke into the silence.

"Why didn't your colleague come, the one who worked on the case in the first place? De Blasio, I think his name was."

Ricciardi replied in a distracted tone of voice.

"He was busy. Tell me, Signora, is the way we came the only way to reach the office?"

"Certainly. From the front door to here, a straight shot. Then through there," and she pointed to a closed door, "you reach another wing of the apartment, the area with the bed-rooms."

The commissario turned his attention back to the desk. A document tray, a desk pad, an elaborate silver inkstand with two wells. A bronze statuette depicting a young fisherman, a leather portfolio tied shut with a ribbon. All of it immaculate, totally clean. Not even a faint coating of dust.

Too clean, thought Ricciardi.

"Was it normal for him to work so late?"

Costanza nodded. It was unsettling how the woman's expression never changed, the wrinkles around her tight lips, her eyes level and empty.

"My husband, Commissario, administered the assets of several very prominent religious institutions. He oversaw their investments, and their financial transactions. He enjoyed the trust of both the bishop and several highly placed state functionaries. He was a member of the Party, and he could have ascended to important political positions, if he had so chosen. He had a hard job, he worked all hours, frequently late into the night. He said that actually he preferred to work at night, because of the silence and the calm, which helped him to concentrate."

Before Ricciardi had time to formulate an answer, the door swung open and a girl walked in. She resembled Costanza in her physique and her eyes, but her complexion was fairer and the oval of her face was much more delicate.

The woman introduced her.

"Commissario, this is my daughter, Carlotta. The gentlemen are here for an . . . examination in preparation for the trial."

The girl made a slight, well-mannered bow. She was wearing a simple pleated dress with white-and-red stripes, fastened at the waist by a belt and with a round collar that was reminiscent of a schoolgirl's smock. Her hair was gathered in two large braids pulled up into a bun in the back. She might be sixteen or even seventeen years old.

She would have been very pretty, thought Maione, had it not been for the expression of profound sorrow that appeared in her eyes. Poor little thing. Before Maione's eyes there passed in succession the faces of his daughters and the face of little Benedetta, whom he thought of as his own every bit as much as the other girls. A long shiver ran down his back: how often it was that a dead person became little more than a puzzle to be solved for someone in his line of work; all too often they simply forgot about the family and the sorrow that death left behind it.

The girl spoke in a harsh voice.

"Then we need to help them, Mamma. Because the man who ruined our lives must be made to pay."

Ricciardi cleared his throat and addressed Costanza.

"You have another child, don't you, Signora?"

"Yes, Antonio. He's twelve years old. He's away at boarding school now. We preferred . . . that is, I preferred to send him away before school started, in order to keep him far away from . . . from all this."

"That night, I'm assuming you were all at home. What time did you see your husband for the last time? Did he come to say goodnight to you, or . . . "

"I brought him a glass of milk and told him that I was going to bed. It was ten thirty, or maybe a quarter to eleven, I didn't look at the clock. I'd read a book in the living room, then I'd dozed off. When I woke up, I just assumed that he was still working, and in fact he was."

Ricciardi spoke to the girl.

"What about you, Signorina? Did you see him afterward, or before?"

Carlotta shrugged her shoulders.

"I'd been asleep for at least an hour when my mother went

to bed. I went in to kiss Papa goodnight, as I do every evening, and then I went to my bedroom. I sleep in the same room with my brother, and it usually takes him a while to fall asleep, though once he does, nothing can wake him up. He always wants me to read him something. I remember that recently I had been reading him *Treasure Island*. After he fell asleep, I dropped off too."

Maione, with the expression of someone compiling a questionnaire, asked, while looking at his notebook: "Excuse me, Signora, you said that the bedrooms were in that direction. Are they far away?"

Costanza pointed to the closed door.

"Behind that door is a short hallway, a living room, and then the children's bedroom and our own . . . my own. Excuse me, I'm still not used to it."

Ricciardi saw the armor that the woman had constructed for herself begin to give way, and felt pity for her.

"Signora," he asked, "we read in the police reports that the day before the murder the Count of Roccaspina had an argument with your husband, here in your home. Could you tell us what happened?"

The woman stared into the empty air in front of her.

"It was in the afternoon. This wasn't the first time that . . . that he had come here. They had met at the yacht club. Ludovico, out of pure fellow feeling, had loaned him some money, but when the repayments came due he hadn't been able to settle up, and so my husband had offered a series of extensions. I know that because I gave him a hand keeping the ledger books and I saw the transcriptions and the extensions."

"Who was at home?" asked Ricciardi.

"Me, the housekeeper, and the chauffeur. The children were at school. He had no appointment; Ludovico usually warned me if he was expecting anyone."

"And what happened?"

"I didn't see him arrive, my housekeeper let him in. After a few minutes though I heard him shouting, followed by my husband's voice. I walked toward my husband's study, because I was worried, but before I could make up my mind to go in and find out what was happening, the door flew open and he stormed out. He was clearly quite upset. He didn't even speak to me: he just left."

"Miserable coward," the young woman murmured through clenched lips.

"And you didn't hear what they said to each other, Signo'?" asked Maione.

"No, it didn't last long. A couple of sentences, no more than that. I went in to Ludovico's office to see if he was all right, and he was calmly writing. I asked him what had happened, but he just shrugged his shoulders and said to me: 'No, it was nothing, absurd things.'"

Ricciardi repeated: "Absurd things? Is that all?"

"That's all. My husband never liked to talk about his work meetings."

The commissario asked: "Were there a lot of people who owed your husband money? Did he have a lot of arguments like that one?"

Before the woman had a chance to reply, her daughter hissed: "It seems like the one standing trial here is my father. What are all these questions for? That bastard murdered my papa, and he even confessed. He's ruined our lives, he's put us in a situation where it's unclear how my brother and I are going to be able to survive, and you come in here and ask us, four months later, if anyone else had come to . . . "

"Signorina," said Ricciardi very seriously, "we know very well that Roccaspina confessed to the murder. But in the course of a trial, the counsel for the defense has the right to set forth alternative theories of events, and the hypothesis of another guilty party is usually the principal one."

The young woman held the commissario's gaze with fierce pride. Only her quivering lip betrayed her extreme youth.

"But the confession is a piece of definitive proof, don't you think? That damned killer told us in excruciating detail exactly what he did, right here in this room."

"A confession can be retracted until the very last moment. Perhaps the magistrate sent us here precisely to prevent such an eventuality."

The mother broke in determinedly.

"In any event, we've told you everything we know, what little that might be. One sure thing, Commissario, is that my husband is dead. And that a man admitted to having killed him, explaining how and why. For the world at large, the case is closed."

The daughter, looking at the desktop with eyes brimming over with tears, added in a low voice: "For the world at large, maybe. But for me, it will never be closed. Never."

She reached into the pocket of her dress, pulled out a handkerchief, and pressed it to her mouth, then she turned and hurried away. Maione shifted his weight from one foot to the other, the way he always did when he felt ill at ease.

Costanza suddenly said, perhaps mainly speaking to herself: "I'll never be able to thank God enough that my children didn't have to see him, lying in his own pooling blood. Maybe they'll be able to find peace, at least.

"I certainly never will."

XXI

Let's get moving, thought Nelide. Let's get moving. *L'acqua ca nu' camina, feti*, still water stinks.

In truth, you could say anything about Nelide except that she lazed around. She always found something to do, and if she couldn't she'd come up with something, or she'd resume the round of household chores, rewashing things that had already been washed, polishing things that had already been polished, ironing things that had already been ironed. She was driven by an appalling natural energy, further enhanced by a fear of failure and her youthful age.

Though actually, to look at her, it's not as if it was all that easy to guess her age. Stout, solid, and massively built, short but broad-shouldered and with extremely powerful arms that were just slightly longer than normal; a wide, short neck, an irregular face with a pair of bright, dark eyes, narrow lips topped by an unmistakable fuzz; bristly chestnut hair pulled back very tight into a bun and covered by a bright white cap. Those who had known and admired Rosa's frank wisdom recognized her features: Nelide resembled her closely. She however knew that she was only seventeen, and she knew that she was unequal to the task to which she'd been assigned.

Carefully arranging the ingredients for dinner on the kitchen table, the young woman heaved a sigh. *'A merola cecata, quann'è notte face 'u niro*, she thought, the blind blackbird makes its nest at night.

When her poor aunt had started to fall ill and realized that she didn't have long left for this world, she had moved up the schedule and summoned her niece to her side in order to complete an education that would have required a great many more months yet to come.

Rosa had been a crucial point of reference for all the numerous members of the Vaglio family. They all worked on the vast landholdings of the Ricciardi di Malomonte family, running the estate with absolute competence and rectitude. They were responsible for managing the farmhands, the share-croppers, and the shepherds who used the fields and meadows, the hillsides and the fruit orchards that prospered around the castle, further south in Fortino, in the lower Cilento. And they were all by and large replacable, as long as they remained honest. All of them, except for the one who looked after the Baron Malomonte himself. The person who was in charge of the tenuous, fragile relationship with the man who was the owner of the entire operation but showed an utter lack of interest in that fact.

'U Pateterno manna 'a frisa a chi nun tene 'i rienti, someone might well have said, God gives bread to those who have no teeth. And there were those among the farmhands who, jokingly around the fire, would say it every so often, referring to Ricciardi. But they'd say it under their breath, lest they be overheard by any of Rosa's countless brothers and sisters, or any of her many nieces and nephews. Because the veneration, the devotion of the Vaglios toward the barons of Malomonte was so slavish and doglike that they refused to admit any negative commentary.

The masters had never bothered with their own wealth, this was a known fact, accepted for generations by now. They had an inclination for more immaterial things; they loved books, sentiments, passions. The concrete work, managing their goods and assets and tending to them, fell to the Vaglios. So it had always been, and so it was meant to be. Still, it was complicated.

The problem wasn't cooking, washing, and ironing, pursuits in which Nelide was even better than Rosa, because she possessed an unequaled strength and aptitude for hard work. *Si 'a fatica fusse 'na cosa bbona, la facissiro li prieviti*, as the saying went where she came from, if hard work was enjoyable, then priests would do it. But to her, hard work was nothing. The difficult thing, for her, was to interpret, translate, and report. To read the expression on the face of that slender, skinny man, whose feverish eyes were such an absurd color, a hue reminiscent of the mountainside in springtime, when the sunlight at dawn begins to light up the new green leaves, or else the depths of the little lakes that form after a heavy downpour. A man who, on the one hand, inspired fear in her and who, on the other hand, prompted the same desire to protect him that had driven her aunt. Her task, she sensed, was to ensure that his life was untroubled, to the extent that she was able.

But she was seventeen years old, she was just a girl. How would she succeed in her task with no one to instruct her?

For dinner she planned to make *ciauledda*. This was the ideal time of year for it, the necessary vegetables all attained ripeness at the start of that month. Of course, she'd send for the ingredients that could be preserved from her village, both so that she could be sure that they were genuine and because that way she saved money. This had been Rosa's first precept, ensure that the large pantry was always packed full, and never use products whose provenance wasn't certain, unless to do otherwise proved absolutely necessary. And so, every three months, a cart set out from Fortino, piled high with all manner of nonperishable provisions.

To make *ciauledda*, though, she needed fresh vegetables, and Nelide had ventured out to buy them from the vendors in the neighborhood. *Chi face ra sé fa pe' tre*, it's true. If you do it yourself, you do it for three, the saying goes. But you can't always follow that rule.

She'd gotten into line at the stall of one vendor who was yelling more than all the others, surrounded by women who were laughing and chattering. She had supposed that it was because of the quality of his merchandise, and then she had realized that those foolish hens actually only wanted to attract the notice of the vendor, who was a dark-haired young man, with curly locks and big eyes, who talked and talked and laughed loudly. She had just turned to leave when the vendor called after her.

"Hey, lovely Signorina, where do you think you're going? You won't find Tanino's vegetables anywhere else!"

The foolish hens surrounding him had turned in surprise, unable to believe their ears: handsome Tanino, also known as 'o Sarracino, the forbidden dream of all the marriageable young women of Santa Teresa, to say nothing of a great many married women, was calling out to that freak of nature?

Nelide had stopped, then she had slowly turned around. She had leveled her eyes directly into Sarracino's and had replied: "I don't waste time. I work. Good day to you."

Tanino had been left frozen in place, with a smile plastered on his face, and in the sudden silence that had ensued, he had murmured, in an offended tone: "Why, what are you saying, that I'm not working? Look here, these are the finest vegetables in the quarter, and they sell like hot cakes! Don't you believe me?"

Nelide had furrowed her brow and imperceptibly ducked her head into her broad neck. She was the very picture of mistrust.

"Terra comme lassi, usu comme truovi," she murmured under her breath, different places have different ways. "But where I come from, the vegetable vendors sell vegetables and the charlatans bark their wares. Have a nice day."

And she'd turned on her heel and left, while a pretty serving girl laughed raucously, telling poor Tanino who stood there, openmouthed: "Sarraci', you've finally found someone who can put you in your place!"

Now, though, Nelide was gazing perplexed at onions, bell peppers, eggplants, zucchini, and potatoes arrayed before her like an army awaiting orders. She didn't like those vegetables. They lacked personality. And the one thing that *ciauledda* demanded was that each individual ingredient maintain its specific identity, lest the dish turn into a shapeless, flavorless mass. Perhaps she should have given a chance to that charlatan who claimed to be a vegetable vendor.

Zi' Ro', she thought, and what would you have done?

She had developed a habit of talking to Rosa. A little because she was asking for help, and a little to keep from feeling all alone in that apartment that, by her standards, was enormous and deserted.

Nu' mangià cucozza ca ti cachi, nu' passà lu mari ca t'annichi, don't eat pumpkins or you'll get diarrhea and don't cross the sea or you'll drown. Her aunt's reply reached her loud and clear, as if she had been sitting on her usual chair, her powerful pudgy hands clasped in her lap as she watched her work.

Nelide was pragmatic and unshakable. To her, all that existed was what she could feel and see, and she accepted it without discussion and without asking too many pointless questions. Rosa was dead, she knew that, she had transported the corpse back to her hometown, together with His Grace the Baron, in a long and sorrowful voyage. She had attended Rosa's burial without weeping any pointless tears for an event that was such a natural part of the cycle of life. She knew, to an absolute certainty, that her aunt's spirit, the aunt who she felt was closer to her than her own mother, would never abandon her. But she also believed that she would never again hear her voice or sense her presence.

Instead, a few days after her return home, there Rosa was. As if she'd just returned from a brief, necessary trip. Nelide had found her close by her one time when she had discovered a crack in a terra-cotta cook pot, and was wondering whether there was a way to repair it rather than having to buy a new one. Out of the corner of her eye, she had perceived a movement, as if someone had just crossed the room; but no one was there. Then she had heard a whisper behind her left shoulder.

Put the pot on a high flame, with a little water and some sugar. Then spread the mixture over the broken part: it will carbonize and seal the crack.

Grazie, Zi' Ro', she had said, thanking her aunt, and then proceeded to repair it. From that moment on, every so often, she'd felt her nearby; and maybe she had become chattier now that she was dead than she ever had been when she was alive.

She started cutting the tomatoes, thinking about what cheese she would serve the baron to go with the *ciauledda*; the cheese was fundamental.

An aged pecorino, the one that's in the pantry, on the middle shelf, Rosa said. Nelide nodded, seriously.

She'd be able to do it, she thought.

She'd be all right.

XXII

Ricciardi had lingered in the office to flesh out De Blasio's crime reports with the new information. For a while, Maione had stayed with him, but he had finally given in to his superior officer's repeated invitations to go home for the night. It was the commissario's impression that the brigadier didn't give a lot of credence to the theory that the murderer was someone other than the count of Roccaspina. He especially sensed skepticism because, after all, the only evidence weighing on the other plate of the scales was the strong conviction of the count's wife.

Ricciardi, however, who was generally cold and rational, couldn't rid himself of the impression that the woman might be right. Arranging in the lamplight on his desk the various scraps of information he had assembled, he realized he didn't have much more material than what his colleague had examined in the immediate aftermath of the murder. Certainly, there was no murder weapon, and it struck him as strange that all this could have happened without anyone hearing a thing. But in theory it was possible, just as Maione might be right when he said, with a dash of cynicism, that whoever had heard anything was taking care to keep that to themselves to avoid inconvenient entanglements.

Before leaving the Piro home, he had asked the widow if everything was the same in the study as it had been when the lawyer was killed. Laconically, the woman had replied that, of course, they had put away the papers upon which her husband had collapsed, but all the furniture and accessories were as they had been. He had then asked her whether anything was missing, and she had said no. Then Ricciardi had recorded the presence of a paper knife, two pens, and a silver metal punch: all of them objects which might have been the fatal weapon, but which had not in fact served that macabre function.

Another point which remained to be cleared up, the commissario asked himself, as he closed the door to his office and headed off down the stairs: with so many objects available, why use anything else? And why carry it off, only to dispose of it in a ditch or in the sea or down the mouth of a sewer? Maybe, at first, the murderer hadn't planned to confess. Maybe he'd made that decision only after a sleepless night, spent tossing and turning in his bed in the solitary room next door to that of his wife, who lay there confident her husband had never set foot outside of their home.

Maybe, he thought, Maione had a point. Maybe it really had been the count who committed the murder. But he had kept his eyes fixed on Bianca's eyes, with their indefinable color, and in them he had recognized the firmness of absolute conviction, the certainty of truth. He wondered whether it hadn't been precisely that ineradicable impression that had left in him the sense of uneasiness that had, in turn, made him believe that there was still something more to be investigated about that murder. Or whether what it was really about was his need, in that terrible phase of his life in which he so greatly feared every new day, to have something to hold onto.

To keep from going under.

That's what he was thinking when a man emerged from the shadows along the side of the broad thoroughfare that would take Ricciardi home. He was holding a visored cap in one hand, and Ricciardi could make out the silhouette of a large black car. He recognized Livia's chauffeur.

"Commissa', *buonasera*. Forgive me if I intrude upon your

privacy," the man said, clearly uncomfortable, "but my mistress asked me if you could please come with me."

Ricciardi was surprised.

"And where is it I should come with you? It's late, I've had a long day and . . . "

The chauffeur heaved a deep sigh. The task he had been assigned was not one he liked.

"The signora said that it's for an important reason. That's what she said. And she asked if you could please come with me."

Ricciardi looked at his watch.

"Tell her that it's dinnertime and that . . . "

The man repeated, like a scratched record: "The signora asked if you could please come . . . "

" . . . with you, I understand. All right, let's go."

The chauffeur, visibly relieved, deferentially held the car door open for him as he got in. In a matter of minutes, after motoring through the empty streets, they were pulling up in front of the building where Livia lived. A housekeeper was awaiting them in the courtyard, and with a bow took charge of Ricciardi and accompanied him into the house, inviting him to make himself comfortable in the living room.

Ricciardi sat down on the sofa. The light was subdued, the music of an orchestra came over the glowing radio. After a few minutes, announced by her usual perfume, Livia entered the room.

She was wearing a cream-colored silk housecoat that hung down to her ankles, fastened at the waist by a broad sash. Her feet were shod in a pair of coquettish slippers, with low heels and pink pom-poms. Her hair hung loose, freshly brushed, and formed a gauzy brown halo around her lightly made-up face. Ricciardi decided that she might not be dressed to go out, but that she had certainly prepared meticulously.

"*Buonasera*, Livia. What's happened?"

The woman laughed.

"Ciao, Ricciardi. Does something necessarily have to have happened for you to come pay me a visit? I just thought that, instead of trying for the umpteenth time to talk you into taking me out to the theater, and being met with the usual polite refusal with all the usual excuses, I could try to organize a kidnapping."

Ricciardi shook his head, amused in spite of himself.

"Well, is that right? I'm in such pitiful shape that I need to be kidnapped to keep from splitting myself between home and work. You should talk that over with Bruno Modo, you both have the same opinion about my case. Excuse me, but I've had a complicated day and . . . "

Livia went over to a side table upon which stood a cluster of bottles and glasses.

"You always have complicated days, Ricciardi. You just mentioned the doctor, and you've given me an idea. Let's just pretend that tonight I'm acting as your physician, and I'm ordering you to take a medicine that will help you to rest easier. All right? Drink a bit of this cognac and let yourself go."

Ricciardi protested.

"Livia, I haven't eaten dinner and drinking on an empty stomach certainly won't do me any good. Listen, I promise you that . . . "

Livia handed him a glass, pretending to be confident and determined.

"No arguments. Empty stomach or full, a little shot of brandy will let you see life from a different point of view. And you know very well, I'm quite stubborn: I'm not going to let you go, unless you take your medicine."

The commissario sighed and accepted the glass. The liquid scalded his throat as it ran down, giving him a faint but immediate sense of vertigo.

Livia had taken a seat in an armchair facing him. She looked at him the way a lioness eyes a gazelle at a water hole.

Ricciardi noticed that her housecoat had pulled open

slightly in the front, displaying the generous curve of her breasts. Continuing to gaze at him from over the rim of her glass, Livia crossed her legs and started playing with her slipper, which she coquettishly dangled from her bare foot.

Ricciardi took another sip.

"Well then, Ricciardi, how are you doing? And don't talk to me about work, if you please, you know that that's not what I'm talking about."

"I don't have much besides my work, Livia. It's a constant commitment, and I'm happy that it is."

Livia took a cigarette out of the silver case on the coffee table and lit it. She gracefully let out a plume of smoke straight up into the air. The music continued to flow softly, as did the air from the September evening, pouring in through the half-open window.

"I meant, how you're doing inside. If you're feeling a little happier now that you've returned to service after your loss. By the way, how is the new housekeeper working out, the one that . . . I can't remember her name."

"Nelide. Her name is Nelide. She's very good, in fact sometimes I almost think that she's . . . she's good. But I miss Rosa, terribly. More than I ever would have thought."

Livia got up from the armchair and, her hips slightly swaying, went over to sit on the sofa, next to Ricciardi.

Now the commissario's head was spinning even faster.

"It's only logical that you miss her," the woman said to him. "You grew up with her, she's taken care of you since you were born. Like a mother, even more devoted than a mother. But life has its phases, and that phase had to come to an end eventually, don't you think?"

Her voice had dropped a tone, until it faded to a whisper. Now that he had her close to him, Ricciardi realized how inebriating that perfume was and how irresistible the lines of her body, sheathed in silk, really could be.

He could almost convince himself that he had been drugged, if he hadn't known that Livia herself was a kind of drug: the most beautiful and seductive woman that you could ever hope to meet. Sitting stiffly on the sofa, he took another sip of cognac.

Livia moved even closer to him, whispering just inches from his ear.

"Have you ever thought that now you could allow yourself to sample another type of happiness? To share a little bit of your life with someone else?"

Ricciardi would have liked to stand up, but somehow he couldn't do it. Suddenly, Livia put a hand on his leg. He could feel its warmth as if there were no trouser fabric between hand and leg. He looked down at that hand and it seemed like an animal endowed with a life of its own: the long fingers, the finely enameled and well cared for fingernails, the soft brown flesh. A ring with a gold knot, a bracelet of red and green stones.

He looked up and his gaze met Livia's eyes: a pair of dark lights, as liquid and alluring as an abyss. Her lips half open, her teeth gleaming white, her neck bare and throbbing. She irradiated life, desire, love. Her chest was heaving under her house-coat, just a breath away from his arm, her thigh pressing against his.

The savage perfume took on another equally subtle hue, a harsh aftertaste that told quite another story.

Ricciardi leapt to his feet, his heart in his throat. His mind and his heart were fighting a terrible battle against every fiber of his being, his body which was eager to lunge into the whirlpool.

"Livia, I have to go. Now I really have to go. Forgive me."

The woman's eyes filled with tears. Her teeth clamped down on her lower lip, while her cheeks burned red.

"But . . . but why? I know it, I can feel that you desire me.

I know men's desires, and I can feel yours. Then why don't you take me? Why not?"

Ricciardi opened his mouth, and then shut it again. Then he said: "I . . . I can't do it, Livia. I'm not . . . I can't. Don't ask me why, I beg of you."

The tears began to roll down the woman's face.

"It's me, isn't it? You don't have enough respect for me. You think that I'm just a superficial little woman, a stupid woman who knows nothing about love. One who only knows how to flirt, who . . . "

He interrupted her.

"No, no, what on earth are you saying? You are absolutely perfect, you'd make any man deliriously happy. You're beautiful, well read, and intelligent. It's me that . . . "

Livia seemed not to be listening.

"You think I want who knows what from you. But I don't, you know? I don't want a family or children, I don't want a home or money. All I want is you, because it's you I've fallen in love with. It's the thought of you that gives me life, that makes me want to laugh and sing. Only you have this power over me, and not one of the other hundred or so men who send me flowers or come here to wait hours to see me, even though I never receive them."

Ricciardi tried to calm her.

"I've told you, but you refuse to listen to me. I told you from the very beginning, I never offered you any illusions. I can't have a woman near me. I just can't."

Livia leapt to her feet. Now she was a wounded wild beast: her dark eyes glittered in the low light, her arms hung at her sides with fists clenched, the muscles of her face were rigid. Her lips spat out the words.

"You're a damned liar! The truth is, you're thinking about another woman, and I know exactly who that dreary little wench really is, that nothing of a girl, that lifeless kitty-cat you're in love with. Well, just so you know, she has a fiancé already. She wants nothing to do with you. So please, stop coming around spouting lies!"

Ricciardi stood in silence, staring at her face. The image of Enrica kissing a man through the branches of the trees, beneath the moonlight, appeared before his eyes again as if he were back at Ischia, the night that Rosa died. Right then and there, for the first time, he felt the stabbing remorse for having gone after Enrica, instead of holding his *tata*'s hand as she breathed her last.

Remorse. Regret. The life that he had had, the life that he'd never have. The past, the future.

"No, Livia," he said in a cold whisper. "Not even her. I don't want any woman near me. I can't."

The refrain of that song, which came to him in the night: Go away, moth. Go away. Don't burn in my flame.

He looked at Livia once again, her magnificent body, her bosom heaving with her tears, the black smears of makeup oozing down her cheeks. A promise of transitory, illusory happiness.

I'm saving you, by not wanting you. Don't you understand that? I am hell, I carry hell inside me. Run, if you can.

You don't know it, but happiness is always an illusion. It's always a dream that you chase, and life is nothing but that pursuit.

For the others. But not for me.

I have nothing to pursue.

He set down his glass, turned, and walked away.

T he old man ends the refrain with a strange chord. The young man has never seen or heard a chord anything like it, and yet people say he's a virtuoso, he's had prestigious teachers, and he has a natural gift for music. He's there to learn something new, certainly not technique. But he's never heard anyone play a chord like that one.

The sound that comes out of the instrument is interlocutory, preclusive, but also sorrowful, full of melancholy self-awareness. A chord of sorrow and pity, a sound of yearning for the future. He sits, openmouthed.

But Maestro . . . that chord you just played. What chord is it? How did you . . .

And he curls the fingers of his hand in the air, in an attempt to imitate.

The old man stares into the middle distance, the empty air, following the beam of light that pours in from the window, from the sea. He grimaces in annoyance.

It doesn't count. It doesn't count for a thing. It's just sound, if you don't follow the story. Did you hear it, the story? The way what he said in the first line pointed the way to the refrain?

The young man remains with his fingers curled, in search of the memory of a chord. He's overwhelmed by the idea that the old man was capable of performing such virtuosity and yet he minimizes its value so brusquely.

I . . . yes, Maestro. I listened.

The old man turns toward him, his gaze grim, his brow furrowed.

And what did it say. Repeat to me what it said.

The young man shifts uneasily on the stool.

It said: Watch this moth . . .

The old man slams his hand down flat on the little table in front of him. The half-full glass of water overturns and a number of sheets of paper scatter across the floor.

Not the words, dammit! Everyone knows the words! The story, I said! Tell me the story that he tells!

The thunderous voice, the noise of the objects, the sound of the hand all make the young man jump and the pigeons burst into flight off the rain gutter, in a frantic churning of wings.

The young man experiences a fit of anger and confusion. Just who the hell do you think you are, you damned old man, arthritic and half blind as you are, to speak to me like that? Don't you know that last night there were two thousand people who came to hear me sing and play? Don't you know that pretty soon I'm probably going to get a contract for a tour like nothing you've ever even dreamed of?

He realizes that the old man is expecting an asnwer, and replies, tersely: What he sees. He tells what he sees, a moth getting close to a candle's flame. And he tries to shoo the moth away, because he understands that otherwise it will die. That's what he says.

The old man, surprised, smiles and nods.

That's right, exactly. Good job. He tells only what he sees. And he makes us see it too, as we listen to the song. And you, as you sing, have to make your listeners see it too, you have to take them to a room at night in late summer, with a hot wind that brings moths inside, in search of light.

Yes, Maestro. And the instrument must tell the story along with me.

Once again, the old man nods, smiling that toothless smile.

That's right, together. Not accompanying you, but singing the same story along with you. Do you understand now?

The young man heaves a deep sigh. He's not sure why, but he senses that the old man is telling him something that's very important for his art. And yet he refuses to explain that chord.

Maestro, I wanted to know, again, if it's possible, how you can pull a story out of the instrument? I understand, you have to sing a story, but I . . .

The old man caresses the neck, with his trembling fingertips.

No-o-o, that's not something you need to worry about. I've seen you play. You have nothing to worry about. You just need to think about telling the story, the instrument will take care of the rest. Now listen to me closely.

The young man assumes the old man is going to start playing again, and he readies himself to listen. Instead the old man goes on talking.

Remember, he's replying to the woman's letter. She's told him that she loves him, that she wants him: the man is explaining that the two of them can't be together. He showed her this little moth that comes in through the window, that starts to flutter close to the flame. But why did he show it to her? What is he trying to say? Do you know?

The young man heaves a sigh, eyes wide open.

No, Maestro. I don't know.

The old man nods, like a teacher responding to a student's correct reply.

No, that's right. You don't know. So he tells you. And how does he tell you? By talking about her, directly to her. And it's here, in the second verse, that he answers the letter; that he begins to answer. It's not just that he could hurt her, but more importantly, it's she who could rip his heart out of his chest. And why?

The young man is baffled, he doesn't know what to say. He whispers: Why, Maestro?

Because, young and inexperienced though she may be, she's still a woman. A capricious, fickle, beautiful, and desirable woman. While he, who is entering the autumn of his years, who is watching his summer end, like a candle burning down, would no longer have the time to be reborn from the death that those lovely smooth hands might deal out to him. That's why.

For no good reason, the young man feels completely inadequate and deeply moved. He thinks it over, while the old man observes him with a half smile on his face. And he finds the reasons.

Inadequate, because he thinks that maybe, in order to sing such a sorrow, a person must have experienced it. Deeply moved, because he's sung that song a hundred times, and he's never really listened to it.

The old man resumes, in a low voice.

Then he prepares the refrain with the second verse, and they're the same words as before. But the meaning, that changes. It's different. Just as we're different, as we listen to it now, as we watch the little moth with fear and sorrow as it flutters around the flame. He tells her: I'll do without you. Because this love can kill me.

He turns his eyes to the small, narrow neck of the very old instrument he's holding in his hands.

And he begins to sing again.

Carulí, pe' nu capriccio,
tu vuo' fà scuntento a n'ato
e po', quanno ll'hê lassato,
tu addu n'ato vuo' vulà.

Troppe core staje strignenno
cu 'sti mmane piccerelle;
ma fernisce ca 'sti scelle
pure tu te puo' abbrucià.

Vattenn' 'a lloco!
Vattenne, pazzarella!
Va', palummella, e torna,
e torna a 'st'aria
accussí fresca e bella!
'O bbí ca i' pure
mm'abbaglio chianu chiano,
e ca mm'abbrucio 'a mano
pe' te ne vulè caccià?

 (Carolina, for some caprice,
you want to make another man unhappy
and then, once you've left him,
you want to fly to yet another.

You're clutching too many hearts
With these little hands of yours,
But it turns out that you can
Also burn these wings of yours.

Get out of here!
Get away, silly thing!
Go, little butterfly, and go back
go back into this air
so cool and clear!
You see that I, too,
am slowly being dazzled
and that I'm burning my hand
as I try to shoo you away?)

XXIII

There is a moment, in every night, that is a crossover point. It's not the same for everyone, of course. It comes when the territory of consciousness begins to blur, like when you're walking through the countryside in a winter dawn and the fog conceals everything in a dreamland.

At that moment our fears push forward into the midst of our decisions and break them apart, one stone after the other, and they begin to build the dreams that will ensue only to dissolve in silence when morning comes.

At that moment all our certainties cease to exist, hunger becomes less urgent, and even pain steps aside to let our farthest-flung passions walk onstage, the passions we have kept safely shut up behind the door of reason.

Mothers know that moment, and they run a hand over their children's foreheads to soothe their eyes and their souls, letting them imagine that it is them, their mothers, behind that fog, that they might move forward into it comforted by that memory of maternal tenderness.

What happens is that you feel strong, at that moment. That it seems possible to knock down obstacles effortlessly, solve matters beyond the shadow of a doubt. Or that you feel weak, and every obstacle seems like a mountain without handholds or escape routes. What happens is that you become afraid of feeling strong.

Afraid you will not be able to make it through, to stick to your decision.

But even more afraid that you will.

*

I'll do without you.

I'll do without your face and your laughter, your flesh beneath my hand. I'll do without your voice whispering in the shadows of our absurd early morning trysts, those half-hours that give a jump-start to the rest of my terrible day.

I'll do without you because I have to. Because I owe you that.

I'll do without you because you believed in me when no one else did, and I believed less than anyone. Because you gave me the strength to smile at the sun, to hold my head high. Because you pulled my life out of the narrow tunnel of a couple of dice tumbling into fate, a horse's nose a couple of inches ahead of another horses's nose. Because you told me that destiny lay not in those cards yet to be turned faceup, but in your smile.

I'll do without you, because no one can get between the two of us. Because if it's going to be a life, it can't be born in blood, but rather out of the tenderness you've bestowed upon me.

I'll do without you because of the decision you made, because your hand is the hand of my joy, not the hand of the death that I caused.

I'll do without you.

And I'll die every single day, gazing into the flame of the candle from which I shooed you away.

A crossover point.

A slender veil that can stitch up the virginity of a dream, that can keep truth on one side and madness on the other.

A curtain made of memories and hopes.

I'll do without you.

I'll have no trouble doing it, because you're no longer the man I met, ravenously hungry for life, happy about everything that hit you in the impetus of sunny days and blue skies.

I'll do without you, because it will be easy for me to remember the long months of silences, when you stopped searching for absurd justifications of the things you did and what you'd turned into. It will be easy for me to remember your returns home, the uncertain sound of your drunken footsteps, your fumbling among the papers and the glasses on the other side of the wall.

I'll do without you, the way I've learned to do over the years, when I finally understand that the false mask of the man that you are was nothing but a lie, a squalid falsehood disguised by the face I thought I'd fallen in love with. Because what I don't forgive you for, what I can never forgive you for, is that you left my eyes with the memory of your face as it is now, shattering the image of our youth, an image that was the image I had of myself.

I'll do without you, once I've figured out why. Once I've learned the reason for all this, and I can finally stop puzzling through the nights. Because I know that you lied to me. I know you did.

I have to understand. I have to know. Then, at last, I'll be able to do without you.

And contemplate the emptiness of my life.

It was just a moment.

A tiny, simple instant, a tick of the second hand on the watch, not even the space of one complete breath.

A glint of awareness, vivid, terrible, and brightly colored, that comes just before the oblivion of silence.

I'll do without you.

It will be necessary, and I'll succeed. I'm already getting used to it, in the seemingly normal days that must flow past, untroubled, to keep anyone from guessing that these are the days of my new life.

I'll do without you, and I'll be sorry about it, because you were the dream of a different, brilliant future, full of fun and laughter. But dreams don't last long, as we all know, even the loveliest ones make way for the morning.

I'll do without you. And as far as that goes, perhaps, I knew from the very beginning that we weren't going to be allowed to get away with it. But it was nice to dream of it, when I felt your knowing, trembling hands on my flesh, when I heard you whisper your nectar-sweet illusions.

Then I'd forget that it was going to prove impossible. Then I'd listen the way you listen to a fairy tale, and you believe in the story that everyone, and I mean everyone, is going to live happily ever after.

I liked to let myself be talked into it, and pretend that we were going to live in the light of day. That when people looked at us, their eyes wouldn't be filled with ill will and malice, and that all told, when it came to it, we too would have our chance.

I'll do without you, and I'll look forward. Forgetting that I ever dreamed and smiled and felt my heart beat in a doorway early one morning.

Forgetting the blood shed, and that long, flaccid, wet gasping breath that whirled through the air.

I'll do without you. And I'll live my life.

How long does an instant really last? Can't it stretch out into infinity, if it's kept alive by a simple fantasy?

If through the window cracked open onto the September night, the words of a distant song arrive, in an ancient, unknown language that speaks of flames, moths, and hearts gripped in small hands.

If those words drop like seeds borne on the wind, and they take root in the unconsciousness of a mind yielding to the pounding blows of sleep. And weeping.

And if those tears sprout leaves, and bitter fruit.

*

I'll do without you. Now I know that. You told me yourself that's what I'll have to do.

At last, maybe I can. Perhaps I can find a way to be reborn.

I believed that I was alive because I had you. Because I looked forward and it seemed to me that you held in your hands both your future and mine.

I believed that we were going to be able to laugh together, and cry as well, if we felt like it, opening so many different parentheses in the midst of so much solitude. I believed that I was going to be able to get you out of the prison in which you had stubbornly taken refuge.

I wanted to feel your flesh and no one else's beneath my palms. I wanted to give you flavors you'd never tasted, teach you how to reach paradise and never set foot on earth again. I wanted to tell you about all the days you didn't even know you had in your pocket and open your heart to yourself. Your heart and mine.

I was certain that it was going to be tonight, our night. That the sun, our sun, was going to break through your shadows and mine, and that it would warm us so much that neither you nor I would be able to do without it.

I'd prepared everything, foolish woman that I am. I'd even thought about these sheets, the pillows that absorb these damned tears I can't seem to choke back. I'd thought about the music, the liquor, and your weariness.

I'd believed that once that pointless dream you were pretending to cherish had been swept away, you'd finally understand that I'm a real woman, made up of petals and tears and laughter, and that you'd choose life. I've never been as explicit as I was then, I'd never known so well what I wanted. I'd never been so sure of myself, of my beauty and my desire.

And now, now that I know I'll do without you, I hate you.

I hate you for what you've condemned yourself to, and me

along with you. I hate you for not being what I was sure that you were. I hate you for the image of your shoulders, indifferent to my pain and grief, when you turned your back on me and left. I hate you for the frustration, for the humiliation.

I hate you because I loved you.

I'll do without you, because not even the dream of a rebirth can be enough to pay for this suffering. I'll do without you, because a love like this can kill a person, leave her burning in the flame of a lonely candle in the night.

I'll do without you.

Then the consciousness hunkers down, squatting patiently in the night. And it gives way to tangled dreams.

And desperate nightmares.

XXIV

It had been a long time since Ricciardi last set foot in prison.

Unlike many of his colleagues, he didn't enjoy taking people to jail. In any case, it represented a defeat to him.

He had pondered at considerable length, when he first began his career, about what it meant to him to be a policeman. He, a constant witness to the sorrow of life's last instant, knew perfectly well that at that point nothing can be fixed, that no preexisting order can be restored. But he also knew that the only relief, however marginal and transitory, that he could offer his own soul was to track down whoever had been responsible for that sorrow. In the final analysis, he was doing it more for himself than for the victim, who by this point really couldn't enjoy any relief.

But every time he found himself looking into the eyes of someone who had put an end to another person's life, he often detected an even greater and deeper pain there. Leaving aside the issue of repentance, someone who had killed suffered and would continue to suffer for every single day of life that remained to them.

That was probably why he'd stopped taking to prison those arrested for the murders he'd successfully investigated. He didn't see how he could interpret that as a victory, something to celebrate with that act, depriving someone of their freedom, perhaps for the rest of their lives. Taking pleasure in someone else's suffering only filled him with horror.

And now, as he was setting out for the prison of Poggioreale where he had arranged to meet Counselor Moscato, he was very pleased to be a virtual stranger to the prison guards.

Moscato was waiting for him at the corner of the street that led to the prison's front gate. Moscato had called him that morning, informing him over the phone that by a singular piece of luck he'd managed to procure the interview immediately, and that they'd therefore need to take advantage of that opportunity. In part because, he had added, Bianca was pestering him relentlessly.

It was strange for Ricciardi to see the lawyer in such a different setting from the last time. At the yacht club Moscato had been relaxed, speculative, and serene. Now he seemed brusque, worried, and even a little ill at ease.

"Ah, Commissario, *buongiorno*. I apologize for giving you such short notice, but in order to procure this opportunity I had to presume upon a number of my acquaintances, and I don't want to embarrass myself."

Ricciardi shrugged his shoulders.

"It's fine with me, Counselor. How should we proceed?"

"We'll tell them that you're accompanying me in, as we had agreed. I'll make it evident at the entrance that you're one of my assistants, though I won't explicitly say so, otherwise I might later be accused of having smuggled someone into the prison under false pretenses, which would be a very serious crime, as you know. Do you think that anyone is likely to recognize you?"

"I doubt it. I haven't been here for quite a while, and in any case I've only been a few times before. I generally let my officers run my prisoners in. What are we going to say to the count?"

Moscato gestured vaguely with one hand.

"I don't think that's particularly important. You see, Romualdo is . . . it's not easy to speak with him, these days. I was here ten days ago, not because I had anything to talk to him about, but because I was hoping that he'd change his mind, that he'd give me a little something more to work with, in other words. And when I was here, I found him . . . well, it's not easy to speak with him."

Ricciardi understood. The reason for the lawyer's attitude, for his unmistakable malaise, was in fact the upcoming meeting with his client. He wondered why.

Clustered around the entrance was the usual, perennial cast of characters. The families of the convicts were milling around beneath the high gray walls, trying to let their loved ones know, with occasional shouts, that they were there. Ricciardi thought that this was what purgatory, if such a thing existed, must be like: the despairing sorrow of parting, of a love kept far away by a partition wall. Women, old men, children with creased, weary faces, sitting on the ground waiting for nothing.

As the two men approached the iron gate, a number of women tried to grab them by the hems of their jackets. Counselor, counselor, they kept saying: take us inside with you. Take us to see our son, our husband. Let us touch his face, let us kiss him; and if you can't take us inside, here, take this, it's a note with his name, we had the scrivener write it out for us, you talk to him. Tell him that we love him, that without him out here is the real prison. Tell him not to worry, that we're waiting for him, that we think of nothing but him. Tell him that, counselor.

For the love of God, please tell him that.

A trolley car went screeching past near the sidewalk. The people crammed inside averted their eyes, unwilling to gaze at those people. Was that out of habit? Shame? Perhaps it was just a secret happiness at not being in the same situation.

Moscato shook off the hand of a pale young woman who was grabbing him by the sleeve.

"For pete's sake, Signo', don't touch me! Just look here, the stains your fingers left on the fabric. Why, what manners! This is what you always do out here! I've told you a thousand times that I can't summon your husband, I can't meet with anyone for you, talk to your own lawyers if you're looking for legal assistance!"

A toothless graybeard commented, in a loud voice: "Sure, and do you think that if we could afford a lawyer we'd be out here asking for the charity of taking a message inside? Are you of all people pretending that you don't know that there's one kind of justice for the poor and another kind for the rich?"

The ashen-faced young woman turned to look at him, her eyes wide with terror.

"Papa, be quiet! Counselor, pay him no mind, he's just an old man and . . . "

Moscato gestured with one hand.

"Don't worry about it, Signo'. I didn't hear a word he said. But tell your father, or your father-in-law, or whatever he is to you, that he should think before he speaks, because around here, we all do our jobs and we're just trying to make a living, it's certainly not our fault that not everyone can pay us."

The large door swung open with a muffled shriek. When the guard appeared in the opening, three women with bundles in their hands stepped forward, asking permission to take the contents of those bundles to their sons and husbands. Some of them called the guard by name, as if they knew him, but he showed no sign of even glancing at them. He did, however, greet Moscato, and ushered them in.

As he had hoped, Ricciardi encountered no familiar faces. The lawyer had handed him his own voluminous leather satchel, packed with papers and documents, just as he would have done with any assistant. As they were waiting for their identities to be recorded, he whispered to Ricciardi: "Unlike conversations with family members, it is forbidden for guards to listen in on interviews with lawyers. They are required to be present, but they keep a certain distance, which means we'll be able to talk without fear of being overheard. Romualdo is . . . last time it was hard to keep his attention, I'd say. What do you want me to ask him?"

Ricciardi thought it over.

"I need him to talk about the murder. He needs to say what he remembers, talk about his relations with Piro. I need to understand if he gets caught up in any contradictions, if he has any hesitations or doubts. And most important of all, whether he's thought about it, whether his time in prison has led him to reconsider the possibility of retracting his confession."

Moscato nodded, doubtfully.

"Frankly, Commissario, the whole thing strikes me as pure folly. If Bianca hadn't insisted so relentlessly, and if it didn't break my heart to see her in such dire straits, I wouldn't have inflicted this visit upon myself. You see, I believe that people's wishes should be respected. If this is what Romualdo wants, then this is what he should get."

Ricciardi stared at him, grimly.

"Counselor, I understand what you're saying, and in part I subscribe to it. But I also believe that the truth must be respected. And it's up to us policemen to make sure that that happens."

A guard came to call them.

As they were walking down a long hallway immersed in an eerie silence, the lawyer murmured to Ricciardi: "Romualdo, at his own request and thanks to my intervention, is in solitary confinement day and night. He was terrified at the thought of having to coexist with other prisoners, and his prominent name, my own requests, and a couple of friendships in the right places took care of the matter. I wasn't in favor of it: sometimes a little company, however unpleasant it might be, can provide a necessary distraction in these situations; but he was quite adamant. Unfortunately, subsequent events have proved me right."

Before Ricciardi could ask the reason why, they came to a door that led into a large, rectangular room with a long table at the center and two benches along the sides. Along the walls, up high, were a number of decorated scrolls containing moral precepts set forth in handsome calligraphy, and beneath them, figures of bishops and saints. At the center of the wall were portraits of Il Duce and the king, the former considerably larger than the latter.

The lawyer took a seat on one of the benches, gesturing for the commissario to follow suit. Through the window, which was opaque with layers of dust, came a milky light. There was a stale odor in the air, a stench of mold and old paper, as in some poorly kept library.

After a few minutes, the door swung open and a guard came in, leading a prisoner, chained hand and foot.

Ricciardi had met Romualdo Palmieri, Count of Roccaspina, some two years ago. He remembered him as a disheveled, unshaven man, but handsome to behold: feverish and distracted, obsessed with his demon, dressed in a wrinkled but well made suit and a walking stick that he waved in the air a little too freely. And he'd seen a photographic portrait of him during his recent visit to the contessa: a bit younger, smiling as he stood next to a racehorse, one hand resting on the back of the animal, which was held on a pair of reins and a bit by a stable boy.

The derelict who was shuffling toward the bench on the opposite side of the table, taking one short step after another in a jangling of chains, was quite another person. The commissario experienced a lengthy shudder of pity.

Inasmuch as he was simply a defendant who had not yet been convicted, he still had the right to wear his own clothing instead of the striped uniform made of rough canvas. In fact, he wore a shirt that had once been white and a pair of black trousers. On his feet were a pair of shoes, also black, quite down at the heels, and lacking laces.

What was most striking was the size of the clothing compared to the man's physique. He looked like a boy who was playing at wearing his father's clothes. His skinny neck floated inside the collar, and his bony wrists stuck out of his sleeves, reddened where the iron shackles had worn away at his wrinkled, opaque flesh. His trousers wouldn't have held up if they hadn't been tied on with a filthy length of twine, though even so they looked as if they were about to fall down from one minute to the next.

His face really was frightening, and it had nothing in common with the image that Ricciardi recollected. Shaven practically bald in accordance with prison regulations, his cheeks were hollow, his lips chapped, his eyes sunken into the orbits that stared dully out into the empty air.

The guard held the man up as he took his seat, then touched the visor of his cap in a gesture of respect, turned toward the door, and ran his gaze out into the hallway. The greatest degree of privacy that could be allowed for an interview.

The count said nothing, his eyes fixed on a point somewhere in front of him. The lawyer shook his head, the expression on his face betraying a sense of profound pity.

"Romua', I don't understand what you've gotten into your head. Have you decided to let yourself starve to death? Don't you understand? You're worse off than you were ten days ago, I . . . "

The man suddenly jutted his chin forward, staring at him.

"No. Not ten days. Twelve. Twelve. Time is important, Atti'. We can't make mistakes in counting. And even though I don't have a watch like you do, of course, I can tell you from the position of the sun in the sky that it's been twelve days and almost two hours."

"Ten, twelve, what difference does it make? You look like a lunatic to me, that's what you look like. Oh lord, it's not as if you were ever quite normal, even when you were a kid you tended to rave a little."

Romualdo bared his yellowed teeth and ulcerated gums in an attempt at a smile.

"Eh, when I was a kid. When I was a kid, I didn't understand a thing. Now I do, now I understand."

Moscato clucked his tongue.

"And if you understand, then you should also understand that you need to eat and you need to keep up your strength. Otherwise, as God is my witness, I'll arrange to have you taken out of solitary confinement, and then you'll see what it means to be in really bad shape."

The count leaned forward.

"No! No! If they put me with the other prisoners, I swear that I'll kill myself. I'll do it, you know? I've even decided how to do it. But listen, what about the trial? Where are we with that?"

The lawyer heaved a sigh.

"I've studied documents and precedents, but for that matter you know the situation well yourself and, even though you've never practiced, you are a lawyer. The formal preliminary investigation has been concluded, the true bill has been handed down, and we're waiting for the clerk of the court to present the chief justice with a request for trial. At that point, the court is called into session and the date of the first hearing is set. And that will be when I'm expected to submit a list of witnesses."

"Witnesses? What witnesses? I've already told you that there won't be any witnesses, and there's not going to be a presentation of evidence by the defense, or even a formulation of a defense theory."

"Romua', I . . . "

The count answered decisively, spitting drops of saliva from his chapped lips, drops that fell on the table.

"I don't want you to do anything. You just need to make sure that no aggravating circumstances are introduced against me, that there is no reason to think we'll be facing more than the minimum sentence."

The lawyer threw his arms wide.

"I don't understand and I never will. You don't want me to defend you, you don't want me to try to get you off, but you do want the shortest possible sentence. In other words: you want to be found guilty, but you want to get out as early as possible."

"You don't need to understand, you just need to do what I tell you to do. It was a crime of spontaneous rage, there was no premeditation. I murdered him on impulse, so the prescribed sentence is twenty-one years. And that's what I expect to get. I'll always behave impeccably and you'll be in charge of submitting the various pleas to shorten my detention. Is that clear?"

"You know, there's always the danger of trival motives. That's an aggravating circumstance that frequently . . . "

The prisoner shook his head vehemently.

"No, no, I've explained this to you at least ten times: it was a major debt, as you can see from the promissory notes. And then I want you to say that he had insulted me, that he had denigrated the honor of my name, of my family. The judges are descended from the nobility, they'll take that into account. You don't need to worry, it'll all go smooth as silk."

Ricciardi decided to break in.

"That is, if you even make it alive to the trial. You look like you're in pretty bad shape."

Until that point, Roccaspina hadn't even seemed to be aware of his presence; his eyes, at first staring into the middle distance, were focused on Moscato's eyes and hadn't left them. But now he slowly turned his head to look at his new interlocutor, with a smirk devoid of all cordiality.

"*Buongiorno*, Commissario. How strange to see you again

here. May I ask why you've decided to poke into matters that are my business, what's more with the approval of someone who is supposed to be *my* lawyer?"

A chilly silence descended. Moscato muttered: "Romua', you see, the fact is that Bianca . . . But wait, do you two know each other?"

The prisoner replied, never taking his eyes off Ricciardi: "Ah, didn't he tell you? I had the honor to cross paths with him almost two years ago; at the time, if I'm not mistaken, he was working on the murder of Gaspare Rummolo, an *assistito*. That was a nasty affair, wasn't it, Commissario? That time you had to find the guilty parties all by yourself. Here you had my lawyer to carry you in here."

"Compliments on your memory, Count. We only spent a few minutes together, and yet I remember you, too. You were in much better form at the time, if I may venture to say so."

Roccaspina snickered, then turned to look at Moscato.

"Attilio, you owe me some explanations, I think. You wouldn't want me to recuse you and be forced to serve as my own lawyer, would you? That wouldn't be a very good advertisement for your services, since, as you tell me, our case is in the spotlight of public interest." He turned back to look at Ricciardi. "A humble appearance, Commissario, is an unmistakable symptom of repentence and suffering. You may not be a lawyer, but surely you can guess how much that counts for the judges when it comes to the decision to apply mitigating circumstances in the formulation of the sentence. Don't worry, I'll be back in fine form in no time. It's all going according to plan."

Moscato massaged the root of his nose with two fingers.

"Romualdo, the commissario is here at your wife's request. You know very well, she can't get over the idea that you're innocent. This attitude can create talk and annoy the court by interfering with your strategy, which, by the way, let me be clear, I neither understand nor support. Bianca . . . "

The count cut him off, turning brusquely to address Ricciardi.

"My wife is deceiving you, Commissario. She tried it on with Attilio, here, and with your colleagues during that aborted investigation that was undertaken. She even went and talked to the investigating magistrate, I've been told. Poor woman, it's understandable enough: solitude, I'm sure you know, plays some terrible tricks. But you'll see that in the end she'll come to terms with reality and resign herself. And after all, it's better for her if I'm behind bars. The enormous mass of my debts won't crush her, and maybe she'll even be able to save the palazzo from the wreckage."

Ricciardi sat motionless, curiously observing that shaven head and that chilly glance that made the man sitting in chains resemble nothing so much as a strange bird.

"Why are you doing it, Count? I don't understand. It can't be because of the debts." He stopped and looked away. Then, continuing as if talking to himself, he resumed: "Even suicide would be less painful than this. And it can't be out of love, because then you'd accept your wife's help. So what's the reason?"

Romualdo fell silent. His eyes suddenly welled up with tears, as if he were thinking back to some memory.

Then he coughed and replied: "I'm doing it because it's true, because I killed him. Because that shady bastard, that shameless loan shark, died at my hand, and I'd never allow anyone else to be accused of a crime I committed. That's why."

Ricciardi drove in.

"And yet no one saw you go in or leave. No one heard any screams, no one heard the sounds of a struggle. And your wife . . . "

The count slammed both fists down onto the table. The noise, amplified by the fact that the room was practically empty, as well as the twin wrist shackles and connected chains, was violent and unexpected. The guard at the door started and turned to rush over to Romualdo, shaking him roughly.

"Oh, you animal, what do you think you're doing? Just thank your lucky stars you're already in solitary confinement, otherwise . . . "

Moscato raised one hand.

"No, no, thank you, but it's all right. It's my fault, really, I brought up a subject that . . . "

The guard reluctantly released his grip, shooting a suspicious glance at the prisoner.

"Anyway, it's time to get you back to your cell. The interview is over."

Before getting to his feet, Romualdo smiled. When he bared his teeth, Ricciardi thought, he looked even more wasted than before. He brought to mind the corpses that Ricciardi saw in the streets, starving vagabonds whose weakness had pushed them under the wheels of trolley cars and automobiles.

Romualdo seemed to be speaking to the commissario, though he looked neither him nor his friend and lawyer in the face.

"Are you familiar with cockroaches? They're very interesting creatures. In my cell I have a whole family of them. They keep me company, they're formidable runners. I'm thinking about breeding them and racing them competitively, I might make bets with myself. I don't understand why they should be swept out or even crushed underfoot, they're perfectly inoffensive."

The guard lifted him out of the chair as if he weighed nothing and walked him to the door. As he left the room, Count Romualdo Palmieri di Roccaspina was chuckling.

XXV

M oscato was fanning himself with his hat, as he sat at the little table in the café just outside the prison.

"Commissario, do you think he's gone crazy? The loneliness, his remorse . . . every time I see him, he gives me the creeps worse and worse."

Ricciardi pensively sipped the dense black liquid.

"I couldn't say. I didn't see any signs of remorse, in any case; if he did it, then he's very glad he did."

Moscato thought it over.

"I wouldn't know about that. His attitude was strange from the very start. First of all, he didn't call me, I could have gone in with him, I'd have taken advantage of the fact that the cops . . . excuse me, Commissa', that the police, at least at first, were stumbling around in the dark a bit. Instead, it was Bianca who alerted me, when Romualdo had already been detained."

Ricciardi grew more attentive.

"Are you telling me that at first, the count wouldn't even accept a defense lawyer?"

"No. And you've heard him, he wasn't born yesterday when it comes to legal procedure. He knows perfectly well what he's looking at, and he doesn't seem to be afraid. In fact, today he threatened to recuse me as a lawyer, which is the last thing we need: it would be a matter of considerable disgrace for everyone, from the court on down. But what about you, why didn't you tell me that you had already met him? That wasn't a very clever move, if anyone happens to learn that I smuggled you into the prison . . . "

Ricciardi shook his head no.

"I thought you already knew it, actually. Otherwise, why would the contessa have come looking for me of all people? For that matter, I'm surprised that he recognized me, we only met for a brief time and, as the count pointed out, that was two years back."

Moscato nodded, uncertainly.

"This story just gets stranger and stranger. And then there's Romualdo's relationship with Bianca: you must certainly have heard that they no longer lived as husband and wife; Romualdo confided in me about that fact many many months ago. What's more, you heard him yourself, depending on how this case turns out, it could even mean the rescue of the palazzo and the few possessions remaining to them."

"But his creditors would have the right to demand payment from the contessa, wouldn't they?"

The lawyer smiled.

"Certainly, if they were normal creditors, but here we're talking about a completely different circle of operators. People that have no interest in stepping out of the sewers they inhabit. No, Romualdo is right. Bianca can only benefit if he is convicted."

"Then maybe that's why he accused himself of the murder. To protect his wife from ruin and disgrace."

"How melodramatic you are, Commissario. And now a man, to escape the clutches of a couple of ill-intentioned scoundrels, takes the blame for a murder he didn't commit? Can you guess how many of my clients I've helped to escape on the first freighter sailing for America or Australia, or by night aboard a train for northern Europe? Much easier, more painless, and with the same positive effects. And then, if you'll allow me, there's still another question."

"What's that?"

The lawyer put on a concentrated expression.

"I've wondered from the very beginning: let's say that Bianca's right, and that for some unknown reason Romualdo has lost his mind and has confessed to a murder he didn't commit. Well, how did he know what had happened? He lives nowhere near the victim and it was the early hours of the morning, which means news of the murder was not yet publicly known. If it wasn't him who did it, then how would he have known about the murder?"

Ricciardi had to admit to himself that he hadn't considered that angle.

"That means the only explanation is that it was him, is that right? Or at least that he was present during the murder. Which would mean that the contessa is a liar."

Moscato shrugged his shoulders, fanning himself with his hat all the while.

"Maybe she just fell asleep and didn't hear Romualdo go out and come back. Or else she has the time wrong. Sometimes, Commissario, we believe what we want to believe, with all our might."

Ricciardi sat a minute thinking. Then he said: "You see, Counselor, I've always cherished the belief that all the various motives that can lead to murder can actually be broken down into one of two, just two basic motives. I don't believe in outbursts of madness, I don't believe in perversion, I don't believe in illusions. I believe that people kill either out of hunger or love. That what arms the killer's hand is always either the determination to ensure his own survival and that of the people he loves, or else the passion that stirs a heart."

Moscato stopped waving the hat and stared at the commissario as if he were laying eyes on him for the first time.

"Interesting theory. But I deal with lots of different kinds of people, you know, and I see some really strange things. Sometimes, there's no motive at all. Sometimes a red haze settles over their gaze and they just stop thinking. You heard what

Romualdo said, didn't you? An unpredictable act, and therefore unexpected. He found himself face-to-face with a man who the day before had offended him, insulted him, had refused to give him more time to pay, and who might even have threatened to expose him to public mockery. These are things that might be sufficient to make you lose your sanity."

Ricciardi shook his head.

"And they might push you to grab someone by the neck, or punch him in the face. But would they drive you to grab a sharp object and stab him in the neck? Certainly, if you're in a state of desperation it could happen. But you wouldn't go home afterwards and go to sleep, and then get up the next morning and walk in and confess."

The lawyer listened, attentively.

"And just what kind of hunger, in your opinion, can lead to a murder like this one? What kind of hunger can afflict someone who's already lost everything, and by his own hand?"

Ricciardi said nothing, as he continued to follow the thread of his thoughts.

"Counselor, you've known Roccaspina since you were in school together. You grew up together and it's clear that you're on terms of great familiarity. Tell me something: Is he a man given to fits of rage? Is he a violent man, someone who has difficulty controlling himself? Can you think of any instances when you saw him react in an exaggerated manner? I beg you, make an effort to remember."

Moscato sat raptly for a couple of minutes, turning over the years of friendship with Romualdo in his mind. In the end, he shook his head.

"No, Commissario. To be perfectly honest I don't feel ready to describe Romualdo as a violent man. A man who operates on his instincts, yes, a sentimental man, given to outbursts of affection, generous and spontaneous to a fault, and I'd imagine that these characteristics could even turn into a predisposition to violence given certain desperate situations. But in all fairness, I can't recall a single instance of him raising his hand to someone."

Ricciardi nodded gravely.

"Tell me something else; I'm asking you this because perhaps, because of the profession you practice, you might be aware of situations that can't be seen from the outside: in the circles that you frequent, except for the count, can you think of anyone else who might have had reasons for resentment against Piro?"

The lawyer burst into laughter.

"Commissario, are you joking? Piro was a social climber, a loan shark with a white collar, a character who was, to say the least, quite equivocal. He raised money from the institutions that he represented, and his sole interest was in making money; how he made it was no object, and he loaned that money out to debauchees who had fallen victims to various sins and bad habits. And in order to be certain he'd be paid back, he regularly threatened to diffuse the information that he possessed, in order to create scandals."

"And so?"

"And so, believe me, there must have been at least a dozen people celebrating his death. But even if it had been one of them, the question remains: why should Romualdo have taken the blame for the murder?"

That was true, there was no getting around that question, and Ricciardi had no answer.

All theories eventually fetched up against that brick wall.

XXVI

The interior of the church of San Ferdinando still offered a pleasant sensation of coolness compared to the outdoors. That is the way it would remain until late October, Cavalier Giulio Colombo thought to himself as he dipped his fingers into the holy water font to cross himself.

He looked around, letting his eyes get used to the dim light. A shaft of multicolored light penetrated through the rose window on the façade and fell in the midst of the nave. Before the image of the Madonna, a small group of elderly women were reciting the rosary, as always, producing a constant murmuring. In the air was the penetrating odor of incense and candles. Nothing could be more reassuring, and yet Giulio was agitated, ill at ease, and would rather have been anywhere but there.

He'd never needed to force his basic nature. His work, his family, his few trusted friends didn't require a personality any different from his own: calm, serenity, conviction, solid ideals, honesty, willingness to sacrifice, perhaps a little stubbornness, solicitude toward those who need a helping hand. Sure, every so often his wife would upbraid him for his extended silences, but she was already there to do all the talking, and she more than sufficed.

Nothing thus far had required that he modify his vision of life. Everything had always run on a highly buffed inclined plane, and if the cavalier had any real concerns, they came from outside, from a world that was taking a turn he didn't like, with the growing militarism and those proclamations of the greatness of a nation struggling under a burden of debt to its own august past. All the same, Giulio was too old to fear being called to bear arms, and his eldest son was too young; as for Marco, his son-in-law, well, if things turned out that way it would be hard to hold him in check, fervent Fascist that he was.

But now something was happening that, perhaps, might require an intervention to change the natural flow of events.

The conversation that he'd had the day before with Enrica had thrown him into a profound state of anguish.

If she had asked him for help, if she had burst into tears, if she had told him she planned to run away, he would have had no doubts and would have known just what to do: against everything and everyone he would have fought for his daughter, saving her from her mother, from social conventions, from the squalor of a reasoning that had little or nothing of the sentimental about it.

Likewise, if he had glimpsed in those eyes so similar to his own a resolve devoid of uncertainty, if he had perceived a firm heart, unwilling to look back, then he too, like the rest of the family, would only have been impatient to meet this much ballyhooed Bavarian officer, and he would have fought to stifle his own prejudices against Germany and the Germans.

The problem, the cavalier reflected for the umpteenth time, sharpening his myopic gaze in the direction of the altar, was that Enrica hadn't convinced him one way or the other. More than decisive, she seemed to be resigned. And he wasn't willing to accept that his eldest daughter, his beloved, sweet little girl, the companion of gazes both complicit and silent, was having to resign herself.

The risk of unhappiness, Giulio Colombo thought to himself, feeling a stab of pain in his chest, is still better than forced serenity. Strange that he of all people should have that kind of thought, he who always seemed to be cocooned in a tranquility laboriously constructed and defended with claws and teeth. But the future that he wanted for Enrica was different, it didn't admit any hesitations, because the cavalier was well aware that wholehearted laughter, a heart that flies high over the clouds, the deep breath that you take as you enjoy life all exist only outside of the tiny, orderly cell of everyday certainties.

That is why he had gone to the church. He'd thought it over all night long, pretending to sleep lest Maria's antennae swivel into alert, picking up on variations in his rate of respiration, or other indicators of his state of mind.

Not that he was particularly religious. His pragmatic liberal mind, his logic had taken him far from the banks of a faith which he sometimes missed. He took his family to Mass every Sunday, he watched over the Catholic education of his children, and he adhered to principles that fully coincided with Christian precepts. Still, he felt that it was up to the individual to construct his own best fate, albeit in full respect of his fellow man. He couldn't imagine the existence of Someone who, according to vast and inscrutable designs, moved the world and everything in it like a puppeteer at the Villa Nazionale on a Saturday afternoon.

Precisely because he had faith in his fellow man, that was why he was there. He had decided that if there was anyone capable of telling him what to do, and even helping him to put a strategy into operation, it was surely Don Pietro Fava, the assistant parish priest. Don Pierino, to be clear.

The shop's proximity to the parish church, just a short walk away, and the fact that the diminutive priest was so talkative and in such constant motion, had led Giulio Colombo to form a friendship with him.

The two of them didn't resemble each other in the slightest: one was tall, formal, silent, and secular; the other was short, always in motion, noisy, and—especially—profoundly enamored of God, whose presence he detected everywhere. And yet they had immediately found common territory where they could meet, in the realms of music, books, art, and people, sentiments, and also politics, with an emphasis on peace and dialogue. Don Pierino often came to see the cavalier and, if he happened to find him unoccupied by customers, he'd drag him into lengthy and highly amusing conversations, which would however be cut off abruptly when the priest opened his eyes wide at the sight of the time on the shop's large pendulum clock, whereupon he would shout a rough farewell and hurry off to administer some unpostponable pastoral comfort to a needy parishioner.

That day it was Giulio who needed him.

He found the priest in the sacristy, with his eyeglasses on the tip of his nose, intently stitching up a tear in his tunic.

Colombo smiled, shaking his head.

"But by all that is holy, Don Pierino, haven't I told you a thousand times that if you ever need to have work like this done, you need only come to see me? I have a seamstress on salary to take care of alterations to gloves and hats, and she's often sitting there with nothing to do. She'd be all too happy if we gave her something to work on."

The man of God looked up, peering over his lenses.

"Oh, Cavalier, what an honor! You know that I love to stitch and iron, I have the soul of a housewife. But you, rather, what are you doing here? Have you had a sudden calling to become a cloistered monk and you'd like some advice on how to break the news to your delightful lady wife?"

Colombo took a chair pushed against the wall and sat down.

"Not exactly, maybe some other time. Certainly, the prospect is an interesting one. But today I'm here about another matter, Don Pierino. Something that's been weighing on my heart."

His tone of voice, more than his words, worried the priest,

who immediately put aside the torn tunic, the needle, and the thread, and took off his glasses.

"What's going on, Giulio? There's a look on your face I've never seen before."

The cavalier heaved a sigh and ran a hand over his face. Now that he was face-to-face with his friend, he was starting to think that bringing him into the matter was an act of selfishness, and possibly pointless as well: What could a priest tell him about a problem that involved a woman's emotions?

"I don't know. Maybe it was a mistake to come here, forgive me. It's just that . . . sometimes we need to speak aloud about what's churning in our heads. That's all."

Don Pierino smiled.

"And do you think I don't know that? Things don't become real until you speak them aloud. It's necessary. Words are body, blood: If we priests don't know that, then who does? We celebrate the Word. And from dawn to dusk, in confession, we see people understand the things they have done only in the moment that they hear their own voices recount them."

"Then do you think I should say confession?"

The other man replied seraphically.

"Goodness gracious, no. In confession, you're just a crashing bore, never an impure act, never a wicked thought. And to think that you shopkeepers are all thieves deep down inside. Just talk to me."

So Giulio Colombo talked.

He started from the beginning. Of course, Don Pierino had known Enrica for years, but he still felt the need to describe her personality, her attitudes. He told him about last summer, the letters, the distress. He told him that he had confronted the man about whom his daughter had written him, the short conversation that they had had. About what had happened next, that is, how she had met Manfred, her return home, and the conversation he and his daughter had had just the previous day.

He allowed his deep-felt, instinctive conviction to emerge that his daughter, in spite of what she might tell him—and perhaps she was just trying to keep him from worrying—in the secret spaces of her soul might be condemning herself to a dull, persistent, morbid state of unhappiness.

Don Pierino listened all the while in silence. If there was one thing he had learned in his many years of priesthood, it was that people had a need to be listened to. In the end he reached out his hand and laid it on his friend's arm; Giulio had become so heartfelt as spoke about a person he loved so well that he hadn't even realized that his eyes were reddened with deep emotion. Without any real reason why, but following the hidden path of an impulse, Don Pierino asked the name of the man Enrica was in love with.

Giving voice to a hidden thought, Giulio Colombo knocked down the last wall of his personal reserve.

The name fell into a rapt silence. From the half-open door into the sacristy came the monotonous litany of the little old ladies.

Don Pierino nodded, pensively.

"I know him. I know Commissario Ricciardi. And this explains a great many things."

XXVII

I t was already late afternoon when a barefoot boy wearing a tattered sleeveless shirt at least four sizes too big for him came dashing into the guardroom, on the ground floor of police headquarters.

He was panting and at least twenty seconds ahead of Amitrano, the officer on duty at the front entrance. The *scugnizzo* looked around proudly. His skin was brown as old leather, his knees were ravaged by scrapes and cuts, he had the marks of ancient chilblains on his feet, and he was absolutely filthy.

"Brigadier Raffaele Maione!" he said in a loud voice. "Who here is him?"

Amitrano grabbed him by the scruff of the neck, hauling him off the floor and wheezing.

"Rude thing, little animal, let me show you right now just what happens when you forget to stop at the front door, I should have just shot you in the legs . . . "

Maione, who was compiling the duty roster for the following day, wearily raised his hand.

"Amitra', just drop it. I'd be curious to see what happens the day that an actual ill-intentioned individual manages to slip in here, maybe to take vengeance for an arrest or a simple stop. Whether or not you're standing watch at the door seems to be immaterial."

The boy, who wasn't even remotely intimidated, said in a hoarse voice: "It's true, we can get in here whenever we like. And there's nothing you can do about it."

Maione raised his voice.

"Hey, now, don't you even think of it, understood? Or I'll kick you black and blue in the seat of the pants so you won't be able to sit down again as long as you live! Amitra', let go of him for a second and let me hear what he has to say. Then slam him in a cell for a month, so we can see who's afraid of who!"

The boy rubbed his neck, glaring ferociously at the officer who was keeping his eye on him.

"Oh sure, do you think I'm stupid? You can't put me in jail because I haven't done anything wrong. I've only come because I have a message to deliver to this certain Brigadier Raffaele Maione, and they paid me to deliver it. Otherwise, I never would have come to catch a whiff of the stink in this place!"

Maione advanced, towering over the boy, who however showed no signs of fear.

"What about, instead of putting you in jail, I knock you black and blue and pound you silly? Then I'll just say that you fell down the stairs while we were chasing you, because you'd scampered into police headquarters without stopping when told to halt by Amitrano here. Come on, shall we make a bet?"

The subdued tone of voice and the determined expression, more than the sheer size of the brigadier, convinced the boy that he'd dragged it out long enough.

"Well, so you're Brigadier Raffaele Maione?"

Maione nodded, disconsolately.

"Yes. And I'm pretty sure I know exactly who's sending me this message. Anyway, come on, out with it."

The boy took a deep breath and declaimed: "My dear Brigadier, you-know-who wishes to see you in the place that you know. Which would be, not the same place as the last time, where there was a waiter who's not on duty now, but that other place, where the two of you once met that time when it was raining. It will be easy for you to recognize you-know-who immediately, because as usual she'll be the loveliest of them all.

She awaits you anxiously. But, take my advice, if there's some-one with her, pretend you don't know her, or you'll both be in trouble deep."

The singsong litany had been recited as if it were a Christmas poem, in a high, precise voice. The boy had been instructed well.

Amitrano, pondering the thought that his superior officer might be arranging some romantic tryst, put on an expression of cunning innuendo; then, in view of the brigadier's undis-guised determination to slaughter him, he gulped, turned his gaze to the wall, and kept it there.

Maione recovered from his surprise.

"*Guaglio'*, I have no idea who sent you or why, and I haven't understood a single word that you said. What I can guarantee to you is that Amitrano, here, is going to hold you until I get back, and if I don't like what I find when I get to where I'm going, and I have a pretty good idea that I'm not going to like it one bit, then you're going to experience such an unhappy fifteen minutes that for the rest of your life, whenever you happened to be in the neighborhood, make sure you take the long way round so you don't even clap eyes on the front entrance. Do you understand me loud and clear?"

The boy executed a perfect military salute, stamping the sole of his bare foot, hard as tanned leather, on the floor.

"Yessir, Commandant, sir!" he said and then, twisting around with lightning agility, he left the room, whipping under and between Amitrano's legs. Meanwhile, Amitrano had still been focusing on a section of the wall that was entirely blank.

"What are you doing, you idiot?" Maione shouted at the officer. "Catch him, why don't you?"

Amitrano snapped to and lumbered off in pointless pursuit, awkwardly overturning the side table upon which stood the pitcher of ersatz coffee, which shattered onto the floor, in a spreading puddle.

A voice floated up clearly from the courtyard.

"Brigadier Raffaele Maione!"

What followed was a long, strong, and skillfully modulated Bronx cheer that split the early evening air.

Maione ran a hand over his face and murmured: "Sweet Virgin Mary, how I hate this city. How I hate it."

Then, wearily, he headed toward the place that he knew, which wasn't the same place as the last time.

The tiny café at the corner of the *vicolo* that twisted and turned up the steep side of the Spanish Quarter had, as every policeman knew, a private room in the back. There the bar's proprietor, whom everyone called Peppe but whose real first and last name no one knew, was willing to accommodate any sort of activity that he was best advised to keep concealed from open view.

Sometimes people played cards there, other times they played craps; from time to time people slept there who didn't want to show their faces out on the street, and others met their lovers there if they couldn't, for whatever reasons, make use of any of the many small pensiones in the center of town. Others went there to get drunk in privacy, only to throw up in the internal courtyard and fall asleep on the cot. Peppe allowed the place to be used freely because he was a good-hearted person, and he made quite sure that nothing dangerous or criminally punishable took place in there. His coffee was first-rate and in his back room you could argue until all hours of the night about the exploits and achievements of the city's soccer team, only recently founded but followed with spasmodic fanaticism by ever broader swaths of the population.

Maione had immediately understood that the *scugnizzo*, in his obscure rigmarole, had been referring to this place; this was where the person he believed must be the sender of the message had waited for him in the rain the previous fall, when he was investigating the murder of a poor orphan boy, immediately prior to the car crash in which Ricciardi had been injured.

The memory brought Signora Rosa back into his mind. It was incredible how, even though he had only met her a couple of times, he now missed her too; he didn't dare to imagine what kind of constant suffering must be tormenting his superior officer, who was so disinclined to share his feelings.

As he walked into the café, he shot a questioning glance at the proprietor, who was busy behind the bar drying coffee cups with a rag. The man shrugged his shoulders with a comical expression of bafflement and tilted his head toward the door that gave onto the famous back room. Maione looked around somewhat furtively and slipped through the door, shutting it behind him.

The room was barren, with a small table, four chairs, a straw pallet, and a few wooden crates stacked up by the wall. At the center, dressed in a long black dress, with a hat of the same color, and a veil covering his face, was Bambinella. The brigadier's astonished gaze was captured by a pair of cowhide shoes, with stiletto heels and of such a vivid red that they seemed lit from within.

"I knew it was you all along. But what the hell is this getup?"

Bambinella lifted the veil with an exaggeratedly graceful gesture of his large begloved hands.

"The shoes, eh, Brigadie'? They give me away, don't they? I know, I ought to have put on a more understated pair, but what am I supposed to do, I just don't own any sensible shoes, and then, I simply couldn't resist: the black dress with the red shoes is entirely too cunning! And I'm wearing some undergarments that . . . "

"I'm going to go ahead and strangle you right here and now," Maione interrupted him, "and that way we can get it taken care of once and for all, go ahead and shut down this bar where too many strange things happen, and put up a plaque out front in memory of the wonderful day that that saint, Maione, throttled Bambinella to death! In other words, are you saying you've taken me for one of those cops who take a bribe to let you keep working? Do you or don't you know that I have a reputation? You send a miserable little urchin to get me, and he razzes me openly inside police headquarters, you tell me to come to this filthy dive, and then you tell me all about the horrible dreck you dress up in?"

Bambinella let loose with a coquettish, gurgling giggle.

"Oooh, did Gioacchiniello behave like a scamp? I'm so sorry, Brigadie', but that little boy certainly has his reasons for being mischievous with you, after all, you've arrested his father, three brothers, and even his grandpa, so you can understand those are the kinds of things that will put you in a mood with someone."

"Well, when you see him, tell him that it's my intention to arrange for a family reunion just as soon as I can: happy and cozy all together, sheltered from the rain and the scorching sun, and all at taxpayers' expense. Now tell me what it is you want, and don't waste any time, because who knows what people might think if they saw us all alone in here together."

Bambinella put a hand to his chest.

"It's true, how exciting, it's our very first love nest, Brigadie'! Darn it all, if I wasn't already going steady I'd suggest we do things that would justify exactly what they . . . "

Maione let himself fall onto a chair, disconsolately.

"You know something? You've convinced me, Bambine'. Now it's time for me to shoot myself. I can't go on like this, and if you ask me, even if I did go ahead and murder you, you'd find some way to go on persecuting me, maybe by appearing in my dreams."

"Why, how romantic you are, so you dream of me! But what nasty thoughts, though, Brigadie'. Life is so lovely, so full of love and happiness, believe me, don't shoot yourself. No, listen, instead I have some fairly interesting news for you, that's why I thought it was best for me to come see you rather than making you climb all the way up to where I live, which is bound to be dangerous because my sweetheart, I don't know if I told you this, is quite jealous and . . . "

"Oh, lord above, yes, you told me that. So what news do you have for me, if I may ask?"

In his turn, Bambinella took a chair and sat facing Maione, crossing his legs with an exaggeratedly graceful motion.

"Now then, listen carefully: this Roccaspina, the count who confessed to the murder, isn't a bad person. Yes, he has a bad gambling habit and he's run through his entire fortune and estate, and he's practically enriched every owner of a gambling den in the city as well as all the bookmakers working the racetracks, and he owes a great deal of money to a great many people, but it's not like he has any other bad habits."

Maione made a face.

"That already strikes me as a pretty bad habit, no? What else would a man have to do, to say he has bad habits?"

"Oh no you don't, Brigadie', you of all people can't get this kind of thing so wrong. Normally people who have one bad habit have lots of others, either because they don't have principles in the first place or else because they don't have a lot of trouble getting around them. And so they run to women, they drink, they smoke opium, and so on. For instance, when I was still a working girl, I had lots of customers who came to me after getting out of the gambling dens either because they wanted consolation for the money they'd lost or else because they wanted to spend the money they'd won. But this Roccaspina, on the other hand, once he'd run out of money, which happened quite frequently, would go straight home. And that's where things get interesting."

"How so?"

"At home is his wife, a beautiful woman who was once famous throughout the city because she was, in her circle, the most desired of them all. A serious woman, though, never a lover, and believe me when I tell you that if she had had one, I would have known about it. Now a girlfriend of mine who works for a doctor near them is a friend of this lady's housekeeper, and even though they haven't paid her for years, she still stays with them because she doesn't know where else to go; she's elderly and then she's fond of the lady because she raised her from a child. Just think that . . . "

Maione emitted a low growl that Bambinella interpreted correctly.

"In other words, she has a suitor. An important man who is driven everywhere he goes in a great big car with a chauffeur, a certain Duke Marangolo of I-Don't-Know-Where, who shows up every so often, dumps off a ton or so of flowers, and waits in the front hall until she sends her housekeeper to tell him that she has a headache; then he heads off with his tail between his legs. Apparently he was there the very same evening as the murder; now I couldn't say whether this information can be useful to you, but it's the only somewhat strange thing I've learned about that household. Aside from the fact that Roccaspina, for a while now, had been leaving home every morning at 7:30; when his housekeeper asked him where he was going, he replied that he was going to Mass to ask for the grace to win a nice round sum to take care of his money problems. The housekeeper thinks it must be true, because she says that he believes firmly in the evil eye and good and bad luck, people who have the bad habit of gambling always believe fervently in those things."

Maione listened with great concentration.

"What about Piro, did you find out anything about him?"

Bambinella interlaced his long fingers.

"There things were simpler, in Santa Lucia there are lots of old girlfriends of mine, working as housekeepers. And then in the palazzo next door to Piro's building there's a private brothel where seven girls work, and even a couple of members of the competition: you no doubt know that they come in handy because there are some clients who like to get under the bed while . . . Hey, okay, what kind of manners are these, Brigadie', you're breaking my arm, and I'm a delicate girl! And anyway, he was a moneylender. His office was just full of high-society types who were constantly coming and going, unsuspectable people. One of the whores has a client who's one of them: she says that Piro threatened to let everyone know what kind of financial shape they were in. In other words, he was blackmailing them."

"And in personal terms, do we know anything? I don't know, relationships, lovers . . . "

Bambinella shook his head.

"No, no. That man was someone who only thought about money, Brigadie'. His wife is a sad one, with a long face on her that her husband's death didn't even really change at all, while his daughter is a young woman who's growing up, a little livelier than her mother, and the two of them fight occasionally, but still, she's a good girl from a respectable family; the son, on the other hand, is just a toddler, a child. A respectable household, but there aren't many people in this city who shed a single tear when Piro died, because he really was just a stinker."

The brigadier thought it over. He was comparing the information Bambinella had just given him with the impressions he'd garnered during his time in the victim's home.

"If they're such respectable people, then why is there all this talk about them? Who told you what kind of people the wife or the daughter or . . . "

"Let's just say that that was luck. One of the girls who works in the brothel had an understanding with the chauffeur. Free of charge, because he didn't have a penny to his name and couldn't afford certain fees. At any rate, this chauffeur was telling stories to this girlfriend of mine, that's all. But now though, he can't tell her anything else, because they let him go."

"What do you mean, they let him go?"

Bambinella shrugged his shoulders.

"Well, Brigadie', in the first place the loan shark lawyer is dead and so they really don't need the chauffeur anymore all that much. And then they told him that what they need most right now is money, and that they can't afford to keep him on anymore, but according to him they're still filthy rich and they didn't sell the car, which means they still need a chauffeur. In other words, he has nothing but bad things to say about them, in part because he no longer has any excuses with his wife and he can't see my girlfriend anymore. And she's sorry about it too, because she says that he, the ex chauffeur, has a nice big . . . "

Maione leapt to his feet.

"All right then, Bambine', if there's nothing else, it's time for me to go. Do me a favor and continue to keep your ears open for anything else concerning this story."

Bambinella stood up, smoothing his dress.

"Yes, but eventually we'll have to stop meeting here, Brigadie'. My boyfriend has a lot of friends, and if they see me come out of this bar together with you looking all rumpled like this, who knows what they'll go tell him. The one time I get a straight razor taken to my face, shouldn't it at least be for something that actually happened?"

And he laughed his usual neighing laugh.

·

XXVIII

He had thought it over at considerable length before taking the initiative. He knew he was taking responsibility for a major risk, and risk, he had always been told, was something he should avoid. At all costs.

All the same, he really was worried. After all, he considered, the job he'd been assigned was quite precise. To whatever extent possible and, of course, while maintaining absolute secrecy, he was to ensure that Signora Livia Vezzi Lucani be put in no danger and live contentedly.

This wasn't an assignment like the others, and Falco was well aware of the fact. He generally spied on individuals suspected of being subversives or criminals, or both things. And when he did, that meant long stakeouts on a bench with a newspaper in his hands, in the bright sun; or at the corner of a narrow *vicolo* with an open umbrella under the pouring rain; on a bridge, holding his hat with both hands to keep the wind from carrying it away. Waiting the whole time for a street door to open and someone to come out so he could jot down a time in his notebook and finally go home, cursing the day he had accepted a certain change of headquarters or job title.

A job like any other, Falco told himself. He knew perfectly well how untrue that was, in his case, merely a pat phrase, and yet he liked to imagine he could say it. No, this wasn't a job like any other, and the more the days, months, and years went by, the less true it was.

Looking after Livia had been strange from the very beginning.

When his superior officer had summoned him to give him the assignment, he had seemed almost embarrassed. He had gone into the office—a nondescript, anonymous room in the back of a shop, which ostensibly sold baskets and hampers, though the merchandise changed every day—believing that he was about to be sent to keep an eye on a group of activists who'd been sent into internal exile and who were suspected of wanting to form an association opposed to the Fascist party. Falco was well aware that he was one of the best agents: he was admired and respected, all his previous missions had been carried out with absolute precision and punctuality, without overdoing things, and above all, while preserving complete secrecy. Falco was reliable, people said in the business—reliable, discreet, and invisible. The last case he had worked on had culminated with the arrests of eight people who seemed to have no connections, but who were actually writing each other and who were even meeting, leaving the small towns where they lived to assemble in the city. A success of a certain prominence, at the end of a painstaking campaign of stakeouts and shoe-leather that lasted a year and a half. He therefore expected that the nameless, ageless little man, anonymous and laconic, perfectly forgettable if it weren't for a scar on his forehead that looked like a comma and small, bright eyes that darted constantly from one side of the room to the other, had something important in store for him, something very important.

He remembered that evening. He had received the note summoning him via the established dropbox, a strolling candy vendor in the Villa, whom he had asked for a colored balloon and had received in reply nothing but an intense glance and fleeting gesture of acknowledgment, after which he had found himself alone in the presence of the man with no name. Without any preamble, and never once looking him in the eye, the nameless man had briefly apprised him of Rome's satisfaction for the excellent work he had done.

Falco had gotten the impression that his superior officer was paying him those compliments unwillingly, which gave him a faint shiver of pleasure. That veiled annoyance could only mean that the little man with the comma on his forehead was feeling threatened by his underling.

Then the little man had explained what his new assignment would be.

At first Falco hadn't been able to believe his ears, and he'd struggled to preserve his proverbial impassive demeanor: this was the umpteenth test to which he was putting his poker face, he told himself. He'd heard about many colleagues whose careers had come to a sudden halt after questioning an order or a strategy. And so he had nodded, expressed his thanks, and settled down to listen.

A singer, indeed a former singer, the widow of a great tenor. Who had moved to this city because she had fallen in love with no less than a police officer, a strange commissario who'd been under their surveillance for quite some time, someone who often operated outside of standard procedures, but about whom, as he had read in the reports, nothing unorthodox had been found, save for a suspicious lone-wolf tendency and the lack of any bad habits.

The woman had to be protected, his superior officer had explained to him, she was very dear to people at the highest levels, and she must not be exposed to the slightest danger. He realized how singular this request must seem, but they had instructed him quite specifically that the assignment should be entrusted to one of his best men. Falco had tried to discern whether there was irony in those words, but as usual, he had been unable to detect any. He had taken the scanty information transcribed onto a single sheet of paper and the woman's file, he had left with a cold, formal salutation, and then he had spent the night studying, clinging to that one phrase: very dear to people at the highest level.

Later, he would learn that Livia was one of Il Duce's daughter's closest friends.

He had remained in the shadows, as instructed, to keep an eye on her as she moved into her new home. He had constructed a protective network around her to ensure that nothing bad befell her in a city where nothing was ever quite what it seemed. Then, in the aftermath of several unforeseen mishaps, he had been forced to ask her for a face-to-face meeting.

That was the kind of thing that, if possible, should always be avoided. The very existence of the organization—even though people were talking about it everywhere, and in increasingly concrete terms—was never supposed to be revealed, and most especially not to anyone who was the subject of its surveillance. But in that case Falco had been forced to arrange for the woman's collaboration, to keep her from getting herself into trouble.

He thought back to that first meeting now, as he climbed the staircase of the magnificent palazzo where Livia had chosen to live. He remembered the encounter and the stirring emotions he had managed to conceal under his customary impassive front, but only by virtue of the long training and practice to which he had been subjected.

Before that day, he had observed her from a distance, by and large, save for a few cases, at the theater or on the street, when he had pretended to cross paths with her by chance or taken an adjoining box. And he had studied her in the countless photographs printed in the newspapers on the occasion of receptions, inaugurations, or theatrical premieres, portrayed with leading figures of Fascism. He knew who she was, and he believed that he knew what she was like.

Then he had come face-to-face with her.

Beauty, thought Falco as he rang the doorbell, is something you can't define until you have it before you. Beauty is a matter of tiny movements of the facial muscles, a flicker of eyelashes, a movement of the fingers. Beauty, thought Falco, moves through the air like radio waves, and if you're too far away, you can't perceive it for what it is. Beauty hits you in the chest like a sudden blow, and its memory produces an echo that, afterward, you'll have to deal with forever.

Falco had become very pleased with that assignment, which he had at first experienced as a professional purgatory, after actually meeting Livia. After his nostrils had inhaled that strange perfume and his eyes had locked with that dark, profound gaze, and then run down over the soft, lithe outlines of a statuesque body, a tacit promise of an unattainable paradise.

It had been second nature, since that moment, to protect her. And it was a pleasure every time to see her and speak to her. All the same, he only became aware of a more substantial sentiment when he heard her sing.

He loved music very much, it was his only weakness. The only message of beauty that came to him from a past that he'd been forced to forget, though without any excessive regret. He remembered having attended an opera in which Livia had been one of the performers, but on that occasion his chest hadn't quavered the way it had when, on the terrace of the apartment where he was waiting to enter, he had heard that wonderful woman's voice shape the notes of a song that had never been sung before. That was when his calloused old heart had skipped a beat, only to begin galloping crazily; that was when he had felt for the first time a sensation of bewilderment and innocence, turmoil and weakness; that was when, almost incredulous, he had felt his eyes well up with tears.

Two months had gone by. Two months in which he had been forced to take into account his awareness of a new emotion, in all likelihood in direct contrast with his professional duties. Two months in which he had tried to find a precarious balance between his profession and the fact that he was a man.

By limiting his desire for more frequent opportunities to see her, focusing on the vague expression of disgust that appeared on Livia's face every time she found him in her presence. Doing his best to persuade her, little by little, that all he wanted to do was protect her, help her to steer clear of the dangers to which she herself and her fragile emotions might expose her.

All of this in the dull, painful awareness that she loved another man. Another man who, for no good or understandable reason, remained unattainable to her, possibly because he was—in his turn—in love with someone else.

And now an investigation undertaken strictly to gratify Livia's wishes, a simple piece of research that ought to have been mere routine, had put him face-to-face with something he never would have imagined. By an indirect and very marginal path, his job of protecting Livia had unearthed the presence in the city of what looked very much like a spy for the German military.

The dossier was classified and his office had not yet been entrusted with the matter, but Falco's well trained eyes and ears could not be fooled. Major von Brauchitsch, newly seated as the cultural attaché at the German consulate, was marked with a finding of top alert and had already been placed under confidential surveillance twenty-four hours a day; and for the past month and a half he had been carrying on a lively correspondence with the young woman who lived right next to Ricciardi, the same young woman who had been friends with the late governess Rosa Vaglio and who was, in all likelihood, the object of the commissario's romantic attentions.

This new development—while on the one hand it certainly complicated his assignment of protecting Livia, who might face consequences from any potential contact with the German that were impossible to calculate in advance—on the other hand did open some interesting possibilities for Falco. It would surely not go unnoticed that he had been able to gather information about this man, about what he did and who he saw. One of his men, for instance, had just learned that the major had paid a call on a florist and had sent a bouquet of roses to Enrica's mother. The note enclosed with the bouquet had announced a visit to their home that evening, as he had learned from the shopkeeper, who by a lucky but hardly uncommon fluke of fate turned out to be one of the organization's informants.

Falco was planning to draw up a report to inform his superior that he had found a channel that might allow him to keep a closer eye on von Brauchitsch's movements; a discreet sidelong vantage point that would, nonetheless, offer a finer view than simple stakeouts or reading his mail. This would allow Falco an unexpected prominence, allowing him to move up through the mysterious hierarchies of the structure in which he worked.

Before doing so, however, he would need to make sure that Livia understood what risks she was facing by being even indirectly exposed to the major's maneuverings. That Ricciardi unquestionably posed a danger, in both one sense and the other. Ricciardi could hinder the consolidation of the major's relationship with Enrica, just by asking the young woman not to see the German officer again, or Ricciardi could become an insurmountable obstacle to Falco's contacts with Livia, if instead he were to decide to accept the attentions of the lovely singer. It would be useful, opportune, and enjoyable to find a way to get rid of this Ricciardi, once and for all if possible.

In this context, he had arranged to intensify the surveillance of the policeman. Perhaps he'd stumble upon some excuse to throw him into jail, or send him into exile somewhere far away. Never give up hope.

Clara, Livia's housekeeper, answered the door; instead of her usual sunny smile, however, she now wore a baffled, unhappy expression. Falco even had the impression that she had been crying. He asked her if everything was all right, and the girl shook her head, lips quavering, incapable of speech.

Falco took fright. Could something serious have happened to Livia? Still in silence, Clara led him directly into the living room, which was shrouded in evening shadows. Usually the young woman was quite a chatterbox and to get rid of her he was obliged to tell her in no uncertain terms that she could leave. This time, instead, she seemed to be in a hurry to leave him alone. She hurried off without even bothering to turn on the light.

Falco reached his hand out toward the light switch, but a scratchy voice coming out of the darkness stopped him.

"No, please don't."

He sharpened his gaze and made out Livia's shape, stretched out on the sofa. The air was dense with the odor of smoke and alcohol; on an impulse he went over to the window and threw it open, leaving the curtains closed. Livia started coughing uncontrollably.

"What's the matter, Signora? Aren't you well?"

Livia didn't answer. She was singing to herself, her voice slurred, an unrecognizable singsong. The man realized that she was drunk.

He switched on a lamp that stood on a side table. Livia was dressed in a housecoat that hung open in the front and was stained with liquor. On the floor beside her lay an over-flowing ashtray and two bottles: one of them lay on its side and had created a small puddle of liquid on the carpet, the other was half empty. At the end of her arm that splayed out into the empty air, her hand gripped a precariously balanced glass.

"Here you are, my dear Falco, the man without a face and without a name. They sent you to take me back to Rome, didn't they? They asked you to come sweep up the fragments of this heap of wreckage of a woman, isn't that right?"

Even in her unmistakable state of intoxication, even shabby and dirty as she was, even dreary and disheartened, she struck Falco as alluring and beautiful. He perceived her need for help. Her malaise conferred upon her a weakness that stirred a certain tenderness within him.

"Signora, you're anything but a heap of wreckage. Come now, put down this glass. How long have you been sitting here? Have you had anything to eat?"

He lifted her to a sitting position, supporting her. She let him do as he wished, then softly began to cry. Little by little, the sobs grew louder and more uncontrolled, and then they subsided, ebbing into an unbroken stream of tears that striped her face, cutting through the gooey layer of smeared makeup. She looked like a heartbroken little girl.

"I beg you, Signora, tell me what's happened. Did someone . . . "

Livia opened her eyes wide, as if she were seeing him for the first time. Then she said, in a harsh and hissing voice: "Yes. Yes. Someone has hurt me. Someone is hurting me, wounding me, ravaging me, murdering me. If you want to defend me, if you want to save me, if it is true that you are here to protect me, you need to rid me forever of the sight of him."

"Signora, but what . . . "

"He's a pervert. A damned pederast, a homosexual. He's not interested in women because he prefers men. It's obvious, this has to be the reason. And I was so stupid, so damned stupid, that I never understood it."

The words fell between them like the drops of a scalding rain. Falco said nothing, his hand supporting her arm. He could smell the toabacco and alcohol on her breath. Yes, she was drunk, no doubt about it, but what did that matter, really?

"Are you positive about this, Signora?"

She nodded, repeatedly. Then she burst into tears again, sobbing into the handkerchief that he had handed her.

Falco, practically under his breath, murmured: "This explains everything. Don't worry, Signora, you have me here to protect you."

XXIX

Maione and Ricciardi had just finished going over the information they'd gathered during the course of the day. They agreed that, with the evidence at their disposal, it would be difficult to support the hypothesis that anyone other than the Count of Roccaspina had murdered Piro.

"But let me understand this, Commissa': he admits he murdered him, and he confirms the confession, but he'd like to be released from prison as soon as possible. And why do you find that so strange?"

Ricciardi paced back and forth across the room.

"Because, all things considered, except for the quarrel the day before, and then his own confession, there is no evidence that it was him. How could we have ever identified him as the murderer? He could have relied on his wife's testimony, and as you know she is quite certain he was at home that night."

"And so?"

"And so, if you don't want to be in prison in the first place, then why do you want to be sent there?"

Maione, sitting in his usual chair, thought that over.

"A person might have a conscience, Commissa'. Maybe the count realized: If I don't step forward, someone else might go to prison in my place. Bambinella told me that, deep down, Roccaspina, aside from his fixation on gambling, is a decent person. Perhaps then and there he wasn't sufficiently clear-minded to understand that he'd be losing his liberty for a long time to come."

Ricciardi shook his head.

"To me, actually, he seemed pretty lucid. I don't know, it's as if something were eluding me."

The brigadier was following the thread of his thoughts in the light of the information brought to him by Bambinella.

"What strikes me as strange is the fact that they fired this chauffeur, so unexpectedly. All right, I understand that the dead man was dead and therefore would no longer need to be driven here and there, but it's also true that people care very much about keeping up appearances, letting everyone think that they are still rich, that nothing has changed. Otherwise who's going to marry the *guagliona*, the young lady? Maybe we should have a chat with him, this chauffeur. Maybe he can give us a little information."

"All right, tomorrow we'll talk to the chauffeur, too. The problem is that this is an old case, something that everybody figures is wrapped up and done with. It's hard to get people to willingly cast their memories back. But one thing I'd like to understand better is our client, the contessa. This suitor, the Duke Marangolo, what was he doing at the Roccaspina residence the night of the murder? A slightly odd coincidence."

Before Maione could come up with a retort, the door swung open without anyone having knocked.

"Why, in here we have people working right into the evening. Very good! My sincere compliments. That means that in this city, as I have been claiming, it's not true that we have nothing but lazy good-for-nothings!"

Maione, who had his back to the door, leapt to his feet, knocking the cap off his head, then he scooped it up, swearing under his breath, and put it back on, first backwards, then the right way round.

"*Buonasera*, Dottor Garzo," said Ricciardi. "I didn't think there was anyone still here at this hour. We were just going over the duty roster for tomorrow."

The man's overcoat was draped over his arm, which meant that he was in fact leaving the building. He ran the back of his hand over his narrow, well trimmed mustache with a gesture that had long since become notorious at police headquarters, as well as the object of endless secret ridicule and mockery.

"Certainly, certainly. Because, as we all know, everything is under control and there are no investigations of any real seriousness underway. That's right, isn't it?"

Garzo, to whom Ricciardi reported directly, was in charge of supervising all the investigative activities of the city's police department. He was puffed up and conceited, and he loved to think that he was in charge of the situation. In reality, he was a bureaucrat who was very skilled at maintaining relations with his superior officers, but entirely incompetent in the specific responsibilities of policework.

Maione and Ricciardi held him in utter contempt, and they struggled to conceal that fact.

"Certainly, Dottore. Everything is under control."

Garzo nodded again, then, winking behind the thick lenses of his eyeglasses, said: "And yet you continue to receive visitors, I see. Perhaps the brigadier ought to leave you alone, Ricciardi, since you're expecting company."

Ricciardi and Maione exchanged a glance.

"No, Dottore, I'm not expecting any visitors. We were just saying goodnight, our shift is over and . . . "

Garzo grimaced in a way that was clearly meant to be a sly grin, but which actually produced an idiotic leer.

"Then let me inform you that, though you may not be expecting anyone, there's someone waiting for you. There's a veiled lady sitting outside."

Maione glanced at Ricciardi and headed over to the door. The commissario pretended he had just remembered, and slapped his forehead with his palm.

"How stupid of me. It's a personal visit, Dottore. She's a friend who . . . "

Garzo put on the face of a man of the world.

"Ricciardi, Ricciardi. I understand. But take it from me, the office is serious business: don't let me hear any complaints about who you entertain in your office, someone much less indulgent than yours truly might see you. Since this is a pretty quiet period, just ask me if you can take off early if you're planning to . . . meet someone. Understood?"

Ricciardi took a long, deep breath, methodically counting to ten.

"*Grazie*, Dottore. It's just a piece of information I'm expecting to receive, I assure you, otherwise I'd have never . . . "

Garzo's smile widened.

"That's quite enough. We understand each other. And I promise on my honor that I won't breathe a word of this to anyone, least of all the widow Vezzi. See you tomorrow: this evening I have the theater."

He turned and left, as stately as a ship steaming out of harbor, stopping at the threshold for a moment to glance curiously at the mysterious female visitor that Maione was ushering into the office.

When the door closed behind him, Ricciardi spoke to the woman.

"Contessa, it's not exactly an intelligent move to keep on coming in here. The man you just saw leaving here could suspend us from duty in the blink of an eye, which would mean we'd have to stop investigating a murder that, as far as the police are concerned, has been a closed case for months now. I thought I'd made myself clear on this point."

Bianca lifted her veil and calmly gazed at Ricciardi.

"*Buonasera* to you too, Commissario. Forgive me, I hadn't quite realized the clandestine nature of our meetings. I'd naïvely supposed that a citizen had every right to expect support from the police, if it's a matter of bringing to light the truth about a murder that is still shrouded with too many shadows."

Ricciardi accepted the point. He had been rude.

"I apologize, Contessa. *Buonasera*. You are quite correct, you'd have every right to much greater satisfaction, but as you know, the preliminary investigation has been completed and . . . "

Maione coughed gently, scuffing one police boot across the floor, the way he always did when he wanted to attract his superior's attention.

"Commissa', forgive me if I break in, but it might be better if you accompany the signora outside of the building. That imb . . . I mean Dottor Garzo, just might decide to come back to see if we're still here, and if we are, he might decide to demand an explanation."

Ricciardi nodded.

"You're right, Raffaele. Come with me, Signora. We can talk in the street."

XXX

The September evening was an invitation to stroll and out in the street, people were lingering in front of the shop windows. With a view to lengthening the shopping day, merchants were keeping their establishments open later than usual.

Ricciardi was walking side by side with the Contessa di Roccaspina toward the large piazza where everyone slowed to a stroll to enjoy the gathering sea breeze. They seemed like any of the many couples busy getting to know each other better, but the subject of their conversation was very different from what you might have expected based on their appearance.

"Well, Commissario, you met with the lawyer today, I understand. And you've also . . . Did you go to Poggioreale prison?"

"Yes, Signora," Ricciardi replied. "I went there. And I have to confess that I'm still quite confused."

Bianca walks into the large visiting room and sits on this side of the thick metal grate. Beside her is a skinny woman holding a little boy on her knees. The little boy is crying.

"How . . . how is he?"

There are so many people. All the seats are taken. There are women, mostly, and children; but also old men and women. Here and there, people dab nervously at their tears, while others laugh as if they were perfectly at ease.

"I can't tell you, Signora. Certainly, his appearance wasn't very reassuring."

Bianca clenches her hands in her worn gloves, feeling guilty because she'd rather be anywhere but here, because she wishes she'd never come. The prisoners, led by guards, begin to come in.

"That place. That place is . . . is terrible, don't you think?"

There's an intolerable stench. Smoke, mold. Filth. Sweat, bodies, fluids. Bianca presses a handkerchief to her nose, inhaling the perfume to ward off the smell. She notices that many of the visitors are glaring at her angrily, because she is an intruder, a strange, incongruous intruder who has nothing in common with that place, and nothing to do with any of them. And yet.

"Yes. Yes, I understand. Even though I went in with the lawyer, so I'd imagine that the situation is quite different for . . . for family members, I mean. Or at least, so I'd have to believe."

Bianca observes the prisoners stretching out their hands, touching the grate, doing their best at least to brush the fingertips of their family members through the rusted bars. The guards tolerate it, turning their bored gazes elsewhere. Last of all enters Romualdo, and with downcast eyes he sits down across from her, in silence.

"The last time I saw him . . . I haven't gone very often. Perhaps not as often as I should have."

"Why not, if I may ask?"

For a long time, he keeps his eyes downcast. Bianca doesn't know what to say. She waits. Last time, the only other time, Attilio was present and in practical terms, he'd done all the talking, obtaining a few monosyllabic replies. Now she'd like to ask him how he is, but her voice sticks in her throat.

"I don't know. Uneasiness, I guess. We never even spoke when he was out and a free man, and inside there, to see him like that . . . "

Skinny. My God, how skinny he's become, thinks Bianca. That bony neck sticking out of his shirt collar, his clean-shaven head, the whiskers gone too. He looks younger, she thinks, and yet much, much older too. What did you think you could do here? What makes you think I want to see you at all?

"Another thing is that it was my impression that he wasn't particularly happy for me to come visit him."

"I don't think that's it, Signora. Sometimes, you know, people are ashamed to be seen in certain conditions."

I'm still your wife, she replies. Her voice is low, flatter, harsher than she would have liked. The pale woman beside her gives her a glance of comprehension and then turns back to look at the old man across from her. That must be her father, she thinks. Romualdo raises his eyes and stares at her. He says: We have nothing to say to each other. We've never had anything to say to each other.

"But to you, did he say anything to you?"

"He recognized me. I didn't think he'd remember me, given the situation he's in, as well, but in fact he remembered perfectly."

"He remembers everything. But sometimes he just wants to forget."

Not far away from them, near the café's outdoor tables, a tall young man was playing a mandolin with virtuosity and passion, and singing a song with heartfelt intensity.

The old man sitting next to Romualdo is weeping, though he smiles at the child. Every so often, he irritatedly wipes away a tear, as if brushing off an insect. He speaks quickly, while the pale woman listens attentively, and cries as well. Romualdo shoots her a glance and says: You see him? He's old, isn't he? You assume that he's her father, but really he's her husband. He's my age, only he's been in here for ten years. I won't wind up like him, of that you can be sure. I won't wind up like him.

"What is it that he wants to forget? Tell me: Everything can be important."

"He . . . he's aware of what he did. He knows it. And he wanted to change, I believe. Change everything."

But what about you? What happened to you? he asks her. There was a time when you laughed, you know? You laughed and you could even shed tears. Once we were walking on the grounds of your parents' villa and we saw a puppy. You don't remember, do you? I do. It was sick, it was whimpering to break your heart. You burst into tears, there was nothing I could do to cheer you up. I had to take you away. But now you've lost your heart. You've always behaved impeccably, no doubt about that, but what kind of wife have you been to me? I've never felt you close to me. Always icy. Always distant.

"What did he want to change, your husband? Did he have specific plans? Something that might have led him to . . . "

"No, no, Commissario. At least not as far as I know. He was just well aware of what his life had turned into."

As he sang the song, the young man with the mandolin seemed to tell a story that had something to do with himself. A couple of girls at a table looked at him and laughed. He was poorly dressed and ill fed, but he was singing with all his heart, his expression rapt, as if he were following some distant thought.

He goes on talking, his eyes fixed on her, his lips clamped in disgust. I'm more alive than you are, he tells her. I'm more alive, even though I'm deprived of liberty, of decent food, of clothing, of soap to wash myself. I'm more alive, though I have no name and no dignity, I have no peace and no sleep. I'm more alive than you, because my heart still beats. Does your heart still beat, Bianca? How long has it been since you felt the beat of your heart?

The young man sincerely tells a moth to go away. To avoid being burned, along with his hand.

"Signora, I can't fathom your husband's attitude. He seemed determined to confirm his confession, to obtain a guilty verdict. But then he told his lawyer to do whatever he could to obtain a reduced sentence, to get him out of prison as early as possible. It seems like a contradiction, don't you think?"

"Is that what he said? I don't understand, Commissario. I really don't understand."

She says to him: Why, Romualdo? Why did you confess? I know that it wasn't you who committed the murder. I know that you were at home, in your bed, that night. He laughs, and it frightens her, because he laughs mirthlessly, with desperate fury, as if he were weeping. The old man next to him turns for a moment to glance in his direction, then goes back to talking to his woman. Romualdo says: what do you know about where I was? About where I am, and where my heart is? You know nothing about me. All you know how to do is judge, you're cold as marble, sealed up in your tomb even though you aren't dead yet. You've never experienced love, Bianca. But I have, to my good fortune. I have. And I have so much life left to live.

"Don't give up trying to find out the reason why, Commissario. I'm begging you. I know that it's difficult, I know that if you're not allowed to rely on the full resources of an official investigation, it isn't easy to get answers, but I'm pleading with you, don't stop. Because I know that it wasn't him. I don't love him anymore, that is true, and this determination of mine to find out the truth goes against his wishes, but I need to understand what his plan is. Because he's not crazy, even if he acts like he is. He's not crazy."

Ricciardi seemed to be lost in listening to the song of the young man with the mandolin, his brow furrowed as if he were trying to remember where he'd heard it before.

"No, I won't give up, Signora. Because I know what it means to feel as if you're behind bars even if you're out loose on the street. I know what it means to be a prisoner of yourself. I know what it means to stare at a ceiling waiting for either dawn or sleep to come, and neither one ever does."

Bianca was thinking that it had been a long time since she'd felt as close to someone as she did to that green-eyed stranger.

He tells her: now everything is taken care of, Bianca. You can rescue your few, miserable possessions. The stones of the palazzo, those few pointless sticks of furniture that still remain, the jewels that you hid from me . . . And you were right to do it, because I'd have lost those, too, in my attempt to regain the splendor of days gone by, and the love in your eyes. Pointlessly. And you'll give me a life, a new life. Which I'll know how to rebuild for myself.

"I can't help but think that he did it for me," the contessa said in a low voice. "To save me from his debts, to fix what could be fixed, by disappearing. Without love, I'm certain of that, just to pay me back for the life he took away from me."

Ricciardi nodded, without taking his eyes off the mandolin player.

"It might be, even if it's a demented solution, as your lawyer points out, and he could have obtained the same effect by just running away. In any case, all we can do is find out what happened. Discovering the reasons why will be up to you."

The young man with the mandolin let out a last, heart-breaking chord. A man stood up and handed him some money, while the woman he was with dabbed at her eyes with a handkerchief. From the tables there arose a brief, awkward round of applause.

Bianca said: "Thank you, Commissario. Let me thank you from the bottom of my heart."

Ricciardi turned toward her, his gaze harsh.

"Don't thank me, Signora. There are a few things I'm going to need to understand about you, to have a complete picture of the situation. Where can I get in touch with a certain Duke Marangolo, and how can I arrange to speak with him?"

The guard says: time's up. Back to the cells. The old man grips the grate with both hands and his wife does the same. The child weeps in despair. Romualdo gets up hastily and says: don't come back, Bianca. Don't ever come back. I don't want to see you again, it will take me a long time to recover from your contempt.

Start yourself a new life and remember nothing of our time together. He turns and leaves, and never looks back.

The contessa blinked in surprise.

"Carlo Maria? But why on earth would you want to . . . No, fair enough, and I certainly don't want to meddle. I'll get a message to him first thing in the morning, and you'll be able to meet him at the same club as Attilio, at aperitif time. He'll answer any questions you might have for him. But I beg you, don't imagine that I have any reason to . . . Carlo Maria is a good friend. If you think it necessary, then go ahead and speak to him."

Ricciardi looked at her for a long time.

"Yes, Signora. I do think it necessary. I know that the evening of the murder, this man came to your home when the Count wasn't there."

He'd hurled those words at her as if they were an insult. Bianca blushed beneath her black veil.

"It's true, Commissario. But I refused to see him. Perhaps your informants haven't reported all the details to you."

And she left, without turning to look behind her.

XXXI

Manfred talked, and the eyes of the whole family were glued to him.

Almost the whole family.

Giulio Colombo was watching Enrica.

The day had been so different from the usual run of events. The early-morning arrival of flowers for Maria, accompanied by a discreet note in which the German officer thanked her for the invitation to dinner, accepting joyfully, had put into motion a succession of activities that verged on the frenetic. Luckily Giulio, who even in the midst of such extraordinary events as these still had his shop to run, had managed to avoid the family chaos, which was only heightened by his wife's immense anxiety.

This wasn't the first time that the Colombo family had entertained a visitor with a view to a daughter's marriage. The parents of Susanna's husband Marco had been guests many times prior to the wedding, but in that case everything had taken place well within the standard confines of tradition, and Susanna herself, though still quite young, had worked energetically to ensure the perfect functioning of that secular ceremony which attached to an engagement. Now Susanna, as Maria liked to emphasize when speaking with Enrica, every time the opportunity presented itself, was a daughter who had never caused her mother any worries. A real woman ever since she was a young girl, who had put marriage, children, and a home of her own first as her dream and lifelong ambition.

Well, maybe not the part about the home of her own, Enrica would have replied, if she hadn't loved her sister so well, seeing that Susanna still lived with them, nor were there any indications of plans to move in the near future. Still, though, Susanna, who was indeed the younger sister, already had a two-year-old boy and had been married for three years, after a five-year engagement. While Enrica had spent all that time stiching a dowry that perhaps she'd never even use.

Over time, Maria had tried to arrange meetings with the families of acquaintances who had a son of the right age, hoping a spark would fly. With one of these, Sebastiano, Enrica had even agreed to go and get a cup of coffee but then, like always, the thing had withered on the vine.

But now, everything was different. Now it had been she, Enrica, who had met a man, who had spoken to him and who had undertaken a correspondence, and who had told her mother, you know, Mamma, there's this person I've met, he lives elsewhere but he comes to the city on business, and so, if it's not too much trouble, well, I think I'd like to invite him over sometime. Maybe for dinner. You know, Mamma, he's all alone, we made friends on Ischia, he was there to take the waters at the thermal spa. Oh, and Mamma? He's a German officer.

And I think he's interested in me.

These few phrases, dropped casually by Enrica in infrequent moments of confidence over the course of a month, after her return from the summer colony where she had worked as a teacher, had caused an earthquake in the Colombo home. Starting with her first, cautious confession, Maria had begun to lay siege to her daughter, and with her own anxiety she had soon infected one and all. That her elder daughter, whose discretion and shyness were proverbial, should meet a man and now want to invite him to dinner constituted a momentous event.

Manfred had arrived in uniform and with another bouquet of flowers, this time for Enrica. He was handsome, fair-haired, athletic, and beaming, and also quite talkative, and he had eaten with gusto, moaning with pleasure and paying effusive compliments to the mistress of the house for each individual dish. Then he had opened a capacious leather bag and extracted presents for every member of the family, overlooking no one: carved wooden animals for the littlest one, an elaborate pipe for Giulio, a silk scarf for Susanna, and cigars for Marco. For Enrica he had brought a silver necklace with figures dressed in the folk costumes of Bavaria, and a hand-illustrated book.

He had shown himself to be an interesting conversationalist, and with his perfect Italian, rendered more exotic by that strange, slightly harsh accent, he had expressed a profound love for the art and the culture of that city. You truly are lucky, he had said, to live in such a wonderful country, with a great past and a great future.

He had then explained the extremely favorable view that the new Germany had of the Italian model; in fact, his presence in the city was proof of the fact, he had added. He was going to provide logistical support for a team of German archeologists working on excavations in the area around the volcano, but he was also going to find the time to satisfy his curiosity concerning the countless other treasures of the local area, which he was sorry to say he only knew superficially. He'd accompanied every phrase with a meaning glance at Enrica, and by so doing he fed Maria's enthusiasm. Enrica's mother, in fact, was happily surprised to learn that her daughter—a rather ordinary woman, she had to admit deep in her heart—was the object of the attentions of such an extraordinary man.

The young woman, as was typical of her, displayed an absolute tranquility. She smiled at witty asides, she listened, she weighed in with her own infrequent yet apposite observations. She had given in to pressure and was wearing a pink muslin blouse with a floral motif that she had embroidered herself, which offered an opportunity for her mother to emphasize, as if in chance passing, how skillful her daughter was. She also wore a string of pearls around her throat and two small pearl drop earrings, just to make clear—again in compliance with the wishes of her female parent—the importance of that new visit in the bosom of the family, far from the place where the couple had first met.

In other words, Enrica was behaving the way anyone would have expected. You couldn't expect a bold and shameless attitude from her but Giulio, who was observing her every slightest reaction, had detected signs of genuine interest toward this guest.

He had paid close attention to his daughter the whole time, trying to detect whether, and to what extent, that man might represent the future universe of her emotions, making her a happy wife and mother. This wasn't an easy thing to figure out, not even for someone who, like Giulio, knew her thoroughly and who frequently, because of their great similarities, could even guess at things the young woman preferred not to show outwardly.

Everything had unfolded in the most impeccable manner imaginable, thought Giulio. The dinner had gone swimmingly. Nothing to criticize. In the excited running commentary that would no doubt continue until late that night and well into the days that followed, Maria would allow as how she was quite contented. And equally contented with the behavior of Enrica, who was now laughing gaily with the others as the major told them of his awkward falls as a young boy, when he had decided to become a mounted soldier in the cavalry.

Still, there had been a moment, a single moment, that hadn't escaped Giulio's notice.

It had happened after dessert, a spectacular *zuppa inglese alla napoletana*. Maria was declaiming the culinary skills of Enrica, who had put together the masterpiece, and had tried to persuade her to explain the recipe. Enrica had retreated shyly from the spotlight, of course, and so her mother had begun to describe how the delicacy was prepared while Manfred, Marco, and even Giulio served themselves a second portion. Ricotta, shaved chocolate curls, sponge cake soaked in rum, two shots of Henry's herbal liquor to be added to the filling; Maria narrated and the German officer listened raptly, chewing with unmistakable gusto.

Enrica had gotten up to clear away the dirty plates and on her way to the kitchen she had shot a rapid gaze toward the window across the way. It was such a fleeting gesture that it was practically imperceptible, and Giulio was certain that she'd done it without even realizing it. But he *had* noticed, and he'd seen the slight jerk of her shoulders when she had understood that, behind the drawn curtains, the window was illuminated from within.

Upon her return, the young woman once again had a nice smile on her face and she had once again disposed herself to listen attentively to the conversation, which had in the meantime been enlivened by a comment from Marco, who had appeared to be very pleased with himself when he came out with the observation that the only thing wrong with that dessert was the adjective "inglese," which means English.

From there the conversation had turned to matters of international relations, with Susanna's husband advocating his usual extremist positions, maintaining that mainland Europe was suffocated by the unacceptable ambitions of the English—Perfidious Albion—to exert dominion over the continent, while Manfred, in more muted tones, shared his views. In other circumstances, Giulio would have weighed in, arguing against the militarism with which both Italian Fascism and the new government of Germany were imbued, but not on that occasion.

For starters, it would have been rude to their guest, who was after all a soldier as well as a representative of the German nation in Italy, and then there was the fact that the cavalier had other things on his mind. He was trying to figure out what his daughter was concealing in her heart. Whether there was already a war raging in that heart, so tender and inexperienced.

He wondered what Don Pierino would have done, and he wondered what feelings were concealed by those drawn curtains just across the street.

As the Good Lord would have it, the evening finally drew to an end, with the children leaping madly around Manfred, begging him not to go and to tell them more stories about his hometown on the shore of the lake, up north in Bavaria, and its strange customs. The major apologized for the intrusion and for his prolonged stay but, he added, leveling his eyes at Enrica, he had enjoyed himself so thoroughly that he had completely lost all notion of time.

With a low and heartfelt voice, he addressed Maria.

"You know, Signora: I'm a widower and childless. I've been alone for many years, always traveling on duty. At times I feel quite sad. But I still dream of having a family of my own, just like your own. And happy, mischievous children, like this one here."

He took little Corrado out of Susanna's arms, tickling him till he squealed with delight. When he set the little boy down, he scampered to the safety of his parents with a finger in his mouth, though he continued to look at Manfred without letting him notice.

Manfred went on.

"Sometimes people have certain prejudices against soldiers like me. People assume that we're superficial, interested only in advancing our military careers and yearning to risk our lives on the battlefield. Believe me, that's not true. A soldier is a man like any other, and a man needs a home to return to. Otherwise, he isn't really complete."

With that brief oration, uttered just as he was leaving, Manfred declared the real reason for his visit. And they were, to the letter, the exact words that Maria had been hoping to hear.

Signora Colombo burst into a broad smile.

"Major, you must surely have realized that you are a very welcome visitor to this home. As long as you are in our city, understand that you can rely upon our family as if it were your own; if you please, you're welcome to come back here every night. We would all be very happy: first and foremost your friend Enrica, whom we must thank for having brought you here, and of course, my husband. Isn't that right, Giulio?"

Called into the conversation, the cavalier courteously confirmed.

"Certainly, certainly. Come whenever you like."

Enrica had the exact same smile as the Mona Lisa.

Giulio wondered for the umpteenth time what she could be thinking about.

And especially *who* she could be thinking about.

XXXII

Certain evenings were worse than others, thought Ricciardi.

Not that there was an actual reason why. Maybe it was something in the air. A special sweetness that worked its way under his skin and stretched its fingers to clutch his heart, compressing it in a vise grip that made it hard just to breathe.

And so he'd been relieved to accept the friendly obligation to take Bruno Modo out to dinner. Informed of the unusual development, Nelide, without any change in her expression, had begun to put away the ingredients she was planning to use for that evening's dinner, and in response to the commissario's question as to what she would eat when she was alone, she had shrugged her shoulders and decreed: *chi cucina allecca e chi fila secca*, which meant that she had had a taste while she was making dinner and was no longer hungry.

The proverb meant something else, to tell the truth (those who cook, get to taste, while those who spin, since they have to wet the cotton with their tongue, always have dry mouths), but Ricciardi understood its meaning. Nelide's habit of speaking in proverbs was helping him to rediscover the dialect of his homeland, which he thought he had forgotten, and really he didn't mind it a bit.

What he missed about Rosa wasn't the way she took care of him, it was feeling her eyes watching him; he missed her almost tangible presence in every corner of the house.

And yet, that evening there was something else provoking his anguish.

His mind had latched onto the case that he was working on, a case that might not even exist, with a prisoner accused of murder who might actually be guilty of that murder. His mind was fleeing, but it had nowhere to take shelter. As he was getting dressed to go out, he noticed that the windows in the Colombo home across the way were all lit up.

He'd pulled the curtain open just a hair and had taken a peek.

Quite often, in the past, when the woman he'd fallen in love with was nothing but an image behind glass, a seamstress embroidering, blurred by darkness and distance, before he could even attribute a specific color to Enrica's eyes, before he had savored the touch of her lips in a sudden, fleeting kiss under an improbable snowfall, before hearing the sound of her voice, he had fantasized about that family.

About how nice it would be to be part of so much untroubled happiness.

They weren't eating in the kitchen the way the usually did. That evening they were dining in the formal dining room.

Through the balcony door, left ajar to let in a little of the cool September air, Ricciardi had glimpsed a headful of blond hair, a uniform.

And his memory had been assailed by the recollection of a delirious night on Ischia. Through the leaves, a blond head of hair leaning in toward Enrica's face. For a kiss.

He had suffered over that kiss every bit as much as he had suffered over his *tata*'s death. A different kind of pain, but every bit as intolerable. It was irrational, it was completely absurd, but that's the way it was.

So it turns out that the thing had continued. Which meant the relationship was developing, as was only natural. And the family, by welcoming the man into their midst, was now sanctioning the daughter's preference.

He wasn't surprised, nor did the sight cause him any additional sorrow. He felt only the burning sting of exclusion.

Once again he found himself looking out at life, his face pressed to a plate-glass shop window.

He went out in a hurry, heading in the direction of the hospital, but he hadn't even needed to go that far. Bruno met him halfway, strolling down the street with his hands in his pockets, whistling a little tune, his hat pushed back from his forehead and the inevitable dog trotting along a few yards behind him.

"Oh, here you are. One need only step out into the night to meet vampires. Some might run into Count Dracula, others instead might meet up with the Baron of Malomonte, and each of us gets the monsters they deserve. Let's admit it, in Transylvania there's quite a different class of creatures, but here at home, as usual, we have to settle for imitations."

Ricciardi's reply was quick in coming.

"Listen, if you're looking for finer company, then you can always go to one of those places you like to frequent. I'm sure the people there would be far more agreeable than I am."

Modo laughed.

"No doubt about it, it's true. But it would cost me too much, whereas tonight, as per our agreement, you're picking up the tab, because it's a well known fact that you're filthy rich. Perhaps I won't be treated to the silvery peals of feminine laughter, but I'll fill my belly at your expense and if I'm lucky, I'll get good and drunk into the bargain."

Ricciardi snickered.

"Yes, yes. I'm convinced that it was silvery feminine laughter you were thinking of. And I never doubted for an instant that I would be left to settle the check. Come along then, show me this new trattoria someone told you about. Let's see if the wine is really so bad that you can get drunk on less than a liter."

The doctor tilted his head to one side and narrowed his eyes, observing his friend's face.

"What's wrong with you? We know each other so well that I am able to detect even the subtlest gradations in your customary tedious dreariness. That worries me: does this mean that I'm refining my diagnostic abilities to the point that I can actually distinguish among the various stages of mental illness?"

The commissario took some time before answering. He took a step or two, then said: "You know, there are certain days that are grimmer than others. I'm digging into a case that isn't a case, and I'm doing it secretly; the story of the loan-sharking lawyer who was murdered in June."

"Interesting . . . Go on, tell me more. That way, as usual, I'll open my mind to you and you, through my merit, will solve the case. Every so often it seems to me that it's an authentic tragedy for the other branches of knowledge that I became such a first-rate doctor: I could have aspired to become anything, even a policeman."

They stopped outside a door that stood ajar, out of which came the unmistakable laughter and music of a local neighborhood eatery. Ricciardi looked crestfallen.

"No doubt about it: I'll leave here tonight with a splitting headache, oppressed by third-rate wine, bad music, and your now-proverbial idiotic opinions. Come on, let's go in. Yank the tooth and the pain is gone."

Modo patted the dog on the head and then the dog went off to sniff an interesting streetlamp not far away. For a while, he'd wander off to inspect the neighborhood but then, at the right moment, as if by magic, he'd show up outside the trattoria's front door.

The doctor spoke softly.

"*Ciao*, dog. You certainly understand humans. And in fact, you chose the finest of them all for your companion."

During their dinner, which proved much better than they'd expected, the commissario told Modo about Bianca and her husband. He didn't often share his own thoughts about his work, but this case was so different from all his others that he thought talking about it to someone other than Maione might help him to clarify his thoughts.

The physician listened to him carefully, then seemed once again to scrutinize his face.

"I'm just trying to figure out what drove you to take on this case. All right, I understand that you need something to take your mind off the death of Rosa, and that you foolishly fail to appreciate the delights of the brothel as an adequate pastime, but an old, closed case, long since filed away and forgotten about, with a confessed murderer who refuses to be swayed, strikes me as a pretty stupid distraction even for someone like you. What is it about Piro's murder that appeals to you?"

Even the wine, in defiance of their expectations, was good and flowed freely. Ricciardi could hold his alcohol well, and as far as he could remember, he'd never been drunk in his life. Still, when he drank, he became even more somber than usual and so, as a rule, he tended to avoid it. Moreover, he had the disagreeable impression that alcohol only strengthened the Deed, another excellent reason to avoid hoisting a glass.

That evening, however, wasn't just any ordinary evening. That evening he'd glimpsed a handsome head of blond hair through a window.

He threw back another glass and poured out some more of the amber liquid for Modo.

"I don't exactly know. There's just something that doesn't add up: details, trivia. Starting with the attitude of the Count of Roccaspina. And his wife's attitude, too."

The doctor drank and smiled, somewhat vacuously.

"Well, I'd stop and focus a little more carefully on this lady the contessa. Because, as I was listening to you, it almost struck me that you sort of had it in for her. And yet you accepted her summons, and now you're investigating to confirm or deny what she's claiming. And why would you be doing that?"

Ricciardi fell silent, staring down into the empty plate before him on the table. Then he said, in a low voice: "She's suffering, you know. She has beautiful eyes, she's a young woman, she has a name and a reputation. But she's suffering. And not out of love, because I can't detect any love in her words, in her gaze. She doesn't hate him, but she certainly doesn't love him. And yet, she's suffering, and she's alone. I can't make any sense of it."

Modo smiled from ear to ear, and threw himself back in his chair after tossing back his glassful of wine with gusto.

"Aaahhh, now we've come to the point. *Cherchez la femme!* You're intrigued by the contessa, Riccia'. In other words, you like her. Just wait and see, we'll find out that a human heart beats in those trousers after all."

In spite of himself, Ricciardi smiled and launched into an attempt at self-defense, once again filling his friend's glass to the brim as he did so.

"Don't talk nonsense, Bruno. You know that there are certain things I'm not cut out for. It's just that I can't stand it when I'm incapable of deciphering certain sentiments, because then I'm unable to understand what drives people. I'm interested in comprehending motives: whatever it is that drives her to take so much trouble to prove her husband's innocence, and whatever it is that drove him to declare himself guilty, since he wants to spend as little time in prison as possible."

Modo drank, and this time he poured a glass for himself alone, rather hastily.

"Your theory, Ricciardi. The one you explained to me a long time ago. People kill for hunger or love. By hunger, of course, we mean material need and by love, all emotions. Whose child is this murder? Hunger's or love's?"

Ricciardi thought it over at length. He raised his glass and admired the hue of the wine against the light. Then he murmured: "Hunger, I think. He was a loan shark, he lent out money and then demanded repayment, threatening to unleash scandals. It's a murder caused by hunger, arrogance, and power, prostration and desperation."

Modo had had roughly the same amount to drink as Ricciardi, but unlike the commissario, he seemed quite drunk. He was slurring his words.

"Then seek the hunger. Try to figure out why and in what way that hunger could be at the root of what happened. That world, the wealthy, the nobility, is full of poverty like any other environment. It's just that there, they conceal themselves. You have to flush them out into the open. Get them to talk, Riccia'. Go where they go: the club, the theater, the café. If only you knew how often I see them, in the brothels, and what dreary perversions they have. Go and see them."

Ricciardi nodded, grimly.

"I'll do that. You know that I never feel very comfortable in those places, but I'll go all the same, tomorrow first thing."

The physician chuckled, resting his chin on his knit fingers.

"Go on, after all you might learn something interesting. By the way, whatever became of the lovely widow Vezzi? Do you know that the whole city has been talking about this magical creature who has fallen in love in some incomprehensible way with a horrible and miserable policeman?"

The commissario put on a sad expression.

"Don't worry, people will stop that talk soon enough. I've put an end to this misunderstanding once and for all. Another moth has been saved from the flame."

Modo blinked rapidly.

"What the devil are you talking about? Misunderstanding, moth . . . It seems to me that you're drunk. I don't know how you're ever going to get home. I certainly can't take you, I can hardly stand up myself. In fact, I think *you're* going to have to take *me* home."

Ricciardi called the proprietor and asked for the check, then he helped Modo to his feet and, to keep him from falling, stretched his arm around his friend's waist, letting Modo place his arm on Ricciardi's shoulder.

The doctor sang at the top of his lungs the whole way home about pale young ladies, notaries with whirling capes, gazes out windows, and love letters discovered in Latin books many years later, none of which did much to make the situation any cheerier.

As if that weren't enough, the dog insisted on snarling dully and continually, turning to look behind them and stopping every so often. They were forced to slow down more than once and call to him.

Along the way, the commissario was forced to withstand the lamentations and curses of an entire family that perished in a car crash: the father run through by the steering column, as he shouted at his daughter to take her hands off his eyes because when he was driving was no time to play games; the little one virtually decapitated by impact; the mother and the little boy calling out to each other.

He shouldn't have drunk all that wine.

Outside his front door, by now completely soused, Modo tried to kiss him on the lips and called him his beloved, perhaps mistaking him for one of his whores. Ricciardi managed to break free, though with some effort, and took Modo upstairs to bed, leaving him in the dog's safekeeping.

From the darkness, two chilly eyes had observed the whole scene.

XXXIII

After the usual comparison of notes with Brigadier Maione, Ricciardi headed off to the yacht club to meet Duke Carlo Maria Marangolo.

He wasn't expecting much from that appointment at the hour of the midmorning pre-luncheon aperitif. For some time now it had become clear to him that the aristocracy of that city was disinclined to open itself up and confide in him. And he also suspected that those who belonged to that world would much rather file away as quickly as possible the whole matter of Piro's murder; the fact that it had been committed by a member of the nobility, and what's more, one who was more generally in disgrace, represented an unpleasant thought, and there was no reason to burden the usual giddy round of cocktails and brilliant soirées with such a thought.

That's it, the haste! thought Ricciardi with a sudden illumination as he strolled down the gentle slope that took him toward the salt water. It was the haste that bothered him about the Piro case. Everyone was in too much of a hurry. As if everyone involved was only too happy to divert attention from that murder and move on to something else, anything else.

A haste that might not be part of a conscious strategy to conceal anything in particular, but rather a convergence of various interests.

The interests of the Piro family, who certainly weren't happy to have anyone delve into the origins of the lawyer's wealth. The interests of the police, who had no need to see a murder featured for more than a day or two in the pages of the newspapers while Rome was intent on spreading the image of a country where what reigned was order and prosperity. And the interests of high society, which had just successfully rid itself in one fell swoop of both a shady loan shark and an impoverished, disgraced count.

He moved past the image of the two drowned boys, clutching each other in one final embrace, but this time without stopping to look at them. When there was more than one dead person, then the Deed tended to last at greater length; who could say for how much longer this grim monument to love and grief would remain open to his perception. Perhaps until summer had become a memory and the waterfront was swept by the wind and rain of autumn.

It's not so bad, he thought with bitter irony. I'm the only nutcase who can see them.

As soon as he set foot on the sun-flooded terrace, a uniformed waiter came toward him.

"*Buongiorno*. Please, walk this way."

The man hadn't addressed him by name and Ricciardi didn't remember having met him the last time. So he was expected. He knew that the contessa would alert Marangolo to his impending visit, and he wondered whether she had already suggested to the duke just what to say to him. He was prepared for the possibility that his interlocutor might retail half-truths and even outright lies, but in spite of that, the duke's presence in the Roccaspina home the night of the murder, and in the count's absence, was a circumstance that might certainly bear some looking into.

The waiter led Ricciardi down a hallway whose walls were lined, in glittering display cases, with the trophies won by the athletic teams that worked out of the club, alternating with photographs of the champions who had taken those trophies. Swimming, sailing, rowing, and water polo. The club into which he was now being ushered was one of the oldest ones in the city, and therefore heaped with the greatest spoils of glory, but other similar clubs had sprung up near the parks lining the waterfront, and were starting to compete in terms of sporting achievements, general splendor, and the elegance of their receptions.

The commissario knew it very well, because he had attended a few soirées there, yielding to Livia's insistence. He had been bored to death and had spent the whole time doing what he could to prevent the woman from introducing him to everyone attending, in an attempt to establish him as her official companion.

The thought of Livia, as the waiter was knocking discreetly with a gloved hand at a heavy mahogany door, caused him a stab of melancholy. He had inflicted a great deal of pain upon her, and intentionally so, by humiliating her; he knew that that extraordinarily beautiful and talented woman was in love with him, and what had happened between them must have wounded her to the very depths of her femininity.

But there had been no way to avoid it.

Precisely because he also cared for her, he had been forced to turn her away.

To keep her from being burnt by his flame.

They entered a cozy little room, shrouded in dim shadows. Only a little bit of light filtered through the drawn curtains over a French door, allowing him to guess at the outlines of the walls.

"Duke, your grace," the waiter said in a subdued voice, "the gentleman you were expecting is here."

A deep, well modulated voice replied from the darkness.

"*Grazie*, Ciro. Draw the curtains a little, if you please, and bring us two espressos and a few pastries."

With alacrity, the waiter pulled open the curtains.

And a marvelous view spread out before them.

They were no more than ten feet above the level of the sea and the waterfront extended in a vast panorama to the foot of the hill that plunged down to the salt water, pointing toward the silhouette of the distant island.

Without a doubt, this was a private room, used by prominent citizens for confidential meetings. A *privé*, as the French would have it. Tapestries on the walls, a sofa with two armchairs and a low table, and, over by the window, a green baize table with four chairs, several decks of playing cards, and stacks of chips.

Ricciardi studied his host.

The man was skinny, with his skin drawn taut over his face, and he was dressed in black. He sat with his legs crossed on one of the two armchairs. He could be any age between thirty-five and sixty: his features seemed fairly youthful and his eyes were dark and lively, but his hair was thinning and colorless, the spots on his face and his deep wrinkles those of an old man.

"I beg your indulgence," said the man. "I don't like strong light, much less being surrounded by other people. And, in order to do a thing I do only rarely, that is, meet with anyone, I choose to withdraw to this little room. It's not roomy, it's certainly not fancy, but that painting on the wall," and with that, he tilted his head to indicate the panorama that burst in through the window, "repays the discomfort, or at least I hope it does. I am Carlo Maria Marangolo. Our mutual friend, Bianca di Roccaspina, asked me to place myself entirely at your disposal, and I am only too happy to do so. Please, make yourself comfortable." He pointed to the empty armchair across from his own.

The duke's voice was low, unaccented. It betrayed both intelligence and irony. Looking at him more closely, Ricciardi detected something that had at first escaped his notice: the man's complexion was yellowish and unhealthy looking.

Marangolo was a sick man. That was the reason for the
wrinkles, the spots, and the skinniness. Perhaps also for the
darkness in which he seemed to be hiding.

Ricciardi sat down.

"Thank you for your time, Duke. As I believe you know, I
am trying, at the contessa's request, to understand a little more
about the case in which her husband is involved. I want to
make it clear straightaway that this is not an official investigation, and therefore if you decide to answer my questions, it will
only be as a form of courtesy. Is that all right with you?"

In his turn, Marangolo studied the commissario's face,
without speaking. The waiter came in, set down the coffees
and the pastries on the little table, and then quickly and sound-
lessly left.

"Ricciardi, Ricciardi . . . I once met a Baron Ricciardi di
Malomonte: nobility of Cilento, if I'm not mistaken. He was a
friend of my father's, a remarkable man, a passionate hunter
and horseman. Would you be related, by any chance?"

The commissario confirmed, brusquely.

"He was my father. The contessa . . . "

The duke pursued his line of thought, as if Ricciardi hadn't
answered at all.

"You look nothing like him, though. He was a tall, powerful looking man, very jovial. An open, contagious laugh. My
father was fairly choosy about his friends, and he adored him.
Physically, you're quite different, and you strike me as more . . .
how to put this . . . reserved?"

Ricciardi shrugged his shoulders.

"I wouldn't know, I can barely remember him, I was still a
child when he died. I believe I take after my mother. Can I ask
you a few questions, Duke? I wouldn't want to take unfair
advantage of your courtesy."

Marangolo nodded repeatedly with a half smile, as if finding confirmation for his theories.

"Curious . . . This narrow, blinkered environment is the forbidden dream of many people, who would do anything to gain access to it. And someone like you, who would have the title and the right to belong to it, actually goes and conceals a part of their name."

The commissario gave the duke a chilly stare, well aware that he was being provoked.

"One might imagine that people have the right to frequent whoever they choose, don't you think? In the light of events, perhaps Piro too would have changed his mind. But it seems to me that he was actually very well accepted in this . . . what did you call it? community of yours."

Marangolo took the retort with the same half smile.

"I never said that it's a particularly nice environment. I believe that my propensity to seek seclusion from it says all that needs to be said. Well, now, tell me, what is it you want to know?"

"I am told that the night before the murder, you went to the Roccaspina residence while the count was not there. Could you clarify the reason for your visit?"

Marangolo scrutinized his questioner.

"No beating around the bush with you, is there? You're a direct fellow, Bianca warned me about that. I wonder what the reason is for this fixation, why not simply accept the fact that Romualdo murdered Ludovico Piro? In any case, to come to your question, I wasn't there to see the count, I was there for the contessa. So, to be perfectly clear, as you prefer, I can tell you that I knew he wouldn't be there at that hour. I didn't choose the time haphazardly."

Ricciardi sipped his espresso. It really was excellent. For that matter, it would have been strange to find ersatz coffee in that club that seemed to follow its own rules, high above more ordinary customs.

"Forgive me for the question. I'm indiscreet and I'm not

going to stop, but knowing the overall picture is the condition I set the contessa in exchange for looking into the matter. So I'm going to have to insist: why did you want to see her?"

Marangolo got out of the armchair and made his way laboriously over to the window. He was a man of average height, his spine somewhat curved. Closer to age sixty than fifty, Ricciardi decided inwardly.

The man admired the panorama in silence for a couple of minutes, during which time the commissario concentrated on his razor-sharp, suffering profile.

Then he spoke.

"You know, Baron, I am rich. Very rich. So rich that in my case not even a lifetime of squandering would be enough to dilapidate the fortune I possess. Not that any of it is to my credit, let me make that clear. It all came to me in my inheritance, through a long succession of arranged and rearranged marriages that had only one intent, to amass an immense patrimony. This palazzo, for instance, belongs to me. I've put it at the disposal of the yacht club to have the pleasure of coming here, every so often, to enjoy a first-rate espresso, and because it made me sad to see so many large, empty rooms. The only contribution I ever made to the family fortune is that of never developing any bad habits. I don't like to gamble, I don't like to get drunk, and I don't take drugs, unlike so many of my debauched compatriots who are strolling up and down on the terrace even as we speak."

He broke off for a moment to step over to the table, bend over with some effort to pick up demitasse and saucer, and return to the window. Then he resumed.

"I'm a rich man, and a sick one. My liver . . . hence the yellowish hue of my flesh. Curious, really, if you consider the fact that I'm practically a teetotaler and that I don't frequent brothels, where no matter what the functionaries in charge of medical checkups for the young ladies might say, it is still eminently

possible to catch diseases. Perhaps it's the result of some marriage between cousins, among my ancestors, or else simply fate.
The finest physicians on earth care for me; they come here to
enjoy a few days of very well-paid vacation. They give me some
new medicine or other, and then scuttle back home. They tell
me that I'm getting better, but it doesn't seem so to me. In any
case, I have no intention of missing out on my espresso."

Ricciardi intervened with a subdued voice.

"Duke, why are you telling me these things? I never asked
you . . . "

Marangolo cut him off, brusquely.

"Baron, if I tell you certain things, there's a good reason for
it. Let us take it for granted that we're both intelligent, if you
please: neither of us is here to waste time, you because you
have work to do, I because I have a life to live. Both things are
very, very urgent indeed. Earlier I told you that I have no bad
habits, but I wasn't being entirely honest. I do have one bad
habit. My bad habit is Bianca Palmieri di Roccaspina."

Being called Baron put Ricciardi ill at ease, made him feel
as if he'd left something out, as if he hadn't done an adequate
job of something that fate had assigned him.

"Duke, that's not why I'm here, there are some things you
need not tell me. I only want to know why that evening . . . "

"No, I'm afraid that you need to know everything, Baron.
Bianca was here, this morning, and she asked me to be entirely
frank with you, to tell you in the most complete and detailed
manner exactly what happened. Because, you understand, I
played a part in all this. An important part. And unless I
explain it all to you from the very beginning, then you might
miss something, or I might overlook some detail, which would
make your 'unofficial investigation,' as you called it yourself,
entirely pointless."

Ricciardi was confused.

"I'm ready to listen to you, but if it's something that's relevant to the case, why didn't you issue a spontaneous declaration about it at the time? It would have helped the investigators to reflect, to refrain from archiving the investigation immediately."

Marangolo was gazing steadily at the horizon where the hill tumbled down to the sea. The cloudless sky looked like a papier-mâché panel.

Blue above, blue below.

"It wouldn't have changed a thing. But it changes everything for me, for my conscience. Because you see, Malomonte, the money that Piro loaned to Romualdo di Roccaspina didn't come from the religious entities for which he served as administrator.

"I gave him that money."

XXXIV

Brigadier Maione was reading the report drawn up by officers Camarda and Cesarano concerning a likely suicide that had taken place the day before, not far from Via Toledo, in the very center of town. Sipping the dark swill that Officer Mistrangelo stubbornly insisted on calling coffee, but which might more accurately be described as an assault on the digestive tract of all employees at police headquarters, he grimaced in disgust. He drained the demitasse, pushed it out of his sight, and for the umpteenth time swore to himself that he would never again drink that horrible brew.

The dead man was a high school teacher, a recent widower. According to the report, in the midst of shopping hours, while the street was crowded with pedestrians, without so much as a shout of warning, he had climbed over the railing of his balcony on the fifth floor of a venerable old apartment house that had seen better days, and had imitated a seagull, or a pigeon, or an eagle; the only difference was that, since he had not been endowed with feathers and wings, he had slammed into the pavement and only by a sheer miracle had avoided taking with him, on his last journey, three or four of the afternoon strollers beneath.

Camarda and Cesarano, the police officers who had hurried to the scene of the death, had followed proper procedures, the brigadier noticed as he skimmed the report. Upon the physician's arrival, they had accompanied him upstairs to the apartment, where they had found a suicide note in which the poor wretch had written to his wife that at last, that night, they'd sleep together again. Then they had waited for the morgue attendants and the entire matter had been wrapped up.

Maione thought about what he would do if, by some cruel twist of fate, he were to outlive Lucia. The report said nothing about children: maybe he would have found the strength to go on living in them. Most likely, the flying high school teacher had no children.

As he was trying to dismiss that bothersome thought, he realized that someone was knocking at the door of the officers' wardroom so softly it was scarcely even perceptible.

"Come in!" he called out.

The door opened just a crack and a worried, broad moon face appeared—it was Amitrano, the policeman who just the day before had failed to restrain the bad manners of the *scugnizzo* who had been sent by Bambinella.

"Amitra'," said Maione, "if I didn't have such good ears, you could have stood there knocking until the end of the shift, do you realize that? What the hell do you want?"

The officer was terrorized: he was sweating and his eyes were wide open.

"No, Brigadie', it's just that I didn't want to disturb you. I know that you were drinking your ersatz coffee and I didn't want to interrupt with work matters."

Maione furrowed his brow.

"What are you talking about, Amitra', you seem to be a little dumber than usual today. I'm already at work, and you don't want to interrupt me with work? Forget about it, okay? So what's going on?"

The man spoke in a very low voice and Maione was able to guess at a word here and another there.

" . . . street door . . . someone who . . . chauffeur . . . not anymore . . . "

The brigadier leapt to his feet.

"Amitra', as God is my witness, I'm going to kick that voice out of you! Speak up, loud and clear, because I can't understand you! And come ahead in, damnation, what are you doing half in and half out?"

The officer leapt into the air, as if some mysterious force had catapulted him into the room, clicked his heels, and lifted his hand to his forehead twice in a salute.

"Yessir, Brigadier. It's just that outside, at the front entrance, there's someone who's looking for you. Or at least, it seems to me that you're the one he's looking for, even if . . . that is, he doesn't know the name, but from the description it seemed to me . . . in other words, he says that he's a chauffeur, or at least that he used to be. He would be a chauffeur, if they would let him, but apparently they fired him and . . . "

Maione was exasperated.

"Amitrano, please, speakly slowly and calmly. Let me understand you. I know that you can do it, even if you're a fool and an idiot and I don't know how you were ever accepted onto the police force. How did you understand that this out-of-work chauffeur was looking for me of all people?"

The officer stared at the floor, tracing the outline of a terracotta tile with the tip of his shoe.

"Brigadie', please, trust me. He's looking for you. Don't make me say things I don't want to have to say."

Maione slowly got to his feet, towering a good eight inches over the head of his confused colleague from his height of six foot three.

His voice was low and therefore all the more threatening.

"Amitra', speak. You see, I'm telling you with the utmost calmness. Speak, it'll be better for you."

The man gasped, his mouth opening and closing like a fish's, trying to get a gulp of air. His face was gray. Then he answered, all in a rush: "He said: there's a brigadier who's looking for me, and he's got an enormous gut, an old man, with no hair on his head. That's what he said."

Maione stood there in silence, staring at the top of the officer's cap, while instead the officer stared at the floor, his neck tucked down into his shoulders, awaiting his inevitable doom.

The brigadier nodded slowly. Then he whispered: "And you understood immediately, didn't you? You had no doubts. You came straight here to find me."

Amitrano was sniveling.

"Brigadie', what was I supposed to do? Should I have just sent him away? Then what if it turned out to be something important? And after all, who else could this enormous brigadier be? Brigadier Cozzolino is shorter than me, after all; Brigadier Ruotolo is skinny as a beanpole; and Brigadier Velonà has a thick head of hair. Forgive me, I beg you!"

Maione ran a hand over his face.

"Amitra', I hate you. I really and truly hate you. And sooner or later I'm going to kill you, on my honor; already, I have no idea how you survived yesterday, with the little boy who let out a raspberry in the courtyard, what do you think, that I didn't hear him? And you never even managed to catch him. Let this chauffeur in, and remember: I don't have a gut, I'm just robust; and it isn't true that I have no hair, I just wear my hair very short for convenience's sake. Go on, get out of here. And try not to let me see you ever again."

The officer shot away, grateful that once again destiny had decided to let him live. After less than a minute the door opened to let in a skinny little man, with large, watery blue eyes, who was holding a chauffeur's cap in both hands.

"May I come in? Are you the brigadier who was looking for me?"

Maione looked him up and down.

"I don't know. It depends. Who told you that I was looking for you in particular?"

The little man, as if he were reciting a poem, replied: "Now then, my surname is Laprece, given name Salvatore, and until three months ago I worked as a chauffeur for the lawyer Ludovico Piro, who recently passed away because of his having been murdered. An . . . acquaintance of mine, Signorina Elvira Durante, who is a working girl at the unauthorized brothel of Madame Sonia in Santa Lucia, and who I chanced to run into today, told me that a young lady who is an acquaintance of yours, Signorina Bambinella of San Nicola a Tolentino, who works privately out of her home, but who from what I've been told no longer works because now she has a boyfriend, asked her for some information about me."

Maione stared openmouthed at the man.

"And so?"

"And so, since this Signorina Bambinella told Elvira Durante that this information had been requested by a friend of hers who is a brigadier, Elvira Durante asked her whether by any chance this friend of hers was having his way with her or not. And Signorina Bambinella began to laugh and said no, what on earth are you thinking, he's an old man, without any hair and with a big gut. So I decided to come here to find out why on earth this brigadier should be taking an interest in me, and whether he might by any chance be willing to help me find a job, because ever since I was unjustly dismissed from my position, I haven't been able to find another one, not even with the references that they gave me."

The brigadier seriously considered inflicting punishment on the former chauffeur for the infractions of Bambinella, Officer Amitrano, and the raspberry-emitting *scugnizzo*; then he decided to let him go free on his own recognizance and to take advantage of the opportunity to hear from the man's own lips a little information about the secret investigation that he was carrying out with Ricciardi.

"All right, Laprece, let's forget about how you came to learn about the fact that we were looking for information. Yes, I'm the one who asked the young lady . . . who asked that person to let me have whatever news she could gather. Even though, as you can see with your own eyes, I'm neither an old man, nor hairless, nor even all that fat. So now, tell me: How long did you work as a chauffeur for the Piro family?"

The man put on a dreamy expression.

"For three years, Brigadie'. I was in charge of maintenance of the automobile, a black Fiat 525, 68 horsepower, lovely as the sunshine; you have to believe me, Brigadie', I miss that car as if it were a member of my family."

"And what was the nature of your employment?"

"I drove the lawyer everywhere he needed to go. And the rest of the time, once I'd made sure the car was in tiptop shape, I waited for orders; and then I'd loiter in the general area."

Maione snickered.

"And while you were loitering in the general area, you met Signorina Elvira Durante, who just happened to be loitering herself, and you became fast friends. All right, go on: why were you fired? Did you do something you shouldn't have?"

Laprece put on an indignant expression.

"No, Brigadie', how can you think such a thing? I've always been, what's the word I'm looking for, irresponsible in my professional life!"

Maione sighed.

"Irreprehensible. The word you're looking for is irreprehensible. Then why would they have fired you, in your opinion?"

The man shrugged his shoulders.

"Brigadie', I've asked myself that question a thousand times. They have plenty of money, and they use that car, even though the lawyer has been murdered. They told me that they just had to retrench with their expenses now that the father is dead."

Maione thought it over for a moment and then asked: "Do you remember anything odd that might have happened in the last few days before Piro was killed? I don't know, a particular meeting with someone, an unaccustomed appointment; or maybe he himself said something to you, confided something . . . "

The chauffeur ruled it out decisively.

"No, Brigadie', why would you think such a thing? The lawyer, God rest his soul, had a ferocious personality, the last thing he'd dream of doing is striking up a conversation with me: I drove and he read his papers. Every so often he'd tell me not to go so fast, but I don't remember ever talking about anything else. And we never met anyone either."

The brigadier scratched his head.

"In other words, nothing out of the ordinary."

Laprece reflected for a moment, then murmured: "Now that I stop to think, one strange thing did happen the very same day as the lawyer's murder."

"What was that?

"Now then: the day before we had gone to the convent of the Sisters of the Coronation of Our Lady; you know, after Pomigliano d'Arco, there's the convent and a boarding school. The lawyer was the administrator there and every three or four months he would have me drive him out. There he would confer with the Mother Superior and I would enjoy some refreshments; the sister who worked in the refectory would make me a first-rate espresso and she'd also give me a dish of the biscotti they make there, which are truly something special. This visit went the same as any other. The next day, though, the lawyer ordered me to take him back, as if he had forgotten something. I had never seen him go to the same place twice in two days before."

"And did he tell you why he wanted to go back? Was he on edge, or angry, or . . . "

"No, no. He was silent, the way he always was. And I didn't ask him anything, of course. I was just happy to be able to eat a few more of the nuns' biscotti. In any case, the visit didn't last long, half an hour or so, and then I took him home."

The brigadier had jotted down notes on a scrap of paper to be able to report back with precision to Ricciardi. At the bottom of the sheet of paper, he also made a note of Laprece's address.

"Lapre', listen carefully, make sure we can get in touch with you, because we might have a few more questions at some point."

The little man threw his arms wide.

"Brigadie', there's no one easier to get in touch with than me. You see? I still go everywhere with my chauffeur's cap, that way maybe someone will see me and hire me. But who's going to understand that I'm someone who knows how to drive, if I go everywhere on foot? Anyway, see if you can help me out, even to drive your police cars, for instance."

Maione gave him an unfriendly look.

"Don't you worry about that, we don't neeed anyone. I'm a first-rate driver! Go on, and give my regards to Signorina Elvira."

Laprece heaved a sigh.

"Eh, when am I ever going to see Elvira again, now that I'm unemployed. Lucky you, since you still have a job, because that means you can see Signorina Bambinella on a regular basis! Elvira told me that she's especially good at . . . "

Before Maione could grab him by the scruff of his neck, the little man guessed at his intentions and with a hasty farewell darted out of the room. In the blink of an eye, he had run out the front entrance.

Pretty fast for being a pedestrian chauffeur, the brigadier thought angrily to himself.

XXXV

Marangolo was talking, in a subdued voice, and he seemed to be speaking to the sea and the hill, and the waves that lapped at the rocks and the boats that rode offshore, slowly rocking.

He was speaking to himself, Ricciardi realized.

"When I saw her for the first time, she was sixteen. It was her birthday, July 7th; her parents threw a party at the villa in Vomero where they regularly repaired for the summer. My folks and her folks were friends, even practically relatives; we're all practically relatives, as you know. I was thirty-eight years old, I was a sort of eligible bachelor, and everyone was wondering who I'd wind up marrying. I found the whole thing to be amusing, but I didn't give it much thought, I didn't like the idea that decisions about my life should be made by my father, and I told him so, to his face. I wasn't even supposed to be there, my friends and I had made plans to go to the beach at Posillipo, to spend the day out on a boat. Instead, I didn't go. Instead, I gave in to my mother's request, we took the carriage and rode up to Vomero for the birthday party of the youngest daughter of the Borgati di Zisa family, Signorina Bianca."

He fell silent for a moment, his eyes half closed. A muscle was twitching in his jaw. The sea continued its slow respiration.

"Practically speaking, I hadn't seen her since the day she was born. I knew her elder brother, who was killed in the war, and her sister who lives in Rome. All I could remember about her was some vague recollection of having held her in my arms when she was still in swaddling clothes. There were lots of people, at the reception. The ladies held parasols over their heads, they held their long skirts up with gloved hands to keep them from getting soiled in the grass; the men sweated in their tailcoats, with top hats on their heads. I was resigned to being bored to death. Little did I realize that in a short while my life would be changed once and for all."

He took a sip from the demitasse, with a grimace, and then gave a tug on a bell pull. With a curt nod he ordered another espresso from Ciro, the waiter, and when the man brought it to him, he continued his story, without ever looking to see whether Ricciardi was listening to him.

"She left a few minutes after we arrived. Even now, she's one of the loveliest women in our circle, but that day, as I watched her walk down the flight of stairs leading away from the villa's front door, I all at once felt as if I was in a dream. All of the noise around me suddenly stopped, the air stood still, the summer breeze stopped blowing. Even my heart stopped beating, lest it interfere with the perfection of that moment. Not only was she beautiful, she was an angel come down to earth. Her hair shot out flame caught from the sun. Her neck was that of a swan. Her lips and her nose seemed to have been drawn by a master painter. And her eyes, Baron. Those eyes. Do you know what I'm talking about when I refer to her eyes? During a trip to the Far East I once saw a precious stone that adorned a royal crown, and I felt sure that it was the same color. I spent a fortune to buy it, but once I was able to make the comparison I realized that it was only a pale, futile imitation. That color exists nowhere else. If I can't read the smile in those eyes, life is worth nothing. Nothing."

Marangolo's voice had a hypnotic cadence. Ricciardi felt as if he had been at the duke's side in the very moment he first glimpsed Bianca. He wondered what it must be like when a glance, a single glance, takes you and carries you away. To him, it had happened a little at a time, from behind a pane of glass, looking across at another pane of glass. Two souls separated by two transparent slabs, fragile and impregnable.

The account continued.

"She was young. She was simply too young. I spoke to her, I tried to cast the spell of my immense wealth. What a mistake I was making. How wrong I was. There are women, Baron, who have no interest in that sort of thing. There are women who love a man's weaknesses, not his strengths. I didn't have the wit to understand that. And I lacked the courage to court her openly; the difference in age was too great. Once I realized that I should have, it was too late. Romualdo had already beat me to it."

Another sip of coffee. Now the sun was shining at the window. The man's unnatural complexion became even more evident.

"He was an impossibly handsome young man, too; I have to admit that, together, they were perfect. She seemed happy to me, which is what kept me from fighting for my own life. You see, Baron, all that mattered to me was her welfare and happiness. I only wanted to see her smile. In all these years I've done a great deal for Bianca, and she always thought that it was out of generosity. It isn't true. Mine were acts of extreme selfishness; I was paying a pittance for the food my soul required: that smile. You've seen it haven't you? She lifts her upper lip ever so slightly, tilts her head to one side, and her eyes emanate a strange light, like late-afternoon sunlight, the last ray of light before nightfall. I was there when she became engaged. I was there when she was married. I was there when Romualdo started squandering everything within reach. Including Bianca's soul."

Ricciardi listened carefully. A seagull flew close to the window and perched on a craggy rock, stopping to gaze expressionlessly out at the sea.

Between the duke and the seabird there was a strange, grotesque resemblance.

"I witnessed Romualdo's ruin. At a certain point, I tried talking to him, I wanted to understand what could push a man to such demented behavior if he had had the unspeakable good luck to marry a woman like her. He told me in quite harsh terms to mind my own business. Perhaps I should have put an end to his destiny right then and there. No, Baron, not by killing him, heavens preserve us. That's not my style. I ought to have bought up all his debts and forced him to quit gambling. But I couldn't resist the temptation to find out just how far he would go."

Ricciardi murmured: "And just how far did he go?"

Marangolo turned, slightly surprised, as if he had forgotten that the commissario was there.

"He lost everything he owned. Then he even gambled away money he didn't have. And when the gambling tables of civilized society stopped taking his promissory notes, he started losing money to people who don't forgive those who don't pay."

"And what about after that?"

The duke turned back to look at the sea.

"That's recent history. A year ago, more or less. Bianca came to see me; she did that rarely, a little more often since I got sick. After her fashion, she does care for me, and this piteous affectione wounds me more than hatred ever could."

He coughed into a handkerchief.

"She told me that he'd been beaten. That she'd found a torn shirt and a bloodstained handkerchief. They hadn't been sleeping together for a long time, now, but she could hear him come in and leave. She had heard him moan during the night, and he had avoided crossing paths with her for almost two days, until they finally came face-to-face: Bianca had seen his swollen bruised face and his arms, hanging stiff at his sides.

She was afraid, and she came to tell me so. I asked around and learned what kind of people he'd gotten involved with. He was risking his life, and he didn't know how to get out of that bind. That was when I decided to help him: when I saw the smile die on Bianca's face."

Ricciardi nodded. He had understood.

"And this is where Ludovico Piro comes into the story."

Without turning around, the muscles of the duke's face tightened.

"Exactly. There was this small, pathetic loan shark who was desperately trying to work his way into our social circle. One of those people who had been lured in by the false glitter of a world they don't understand and from which they will always be excluded. He glimpsed the possibility of achieving his wildest dreams the day that I summoned him for an interview, right in this same room, in fact. I told him that he should approach Romualdo and offer him help, at a normal rate of interest. I would finance the operation, he could earn on the margin. Naturally, if and when Romualdo failed to pay back his debt, I would be glad to honor the promissory notes. The only condition was that no one, no one could ever know where that money came from."

The seagull on the rocks let out a shrill cry in the direction of the sea. The sound, so sudden and powerful, caught Ricciardi off guard and made him jerk in his armchair. Marangolo didn't even seem to notice it.

"Soon enough, from one promissory note to another, Ludovico became Romualdo's sole creditor. All the man had left was the building he lived in, whose total worth was less than the amount of the debt, but I couldn't allow Bianca to lose the home she lived in. From time to time, I'd go and see her, but she had guessed something, I have no idea how. The last few times, bringing up some excuse or other, feeling indisposed or alleging some prior obligation, she avoided seeing me entirely. I was hurt, but at least I could tell myself that I had saved her from utter ruin. And that's certainly something, no?"

Ricciardi didn't answer the question. Instead, he asked: "And so we come to that fatal evening, Duke. Exactly what happened?"

Marangolo turned around and went back to sit in his armchair. Now Ricciardi could clearly glimpse on his face the signs of impending death.

"Piro had decided not to allow any further extensions on Romualdo's promissory notes. I have no idea why. I summoned him, but he wouldn't come to see me. I went to his home, but he refused to receive me. I sent word to him that I wished to pay off the debt in full, but he sent word that he wasn't interested. He was determined to ruin Romualdo. He wanted to see him in debtors' prison, or else a suicide. The promissory notes were in his name, I was helpless to do anything about it."

Ricciardi stared at the duke over his interlaced fingers, in the position he always assumed when he was seeking the greatest possible concentration.

"A person might suppose, in light of the story you've just told me, that it was you who desired the count's ruin. You were finally certain that the arc of his existence would soon come to an end, whether in prison or by a pistol shot. And so you would finally be able to obtain what you had yearned for all your life."

The duke started, and in the room's dim light he resembled nothing so much as a skull. He relaxed, morosely.

"So one might think, if it weren't for the fact that I myself am about to die. If it weren't that my liver had decided that I don't have much time left to me, in defiance of the nonsense that I continue to hear spouted by the physicians I pay so generously but who are still determined to bleed as much cash as they can from me. And if it weren't for the fact that I know

Bianca, and I know that she would never, never ever, accept a man out of gratitude or pity.

"You see, Baron, all that Bianca has left to her is her reputation, and the opinion that she has of herself. She has nothing else. A name and an image in a mirror. So I will never have Bianca, for the very simple reason that she does not love me."

Ricciardi stood up.

"Why did Piro put an end to this pantomime? He was looking at enormous, reliable earnings. He could have continued on with it and nothing would have happened. So why did he do it?"

Marangolo put his hands together, fingers intertwined.

"I don't know. I swear that I have no idea. I've asked myself a thousand times, and I just can't seem to fathom why such a miserly, money-grubbing, cowardly man should have decided to wring the neck of the goose that laid so many golden eggs. And paying for it with his own hide, by the way."

"Then you're convinced that it was the Count of Roccaspina who murdered Piro. Is that right?"

Marangolo seemed exhausted.

"Yes, Baron. It was him. Who else could have had any motive to do it? Piro wanted to demand full payment of his promissory notes, the name of the Roccaspina family would be dragged through the legal mud, and it would have spelled his utter ruin. The only alternative would have been to take his own life."

"Then why did you go to call on the contessa, that night?"

"To warn her. To tell her that matters were plummeting out of control, to tell her not to ask me why, but that I knew, that I was certain that her husband might be on the verge of doing something extreme. Except what I had in mind was suicide, not Piro's murder. I confess, Romualdo caught me by surprise: I never thought him capable of such a thing."

Ricciardi nodded his head. The seagull took to its wings

with another shrill cry and vanished from sight. The sea continued its motion in utter indifference, but now it was frightening.

The commissario said farewell to the duke, but just as he was about to leave, he turned around and asked him: "One last question. You knew, or at least you've said, that the contessa would never accept you; and you had excellent reasons for hating the Count of Roccaspina, who took away any chance you might have had of winning her, and who then ruined her youth. So why did you help him?"

Marangolo smiled again.

"Do you really not understand, Malomonte?

"I love her. I will love her until the day I die. And long after that, too."

XXXVI

Enrica had felt an urgent need to go down to the sea.

It wasn't something that happened often. For the most part, if she was free of obligations to tutor children, look after her siblings, or tend to housework, her main inclination was to stay home. Moreover, now they had the change of seasons to think about, a titanic undertaking that involved the putting away of all summer garments and the extraction of all winter clothing, much of which would have to be washed and ironed. But today, giving in to a sudden impulse, she had grabbed her hat and, without a word to anyone, she'd gone out.

She needed to see the horizon, a little blue.

Blue was the color of that city, her father liked to say. You see, sweetheart? Blue is the sky, at least for most of the year. Blue is the sea, when it heaves unexpectedly into view as you come around a curve, or reach the top of a steep incline. Blue is the light that filters into the interiors, through the windows but also the street doors, the minute you open them. A city of blue. And so, he would tell her, if you're looking for equilibrium and serenity, what you should look for is blue. You'll feel better instantly.

Did Enrica lack equilibrium? Was her state of mind not serene? Why did she feel this sudden need? Ever since she was small, she had always been capable of attaining a state of equilibrium without difficulty. Even when everything around her was shifting, changing, or being altered, her personality was capable of shifting her mood to a new point of view. It was a gift, she knew, she wasn't the kind who tended to despair, or cried over spilt milk, or became pointlessly upset. She was sentimental, she was introspective, but she was also quite rational. She knew how to accept change, if it didn't lie within her power to do anything about it.

She adapted.

Then why, she wondered, as she walked down the long, gentle slope that ran down from the large piazza to the sea, did she now feel so uneasy?

Was it on account of Manfred, perhaps?

She had feared that dinner, which she had felt obliged to arrange in order to placate her mother. She had feared this renewed encounter with that officer of a foreign army still remembered as an enemy in war; a widower, a German who was proud of his country, which so many considered with suspicion. She had feared the great differences between his political beliefs and those of her father, between which lay a yawning gulf. She had feared that her mother, in her eagerness to allay the solitude of her unmarried daughter, might behave like a merchant eager to unload slightly defective goods, willing to praise them to the skies in order to sell them off. She had been worried about her young brothers, whose naïveté might have betrayed the gossip among housewives that they had overheard, making them especially dangerous.

She had feared that the evening would end in disaster.

Had she feared it or had she secretly wished for it?

An irritating little voice tried to worm its way into her mind, playing on the opposing sentiments that crowded her thoughts: she hushed it.

Pointless fears all: nothing had happened. Manfred—and knowing him as she did, she should have expected it—had won over everybody, including her father, a man who was seldom inclined to express his feelings; Enrica had caught his glance and clearly interpreted his relief. Her mother, of course, had gone head over heels for him, and by now she talked of nothing else; the following morning she had basically called a general meeting of the other tenants in the apartment house to provide her neighbors with a blow-by-blow account of the dinner, including a pathetic imitation of their guest's coos of appreciation for the food. As for her brothers, they wouldn't set down the carved wooden toys that he had brought for them, and Susanna had launched into a series of intricate, asphyxiating hypotheses concerning the appearance of the children that Enrica would bear after her now inevitable wedding with that athletic, very good looking, and extremely likable major in the German Reichswehr, the "Defense of the Nation," as he had explained the word, which in simpler terms just meant the German army.

Perhaps, Enrica reflected when she finally reached the waterfront and could take a deep breath of salty, briny air as she looked out over the rocks, more than a need for blue, what might have driven her out there was a yearning for silence.

But what about her? What had she felt when she saw Manfred eating out of her dishes, drinking from her glasses, sitting in her living room in the midst of her family? Had she perhaps felt a sense of intrusion, as she had with Sebastiano and the other suitors that her mother had tried to palm off on her?

No. She had to be honest. It had been a pleasure, actually, and she had felt gratified to be the subject of such interest on the part of a man who lacked nothing, to be considered both desirable and interesting. He was well read, sensitive, intelligent, even handsome. There were no dark shadows, no mystery about him: Manfred was exactly what met the eye, and what met the eye was more than satisfactory.

Enrica had admired his conversation, she had appreciated the way he had avoided topics that her father might find unpleasant, in spite of her brother-in-law's attempts to steer him onto more extreme positions. He might even share those opinions, but he had displayed great sensitivity toward Giulio. And she had been impressed by the way he had interacted with the little ones, to whom he had given plenty of attention and with whom he had immediately gotten along famously. He would be a wonderful father, Manfred would.

Of whose children? burst in once again that irritating little voice. Your children? Yes, she replied, mine, and why not? Don't I have a right to be happy too? Can't I have a home of my own, a family of my own? Where? In Germany? asked the same little voice. In Bavaria? And will your children be fair-haired? Will they speak a foreign language?

It will be up to me to turn them into the children I want, she told herself proudly. I will know how to raise them as Italians.

She ran her eyes over the wave-swamped rocks, while the sea stroked the land as if it were velvet. Where are you? she suddenly thought. Where are you now? Why aren't you here with me, to explain?

Lunchtime was emptying the street. The sun was hitting Enrica's eyes through the lenses of her eyeglasses; the light breeze that was blowing in from the sea forced her to clap her hat down on her head with one hand, while the other hand grasped her handbag. She turned around.

And she saw him.

It seemed to her that mind and heart had ganged up on her to play a cruel trick. Her heart skipped a beat; it skipped another. Then it made up for lost time by starting to gallop dementedly in her throat and in her ears. Oh my God, she thought. Oh my God, now where can I run away to?

Ricciardi found himself face-to-face with her as he was leaving the yacht club, his mind full of wind and sand as if he had been exposed to a desert storm. The conversation with

Duke Marangolo had dug into an intimate personal territory that he would never have wanted to stir up, and now he felt quite uneasy. The reference to his father, to his own family, and to a past that he, irresponsibly, had never paid much attention to. To be called by the title and name that he'd turned his back on for so many years, to understand for the first time that he was not, in all likelihood, the man that his parents had hoped he would become, had shaken him to his very foundations.

And then there was love. He had been in the presence of an enormous, extreme sentiment, which had more than filled a life like that of the duke, a life that could have been full of every other sort of thing. The image of a young woman on a July morning and that man's existence was changed once and for all. And yet it was clear that Marangolo would never have willingly given up that unattainable and unattained love. He held it close, he regretted nothing, save for not having done more to help a woman who had rejected him.

He had thought about himself, Ricciardi had. About the punishment that he inflicted upon himself every day, and the love that he felt for Enrica. About the certainty that he, too, would be nothing but a witness to the future of the woman he loved, a future in which he played no part.

On his way out of the building, he had crossed paths with Livia. On the far side of a large plate-glass window, illuminated by the bright sunshine on the terrace of the yacht club, she was laughing in the midst of a court of six men, all of them doing their best to get her to notice them, all of them captivated by her beauty. The two of them had exchanged a brief, fleeting glance, and the woman's laughter had died in her throat, betraying clear evidence of suffering and lack of sleep beneath the cunning little red hat and the hair done up in the latest fashion, under the rouge and the lipstick. Her eyes had filled with pain and sorrow, but only for an instant: she had immediately started laughing again, flirting with her suitors, defying the unfriendly glares from the other women confined to her shadow.

He had hurried out of the club, feeling a sensation of malaise rise in his chest that was a form of nausea with himself, and an awareness that he belonged to neither the world of Livia nor that of Enrica.

Livia and Enrica on the other side of a window, and he always on the wrong side of that glass.

Then, out in the street, while he was trying to concentrate on the Roccaspina case, a woman, the only other human being who was passing at that moment on that stretch of street, had turned around and looked at him.

And she was Enrica.

They stood there looking at each other, both of them overwhelmed by the way that their thoughts had coincided with reality, both of them aware that there was no escape route, no way to avoid an encounter for which neither was prepared, for which they would never be prepared, both of them with their heads full of wind and sand and neither in the slightest degree capable of formulating a thought, much less articulating a word.

Both of them with their hearts in their throats.

Ricciardi walked toward her. He wished that, for once, he was wearing a hat, so that he could doff it in greeting, but as usual he was without one.

"*Buongiorno.* I . . . beg your pardon. I didn't expect to find you here and . . . I beg your pardon."

Enrica wanted to smile amiably. She would have liked to say nothing more than *buongiorno* to you, and then go her way cursing the moment that she had decided she needed to fill her eyes with the sea.

Instead her heart took possession of her mouth.

"My pardon? You beg my pardon? And for what, would

you be begging my pardon? For having written me, for having . . . looked for so long and then turned and left? For not having reached out to me again? For having made me believe that you . . . that you and I . . . "

Her eyes filled with tears, fogging over her lenses. She bit her lower lip and took a deep breath. Don't cry, stupid girl. Don't cry, confound you.

Behind her, a seagull stared out to sea in boredom.

His eyes were wide open, as if he were afraid, as if he were in some nightmare from which he was unable to awaken.

Behind him, the two dead children had their arms wrapped around each other.

" . . . another man."

He had barely murmured. He didn't even know what he wanted to say.

"What did you say? What about another man?"

He let all the air out of his lungs in a single breath.

"Another man?! There's another woman, another person in your life. Or am I mistaken? I, I . . . " and here she tapped her forefinger on her chest, "I saw you. I saw you when you were . . . I saw you."

Enrica thought about the brightly lit window that she had noticed the night before, when she was going to put away the cookware, the warm shiver that she had felt in her chest. And she felt a bottomless rage swell within her, the reaction to her pride, so brutally trodden underfoot.

That man, who had deceived her and abandoned her; that man whom she had seen many times with the woman from out of town; that man who had made her believe that he was in love with her, and now was upbraiding her for having invited a person to dinner. For all he knew, the guest could have been a friend of her brother-in-law's, or a distant relative: how dare he accuse her?

She clenched her jaw and hissed.

"Why, how dare you, you, how dare you talk to me about how there's another man? What right do you have? Have you ever told me, or written to me, that you care for me? I, I would have waited for you for who knows how long, don't you understand that? All I wanted was a gesture, a single gesture and I . . . But what good would it do? What good is all this . . . " She waved her hand in the air, incoherently. The tears were rolling down her cheeks in an unstoppable flood. "What is all this sea any good for, can you tell me that? What purpose does it serve, the sea?"

With that last, absurd question, she turned on her heel to leave.

After a few steps, she stopped and said: "Please forgive me. Allow me to offer my condolences for the death of Signora Rosa. As you may know, I cared for her very much."

Ricciardi remained with a hand half-lifted, his eyes staring into nothingness. He just couldn't understand what all that sea was good for.

XXXVII

Maione was seething with the urge to tell Ricciardi all about Laprece, the chauffeur who had been fired much too summarily, and he was just as curious to hear how the meeting with the famous Duke Marangolo had gone, the man who had been in the Roccaspina home the evening before the murder. And so, the instant they informed him that his superior officer had returned, he galloped down the main staircase.

By now it was evening and the brigadier was beginning to feel anxious; the commissario had left the building at a little past ten that morning and he had been forced to cover for his absence in one of the useless meetings called by that idiot Garzo. He'd made up an urgent phone call from Dr. Modo at the hospital for a suspicious wounding, and he had put in a call to his friend the physician just in case anyone had had the unfortunate idea of checking the situation out. The doctor had stifled a laugh: there were all the suspicious woundings anyone could think to ask for, so really as far as that went there was an embarrassment of riches, and at the very least, there was always the pounding headache he was suffering from, about which, he informed the brigadier with sibylline archness, Ricciardi knew a little something.

Maione had hung up without delving into that statement. He was left with a feeling of uneasiness: the commissario continued to behave strangely, he was no longer the man he thought he knew so well.

His worry rose to the highest levels when, after knocking and pointlessly waiting for permission to enter the office, he had made up his mind to simply open the door himself without it. Ricciardi was sitting at his desk, his head bowed over the desktop as if he were reading something. But there was no document in front of him.

Maione picked up his superior officer's jacket from the floor, where it lay at the foot of the coatrack, and hung it up.

"Commissario . . . Commissa' . . . you're all right, aren't you? Let me get you something, a little water, a cup of ersatz coffee . . . no, maybe not ersatz coffee. Please, Commissa', answer me, you're worrying me."

Ricciardi slowly turned his face up to him. He was ashen, his eyes were sunken, his hair matted to his forehead in messy clumps as if he'd been out in the rain for a long time. The brigadier felt his heart surge in his chest.

"Commissa', what's the matter? Should I go summon the doctor, maybe you have a little bit of a temperature, or maybe . . . "

Ricciardi lifted his hand to stop him.

"No. No. Don't worry, Raffaele. I took . . . I took a long walk, I needed to clear my head. It's hot out, it's very hot, and I sweated a little. Don't worry."

Maione scrutinized him.

"Commissa', forgive me, but I just can't keep from worrying. I know that losing Signora Rosa was a hard blow, I understand that. But you need to recover and find some sort of peace, this habit of not speaking isn't good for you. Let's do this: tonight you come and eat with my family, and you'll see, you'll feel better immediately."

Ricciardi stared at the brigadier as if he were speaking to him in a foreign tongue. Then he smiled sweetly, which was something that, if possible, frightened his underling even more.

"It's not necessary, trust me. I just wanted to enjoy a lovely September day. So tell me, is there news?"

After a moment of perplexed silence, Maione decided to comply with the commissario's suggestion and simply discuss the case they were working on.

He was finally able to tell him about Laprece's visit, with an abundance of details and doing his best to recount the chauffeur's words verbatim. When he was done Ricciardi nodded. Maione couldn't seem to shake the unpleasant impression that he was sick, or drunk, or possibly both.

"Is that what he said? That, since the father was dead, they no longer had any need of him? And did it sound to you as if he was telling the truth? I mean, did he sound sincere?"

The brigadier shrugged his shoulders.

"Well, yes, Commissa', I think so. And how about you, how did it go? What did the duke have to tell you?"

Ricciardi told Maione all about his conversation with Marangolo, leaving out nothing. The tone of his voice was flat, expressionless; his green eyes looked out into the void. The brigadier was increasingly uneasy. In the end he said: "In other words, Commissa', we're gathering plenty of important information but we still can't get away from the likeliest hypothesis, which is that Piro was murdered by the Count of Roccaspina. Even the duke is convinced of it, and the chauffeur didn't say anything particularly interesting."

Ricciardi murmured:

"You're wrong there, Raffaele. The chauffeur did tell us something: Piro went to the Convent of the Madonna Incoronata on two consecutive days, and that wasn't something he usually did. As you know, I don't believe in coincidences. We need to talk with the widow again. We need to figure out if she left something out."

Maione pulled his pocket watch out and looked at it.

"But isn't it a little late, now, Commissa'? Maybe tomorrow . . . "

Ricciardi stood up abruptly from his desk.

"No, we'd better do it right away. Otherwise, she might find out that we spoke to the chauffeur and arrange for him not to answer our questions. Remember, we're moving through unofficial channels and they can block us whenever they like. But don't you worry, you go on home, I'll take care of it on my own."

Maione was already at the door; he was holding Ricciardi's jacket open for him.

"Just think if I'm about to let you go on your own, Commissa'. It's already clear that it was a mistake to let you go on your own this morning. Come on."

They ran into Piro's widow a short distance from her front door, as she was returning home. Her face looked strained and her eyes were red. It looked as if she'd just finished crying.

Ricciardi, faintly embarrassed, said to her: "*Buonasera*, Signora. We wanted to speak with you, but perhaps it would be better if we came by some other time."

"No. No, absolutely no problem; after all, by now I'm used to my troubles. Would you care to come upstairs?"

The commissario shook his head.

"That's not necessary, it's just a quick thing. We only need a minute."

The woman pulled a handkerchief out of her sleeve and blew her nose.

"Go ahead, then."

"The business relationship that your husband had with Count Roccaspina, would you have any idea of its nature?"

The woman made a face.

"That damned murderer must have owed my husband a great deal of money, that's something I know. I told you, I helped Ludovico keep the ledger books."

"And what did your husband say about this large line of credit? Was he not afraid that it might not be repaid?"

"No. He never had that fear. Every time that the sum increased, I would ask him whether it might not be wiser to stop, but he'd laugh and say: this is the surest money we'll ever see. I never knew why. My husband, you see, never liked to talk about certain matters. But he was very messy, and he needed me to take care of accounts."

"And is that how it was up to the very end?" asked Maione. "Right up to the quarrel the day before the murder?"

"Certainly. Until that argument, and I repeat that I have no idea what it was about, Roccaspina was my husband's best client, at least, that's what Ludovico said."

Ricciardi tried to insist.

"And you don't know where your husband got the money that he was lending to Roccaspina, is that right?"

Costanza Piro furrowed her brow.

"What are you trying to say, Commissario? My husband invested the money of the institutions that he administered, paying interest and living off the difference. A risky, dangerous line of work, but Ludovico was a man of great courage and intelligence. He deserved every lira that he earned; his only thought was his family. And now I'm all alone and I don't know where to turn."

She began to cry, sobbing into her handkerchief. Maione and Ricciardi exchanged a glance. Then the commissario said his farewells.

"*Grazie*, Signora. We won't disturb you any further. Have a good evening."

The woman bowed her head briefly and turned toward the street door, but before she could go back inside, Ricciardi called out to her.

"One last thing, Signora. Could you tell me why your husband, the day he died and the day before that, as well, should have asked his driver to take him up to the Convent of the Madonna Incoronata?"

Signora Piro froze in place, with one hand holding the door, as if she'd just been turned into a pillar of salt. She turned her head a few degrees and, without even bothering to look at the two policemen, hissed, flatly: "Now that I think about it, gentlemen, yes, you are disturbing me. You're disturbing me a great deal. And now I'll have to beg you not to come back again, because we already have enough pain and sorrow without you coming around to stir it up and make it worse. I hope I never see you again, otherwise I would be forced to reach out to some of the highly placed acquaintances of my husband, and believe me, there are quite a few, and ask them to help us defend our family's peace. Have a good evening."

And she disappeared into the atrium.

SECOND INTERLUDE

T he old man stops playing at the end of the refrain. The young man observes his hands.

It's incredible the metamorphosis they undergo when they're not moving across the face of his little instrument. On the strings they flutter like butterflies, every single touch is firm and precise, the pressure of his fingers never knows uncertainty. As soon as the last echo of the music dissolves into the air, leaving a legacy of the heartbreaking yearning of the notes, those hands go back to being a pair of gnarly claws run through with tremors.

The young man realizes that once again he's been holding his breath, and he lets out the air in a subdued puff. Pe' te ne vulè caccià, he thinks. The man burns his own hand, in order to shoo her away.

During the second verse something happened to him. He stopped thinking about the execution, the succession of chords, the musical solutions. He stopped following the song with his hands, imitating the path of the fingers across the neck of the instrument, as if he himself were playing or even as if he were accompanying the old man on the guitar.

He stopped.

And he followed the story. The story of the forty-five-year-old man who, in the first verse, was watching the moth flying in circles in the night, irresistibly attracted by its own ruin; and that attraction was the letter that she, the beautiful young woman, had written to him. I love you, don't you understand that? I love you. The man, who believes that love was impossible, tries to *protect her, in the first verse; he says to her: moth, this is a candle, not a flower. It may attract you with its luminosity, but it can't feed you. It can only kill you. And you would only die in atrocious torment.*

That's how the first verse was, and now the young man thinks that this second part means something quite different.

The old man places the instrument in the case and gets up from the armchair. The young man half stands up from the stool, to help him, but the old man gestures to him not to. He drags his steps toward the window, he pulls back the shutter and throws the window wide open. All the blue in the world explodes out of that rectangle, in contrast with the dusty gray shadows that fill the room. From where he sits, the young man looks at the old man's razor-sharp, crooked profile, the intensely fine network of wrinkles, the eye squinting against the light. The trembling hands, gripping the windowsill, as if he were perching, in every way like the pigeons that coo on the nearby rain gutter.

In a soft voice he asks: what's it good for, all this sea?

The young man is still thinking about the verse that has just ended. He's sung it every night for years, but this is the first time he's heard it.

Maestro, he says, the man is afraid. Is that right? He's afraid. He's defending himself, not the girl. At least, not her alone.

The old man doesn't take his eyes off the sea, but he answers him: yes, very good. You're starting to understand the story. The second verse doesn't explain the first one, it doesn't carry the metaphor of the moth into the real world. The girl and the moth are two distinct, separate things. Both of them flutter, the moth from flower to flower, the girl from man to man. Because really, the girl isn't all that naïve and fragile after all, or at least she doesn't know that she is. And so he, yes, is every bit as afraid for himself as he is for her. But do you know what he's saying?

The young man murmurs: yes, I know. At least, I think I do.

He's saying that there's nothing he can do about it. That he can't stop her, that he doesn't have the strength. He begs her to go away, because he is powerless.

The old man turns around and smiles at him, and his creased face wrinkles up a little more.

Precisely, he says. He's explaining to her, or he's trying to explain to her, that she's playing with something that actually burns, wounds, and can even ultimately kill.

The young man raises his dark eyes and looks at the old man standing in the rectangular frame of the window, with all that useless sea behind him.

But then what happened, Maestro? The letter, he . . . Did he answer her? Did he want her? Did she leave? Did she stay? How did it end?

The old man doesn't answer immediately. He drags himself toward the armchair, he sits down with a faint lament. His bones crunch with a flat sound. One trembling hand reaches out to take the instrument and bring it back to his lap, as if his lap were another instrument case.

He says, in a low voice: It doesn't matter. All that matters is the song, that's the story. But it's nice that you wonder what became of the two of them, how it turned out. It's nice because it means you've understood that the song is a story. Bravo.

He plays a chord: sweet and desperate, suffering and piteous. A call for help, an account of an unrequited laceration. All in a single, miserable chord. The young man thinks: I'll never be able to do that. I can never be as good as him; and with his hands in that condition. I'll never be able to play like that. And if I can't play like that, then I can't tell a story.

He only thought it, a series of disconnected flashes in his head, but the old man stops and turns around to stare at him with his eyes sunken in wrinkles.

No, don't even think it. You must merely eliminate the barriers, it takes a little time, but once you've figured this out, that

you're telling a story with your hands, then you'll really be good.
Even better than me, because your hands don't tremble.

   The young man feels a long shiver go down his back; I have
to be careful about what I think, he reflects, absurdly. This one
can hear me think.

   The old man starts to tell his story again with his hands.
For the last verse.

Torna, va', palomma 'e notte,
dint'a ll'ombra addo' si' nata!
Torna a 'st'aria 'mbarzamata
ca te sape cunzulà!

Dint' 'o scuro e pe' me sulo
'sta cannela arde e se struje,
ma c'ardesse a tutt'e dduje,
nun 'o ppozzo suppurtà!

Vattenn' 'a lloco!
Vattenne, pazzarella!
Va', palummella, e torna,
e torna a 'st'aria accussí fresca e bella!
'O bbí ca i' pure
mm'abbaglio chianu chiano,
e ca mm'abbrucio 'a mano
pe' te ne vulè caccià?

(Go on, go back, butterfly of the night,
into the shadows where you were born!
Go back into this resin-scented air
that knows how to console you!

In the darkness and for me alone
this candle burns and suffers,

but that it should burn us both,
that I cannot accept!

Get out of here!
Get away, silly thing!
Go, little butterfly, and go back
go back into this air
so cool and clear!
You see that I, too,
am slowly being dazzled
and that I'm burning my hand
as I try to shoo you away?)

XXXVIII

Ricciardi was walking down the broad boulevard, heading for the office, after an almost entirely sleepless night. It had been difficult to wait for the dawn, with the images that kept chasing each other behind and before his eyes, faces and expressions, and sun and sea and dead children embracing to remind him of his pain and sorrow. And in his ears the confusion was certainly no less, with the words of the duke and Piro's wife and especially Enrica: it all piled up in his weary, vigilant mind, sleepy yet awake, grinding incessantly away at the past and the future to reconstruct a senseless present.

He had run into her, he could scarcely believe it. He had met her on the street after spying on her the night before through the gap between his curtains and he had even spoken to her about that man, thinking back to the night on Ischia and what he had seen from his hiding place in the shrubbery, and she had thrown the blame back on him. But how was it his fault? He was alone. He'd been left with no one to think about him. Whereas Enrica had a family as numerous as an army. And someone who kissed her under the stars.

And after all, what the devil was it supposed to mean: What is all this sea any good for? What could he have said to her in reply?

Ricciardi was walking, his eyes downcast, his hands in his pockets. He was walking, with the same wind and sand in his head as the day before. And the wind whirled crazily around even the few, scattered thoughts he had about the Roccaspina case, and he could tell he wasn't applying himself to it with the proper degree of dedication. The contessa's composed suffering when she'd asked his help would have deserved at least the clarity of a refusal, rather than the neglect of a lack of attention.

The street was gradually filling up with people, a little later than had the network of *vicoli* that extended uphill and downhill. The commissario listened to the calls from one apartment to another, the sound of the shutters opening to greet the new day. This is how it always was, at seven in the morning: another world, a minuscule universe of faces and sentiments.

A festive group of children went running past him, bookbags on their backs. There were schools that had begun to take in students for preparatory courses for the new classes; that was the hybrid period when the last barefoot beachgoers in shorts crossed paths with the first students in school uniforms.

Not far away, the commissario saw a figure that in terms of stature could have just as easily been one of the kids on their way to the beach or to school, but whose uniform eliminated all doubt. When he got close to him, he stopped, intrigued.

"Don Pierino, *buongiorno*. Why are you out and about so early, and in this neighborhood?"

The little priest gave him a broad smile.

"Very simple, Commissario. I was waiting for you. Can you spare me a minute?"

Ricciardi had first met Don Pierino a year and a half earlier, during his investigation into the murder of Livia's husband. They had struck up an acquaintance, even though they were as different as they could possibly be. The priest was cheerful, extroverted, an impassioned lover of the opera, while the policeman, who among other things felt a certain annoyed distaste for performances based on fictional sentiments, was the exact opposite. But they both shared a sincere, profound sense of empathy for the sufferings of others, a territory that was vast enough to accommodate, if not a genuine full-fledged friendship, at least a relationship of cordial amiability.

"Why, certainly, Father," Ricciardi therefore said. "What's going on? Do you need help?"

Don Pierino lifted a hand.

"Ah, certainly, I could use a great deal of help: people falling sick, children who have nothing to eat, heads of households tossed into prison who lack the money to defend themselves from absurd charges; poor women forced to become prostitutes in order to feed their families, victims of loan sharks, you name it, we've got it. But all these are things you already know about, and in fact you are one of the very few who fight on the same side as me. Do you think I don't know that?"

"We do our best, Father. But tell me, now, what can I do for you?"

The priest locked arms with him and pointed to the street leading to police headquarters.

"I'll walk you to the corner, if you don't mind. There's something I want to talk to you about."

They strolled off together.

They really were an odd couple. Every so often they'd cross paths with someone who knew one or the other of them, and the reactions were, according to the specific invididual, quite diverse. Ricciardi had to admit that Don Pierino, without a doubt, was far more liked and appreciated. Certainly, a priest is far more likely to win hearts than a policeman, he thought to himself, but probably his glowering persona didn't help matters either.

"Commissario," said the man of the cloth, "I'd like to ask you to make an effort of imagination. Try to imagine a priest, let's say, an assistant parish priest, beautiful to behold and good-hearted, tall and fair-haired, in odor of sanctity. Can you do that?"

In spite of himself, and despite the miserable night he'd had, Ricciardi found himself smiling.

"Yes, I have no difficulties, especially right now. Please go on."

"Well, now, let us suppose that one day this extraordinary model of beauty and virtue receives a visit in the sacristy from a friend of his, a good and respectable person, but very reserved: one of those people who would sooner let themselves be tortured than let any personal confidences escape them. And let us suppose that this person sits down and starts chattering away like he's never done before, and that the assistant parish priest realizes that his words conceal a great deal of suffering. All right?"

Ricciardi's curiosity was aroused, but he had not the slightest idea of what Don Pierino was driving at.

"Yes, Father," he replied.

"Well then," Don Pierino resumed, slowing his pace, "in your opinion what should that tall and fair-haired and holy assistant parish priest do? Simply accept the information confided in him by his friend, not under the seal of confession, by the way, just to be clear, and try to offer him some spiritual comfort, or else take the initiative to try to lend him a hand?"

The commissario froze in his footsteps.

"Father, if this is something that concerns my work, I beg you, don't be afraid. We operate with great discretion and without revealing the provenance of any information concerning a crime that . . . "

Don Pierino shook his head with some vigor.

"No, no, Commissa', what did you think I was talking about? No murder, for the love of all that's holy! I know perfectly well that in that case I would have been able to speak to you, but I would have come to your office to talk to you there. No, instead, as you can clearly see, I've simply waited for you to happen by on a street corner. I remembered how common it is for me to go and officiate for some poor sick man and run into you around this part of town early in the morning."

"Then what is this about, Father?"

Don Pierino started walking again.

"Now then, Commissa', this is a fairly delicate matter. And trust me, I don't really know where to begin. It seems strange, you know, but it's not necessarily the case that a priest really loves to stick his nose into other people's business. We're supposed to do it as a profession, but we don't like it. At least, I don't."

Outside the front entrance of an apartment house, Ricciardi's eyes were greeted by the sight of the plummeting suicide who had died two days earlier. He was vivid and real; to Ricciardi it almost seemed that if he had reached out a hand he could have touched the man's shattered cranium and the deformed abdomen with the crushed rib cage. Kneeling on the street at the exact spot where he had died, upon a brownish stain that still hadn't been washed away, he kept repeating: My love, I won't spend a single minute more without you.

Caught off guard, Ricciardi started. Don Pierino followed his gaze and focused on the large bloodstain in the street.

"You heard about him, eh? Professor De Stefano. When she was alive, his wife always came to Mass, then, once she died, he stopped coming. I often thought of going to see him, but what with one thing and another . . . "

Ricciardi heard the poor old man's voice pulsate in his head. Love that kills, love that sweeps everything in its path, love that destroys. Two young women walked past laughing, their pleated skirts fluttering in the wake of their brisk strides, swift and full of life, their heels striking the sidewalk, their handbags, slung over their shoulders, swinging at their hips. Life. Death.

My love, I won't spend a single minute more without you.

"Please get to the point. I have to get back to the office."

Don Pierino stared at him with consternation. Ricciardi's change of tone, the coldness of his words had disoriented him.

"But . . . did I say something to hurt your feelings, Commissario? If I did, please forgive me, I talk and I talk and sometimes I don't realize what I'm saying."

Ricciardi ran his hand over his eyes.

"No, Father. Quite the contrary, I hope you'll forgive me. I haven't been sleeping well for a while now, and I always have something of a headache."

"Yes, yes, I understand. We haven't seen each other since I came to see you to extend my condolences for poor Signora Rosa, and to be perfectly frank, you actually don't look especially well. This confirms my instinct that it was a good idea to come and see you. I have a question to ask you, Commissario. Just one question."

"Be my guest."

"How much longer do you plan to condemn yourself to this pain and sorrow that, for whatever reason, you carry in your body?"

Ricciardi stopped again and looked at the priest. Behind him, the horrendous image of the suicide continued to repeat the mad litany of his love. Let's hope that somewhere, even if it's in hell, you have the comfort that you're asking of her, he thought.

"Father, please be clearer."

Don Pierino hesitated, then threw himself into it.

"This tall and fair-haired assistant parish priest of my little fairy tale cares very much about his friend. And his friend adores his daughter, a delicate and kindhearted young woman, with a vulnerable soul. A young woman who might—as she senses that the man she truly loves is moving away from her—make a choice for her own life that isn't perhaps the right one, a choice that she might live to regret, that she might pay for with profound unhappiness. And so the tall and fair-haired assistant parish priest would really like to tell the man who holds this young woman's heart in his hands to stop building walls behind which he himself might someday find he's a prisoner. To tell him to open up to life and emotions."

Ricciardi turned and stared into the empty air, which to him wasn't empty at all.

My love, the dead man said again.

"And in your opinion, Father, what would this man reply to the tall and fair-haired assistant parish priest? Wouldn't he tell him, perhaps, that walls do exist and that he's not the one who builds them, that it is life, and destiny, that builds those walls? Wouldn't he tell him that sometimes you might wish and want, so very badly, but there are some obstacles that are insurmountable?"

Don Pierino shook his head, decisively.

"No, he couldn't tell him that. Because nothing is insurmountable, where there's a bit of genuine will. Happiness is something you achieve, not something you sit around waiting for, as if it were your due. The Lord has endowed us with the ability to choose, Commissario. That is the greatest gift He ever gave mankind."

My love, I won't spend a single minute more without you.

"Loving someone means wishing for their happiness and welfare, Father. You ought to know that. And when you're certain that you yourself are the evil, the harm, then you must stay away from them. To prevent the very person you care most about from burning themselves in the candle's flame."

Don Pierino, struck by the gravity of Ricciardi's last words, remained for a few moments in silence. Then his voice came out sounding slightly more broken and overwrought.

"You see, Commissario, souls are fragile. Beautiful, fragile creatures, made of glass, they let light and heat through, but they're incapable of containing them. Souls are made of glass, and if you treat them too roughly, they're liable to crack and emit inaccurate reflections. Never underestimate the soul, Commissario. Have the courage to gaze deep into it, the surface is transparent, it will let you see."

Ricciardi turned his gaze away from the image of the dead man.

"Tell that to the tall and fair-haired assistant parish priest. Everyone loves as best they can, and in the manner they think best. Have a good day."

And he walked off.

Left alone on the street corner, Don Pierino whispered a few words, his mouth twisted into a bitter grimace: "I will pray for you every day, Commissario Ricciardi. Every single day."

XXXIX

Bianca Borgati of the Marchesi di Zisa, Contessa Palmieri di Roccaspina, had three lire and seventy-five cents in her pocketbook. Which meant that she could afford to take the trolley to Poggioreale, both there and back.

She made up her mind, after thinking it over very thoroughly. She didn't know whether she'd ever unravel the mystery, but she was certain that she wanted to tell her husband, while looking him in the face, that it was all over between them. Whatever else he might have in mind and however he might want to act, when he got out of prison, she wouldn't be there to meet him.

She walked down the alley that ran past the front door of the palazzo, keeping her eyes fixed straight ahead of her, straight as an arrow, as if she were attired in regal garments instead of her usual, threadbare black dress and the shoes whose uppers, with all her tireless buffing and polishing, had been reduced to nothing much thicker than a silk veil. As usual, before leaving the apartment, she had been subjected to the examination of Assunta, the ancient servant who had taken care of her since she was a little girl. Those stern eyes checked everything, from the pin that fastened her little hat to her hair to the strength of the buttons and the clasps on her earrings. Their economic ruin, the financial collapse, the shortness of resources had done nothing to alter the attitudes of her old governess: the Signora Contessa was still and always would be the Signora Contessa, even if she were poor now.

And if was going to appear in public, it would be as the Signora Contessa.

Bianca knew very well that's not how it was. She could feel upon her the eyes of shopkeepers, strolling vendors, the women of the *vicolo*, and idlers who whiled away the day doing nothing but gossip. She thought she could hear their whispers, their malign satisfaction at the last member of a family that had long been synonymous with greatness and wealth. For this, too, she owed Romualdo a debt of thanks.

Now she was on the main street, where she could more easily mingle with the busy and variegated humanity that was out doing its various errands. It was strange, but she didn't really have it in for her husband on account of his bad habit, nor for the devastating effects that it had had on her own life; he had paid and was continuing to pay in person for the many errors he had committed. As for her, once Carlo Maria Marangolo had told her that he considered her to be exceptional precisely because of her ability to distinguish between important matters and trivial details, in the midst of so many people who could see no difference between one and the other. Bianca had replied to him that in this, as in so much else, he was overvaluing her, but her friend's words had still pleased her.

Skirting close to the wall, she went past one of those piazzas that had been reduced to little more than an enormous construction site due to the reclamation of the entire area. She often thought about the public works that the regime had undertaken in the city, and if they were as good as everyone claimed, then the result would surely be a small heaven on earth. She didn't know what to think about that, but she was a bit sorry to lose the little shops and ateliers, the *bassi* or grim ground-floor apartments, the *vicoli* or alleyways, the ancient buildings that were being razed to the soil to make way for square buildings and piazzas, white, with austere rectangular windows. They gave her the shivers, those buildings; they looked like gigantic collective caskets.

A part in this sudden transformation had certainly been played by the earthquake that had struck in the July of two years ago; the city, built of yellow tufa stone, had tolerated the shock rather well, but the fallen cornices had been an excellent excuse to accelerate the project. The desire to destroy, to encourage the desire to rebuild.

For that matter, wasn't that exactly what Bianca was doing?

No, she thought as she fended her way through the vegetable and fruit stalls in a small neighborhood street market. I didn't want to destroy anything. All I wanted was a normal life.

She crossed the piazza in front of City Hall, enjoying the pleasant shadow of the trees lining the center of it. The dark silhouette of the castle loomed like a strong and gentle protector. The children played with balls and hoops under the vigilant eyes of mothers and nannies. There, thought Bianca. A normal life. Children, a home: nothing more, nothing less than what these women have, these women who spend their mornings in the public parks, in search of a little cool air, a little shade from the sun. No luxuries, no holidays in the mountains, no receptions and jewelry and carriages and automobiles.

Maybe, she thought to herself, right then and there an automobile would be useful in getting to Poggioreale prison. The thought made her smile: arriving at the prison with a chauffeur, that way she certainly wouldn't attract attention.

The trolley stop that she had chosen was the one on Via Depretis. She could have caught the trolley at the Piazza Dante stop, it was more or less the same distance from home, but she would have been followed by all the eyes in the whole *vicolo*, feasting on the picture of her, standing in line with the wives and mothers of hardened criminals, murderers and thieves at the entrance to the terrible fortress where Romualdo had chosen to live the next few decades of his life. Because there was no doubt in her mind on the matter: it had been a conscious choice. Her husband was innocent.

The trolley was very crowded, but no one even vaguely resembled that tall, refined, haughty woman, who looked like a queen, with down-at-the-heels clothing but utterly regal beauty. Students, mothers with their children, men with white hats and fancy bowties. Bianca stood off to one side, resigning herself to a wait that, fortunately, was not long. The trolley car came screeching to a halt and a small river of people climbed aboard, intensifying the struggle for room.

With some difficulty, the contessa also managed to force her way on board, though she was largely uninclined to indulge in the shoving and elbowing necessary to make space for herself. She paid the fifty cents to the ticket taker, who shot her a glance of idle curiosity. When he saw her, a well dressed middle-aged gentlemen immediately stood to offer her his seat. She thanked him with a smile and a nod of the head, and sat down. Beside her, a fat woman with two children in her arms shot her a hostile glance; from one of the little ones, who'd been ineptly diapered, came a terrible odor. Bianca pulled a handkerchief out of her purse and pressed it to her mouth.

The woman commented in a loud voice.

"If the signora has such a sensitive nose, she can just walk instead of ride, or cling to the doors like the others!"

The trolley, in fact, was operating with a certain number of nonpaying passengers: a sizable number of *scugnizzi* was hanging on to the back of the car and to the running boards that paying passengers used to climb into the trolley, and they emitted a cheerful chorus of cries at every curve and every time the driver sounded the distinctive trolley horn. The vehicle pushed its way through cars, carriages, and carts drawn variously by donkeys, horses, and men, and which transported all manner of merchandise. As they gradually moved from the center of town out into the less prosperous quarters of the city, the trolley ran along past rows of hovels and shanties that looked as if they were about to collapse in so many clouds of dust, outside of which hordes of children played naked and barefoot amidst chickens and geese.

Who knows how many cities there are in this city, thought Bianca as she tried to keep her mind off the odor and the glares from her seatmate. Who knows how many emotions boil, sink, resurface, and then plunge down again, leaving traces only in those who are touched by them directly.

She thought of Ricciardi. Perhaps she'd thought of him, she mused, because she imagined, by the very nature of things, a policeman must deal with the traces of emotions. By begging the commissario to find out the motive that had driven Romualdo to take the blame for a murder he hadn't committed, she had authorized him to delve with complete impunity into their lives; and therefore, into her own.

She knew that he had gone to talk with Carlo Maria, and she continued to wonder what the two men had said to each other.

A good friend, Carlo Maria. An old, dear friend. She was certain that he harbored delicate and powerful emotions toward her, and had done so for some time. A woman can always tell when someone falls in love with her. Still she had never wanted him to make an open and explicit declaration. He was too dear to her to be met with a refusal.

Now he was sick and she wished she could comfort him, but she was afraid she might be leading him on and therefore wound him. Still, she'd been unable to avoid acquainting Ricciardi with the role that the duke had played in the whole affair. Bianca hadn't wanted to know too much about it, but she was convinced that he had been acting as her guardian angel and that, after his fashion, he had tried to steer Romualdo away from the brink of even greater ruination.

At the very least, as her own husband had told her, he would manage to save the palazzo.

Every morning a number of suppliers brought Assunta various kinds of foodstuffs, and with the beginning of every season, linen for the household. Bianca was certain that it was Carlo Maria who sent all these things, but no one had ever revealed the name of their benefactor.

My poor friend, she thought, you do all that you can, but there are things that lie beyond the reach even of the power of your money.

As the trolley screeched and rocked its way closer to the broad street at the end of which sat the prison, Bianca decided that perhaps Ricciardi, that singular, shadowy individual with the exceedingly strange green eyes, might discover what had really happened, and by so doing, give her a way, perhaps the only way, to find a sort of serenity. Or perhaps she herself would be able to achieve that, shortly, when she looked her husband in the eye for the very last time.

She got in line with the other visitors, keeping her eyes fixed ahead of her; she could feel the eyes of the more curious members of the crowd upon her.

Everyone, guards and members of the prisoners' families, belonged to the same class of people.

Everyone except for her.

With her gloved hand she presented the authorization signed by the warden and issued at Attilio's request. Until the very last, the lawyer had discouraged her from going, because Romualdo did not want to see her; Attilio had even offered to take her there himself, but hadn't insisted when she had firmly rejected the offer.

Bianca suspected that Moscato wasn't particularly happy at the idea of meeting Romualdo, and she had wondered why: perhaps because he knew he'd never be paid, that he would be forced to consider the work he did as a tribute to an old friendship.

They ushered her into the visiting room, which was packed

with people as usual. This time, she felt no uncertainty and sat down, well aware of what would be appearing on the far side of the heavy grate of rusted metal.

Or at least, she thought she was. But when Romualdo came in, her heart leapt into her throat. In the two months that had passed since her last visit, when he had warned her never to come visit him again, he had shrunk to half his former size. He looked like a skeleton exhumed after burial and dressed in the clothing of a healthy man.

In comparison, Marangolo with his terminal illness looked like a veritable athlete.

The stubble of his shaven hair covered his cranium, to the exclusion of broad patches of bald scalp. His flesh, taut over his cheekbones, sagged flaccid at his cheeks, and his eyes were lost in the deep sockets. On his chapped lips, there were clots of dried blood.

The man remained standing in front of his wife. The guard at his side gestured for him to sit, but he refused.

"The signora won't be staying, rest assured. It's a matter of no more than a minute."

Bianca had been left openmouthed. She started to cry, grasping futilely for the handkerchief she kept up her sleeve. Romualdo heaved a sigh of annoyance.

"Spare me your compassion, wife. I have no need of it. What are you doing here? I though I'd made myself clear. I thought that at least I'd be able live free of your visits."

The guard, who was required by regulations to remain present, seemed ill at ease. He was accustomed to conversations of quite a different nature.

Bianca struggled to master her breathing.

"Romualdo, may I ask what it is you think you're doing? Are you trying to kill yourself? Do you want to die behind bars, like some ordinary . . . some ordinary . . . "

Her husband finshed the sentence for her.

" . . . some ordinary murderer, that's right. Which is what I am, some ordinary murderer. I wish you'd keep that in mind."

Bianca didn't know what to say. She had prepared a little speech, but now she couldn't remember even a word of it. She gathered her thoughts.

"I know that you didn't want me to come visit you, and now that I see you I can also understand why. Even your lawyer tries to avoid meeting with you. But I have to tell you this, I've made up my mind to find out what reason you have for doing this."

The man laughed bitterly.

"Yes, I met the henchman you recruited to dig into matters that don't concern you. That's of no interest to me, after all, there's nothing to find out and it wouldn't change a thing. I asked you to turn your back on my life, Bianca. I'm turning my back on yours. Find yourself another man. Maybe my dear old lawyer will find a way to get you to marry that poor Marangolo. Come on, give him a little sweetness and light before his liver drags him down to hell."

The crass, vulgar reference to Carlo Maria was like a knife to the heart.

"That's petty and ungrateful on your part. You're trying to wound me and in the meantime you vent your resentment against the only person that has tried to help you."

Once again, Romualdo laughed, uncontrolledly.

"Help me? By financing a loan shark and allowing him to feed the flames of my ruin? If nature wasn't already taking care of it, maybe I would have arranged to murder him, too. But I don't care what you think. All I want is that you never come back here."

Bianca stood up. A cold fury surged up from her stomach like a column of bile. She regretted ever having felt an ounce of pity for that demon in human form.

"You're right. I've come here today to tell you goodbye, in fact. I'm going to follow this story all the way to its logical conclusion because I want to know the reason for what you did. But whatever the real motive, and I'm going to find out what it is, you can rely on it, it won't change the fact that now you're the opposite of the man I thought I wanted beside me for the rest of my life. I only thank God I never had your children."

The man replied contemptuously, looking her right in the eyes.

"There's more dignity in me, after I did what I did, than you've ever had; you who know just how much that man loves you, and yet you live off him without giving him so much as a gram in return. And do you know why, Bianca? Because you don't have any love in you. You don't know love. And you never will. Now, please, let me get back to my many important engagements: there are cockroaches in my cell that I'll see more gladly than I'll see you."

Bianca bit her lip to keep from bursting into tears and turned to go. Romualdo watched her grow smaller, pushing her way through the crowd of poor people who had come to bring a smile to their relations in prison.

Once she had left the large visiting room, and not a moment before, the count of Roccaspina allowed himself to break into tears.

Then he asked the guard to take him away.

XL

From the atrium of an apartment house, Maione and Ricciardi fixed their gazes on the entrance to the Vittorio Emanuele II high school. It was almost one o'clock and the students who were enrolled in the preparatory courses were about to be let go for the day.

That morning the two men had talked at some considerable length about the Piro case, in part taking advantage of the enduring, extraordinary doldrums in police work. There had never been, as far as they could recall, a period like it: no serious case of violent crime, no murder that might demand immediate action, nor any of those situations that occasionally burst out of the shell of local *omertà* in the more densely populated neighborhoods, where disputes were more commonly settled with the blade of a knife and only rarely did those seriously wounded take their injuries to physicians or hospitals, which were obliged by law to report such cases.

For the past two weeks, practically nothing at all had happened in the city.

There had been a couple of street brawls, certainly, and one or two men had wound up flat on their backs, but nothing that required an actual investigation: a report was filed stating that a certain police officer, summoned to such-and-such a place at thus-and-such time of day, had proceeded to arrest John Doe for wounds inflicted upon Richard Roe, and the matter was settled.

And so Ricciardi and Maione, once they'd quickly worked

their way through their daily duties, had been able to devote themselves to their unauthorized investigation; the brigadier in the vain hopes of distracting the commissario, the commissario in the equally vain intent of ridding himself of the brigadier's solicitous attentions.

They had agreed about how odd the shift in the victim's wife's attitude had been the night before, the instant they had mentioned the lawyer's unusual twofold visit to the convent of the Madonna Incoronata. An inexplicable reaction at the end of a conversation that had been entirely urbane up to that point, if not indeed fully collaborative.

Certainly, they would have to take into account the threat leveled by Signora Piro to reach out to some highly placed invidivual, but in Maione's view, and on this point Ricciardi was in agreement, the woman had made an idle threat: if she really did have that power, she would have unleashed it immediately, the day after their first visit. What seemed more likely was that, just as it was with financial matters, interactions with the notables of the city had been the exclusive jurisdiction of the dearly departed.

So it was worth looking into.

Maione had spoken with the building's doorman, who he thought had a familiar face. Sure enough, as a young man, the doorman had indulged in a few minor thefts that he hoped had long been forgotten, and all the brigadier had needed to do was speculate about the effects of publicizing that chapter of the man's past among the tenants of the building, and his tongue had quickly been loosened, assuring at the same time the man's utter and reliable discretion.

He had thus come to learn that Piro's daughter had already returned to her studies at one of the most respected schools in the city. A partial boarding school with a well established tradition, to be exact, which however also claimed a vigorous inclination to political renewal, since the new headmaster—

himself a "veteran of the Great War and a Fascist from the very outset," to put it in his own words—had just undertaken a rigorous process of application of the principles guiding the Fascist regime to his school.

There were more than a thousand students, nearly all of them members of the Balilla National Fascist Organization, two hundred of them girls. Among those girls, of course, was Carlotta Piro.

The activities on offer were numerous, as Maione soon learned with a phone call to the main office; above and beyond the strict domain of academic studies, there was music, theater, and various athletic pursuits. Even before the beginning of the school year, students both male and female were expected to begin preparing for the numerous extracurricular activities that were planned.

From what they were able to determine, Carlotta was an enthusiastic participant. That day, in particular, she would be taking part in practice for a regional athletic competition. The doorman, visibly perspiring and clearly eager to comply with the brigadier's demands, had no difficulty providing him with the scheduled end of the school day: the girl was let out at one o'clock, because she was invariably home by two.

Talking to Carlotta had been Ricciardi's idea. Even though she had displayed a highly emotional reaction during their first meeting, she seemed more willing than her mother to express her inward thoughts. And she might well remember something that her father had let slip, even by pure chance, concerning the convent of the Madonna Incoronata, something that Signora Piro had failed to remember or for some reason chose not to reveal.

It was worth giving it a try: they had reached a stalemate, and any information might prove useful in giving their unusual investigation a jump start.

The front entrance of the school swung open and the boys

came charging out, all of them dressed in black, in jacket and tie even though it was still quite hot out. The girls emerged after them, in a much smaller group. Carlotta was the only one to wear a black dress, given her recent loss and state of mourning, but like the other girls she was laughing and chatting excitedly.

A young woman who wanted to be happy, the commissario thought. She wanted to forget about the death that had come into her home as quickly as she could.

From the shadows where they had been waiting, the two policemen watched her stop with a couple of girlfriends at the street corner; several young men came up to them and started talking. One of them must have said something very amusing, because they heard a gale of laughter. Another one pulled out a pack of cigarettes, and Carlotta took one.

She seemed miles away from the girl weeping in her home in the presence of her mother.

With a graceful gesture, she removed her silver hair stick and let the chestnut blanket of her hair fall over her shoulders; one of the boys pulled her hair, and she shoved him away with a laugh.

Ricciardi and Maione were almost sorry at the thought that they would soon wipe that smile off her face.

After a little while, the group broke up, bidding cheerful farewells.

When Carlotta walked past the atrium, they called out to her. She started and stared at them in confusion.

"Ah . . . hello. But what are you doing here? Were you looking for me?"

Maione tried to reassure her, jovially.

"In fact, we were hoping we might run into you, Signori'. There's something we'd like to clear up with you, and perhaps you can help us."

The girl narrowed her eyes, diffidently.

"I've already told you everything I ought to. And you also spoke to my mother, last night, so I can't imagine what else you might want from me."

Ricciardi broke in.

"Your mother, Signorina, doesn't seem convinced that we're interested in finding out the truth about your father's murder. And with her rather uncooperative behavior, she's preventing us from understanding several aspects that remain unclear. Now, in the interest of one and all, it would be best if you answered a few questions. Unless, of course, you have something to hide. In that case we'd take very different steps."

The young woman looked startled; she found the idea that she had anything to hide offensive, to say the least.

"My father was murdered. And the man who murdered him, that cowardly dog, confessed and is going to remain behind bars for the rest of his life. What else is there to clear up?"

This was the moment to drive in, Ricciardi decided.

"Your father, in the two days prior to the murder, had his chauffeur take him twice to the convent of the Madonna Incoronata. Do you happen to know the reason for that two-fold visit?"

Carlotta seemed confused.

"But . . . my father never told anyone what he was doing or how he did his job. He was very secretive. I believe that the Collegio dell'Incoronata was one of the several institutions whose finances he administered . . . "

Maione didn't let her finish.

"We know that, Signori'. What we don't know is why he would have gone there twice in two days."

The girl stared at him coldly.

"Well, why would I know that, Brigadier? Or my mother, or my brother, for that matter? Why don't you just leave us in peace? Do you have no respect for the sorrow of a family that now may have no future ahead of it?"

Ricciardi changed the subject.

"Then let me ask you to make an additional effort: let's talk about the quarrel that your father had with Roccaspina. Can you tell us anything about what happened on that occasion?"

The young woman's eyes lit up with renewed determination.

"I was here, at school, but my mother and the housekeeper told me all about it. They told me that the murderer was shouting like a madman. I believe that my father must have refused to give him something he wanted, either money or else an extension in his repayment, and he kept shouting that it wouldn't end there, that if my father persisted in his stubborn attitude, he'd be forced to do something about it. That's right, that's what he said."

Ricciardi seemed lost in thought. Then he nodded his head.

"That matches what we know. Perhaps that's all, Signorina. You've been very helpful."

Carlotta was relieved, but still doubtful.

"My mother and I don't like it when people question whether that miserable coward Roccaspina actually killed my father. He's a foul murderer, he crept into our house in the middle of the night and then took to his heels. We were fast asleep while my father was dying. My mother thought he had simply stayed up late working and I left in the morning thinking that he was sleeping when he was actually dead. He didn't even let us say goodbye to him. We don't like it when anyone tries to save the killer just because he's an aristocrat and has friends in high places."

Here we need to make things clear, thought Maione.

"Don't worry about that, Signori': we are certainly not accustomed to having our investigations run by important persons who instruct us not to follow up certain leads. If it was Roccaspina, he'll serve the sentence he deserves."

She gave him a look.

"And in fact, that's exactly how it will be, Brigadier. That's how it will be."

And she turned and left, with the afternoon sun glinting off her youthful hair.

XLI

F alco made a note of the exact time he saw Ricciardi head off with the brigadier toward police headquarters after speaking with the young woman.

No, his was certainly not "a job like any other," as he himself had said, warding off attention. If you were following a trail, you couldn't allow yourself to be tempted by what you might encounter along the way. Even though it was a risk that one often ran, especially in a city like that one, where relationships and bonds of friendship were constantly intertwining; all the same, it was important not to take one's eyes off the objective, not to allow oneself to be distracted. Certainly, if you stumbled upon something big, you were duty-bound to inform your higher-ups as soon as possible, but in no case could you lose sight of your quarry. Never.

But now, Falco wasn't working. He was following an idea.

He stood up from the café table, folded his newspaper, and stretched lazily in the still-warm air of that early September afternoon. Certainly, though, the summer was hanging on, he thought to himself. It was stretching into winter, it seemed, cutting the length of autumn. That wasn't a good thing: rain made his job easier. It made men like him, who were professional watchers, invisible behind their umbrellas, and it made those who were under observation easier to spot, as the passersby became fewer in number, while the cold forced conversations that they wished to eavesdrop upon into the indoors, in the shelter of cafés and bars.

Rain was better.

Now, though, if nothing else, the weather was perfect for stakeouts; the comfortable warmth presented no danger to his joints and also allowed him to select ideal corners from which to watch and listen.

Falco was pleased, now, that Livia was reacting. He had tried to shake her out of it, persuade her to put on some makeup, get dressed and get out and about. He had worked to leverage her womanly pride, he had told her that she mustn't give the satisfaction of a sorrowful depression to those who had warned her not to move to a provincial city, who had criticized her renunciation of the glittering social life of Italy's capital and her involvement with a man who didn't deserve her and who might not even be particularly attracted to the gentler sex.

Until then, he'd always been very careful to say nothing bad about Ricciardi to Livia. That would have been a fatal misstep. It might have caused Livia to shut him out, by wounding her self-respect. And now it was enough to tell her she was right and steer her malaise toward its logical consequences.

Now, however, there was also the question of von Brauchitsch. He thought about that as he tailed from a distance the Don Quixotesque silhouettes of the commissario and the brigadier. The German major who was the target of the greatest interest and whom none of his colleagues had found a way of approaching effectively. The major had gone to dinner at the Colombo home, and from what he had been able to learn, he had also invited Enrica, the cavalier's eldest daughter, to meet him for a gelato that very afternoon. The very same Enrica, moreover, had met Ricciardi at the exit of the yacht club, down by the sea, the day before.

A coincidence? An opportunity? Falco didn't know, but he felt certain that the matter needed to be followed up on, and with the greatest attention.

He had therefore requested and been assigned, in a brief conversation with the man who had a comma carved into his forehead, to monitor, himself in person, the meeting between the young woman and the German soldier. On that occasion he had also learned of a suspicious stroll that Manfred had taken down to the port, in the area around various military facilities; that was, to say the least, an unusual thing for a cultural attaché assigned to learn about archeology in the Vesuvius region to do. The man with the comma had also informed him of something that, if it wasn't actually a disguise, certainly qualified as a remarkable choice of attire, because according to the report submitted by the agents detailed to him, von Brauchitsch had chosen to dress as a sailor serving aboard a Nordic freighter, with a work shirt, commodious britches, and a cap worn snug and low to cover his head of hair, and as he had come closer to the wharf where the cruiser *Goffredo da Buglione* was tied up he had started to walk around as if lost, though drawing closer to the warship the whole time. When a sentinel, rather belatedly, had called out to him, asking him to identify himself, he'd immediately apologized, speaking in a language that seemed to be Norwegian, and had headed back without any further deviations to the pensione where he was staying.

Everything, in other words, pointed to a confirmation of the initial suspicions, which is to say, that the major wasn't in the city just to ensure that the crew of German archeologists were being given full support in logistical terms. And that clearly meant that Falco and his men were going to step up their surveillance.

The man with the comma had also told him that for now Rome wasn't planning on intervening. Instead, it was important to learn how the information that the German soldier was gathering made its way back to Germany, and therefore, how his orders were conveyed to him. In the meanwhile, it was crucial that they miss none of his moves, not in public, much less in private.

This fit in perfectly with what Falco wanted most, that is, to get rid of Ricciardi, if possible. Enrica, an essential instrument in his surveillance of von Brauchitsch, was at risk because of her past, and perhaps still present, infatuation for the commissario; Livia wouldn't look forward to a new life as long as she thought Ricciardi was still attainable. He knew her a little, by now, and she didn't strike him as the kind of woman to resign herself to a defeat in love. No, if he was to be ripped from her heart, it would have to be root and branch.

From a safe distance he kept his eye on Ricciardi's back, the overcoat that fluttered around his legs. He wondered idly what it was about him that could so capture the fancy of the two women. He could even comprehend the interest of the young Colombo woman: it was understandable that a young woman who had turned twenty-five and was in search of a fiancé with whom to begin a family might fall in love with the first man to look at her through a window. But Livia? A woman who could have anyone she chose, the loveliest and most charming woman Falco had ever met. What's more, a woman with great artistic talent, intelligent and cultivated.

As he was walking along, following the gentle downhill slope of the street, he wondered what it was he actually felt toward her. The protection that it was his duty to afford her had become a personal matter, as well as a professional responsibility, and it filled his thoughts much more than it ought to have, given that it was his job.

Well, he wondered, what of it? Did people in his line of work have some ethical guidelines they were called upon to respect? There was nothing wrong with adding a little spice to one's duty. In fact, it might even sharpen his senses and improve the final outcome.

He wondered whether what Livia, in tears and half drunk,

had said about the commissario was the truth. Not that it really mattered much, the important thing was to be able to construct a plausible scenario. He had learned early that, especially in a field like his own, which consisted of hypotheses and buttressing evidence, far more important than reality was the fundamental perception that could be conveyed.

One way or another, thought Falco as he sheltered himself from the horde of pedestrians all more or less bustling and busy, obstacles were there to be removed. And the more important what lies behind that obstacle, the more conviction and determination would have to be brought to bear. You, Commissario Luigi Alfredo Ricciardi of the mobile squad at the Royal Police Headquarters, you are an obstacle, and not a particularly forbidding one, objectively speaking, but you stand right in the middle of an important thoroughfare, and therefore you most certainly will be removed. And perhaps we already know how.

The night before he had taken a look at the file on the murder of Ludovico Piro. He had become curious about the determination that Ricciardi, with Maione's assistance, had shown in pursuing that investigation, outside of his proper jurisdiction, concerning a case that had been filed away months ago. He knew that his interest in the case had been requested by the Contessa di Roccaspina, who had always maintained her husband's innocence, according to the official police reports; perhaps the commissario felt the need to work on something during a particularly quiet period. Or else he'd just taken pity on the contessa, who appeared to be in dire financial straits.

Inwardly, Falco approved Ricciardi's inclination to compassion: he wasn't a bad person and, perhaps, in other circumstances, he might even have admired him. Ricciardi was good at his job and not particularly gifted at social interactions, and basically, Falco felt that he could sympathize.

But he was an obstacle. And he would need to be removed.

*

Suddenly, Maione swung around, scrutinizing all the pedestrians moving in the same direction as them. His instincts had told him that someone, in that crowd of strollers, was following them.

He let a few seconds pass, and then did the same thing again. He saw no one. Reassured, he went on his way.

XLII

After their rather fruitless conversation with Carlotta Piro, Ricciardi and Maione found themselves faced with a clear alternative: either admit the absurdity of carrying on such a complex investigation, which had run up against a wall of silence and which no one had authorized, aside from their own consciences, or else continue forward in defiance of everything and everyone.

Maione let himself drop into the chair in front of his superior officer's desk.

"Do you know what the worst thing is, Commissa'? That in this private investigation, which we have to pursue secretly, the ones who ought to be most interested in learning the truth are the toughest to question. The Piro family, for example, seems to be determined to make sure that nothing comes to light."

Ricciardi reflected as he looked out the window.

"That does seem to be the case. I believe that the work our victim did had a number of slightly illegal angles to it, and the deeper we dig, the more frightened his family becomes. They can't bring him back to life, but they can defend his memory."

"And they can defend the money that they still have set aside, Commissa'. Someone might even bring a lawsuit to recover some of it, and if you ask me the real fear haunting the signora and her sweet young daughter is that the two of them will be left penniless. That's why they fired the chauffeur, too, isn't it?"

Ricciardi shook his head.

"No. I don't think so. I believe that the chauffeur was fired in order to conceal something else, perhaps the very fact that Piro had gone twice to the Convent of the Incoronata. By the way, Raffaele, do you know where it is?"

"Why certainly, Commissa'. I wouldn't be from this city if I didn't know that. Why, do you want me to go there?"

"We can go together. Most likely, we won't find out a thing, but we need to give it a shot. After all, we don't have any other leads. Even though, out of all this information, there's definitely something that just doesn't add up."

Maione got to his feet.

"I got the same feeling, Commissa'. Otherwise, I'd have already suggested we just drop the matter. You know what I'm going to do right now? I'll take a run down to see if there's a car available, at least the Fiat 501."

Ricciardi immediately regretted having opened his mouth; if there was one thing that terrified him, it was going anywhere in a car with Maione, who was, to be charitable, a terrible driver. But it was too late: the brigadier had already left the room. The only hope he could still cling to was that the car might be out on duty.

Almost immediately, there came a light tapping at the office door; he heaved a sigh of relief and went to open the door, already mentally preparing to head out to the convent by public transportation. Instead, he found himself face to face with Bianca di Roccaspina.

The woman's face was devastated with tears and sorrow. Ricciardi shot a quick glance down the hallway, making sure that no one had seen them, and then ushered her in.

"Contessa, what's going on? We'd made it very clear that it was best you not come here anymore."

Bianca stared at him with reddened eyes and trembling lips; she seemed on the verge of giving into her emotions.

"Forgive me, Commissario. I . . . I just don't know where to go. I didn't want to go home in this state, people, you know . . . All I have left is my dignity. It's the only thing left to me."

Ricciardi felt his heart twist.

"I'm sorry. I'm so sorry. Tell me, has something happened?"

Bianca sighed. She seemed younger than usual, but also wearier.

"I've been at the prison. I wanted to . . . Attilio had warned me . . . He'd told me that Romualdo didn't want to see me, and for that matter I wasn't especially keen on seeing him. But, you understand, I wanted to tell him . . . I thought it was only right to tell him that it's over between us. That I don't love him anymore and that even if this whole affair ended with his freedom, I won't stay with him for so much as another minute. Do you understand me, Commissario? I had to tell him."

Ricciardi felt a surge of pity. For that woman, for the man that he'd seen in prison, and, the reason being some mysterious motive that remained hidden beneath the surface of his consciousness, for himself.

"Contessa, why are you telling me these things? I . . . "

The woman went on as if he hadn't spoken.

"And when I saw him I was frozen to the spot. He's a phantom: prostrate, devastated. There's no trace in him of the man I once knew. It frightened me."

The commissario remembered the count's eyes, sunken in their sockets, and nodded.

On Bianca's face, the tears were streaming freely.

"That voice, Commissario. That voice. It seemed as if another soul had taken possession of his body and were devouring it from within. How can that be, how is it possible to live with a person for years and never really know who they are? Tell me how it can be, I beg you."

She's overwhelmed, thought Ricciardi. Terrorized, bewildered, and overwhelmed. Alone, abandoned, poor, and what's more, a victim of her own dignity. In his mind, the image of

Bianca was overlaid upon that of Livia, she too the victim of desperation, lovely and tortured, her makeup streaking her face; and that of Enrica, by the sea, one hand clamped on her hat, her eyeglasses fogged with tears.

God, thought Ricciardi, what a crime You committed when You invented love.

"I'd have rather sensed hatred, believe me. I'd have rather seen that in his eyes, instead of a mocking contempt, an icy indifference. I had never seen that indifference before. And the worst thing is that in my heart I felt the same thing; until today, I'd never confessed it even to myself. What can I do, now? What can I do?"

She stared at him, her lips compressed and her hands clutching the handle of her purse, her shoulders rigid to maintain a certain shred of dignity. She was staring at him as if he could answer her.

But Ricciardi, the man with a head full of wind and sand, the man whose soul of glass could so easily be shattered into a thousand bits, had no answers for her. He had none for himself, much less for others.

"Contessa, please. Relationships are born, they age, and they die, just like people. I don't know what to tell you, because my life . . . I don't know what to tell you. But I will make you a promise, I'll do everything within my power to provide an explanation of what's happened. The only thing is, I beg you, don't suffer like this. You're a young woman, you have every chance at . . . "

Bianca raised her hand.

"I'm begging you, Commissario. Today, here, at this very instant, I feel as if there is no future for me. And I'm more alone than I've ever been before. I don't even know if I have a soul anymore."

At that point, Ricciardi felt weighing down on his shoulders all the weariness of the sleepless nights, the everyday absence of Rosa, the terrible solitude of his life, Livia's rage, the distance he had read in Enrica's eyes. Absurdly, in the fog of his numb grief, he found himself wondering once again what all that sea was good for.

And as in a dream, against his shy, retiring nature, and in defiance of all reason, he reached out his hand and placed it upon Bianca's tearstained cheek.

Her flesh was silk-smooth and burning hot, full of life and bewilderment. She lifted her black-gloved hand and rested it on the commissario's hand, as if to keep it there. Bianca needed to feel she was still alive; and Ricciardi needed to feel he was still alive, too.

They remained like that for a few seconds, her violet eyes in his green ones, she teetering on the brink of the other's abyss of solitude, in a profound and self-aware contact, as if the two of them were a single thing.

The magic was interrupted by a couple of sharp taps at the door. They broke apart just as Maione came in with a broad smile on his face.

"Oh, *buonasera*, Contessa." He observed the woman for a moment, then decided that he had better not ask any questions and instead addressed his superior officer. "We're in luck, Commissa': the car is in the courtyard. Amitrano says that no one was interested in taking it out because the brakes aren't working right. I told him that I'd take it out for a test spin, that way we don't have to explain to anyone why we're taking it— did I do right? Let's go, if we move quickly we can get back before the end of our shift!"

XLIII

Not even half an hour later, Ricciardi stepped out of the car in the courtyard of the Convent of the Madonna Incoronata with a faint sense of bewilderment: he couldn't even begin to guess how and why it was that he was still alive.

Maione's driving, he knew, was already lethal per se, but combined with the wear and tear on the brakes of the ramshackle vehicle available for the use of the mobile squad, a thirteen-year-old Fiat 501, the likelihood of dying on the way over had spiked to a virtual certainty.

Along the way, they had overturned two vendors' carts, had a close brush with a motorcycle sidecar, knocking it with the front fender, and brushed into the roadside ditch at least three cyclists. The pedestrians, more agile and alert, had managed to take to their heels, but a hen hadn't been so lucky and had perished under the front left wheel, amidst the shouts and curses of the fowl's owner, whom Ricciardi had seen shaking her fist until they vanished around the next curve. And in all this, the brigadier didn't appear to notice a thing, his eyes fixed on the roadway ahead of him and the tip of his tongue sticking out of the corner of his mouth, in full and absolute concentration. He turned the wheel jerkily, without any relationship to the roadway or the potholes, which were increasingly numerous as they ventured farther out into the countryside. Ricciardi hung on tight to the handles with both hands and yet, in spite of that, had knocked his head against the roof so many times that he finally had a fiercely throbbing migraine, as well as an intolerable sense of nausea. When the self-taught driver triumphally screeched to a halt with a terrible shriek of metal against metal in the convent's courtyard, the commissario catapulted himself out of the car, resisting the temptation to kiss the ground like a sixteenth-century navigator.

Maione, smiling, pulled out his pocket watch.

"Twenty-two minutes, Commissa'. There's nothing you can say about it, I'm the best driver at police headquarters. When I took the driving class I was the best, and I'm still the best now."

Ricciardi replied weakly.

"Remind me to talk to the instructor, if we ever get back alive."

The theatrical arrival had at least obtained an effect. Ten nuns and young women wearing uniforms marking them as convent personnel peeped shyly out the front entrance, after first having taken hasty shelter inside.

The brigadier identified himself and asked to be received along with Ricciardi by the mother superior.

A nun who was studying them with great mistrust led them through a maze of hallways and staircases until she reached a dark wooden door, where she knocked. A woman's voice, energetic and brisk, invited them to enter.

The mother superior was a short, overweight woman, with a pink complexion and lively blue eyes; she sat behind an enormous desk piled high with papers. When she saw the two men, she stood up to greet them.

"I am Sister Caterina," she said.

Ricciardi and Maione took turns introducing themselves, then the commissario said: "Mother Superior, forgive us for coming unannounced. We are undertaking a supplementary investigation concerning the murder of the lawyer Ludovico Piro, which took place this past June. Our research is going to contribute to the first stages of the trial. Would you be kind enough to answer a few questions for us?"

The woman's eyes darted for an instant, followed by a smile.

"Why, of course, if it's within our power, we'll do whatever we can to help. Sister Carla, you can go back to your service, thank you."

The nun who had accompanied them shot a final dark glare at the policemen and left without saying goodbye. Sister Caterina took her seat again behind the desk.

"I apologize for the behavior of my fellow sister; we don't get a lot of outside visitors. Now then, poor Ludovico. A grim story, very grim indeed. I won't conceal from you that we have been very concerned: the Mother General of the Order has written us many times to get more information about the accounts. Luckily, though, Piro was a very precise person, and we have been able to reconstruct our financial situation to a very complete degree. Certainly, now we are going to have to find another administrator, the lawyer had been working for us for a very long time; as you can see from the disorder, I've been trying to look after it myself, but I'm afraid I'm not particularly good at it."

Ricciardi got straight to the point.

"We understand, and we have to imagine that the same thing is happening in all the institutions that the lawyer handled. We have learned that he was here the day before he died. Can you confirm that?"

Sister Caterina never stopped smiling.

"Certainly. In fact, I was somewhat astonished when no one came to ask me about Ludovico's visit. I imagine that's because the murderer, may the Good Lord forgive him, was immediately caught."

"Do you mind if I ask why he had come?"

The mother superior shuffled through the papers on the desk with her pudgy hands.

"Of course, I was just looking at the statements now." She opened a large notebook. "Here, he brought us this that day, along with other documents; it allowed us to have an updated starting figure upon which to work. Bank deposits, real estate . . . Let me say it again, Piro was very scrupulous."

Ricciardi took a quick look at the ledger book. In effect, everything seemed to be in good order.

"Tell me, Mother, did you know what businesses Piro invested your cash in?"

Sister Caterina reddened almost imperceptibly, but her expression didn't change.

"Not really, but that's only natural. Piro was our fiduciary agent, and therefore, as the term suggests, we trusted him."

Maione heaved a sigh of irritation, masking behind a burst of coughing a hint of annoyance. He couldn't stand hypocrisy.

"But excuse me, Mother, do you remember any unusual details about that visit?"

The nun shook her head seraphically.

"No, nothing. Piro stayed for about an hour, he ran through the numbers with me, illustrated the financial transactions of the months to come, which unfortunately he was never to undertake, and then he left."

Ricciardi nodded pensively.

"But how did he seem to you? I mean: tranquil, agitated or . . . "

Sister Caterina replied somewhat hastily.

"Tranquil, absolutely tranquil. A perfectly normal visit, no different from all the others."

Maione asked: "And just how often did Piro come to see you, to brief you about these investments you knew nothing about?"

The mother superior seemed to miss the irony.

"At the end of every quarter. He was very regular."

"And he hadn't left anything out, had he? The information that he provided was complete."

"Certainly."

Ricciardi exchanged a rapid glance with Maione. The time had come to deliver the knockout blow.

"So it was strange, unusual, that he should have come back again the very next day, wasn't it?"

The nun was caught off guard. She clearly did not think that Piro's second visit had come to the attention of the police.

She reddened and dropped her eyes to the papers on the desk.

"I don't think I remember exactly, but I don't think that . . . "

Maione interrupted her brusquely.

"Mother Superior, we are certain that the lawyer Piro was also here on the morning of the day he was killed. We have the testimony of his chauffeur, who drove him out here. He told us that Piro didn't stay long. Let me ask you, then, try to remember."

Sister Caterina showed no sign of losing her blush, but she had regained her cold composure. With her eyes trained on Maione's face, she admitted it.

"Yes. Now I remember. It's true, Ludovico came back the next day."

Ricciardi leaned forward.

"And you can't tell us the reason why?"

The woman met and held his gaze.

"No, Commissario. I can't tell you the reason why. It was about a personal matter, and we aren't accustomed to revealing the business of our faithful friends. Even if they are, sadly, dead, indeed, all the more so if they are dead."

Ricciardi and Maione exchanged a quick glance.

"Mother Superior, this is important information that could cast light on . . . "

The nun stood up.

"I really don't think so. Let me repeat, it was a personal matter that can't have any connection to what happened later. And in any case, it was only a request for information."

Maione tried to insist.

"But can you at least tell us whether he mentioned anyone's name, or if . . . "

The nun walked over to the door with brisk, short steps and threw it open.

"I've already explained to you that I cannot and I will not say anything about this matter. And I'm going to have to ask you to leave immediately, because both the convent and the school are in need of a great deal of work, and we cannot afford to waste too much time in these pointless conversations. The trial against the murderer, I feel certain, will have all the evidence required. *Buonasera.*"

Once they were back in the car, Maione slammed his fist on the steering wheel.

"Darn it, Commissa', we'd almost nailed it. You saw it, first she pretended she couldn't remember, then she was forced to admit it, but then she decided not to tell us anything. I assure you, that tea-towel head knows something, as God is my witness!"

Ricciardi ran his eyes around the convent courtyard, where small groups of nuns and young women in navy blue uniforms were observing them curiously.

Then he looked at Maione almost affectionately and said: "If we ever make it back alive, and I'm sure that we won't, there are a few things I want to examine in some greater depth. I've suddenly had an idea."

XLIV

I t hardly needs saying, but Manfred's invitation had created a genuine state of frenzy in the Colombo family. It had been expected of course, but not so quickly.

Those Germans, when they set their sights on something, they don't waste any time achieving it, Maria had said, and with a clear hint of satisfaction, because what the German in question had set his sights on was her daughter; but the concept possessed an unsettling military overtone that sent a shiver down Giulio's spine.

Enrica would have preferred to have the invitation delivered to her in a discreet manner, so that she could postpone that meeting; for more than twenty-four hours now she had spent nearly all her time shut up in her bedroom, claiming a faint malaise caused by the change in seasons and, perhaps a form of influenza caught from one of the children she tutored.

Her father had appeared in her doorway several times, to ask her in a whisper whether there was anything she needed; like her, he was subject to migraines, and he knew just how painful they could be. That was the ostensible reason: in reality he wanted to see what his daughter's state of mind might be. For a deductive soul like him, the condition in which she had returned from a long solitary walk the morning of the previous day made the fact that she was now so indisposed something that could only be viewed as highly suspicious.

But the invitation hadn't been discreet in the slightest. It had burst into the household yesterday in the form of an open note, delivered along with a gigantic bouquet of flowers and received by her mother and sister in the presence of the entire landing, which had been summoned in a plenary session. In practical terms, Enrica had been the last one to know about it.

Manfred asked her to give him an hour of her time tomorrow afternoon. If that weren't possible, he hoped she'd tell the messenger boy who had brought her this note, but, he added in his strange, upright, and slightly gothic handwriting, he ardently hoped that her answer would be a yes.

Since that answer was issued with great impetus directly by the committee of floral reception, a committee which did not include the young woman, that answer was positive and then some. And the appointment was set via messenger boy for four o'clock.

The question, from the very outset, had been one and one alone: what are you going to wear? In the thrill of choosing the outfit, accompanied by a discussion of the tidal wave of alterations that would have to be done on any of the inadequate items in Enrica's scanty wardrobe, no one paid any attention to the distinct lack of enthusiasm on the part of the person in question. No one but Giulio, of course, though he was given the standard justification of a nagging migraine.

Still, he continued to wonder what had happened on that walk, resulting in one Enrica going out the door and a very different one returning home.

The young woman, for her part, was distracted, to put it lightly. The absurd and unexpected chance encounter with Ricciardi had thrown her into a state. She hadn't been prepared for such a thing, and instead of adopting a formal and detached demeanor, she had spoken without thinking, something that to her was roughly as mortifying as walking naked down the street.

She had thought for hour and hours about what she had said and what he had said, and she couldn't get over it. What good is all this sea? she had asked him. What kind of a question was that? What did it mean? She didn't have the faintest idea, and yet right there and then it had seemed like the only sensible thing to say.

The brutal shove that knocked down the castle of certainties that she had painstakingly assembled had come from the man's expression. Had he only displayed indifference, courtesy, or simple kindness, it would have been easy for her to issue a greeting, perhaps with a nod of the head and a smile, and then continue on her way, even if her heart was in utter tumult. But that's not how it had gone: he was even more upset than she was.

The image of his staring eyes, his open mouth, the lock of hair on his forehead was vivid and unequivocal. Surprise, bafflement; even fear. And those absurd words: I saw you. What had he seen? What could he have seen, if not a perfectly ordinary guest sitting at the family dinner table on a September evening?

Deep down, she had to admit it. Manfred wasn't some perfectly ordinary guest on a September evening, he was the man who on a July night had kissed her beneath the moon and whom she had not pushed away, out of a mix of sorrow and fear of the life that awaited her, of the past and the future.

But that kiss, there was certainly no way Ricciardi could have seen that.

With her head elsewhere and without enthusiasm, she had however submitted to the excitement of the female part of her family, with the female neighbors standing in as a sort of Greek chorus; one of the worst moments was the massive offering of horrible jewelry and garish accessories, all of them rejected with perfect courtesy.

As for the dress, the committee opted in the end for a skirt with blouse and jacket, ecru with polka dots, and a cloche hat in the same fabric and matching gloves, with beige handbag and shoes; her mother managed to talk her into taking in the blouse a bit at the waist to highlight her breasts, one of Enrica's better features. The young woman lacked the strength to even object.

At four o'clock on the dot on the following afternoon, her sister Susanna, standing watch behind the shutters, announced Manfred's arrival. How German they are after all, she said, with admiration for his punctuality, as if it were a matter of national pride. Enrica went downstairs and the man greeted her by kissing her hand, sending a grandstand full of family members on the balcony into a collective swoon.

Only Giulio, if he hadn't been at the family store, would have noticed the glance that Enrica shot toward a certain window in the palazzo next door. A window that was shut.

Fortunately, the stroll arm in arm with Manfred hadn't been unpleasant. The major had so many stories to tell about his first period living in the city, and she could take shelter behind courteous and interested monosyllabic replies. He told her about what it was like at the consulate, how lovable the Italian clerks and janitors were there, and the saga of the consul himself. As they walked toward the center of town, facing into a light breeze that rose from the sea, he told her amusing anecdotes about the day he'd spent at the archeological digs; he told her about a German professor who was absolutely convinced he spoke excellent Italian but whom no one could understand, and who generated absurd misunderstandings with the local laborers, who exclusively spoke in dialect.

In short order, Enrica felt a sense of tranquility wash over her. Manfred always had this effect on her. It was like moving through a new territory that nonetheless remained familiar, comfortable, and close to the serenity to which she so aspired. She even laughed, attracting the curious, pleased gazes of the people they crossed paths with. He was in uniform, handsome and exotic, and many young women shot him unequivocally interested glances. That gratified Enrica, though in a fairly bland way; it didn't trigger even a stab of jealousy, even though it ought to have. This too, she told herself, was indicative of something, but she couldn't have said exactly what.

Manfred committed the unconscious error of taking her to Gambrinus. A place of meaning for her, both pleasant and unpleasant. She went there with her father, she'd met Ricciardi there more than once, she'd seen that woman, Livia, there, so beautiful and self-confident in a way she could never hope to achieve. While waiting for a waiter to clear a table for them, she raised her eyes in the direction of a stretch of the sea that extended into the distant afternoon, like a threat. What are you good for? she thought. What are you good for?

She took a seat, while Manfred courteously held out her chair for her. They ordered: she a vanilla gelato, he a glass of white wine. From inside came the muffled notes of a piano, but not far away a skinny young man was playing another song, his fingers flying over a mandolin.

People could say whatever they liked about this city, Manfred commented, but not that there was any shortage of music.

Why, what could people say about the city? Enrica enquired.

The major shrugged his shoulders, gesturing vaguely toward the gentle slope leading up to Monte di Dio. Nothing, you know, the usual things.

What usual things? she asked. Behind the plate-glass window she could see an unoccupied table. Not once but twice she had seen Ricciardi sitting there, his rapt gaze focused outside while he drank his espresso, in front of him a small plate with a *sfogliatella* pastry, half-eaten.

Manfred smiled with a hint of embarrassment. The mess, the dirt. The criminals. What people say.

Enrica narrowed her eyes, behind the lenses of her glasses. A little more than ten feet away, three young women were trying to capture the attention of the handsome fair-haired soldier by giggling, shooting glances, and crossing and uncrossing their legs.

Ah, so *that's* what they say about the city.

The officer shifted uneasily in his chair, though he never stopped smiling. But it's people who don't know the city, that say those things about it, without ever having seen it.

Enrica felt a strange anger surging within her. She knew that Manfred had invited her there to talk about something else, to establish once again the contact of that night in the moonlight, and she understood that, perhaps, her excessive reaction to a perfectly innocent phrase was a way of seizing on the first pretext that came to hand to put off a situation that she didn't know how to confront.

Not yet, at least.

And you, she replied, you who know the city, don't you know how to explain to them that it's something very different? That it has a thousand extraordinary beauties?

Manfred's smiled faded, but only for a moment. You're not being fair, he replied. You know that I never let a vacation go by without coming here, and that I chose this destination among the many that were offered to me. And you know that among the motives that drove me to make that choice there was you.

The table behind the plate-glass window. An empty chair in which a ghost sat, sipping an espresso and looking at her, of all people, her.

That doesn't have anything to do with it, she said. Do you hear this music? The mandolin, not the piano. It seems as if it's being played for tourists, just to get a few pennies of charity. But that's not what it really is: it's an expression of the city, it's the song of the city. It's a story, a story being told. This place tells stories, Manfred. It tells them by talking, playing, singing, and even just with its colors. And you, in that chilly gray place where you live, all you know how to talk about is mess, thieves, and criminals. What about the air? What about the songs?

What about the sea?

Manfred's face darkened. He didn't know what direction this afternoon's outing was taking, but so far he didn't like it one little bit.

That's not what I think about it, Enrica. I love your people, and I love this place, if you love it. I came here to . . .

You shouldn't love it because I love it, Manfred. You should love it for itself. Because it's beautiful, and magical, and even if at times it's a place that seems caught in desperation and dire need of help, it remains the only place on earth where you can be completely happy. Don't you understand that?

The table behind the window. The mandolin that gently emitted its laments. The colors of the women's clothing, the waiters who whisked past in their tailcoats, skillfully balancing trays piled high on gloved hands.

Without warning, Enrica stood up.

Excuse me, she said. I haven't been feeling very well for the past few days. I have a headache. Would you see me home?

In his turn, Manfred got to his feet, looking disconcerted. Of course, darling, of course. Forgive me. Let's put this off to another day, but you can be sure that I'll send another invitation, perhaps tomorrow, or the day after that. We live in a place that's chilly and gray, but we aren't chilly and gray ourselves, and when we find something that matters to us, we don't give up easily.

He extended his arm, gallantly, after depositing some money on the table. The young women nearby shot venomous glances at that vinegary, tall woman, far less pretty than any one of them, but who had the power to bid such an attractive man to come and go like a lapdog. She must be rich, murmured one of them, making all of them laugh.

The skinny young man's mandolin went on telling a heart-breaking story of love and grief.

Before turning around and heading home, Enrica thanked the long strip of blue water that was turning dark as evening fringed the horizon.

After all, she told herself, that's what all this sea is good for.

XLV

Canta lu addu e tocola la cora: iamo a mangià cà è benuta l'ora, murmured Nelide. The rooster is crowing, move your derriere: let's get something to eat, because it's time.

Sometimes she thought she could hear her father's voice, as he battled the fields, the cold, and the heat the way he always had done, with never a complaint. He spoke only in proverbs, her father did. Zi' Rosa used to make fun of him for it, but she remembered every one of them, and used them the same way he did.

Behind her, just on the edge of her field of vision, she glimpsed a movement and nodded; Rosa was there. Her presence made Nelide feel safer and reassured, because she knew that if she got anything wrong, her elderly dead aunt would have wasted no time letting her know, one way or another, correcting her before the error became irreparable.

The home wasn't a problem, though. The problem, the only one that she had, was the Baron of Malomonte.

Rosa called him the young master, because when he was little she had held him on her knee and because to Rosa the baron could only be Ricciardi's father, a big jovial man whose pranks and exploits were still the talk of the town, and stories to enchant with. But to Nelide, to her relatives, and to all the people of Fortino, the only true Baron of Malomonte was that slender, silent man with his large, sad green eyes: Luigi Alfredo Ricciardi. And she was the person appointed to look after him.

The problem was that the baron wasn't well. He wasn't a bit well.

Rosa sighed gently behind her. The young woman narrowed her eyes as she reviewed the ingredients for dinner. Zi' Ro', she thought, don't worry. Maybe he'll get over it. Maybe he just misses you. The way I do.

But things had to be kept running, and that was her job. Certainly, mistakes might be made: *ma sulo chi nun face nienti nun sbaglia nienti*, as they said where she came from. If you don't want to make mistakes, don't try to do anything.

And she also told herself that, in order to feel better, a man must eat well. *Panza chiena core cuntento*, in other words. Full belly, happy heart. And so she had consulted with her aunt and had come to a decision: pumpkins with cheese and eggs, borage pizza, and eggplant Parmesan.

The problem of obtaining the best ingredients was, as always, a matter for some careful thought.

As long as we're talking about Romano cheese, olive oil, and cacioricotta cheese, she could draw on the provisions in the pantry, the ones brought by the donkey cart that came in from the villages.

But the borage, the onions, and especially the pumpkin would have to be bought locally.

Nelide was reminded of that vegetable vendor surrounded by women, 'o Sarracino, that's what they'd called him; but what she needed was vegetables, not theater. And so she went downstairs with her bag, her eyes fixed straight ahead of her, determined not to fraternize with anyone and to head home as quickly as possible. Her stout body, broad shoulders, and powerful forearms, along with her small eyes and square jaw, discouraged anyone from trying to strike up a conversation with that strange woman, proud of being a hick, equally proud of a virtually incomprehensible dialect, and ill disposed to smiling.

Tanino, the bold vegetable vendor, had seen her appear

from a distance and had called out to her over the heads of the young women who surrounded him, pretending to be interested in his wares.

"Signori', and where do you think you're going with that lovely empty shopping bag? Who could fill it up for you, if not your own loving Tanino?"

They had all laughed, perhaps interpreting a second meaning where perhaps the young man had meant no such thing. Nelide stopped, turned around, and shot him through with a grim glare. Then she said: "*Nun c'è 'ngnuranza senza presunzione, nun c'è pezzenteria senza rifietti.* Every crass fool is conceited, every poor man has some lack. That's what people say, where I come from."

She'd spoken in a low voice, as if thinking aloud; but everyone had heard her. Tanino's smile died on his face, while the other vendors laughed even louder. An elderly pasta vendor courteously inquired: "What do you need, Signori'? You're new around here, forget about 'o Sarracino, all he ever wants to do is kid around."

Nelide snarled: "*Vurraina, cocozza e cepudde.* Borage, pumpkin, and onion."

"You'll find them in an hour or so, Vittorio is coming, he's a vegetable vendor a little less in love with his own voice. Maybe you'd get along better with him. Come back later."

Nelide had nodded her head ever so slightly in assent and had then turned to go, accompanied by the murmurings from the alley. She was a tough nut, Commissario Ricciardi's new governess. The old aunt, God rest her soul, had at least smiled every once in a while: this one, never.

Half an hour later she heard a knock at her door. Drying her hands on the front of her housecoat, she'd gone to see who it was, and had found herself face-to-face with an unexpected visage.

There was Tanino, panting slightly but with a broad smile

on his face, and with a bag in his hands. Behind him she could see the whispering heads of a half dozen curious housemaids.

"Signori'," said the young man, "I've been a little unfortunate with you. You never laugh, and I don't know how to converse with ladies who don't laugh."

"A parlà è art' leggiera," said Nelide. Talking is easy. "I don't have time to talk, young man. The gentleman I look after will be home soon, and I have a meal to get on the table."

'O Sarracino smiled.

"And that's why I'm here, Signori'. Let it never be said that Tanino 'o Sarracino let one of his customers go to another vegetable vendor. My merchandise is the best there is, why just look here: a borage that's smooth as silk, a pumpkin that's pure gold, and certain onions that are . . . "

Nelide grunted.

"Yes, yes, all right. How much do I owe you?"

Tanino put on an air of offended nobility.

"Signori', this is my own personal complimentary sampling, to show you that we know how to extend a welcome to . . . "

Nelide looked at him, mistrustfully.

"You mean you don't want money?"

The young man nodded.

"Not a penny!" he declared proudly.

Nelide thought it over for a second or two and then said: "All right. *Arrivederci.* See you later."

And without a word of thanks she took the bag and slammed the door in Tanino's face, to a gale of laughter from the women behind him. The young man called out cheerfully to the dark wooden door: "But remember, Signori'! You said: See you later!"

Lucia had made *polpettone*: a small but extraordinary family event that was generally celebrated for the treat that it was.

Making that dish took time and the costs were considerable,

especially if you took into account the wolves she was raising and feeding, disguised as children. Another factor to be considered was the hunger of Raffaele, who came home evenings staggering with exhaustion, and hungry enough to devour an entire ox, alive. But when it was time for *polpettone*, it was time, and since in that wonderful month of September the brigadier had been given a nice bonus at Ricciardi's recommendation, Lucia decided that the good news should be celebrated with the whole family; they'd think about their own private celebrations later, when the children were asleep, well fed and happy, and the two of them would finally be all alone in the bedroom at the end of the hall, the one with the high bed and the nightstand with the Madonna who, Lucia certainly hoped, would understand the situation and be quite indulgent.

And so she had spent the entire afternoon working on the components that would, before long, make up her justly famous *polpettone*, a magnificent baked meat loaf, under the attentive gazes of her daughters Benedetta and Maria, who seemed to be watching as if they were studying to be the mothers of their own families. With them, Lucia had developed the habit of telling them everything she was doing, step by step.

Take this slice of nice lean meat, you see? It should be nice and big, but tender. You need to flatten it thoroughly, without breaking it, otherwise it will spew out its contents. Season it with salt and pepper. Now, separately you make a very fine mince of prosciutto, garlic, parsley, and a little marjoram. Not too much; marjoram can be terrible, if you overdo it, then all you taste is the marjoram. Now a little bread crumb, squeezed out thoroughly after soaking it in water, with two egg yolks. Mix it all together until it amalgamates, then spread it on the meat and sprinkle it with pine nuts and raisins.

The girls were a sight to behold, eyes wide open, jaws

dropped; Maria, who was the glutton of the two, every once in a while dipped in a finger for a taste, while Benedetta, the adopted daughter, absorbed the lesson like a sponge.

Now you roll up the meat and tie it; you need to preheat the pan, you know we're not done yet. The lard, the pancetta, a few rings of onion, celery, and a carrot. There you are. Then you add a cup of water and a teaspoonful of tomato paste, the *conserva nera*.

At the dinner table, the result of so much effort lasted such a short time that she was almost sorry she had gone to such trouble; but the ecstatic moans and groans from the men of the household were, nonetheless, gratifying.

But Lucia noticed that Raffaele seemed distracted. Not that he didn't gobble down everything that came within reach, let that be clear, but he was uncommonly taciturn, and she didn't like the expression on his face.

As if he were sad.

When dinner was over and the children had been put to bed, and she was drying the dishes while he read the newspaper, she asked him: "Raffae', can I ask what's got into you? You haven't said a word all evening, I don't know if it was really worthwhile making *polpettone* if you were just going to scarf it down like that."

Maione looked up, startled, and put down his newspaper.

"Forgive me, Luci', you're right. It's just that I'm a little worried about the commissario."

Lucia smiled at him, shaking her head.

"You just can't do it, can you? I mean, you just can't help being a father. It's the thing I like best about you, so I can't complain: but with Ricciardi you can't, you know. That's the way he is, taciturn. Like you when I make a *polpettone*."

"Oh, go on, you can joke about it. But he's not his usual self, I know him too well. He's got something inside, right here," and he pounded his chest, "that he can't get rid of. Now he's not even seeing Signora Livia anymore; I was hoping that she'd be the one, such a beautiful woman that . . . "

Lucia hurled a dishrag at him.

"Hey, don't you dare talk like that, understood? Pretty is as pretty does: beauty isn't everything. Maybe one lady is beautiful but leaves a man indifferent, another lady is less so but he falls for her all the same."

Raffaele protested, laughing.

"And what could you know about that? You're beautiful as can be and I'm head over heels in love with you, so we've put together the whole package. On the other hand, he doesn't even seem to think about having a family. And he's already over thirty."

"You see? A person would think you were talking about your son. But he isn't your son, and he has every right to live as he chooses. There are people in this world who don't care about family, maybe he's one of them."

"No. If he were happy, I'd be fine, I'd be happy for him. But the man isn't happy, and no one can get that out of my head. And who knows what he has in his heart."

Lucia walked toward him, swinging her hips.

"I don't know what he has in his heart, but you in your stomach, you're carrying half the *polpettone* I made, and do you know what that means? That you need to digest. And here, in the Maione household, we take care of feeding but also digesting. That is, if the idea interests you, naturally."

Maione leapt to his feet and in a single lithe movement took Lucia in his arms, striding briskly toward the bedroom. She started laughing, but he gently hushed her.

"Quiet, otherwise if those little devils wake up, there's no chance of anyone getting any digestion around here!"

And he carried her off, thinking all the while how lucky he had been to meet her in the first place, one morning almost forty years ago, next to a certain fountain he knew.

Inwardly, smiling, he said: I love you.

XLVI

Inwardly, weeping, he said: I hate you.

In this night of hovering ghosts singing their damned songs of love, I hate you. I hate you with all the strength I have in my chest, for as much as my fibers are capable of hurting and shouting.

I hate you for the way you have occupied my mind, by and large, without leaving me any room to take a step on my own for the rest of my life.

I hate you because you remained alone to guide me like a solitary star in the darkness, and I don't even know if you'll remember my face or my eyes once your days will have taken you away from all this fury.

I hate you for the silence that I bestowed upon you and in which I wrap myself to keep from going mad. I hate you because I had already gone mad, and incurably so, the first time that I saw you.

I hate you.

Inwardly, weeping, she said: I love you.

Now that I've erased the hope of ever having you, I know that I love you. However much my belly might twist with melancholy, I love you.

I love you for the yearning that you gave me for myself, because I had fallen in love with the idea of you and me, of being a woman in the light of day instead of in this perennial night of sequins and smoke and wine, walking on high heels through the gazes of men's eyes and feeling desire upon me, without joy or smiles.

I love you for this solitude, for the beauty of recognizing myself without fake flowers and letters and wineglasses. For having given me the gift of myself as I was before I forgot myself, while I fooled myself that I was caressing the line of my belly and a small dead cheek.

I love you for having made me feel like a woman, for having let me worry about you and for having let me dream of being able to bring peace to that green sorrow of yours, which grows in the soul and in the void like a powerful perverse plant. I love you for the grief I have known, for the grandeur of being able to look it in the face without having to flee from myself, carrying myself on my own back the whole time, like a crushing burden.

I love you for having taught me love without having known it yourself, for having explained to me without words that there is no peace in life, except at last in death. I love you in this desert, where the only sound that can be heard is that of my condemnation, my verdict and sentence, and it is a song of desperation that I do not know but I understand, the way you understand magic.

I love you for the music you gave back to me. And I love you for the back you turned on me when you left.

I love you.

Inwardly, weeping, she said: I hate you.

I hate you in the darkness of a building and a body where I thought I would have you and instead you weren't there. I hate you for the streets you walked down without me, without even explaining to me why you were leaving.

I hate you because I'm still young, and my belly twists in the springtime when I catch a whiff of the heavy scent of flowers and ripe fruit, and out of the night comes the odor of the sea.

I hate you for the hands that you wouldn't let me feel on my flesh, and for the old woman that I resemble.

I hate you because I can't even bring myself to wish you evil, in the name of a sentiment whose name I know, though not its face, and which belongs to another time and another space.

I hate you for the prison you sit in, and the prison you left me in, prisoner of a name that I no longer want but which I don't know how to get rid of.

I hate you for having left me a road that I walk step by step, with no idea where it takes me, and unable to retrace my path.

I hate you.

Inwardly, weeping, she said: I love you.

I love you and God only knows how much I wish I didn't, in order to be born into a new life I don't deserve and which my days demand forcefully, and yet which deep down I don't desire.

I love you because no one is like you, and I don't want anyone to be like you, even though I might perhaps be able to convince myself and imagine and deceive myself, as much as I am able to do what I set out to do, quiet and determined as in everything else in my life. I love you in the light and in the darkness, when I turn around to look at myself and I find myself alone, nude at the center of a room whose walls are lined with mirrors, without so much as a lie to cling to.

I love you every time I hear a song, I love you every time I see a child smiling, I love you if you pet a dog out in the street.

I love you for my heart, which races like crazy every time I walk by a window.

I love you for my eyes, which fill with tears and anger every time I think of how far away you are.

I love you even if I never see you again, and my legs wrap themselves around other hips, and my arms embrace another body.

I love you because I miss you like hell, even though I've never had you.

I love you.

Inwardly, weeping, he said: I hate you.

I hate you for having been forced to deceive you, while the night of blood just past was already silent in the light of dawn.

I hate you for the remorse that sweeps over me at the thought of you, for the closed doors and open windows, for the sea that never stops knocking on dawn's door, and for this immense, cursed summer that can't seem to resign itself to end.

I hate you for that smile you gave me, for having taken my misery and put it on like the most comfortable of outfits, an outfit you wear still.

I hate you because I had to lie to you, and for the time you're going to have to wait for me outside of these walls, for the thoughts you will have of finding me, and yet you'll never find me.

I hate you for the silence to which you and I will be constrained. For no longer being able to talk and talk and tell stories.

I hate you for having had to do what I did, just to love you. And I hate you because I'd do it again a thousand times and another thousand after that, for the blood that I had before my eyes and for the anger that rode my hand.

I hate you.

I love you, said Lucia, laughing, after they had made love. I love you, Brigadier Raffaele Maione.

And I'll love you forever.

XLVII

The solution had come to him in the courtyard of the Convent of the Incoronata, while, resigned to an early and imminent death, he was preparing for the drive back to police headquarters in the old Fiat with Maione behind the wheel.

As always, it had been a sudden, total reversal of perspective. It was enough to change the way you interpreted the facts, and what had previously been contradictory, senseless, and discordant suddenly composed an eminently legible picture, free of inconsistency.

Along the way, he'd paid practically no attention to the disasters missed by a hair and the panicky scattering of pedestrians at the automobile's approach: his mind continued to sort and match the fragments that up till then he had squirreled away one by one, in the hope that sooner or later they would serve some purpose. As absurd as the triggering thought might have been, it now all added up.

He said nothing to Maione. He wanted to continue thinking it over, and he did so for many hours until, in the middle of the night, he collapsed into a deep and dreamless sleep. At dawn he was already awake and ready to see if he could test out his hypothesis.

But at this point, the usual script changed radically. Here it was no longer a matter of going to pick up a suspect and forcing him to confess. Here there were no eyewitnesses to be confronted one with the other.

Here there was no reason to worry about a potential suspect escaping. And above all, here they could not rely upon the official inquiry of the police, on an investigation to be carried out in the light of day to track down the person guilty of the crime beyond the shadow of a doubt. This time, everything was wrapped up and settled, and no one was going to be happy to see a subversion of the order that had been spontaneously restored by Roccaspina's confession.

No one was going to be happy, that was for sure. Not even the contessa, who had asked him to find the truth in the first place. Because if there's a dead man, my dear contessa, the truth does nothing to assuage anyone's sorrow. He had learned that so long ago that it seemed to him he had always known it.

At a brisk pace he made his way through the milky light of early morning to the Roccaspina residence. When he reached the front entrance, rather than ringing the doorbell, he leaned against the wall and checked his watch; a fishmonger, who was laying out his wares in wooden tubs, sprinkling them with seawater, gazed at him mistrustfully. He waited ten minutes. At seven thirty on the dot he set off, heading in the direction that he imagined the count took when he was still a free man, in his strange morning outings that no one had been able to figure out.

First he walked down a few narrow alleys in another section of the city that was preparing for the new day. Every so often, someone would look up and meet his gaze, failing to recognize him as a customary presence, and immediately turn their eyes away. A man, all alone, and well dressed, was interpreted as an intrusion, a potential danger.

Once again, he became an anonymous figure in the broad thoroughfare, which was already alive with the many bicycles of laborers and factory workers, heading out to the construction sites or the plants on the outskirts of town, with women carrying large baskets on their heads full of vegetables, ricotta, and fruit to be sold in the city's piazzas and courtyards. Ricciardi continued walking, mulling over the details of the case that had led him to the path of what he believed to be the solution.

He knew what had happened. He was reasonably certain of it, because it was the only explanation compatible with what he'd been told and what he'd seen. What he still didn't know was the reason why. He knew the effects that certain thoughts and certain passions had on people, and he could also imagine what had propelled the murderer's hand, but it continued to strike him as truly absurd.

He stopped. This had to be the exact spot where the two routes converged toward the daily destination, and therefore the closest useful spot where they could meet and be alone.

He didn't have long to wait. Not even five minutes and he saw the person he was expecting arrive briskly. The person who, according to him, had killed the lawyer Ludovico Piro, whose suffering image he had been unable to hear in its last thought, as that thought had gone through the lawyer's mind on a hot June night, earlier that year.

He emerged from the shadows and greeted that person.

"*Buongiorno*, Signorina Carlotta. This isn't the first time that a man has waited for you at this corner, now, is it?"

The young woman didn't seem surprised. If anything, annoyed. She clenched her jaw and shot a quick glance around, as if she were considering whether to call for help.

"What the devil do you want? I'm going to school."

Ricciardi looked her in the eye.

"I know you are. Just as you were in the months leading up to June. How many months? Two? Three? Months during which every morning the Count of Roccaspina would come all the way to this corner to meet you. What did you say to each other? What did you have in common, with so many years' difference between you?"

The young woman shifted the books fastened with a strap from one hand to the other.

"I don't understand what you're talking about and if you don't stop pestering me immediately I'll start screaming. You have no right to . . . "

"Really? All right then, let's put it like this: either you agree to talk to me clearly and openly, or I'll go straight to the magistrate who's laying the groundwork for the court trial and I'll ask to be heard as a witness. I'm not saying I won't do it anyway, let that be clear: but first I want to understand the motive for the murder."

Carlotta opened her mouth, and then snapped it shut. She narrowed her eyes.

"All right. Let's hear what absurd ideas you've gotten into your head. Even if I still don't understand what right you have to investigate the case of my father's murder. I believe that I'll talk to some of his friends to get an explanation."

Ricciardi shrugged his shoulders.

"As you think best. If you please, let's take a seat in that café. It won't take long."

Carlotta turned and headed straight into the café, where she took a seat at a table set slightly apart from the others, at the far end of the little room. Her confidence in selecting a place to sit confirmed in Ricciardi's mind that this was exactly where the girl had had her meetings with Roccaspina.

He ordered an espresso, and Carlotta asked for a glass of milk. Ricciardi observed her at some length: the delicate features of the young girl were evolving into the woman that she would eventually become: strong-willed, powerful, aware of her beauty. Now that he had her before him, the picture that he had sketched for himself seemed even more convincing.

"I'll speak in hypothetical terms, Signorina. This is all just the fruit of my imagination. And I'm going to imagine that you began a romantic relationship with Romualdo Palmieri di

Roccaspina; perhaps after meeting him in your father's office, or else at the yacht club. A cheerful, likable, romantic man, deep down, a fun-loving gambler. And handsome, too. Very attractive to a young woman who no longer feels she's a little girl, and is ready to be a grown-up woman. You began to see each other on the rare occasions offered by your life as a girl living at home and attending school. For instance, in the early morning; perhaps in this very café, and at this very table. Where you could look into each other's eyes, and whisper sweet nothings. Even a caress or two."

Ricciardi's voice flowed lightly. Carlotta stared into the middle distance; she seemed to be dreaming.

"Then something must have happened. For your father, Roccaspina was the best of business; the money came from Duke Marangolo, who even guaranteed it would be paid back in full. There was no risk: an enormously wealthy man, who was sick to boot, provided the money to lend out, offering sizable profit margins. And in fact for a long time it all went well, with frequent visits and excellent relations. All of a sudden, however, the lawyer, the ruthless profiteer who made all his money by loan-sharking, and who was therefore devoid of scruples or misgivings, decided to wring the neck of the goose that laid the golden eggs. He was no longer willing to act as an intermediary, and he cut off all ties with Marangolo as well."

Carlotta slowly shook her head. Ricciardi went on.

"Actually, he had found out about the two of you. How did that happen? Did he see you, run into you by chance? Did he overhear you talking? Did Roccaspina himself tell him, in an impetus of sincerity?"

The girl didn't reply. Ricciardi continued.

"It was at that point, in any case, that your father stopped giving extensions and refused to lend him any more money. Roccaspina found himself with his back to the wall and came to your home the morning before the murder. You were at school, perhaps that's exactly why he chose that time to come over. They quarreled, bitterly. Everyone heard them shout, but no one understood what they were saying. They were talking about you, isn't that right?"

Silence. Outside, the stream of young people heading to school increased, spreading through the air a cheerful sound of laughter and conversation. The commissario resumed.

"He didn't say anything to your mother, I believe; actually, I'm quite certain of it. He wanted to settle the matter on his own. Who can say, maybe he just didn't want to worry her. He decided to go to the Convent of the Incoronata, where he was the administrator and where, as chance would have it, he had been the day before on business. The Madonna dell'Incoronata is a convent, certainly: an ancient, renowned convent. But it is also a boarding school. And the lawyer Piro, who had visited the convent the day before in his capacity as its administrator, went back to the boarding school the following day, in his capacity as a father."

For the first time, Carlotta looked up at Ricciardi, and her eyes were aflame. The commissario saw the pure hatred that inhabited that mind, but he wasn't afraid of it. He continued.

"I understood it late, I was stupid. I couldn't see. And yet you yourself, when I asked you yesterday whether you knew the reason for that double trip, referred to the Incoronata as the *boarding school*. And Laprece, the chauffeur that you fired immediately for fear he might talk, said the same thing. And you were the one who fired him, not your mother, because when he came in to tell Brigadier Maione about it, Laprece said: Because now that *the father* was dead, they didn't need me anymore.

"You have a strong personality, Signorina. Your mother, who must have guessed something or who you might actually have told what happened, is afraid of you."

The young woman grimaced. She reached into the pocket

of her dress and pulled out a cigarette, lit it calmly, and started smoking while she looked out the window.

Ricciardi went on.

"That very same evening, when you went to tell your father goodnight, unaware of what had happened, he told you of his decision to put you in boarding school to break off that relationship. Just as he had told Roccaspina himself, on the morning of that day. His radical approach to the matter made you see red. He spoke, grim and determined, and you walked up and down in the room, perhaps denying, or else coming up with excuses. When you found yourself right behind him, over by the window, you struck. A single, mortal blow. You were never going to allow yourself to be locked up in a religious boarding school."

Carlotta hadn't changed expression, with her elbow on the table, the cigarette smoldering between her fingers, her eyes focused on the street outside.

"No one saw, no one heard. Impossible to think that at that time of night and with that heat, in such a silent and densely inhabited area, anyone could have gotten in from outside. In fact, no one did get in: the murderer was already inside. And the murder weapon, the one that no one could find? I have come up with an idea of my own."

With a rapid motion, Ricciardi leaned over the table and yanked the hair stick that held Carlotta's hair up in a bun. Her hair, loose now, cascaded over the girl's shoulders, but she didn't even change position. The commissario looked at the object, holding it midway beween himself and her: a silver wedge, pointy and about eight inches long, surmounted by a geometric decoration.

Like in the Rummolo murder. There too, it was a hair stick. And there, too, it was the Roccaspinas.

"Something like that. Your rage, your despair, a burst of madness. You went back to your bedroom, but you didn't get any sleep. I can't imagine how long you thought about what to do. The minutes, the hours were passing and the time was nearing when your mother would wake up and, not finding your father in bed, would go to look for him. And so you asked the only person who would have done anything to save you. Literally anything."

Carlotta crushed out her cigarette in the ashtray and calmly began to gather her hair in her usual hairdo. She picked up the hair stick and put it back into her hair.

"You went to wait for him outside his home, or else here, at the usual place and the usual time. You told him everything, maybe that you had done it for him, or even for the two of you. To keep your love alive. Did he think it himself or did you suggest it to him, that if they discovered the truth, your life would be over? A parricide, a murderer without any mitigating circumstances. Whereas he, if he had confessed, could get the mitigating circumstances of serious motives, the outburst of wrath, tempted by a mocking provocation: everyone had heard the quarrel, everyone knew about his huge debts and the fact that your father held him in his fist. And his name, too, would carry a certain amount of weight, as would the reputation of his family. He convinced himself, or perhaps you talked him into it. And he confessed."

He fell silent. The girl heaved a deep sigh and leveled her cold eyes at him; then, slowly and sarcastically, she started clapping her hands.

"Bravo. Bravo indeed, Commissario! You have a very vivid imagination. I'm very fond of these new novels, and surely you've read some, that talk about murderers and conspiracies, and clever, bright policemen who unveil the mysteries. Have you ever thought of writing one? Maybe I could help you. The plot you just laid out for me is a nice one, but I think it still needs a little work. What do you say, shall we work on it?"

Now it was Ricciardi's turn to listen. The girl began.

"Well, now, let's see. First of all, I think the characters ought to be developed a little more completely, don't you? The protagonist's father, for instance. You said it right, a man without scruples, someone who thinks of nothing but money. But we ought to add, someone who cares nothing for the happiness of his family: a social climber, someone who has no notion of allowing others to choose for themselves. And if the nobleman who made the confession were rich instead of powerful, then the age difference would count for nothing. Nor the fact that he was already married. In the fictional narrative, we could have him introduce his daughter to Duke Marangolo, an old man about to die, in the hopes that the elderly duke might fall in love with her; perhaps that might actually be the occasion on which they first meet the count. What do you say? Nice, don't you think? The young girl whose father wants to toss her into the arms of a wealthy old nobleman instead throws herself into the arms of the penniless nobleman. That strikes me as an interesting plot twist. As is the idea of sending the girl to a religious boarding school, perhaps with a view to the possibility that she take her vows and become the mother superior of the very same institutions that are the source of his income. Sure, vows, just think."

She lit another cigarette, smiling as if she really were thinking about a story to write.

"And then there's the count—we need to do a little work on how we've presented him, too! We ought to explain that he's married, yes, but that he hasn't had any real relationship with his wife for many years. And that's because, let's say, she's a harsh woman, rigid as a piece of wood, cheerless and without any dreams of her own. She hasn't known how to be a companion to him, she's never helped him, she's abandoned him to his fate. There, now she's perfect."

She took a long, contented drag on her cigarette.

"But let's get back to the count. He found in the girl, in her joy of living and her desire for the future, a new hope. What do you say, that could even be the title: A New Hope. If we don't tell about this part, then the character becomes incomprehensible. Everything collapses. And then we have to depict the girl's mother, a weak woman, fragile and petty, ignorant and entirely at her husband's beck and call. Easily manipulated, that much is true, and always dependent on others to know what to do. From the father to the daughter. Perhaps that could be the moral of the story, maybe they remember each other more than she's willing to admit."

She chuckled, ironically, and went on, as if the grip of some delirium.

"And then the secondary characters are very important in stories like this one. The chauffeur, for example: he's a damned busybody who's always sticking his nose into other people's business, and maybe he got to chatting with the lawyer about why he was out at the Convent of the Incoronata twice in two days . . . "

Ricciardi had heard more than enough. He interrupted her, in a flat voice.

"What did you tell him, to convince him? How did you manage to send him to prison in your place?"

The girl smiled, blowing a plume of smoke toward the commissario.

"Ah, ah, ah, Commissario! You're abandoning the world of fiction in order to step into the real world, and that's not how we do. That's a risk that writers run, but they have to resist the temptation. In the novel, now, maybe the girl has explained to the count that when he gets out, she'll be there waiting for him. She'll still be a relatively young woman, she'll love him even more than before, and she'll be so grateful to him that she'll give him a future he could never dream of otherwise. The crazy count only has to make sure he spends as little time as possible in prison."

Ricciardi stood up brusquely. He was having trouble breathing.

"It seems to me that you have no intention of confessing, Signorina. No intention of telling the truth and bringing peace to the many people who are suffering and will suffer for what you've done."

Carlotta stood up gracefully, gathering the schoolbooks she had left on a chair.

"But we're talking about a novel, Commissario. Have you forgotten? I have absolutely nothing to confess. There's already a man in jail, and he's the one who actually killed my poor papa, and ruined my life. And I hope the court grants him no mitigating circumstances of any kind, and that instead they sentence him to death, because that's exactly what he deserves. Now, I'm sure you'll excuse me, but I have to go to school. You know, I have a future to build."

XLVIII

Nothing he could do about it, but Maione would be worried not to find him in the office. Still, Ricciardi decided to go directly to the home of the Contessa di Roccaspina. He felt conflicted. He needed to tell Bianca what he had discovered, but he wished he could spare her the pain of knowing the true motives that had driven her husband to confess to a murder he hadn't committed.

And that wasn't all. He needed to meet with Roccaspina again, and tell him that someone had figured out the way things had actually gone. Help him to regain his sense of reality, force him to think about what he was doing to himself and to his wife by allowing that girl to manipulate him.

Bianca received him immediately, dressed in black as usual. She looked weary, as if she hadn't slept or had slept badly. Looking at her lined face, Ricciardi thought that she seemed far more fragile than the adolescent with whom he had spoken until just a few minutes before, conversing about death and murders in a café in the center of town as if they were inventions, rather than reality.

There was a certain awkwardness between them.

The caress of the previous day at police headquarters had left upon him the memory of the woman's warm flesh, burning with tears and sorrow. And it had transmitted to her, who reached up and accompanied that caress with her hand, a closeness and support that she never thought she would feel again in her solitary life.

Now, however, it was the commissario's job to tell the contessa something that she might not ever have wanted to hear; and he discovered to his astonishment that he was afraid that this revelation might drive her away from him.

But it was his duty to talk.

He told her about his intuition at the convent, of how he'd spent the whole evening and much of the night arranging the evidence in its new context, and how he had found a series of confirming details sufficient to close the circle without many possibilities of error.

He told her how he'd met with Carlotta, waiting for her at the same corner where Romualdo probably waited for her; and he saw her start when he revealed to her that at seven o'clock that morning he had been standing in the street outside her building.

He told her about his conversation with the young woman, and about how she had reacted: her chilly calm, her unruffled equilibrium, her ability to withstand his reconstruction of the truth.

He told her that Signorina Piro hadn't displayed any willingness to confess, and had in fact made a great show of confidence that the count would never retract his story, but would keep her perfectly safe.

When he was finally done, Bianca stared into the air in front of her, shaking her head. Ricciardi was afraid he would upset her, but instead she seemed to be plunged into genuine sorrow.

"A little girl. She's just a little girl. I saw her from a distance, at her father's funeral: she seemed heartbroken, strong but despairing. She was supporting her mother, and holding her brother by the hand. How can a person be so false? I beg you to tell me, Commissario, how can someone be so false?"

Ricciardi cautiously tried to sound her out a little further, to pull her out of that maelstrom of sorrow.

"I've seen things, Signora, believe me. I really have seen

amazing things in my work. And after all, Carlotta resembles her father, if it's true that he was a man with so few scruples that he was willing to make her Marangolo's lover."

Bianca opened up. She smiled sadly.

"Poor Carlo Maria. He has always been a victim of his great fortune. Money makes people lonely: both people who have none and people who have too much. Now that I know what happened, Commissario, I feel hollowed out. I thought I would feel a sense of relief, if for no reason other than that I finally had proof I hadn't lost my mind. Instead I feel like a failure, both as a woman and as a wife. But also as a friend, since I've caused the duke so much pain, forcing him to have dealings with these people in order to help me."

Ricciardi looked at her, tenderly.

"You're certainly not the one who's a failure. It's your husband who fell into a net from which he was unable to extract himself. And I'd like him to understand that, at least."

Bianca stared at him, bewildered.

"But . . . but how can this be, Commissario? Now we know the truth, we know exactly what happened, right down to the smallest detail: isn't that enough to set Romualdo free?"

Ricciardi shook his head.

"Unfortunately, no, Contessa. Unless your husband retracts his confession, we cannot even reopen the investigation. We have no solid evidence, just a reconstruction based on conjecture and vague testimony. Carlotta Piro made no admissions and she does not intend to make any, and there's no question that her family will rally around her. I can't imagine that, after all these months, we'll obtain anything more. I told you about the reticence of the mother superior of the convent of the Incoronata, and I also believe that Duke Marangolo's testimony would be worthless.

"The only possibility is for your husband to change his mind."

The woman ran her hands over her face.

"Commissario, I . . . I want you to know that nothing Romualdo can do will change my decision to stop living as his wife. It's over between us, and the fact that knowing about this relationship does nothing to hurt me is just further proof that he no longer meant a thing to me. But the thought that an innocent man, manipulated by others, should destroy his own life does weigh on me, and greatly. In part because, from what I was able to see, he's not going to survive a lengthy detention."

Ricciardi nodded.

"I think so too, Contessa. And I intend to go right away and talk to him. Could you please get in touch with the lawyer Moscato and ask him to arrange for an interview as quickly as possible? I'll wait to hear from you in my office."

Bianca stood up, staring Ricciardi in the face with those strange and deeply lovely eyes of hers.

"Commissario, I don't know how I can ever repay you for what you've done. You've freed me from the obsession of something incomprehensible that would eventually have suffocated me. You restored my faith in myself and in those around me."

Ricciardi couldn't restrain a half smile.

Then he bowed his head and left.

XLIX

Ricciardi had just finished telling the whole story to Maione, who continued to shake his head in bafflement. "Commissa', forgive me but I truly can't bring myself to believe it. That girl is the same age as my boy Giovanni, sixteen years old, and he plays soccer with his friends, his knees are always scraped up, and I still have to box his ears to get him to wash his hands before dinner. How can I believe that a young girl, a *guagliuncella* like her, could start up a relationship with a man who, even if he is a fool, is still a fully grown man, then kill her father, and still have the lucidity to deceive the police, her mother, the lawyers, and the magistrates?"

The commissario grimaced.

"No, Raffaele. Carlotta didn't trick all these people. All she had to do was trick one person, Romualdo Palmieri di Roccaspina. Then he took care of tricking everyone else. Women, as you know, grow up quicker, so don't worry about your son."

"Eh, Commissa', you joke around, but in the meantime, like you said before, there's really almost nothing we can do. The only thing would be to talk the count into changing his confession."

Ricciardi shrugged his shoulders.

"I'll try to talk to him. The contessa is going to ask his lawyer to request an urgent interview, we'll see what comes of it. After all, here there's still no trouble in sight, is there?"

Maione threw his arms wide.

"Quiet as a church, Commissa'. One of two things must

have happened: either the crooks are all still on holiday or else they're about to fire us all and we can all set up shop and do like the private investigators in America. After all, we'd be pretty good at it, don't you think?"

Before Ricciardi had a chance to reply, there came a knock at the door. It was Amitrano.

"Commissa', there's a certain Counselor Moscato at the front entrance who asks if you can come downstairs."

Bianca couldn't bring herself to cry.

She had locked herself in her dark bedroom and had convinced Assunta that she wasn't hungry and wouldn't eat because of her headache. She continued to contemplate her own life, her memories of past grandeur and present poverty, but she still couldn't bring herself to cry.

She ought to have, really. She had every reason to, and now she could add to that array the fact that she'd been betrayed by her husband.

Betrayed?

In good conscience, could she really say that she'd been betrayed? After all, she hadn't thought of herself as his wife for years.

The answer was no.

She discovered, to her cautious amazement, that she actually envied Romualdo a little, because he had been able to rediscover the power of an emotion, the energy that goes with that. And this energy was strong enough to allow him to make an enormous sacrifice: renounce that very emotion.

Would she ever have that good fortune?

She still felt capable of experiencing love; her heart was hungry, her flesh was eager to be touched, caressed, her mouth wished for nothing better than to laugh.

She still felt alive, but buried in that palazzo which had become a museum to its own memories.

Who knows, maybe she ought to sell the place. After saving it from Romualdo's demon, she ought to get rid of it and use the money to make a new life for herself. After all, her reputation remained intact: she still had her good name. She could rewrite her own destiny.

As she was thinking, someone knocked at her bedroom door. She heard the housekeeper's voice.

"Signo', Duke Marangolo is here. He says it's urgent."

Along the way to Poggioreale prison, Ricciardi informed Counselor Moscato of what he had found out.

The man was clearly disconcerted.

"Poor idiot. I told you, Commissario, the man never grew up. He isn't a bad man, but deep down he's still just a boy: he believes he's immortal. Now he's started skipping his meals, and you've seen the results. He thinks that that's going to make the judges take pity on him and they'll give him a shorter sentence."

"We need to make him realize that all this is absurd. That he's making an enormous sacrifice for no good reason, that the girl, given her age, would serve at most a few years in a juvenile reform school."

Moscato twisted his mouth in a grimace.

"Commissa', the man is out of his mind. All he talks about is mitigating circumstances, legal quibbles, he wants to get out of prison as soon as he possibly can. I thought it was for Bianca, even though whenever I mentioned her name he'd just change the subject: he didn't want to hear a word about her. Instead it's for the viper, Piro's daughter. Bloodcurdling: if this is what she's like at sixteen, you have to wonder what she'll be like as an adult."

Carlo Maria was waiting for Bianca in the living room. He looked simply terrible, his unhealthy complexion highlighting the features of a face full of suffering. He was clutching with both hands at a walking stick that supported his weight.

"*Ciao*, Bianca. At last, you receive me."

She stared at him sorrowfully.

"You know why I never wanted to receive you here. Because I have your welfare at heart much more than many of those around you."

The man said, in a whisper: "Seeing you. Seeing you is the difference between living and dying, for me. Don't you understand? Just seeing you. I could never hope to have you by my side, not anymore, anyway, not since I fell sick. But to see you is such a delight! I feel as if my heart . . . is about to burst."

In his deep emotion, his voice had failed him toward the end of that sentence.

Bianca felt her eyes fill with tears.

"Carlo, I . . . "

The man shook his head.

"I didn't come here to tell you this, Bianca. There's a very serious mattered to be decided, and we're going to have to resolve it immediately."

The contessa grew worried.

"Why, what are you talking about? Has something else happened? Has Romualdo . . . "

Marangolo waved away the count's name as if it were a bothersome fly.

"No, for once this has nothing to with that fool husband of yours. Something very serious is happening, and we have to decide whether or not to intervene. But the decision is up to you."

"Then explain it to me," said Bianca.

Marangolo heaved a deep sigh.

"As you know, I have a great many friends. Friends where you wouldn't expect; people whose names it's better for you not to know. People who occasionally come to see me down at the yacht club and confide in me, tell me things. And so I come to learn things that are exceedingly interesting, I assure you; it's as good a way as any to stay informed."

"Carlo, I don't understand what . . . "

The duke interrupted her.

"Listen to me. Then it will be up to you to decide what to do."

When Romualdo di Roccaspina saw Ricciardi his face took on a harsh expression and he turned to speak to his lawyer.

"Attilio, frankly I can't understand why you persist in bringing this individual here to see me. I don't wish to speak to him. My wife and her absurd idea of . . . "

Moscato waited for the guard to move away and then addressed him in no uncertain terms.

"Romua', shut up. I've had it up to here with your lunatic ravings. The commissario isn't here to listen to anything you have to say. He has some serious matters to tell you about. So sit down and listen."

Moscato's brusque, no-nonsense tone came as a revolutionary change, and it caught Roccaspina off guard.

Ricciardi took advantage of the situation and went on the attack.

"Count, I know what happened. I know, right down to the smallest details, the motives, and the way things went. Listen to me, and I think you'll agree."

He spoke coldly and with precision. He recounted the whole story, reconstructing moment by moment the scenario he had assembled for the murder, the hours preceding it and those that followed it.

As he spoke, going on for several intense minutes, the prisoner kept his eyes fixed on Ricciardi's face without displaying any signs of change in the haggard, long-suffering features of his face, with the exception of a silent quivering of his lips.

Moscato, on the other hand, had lifted his gaze above the table and seemed particularly focused on reading the slogans on the walls of the visiting room. Directly over Roccaspina's head was written: "It is necessary to be disciplined especially when discipline requires sacrifice and renunciation."

When Ricciardi fell silent, the lawyer weighed in.

"It makes no sense to go on maintaining this position, Romualdo. She's a young girl who doesn't even know what she wants from tomorrow, let alone trying to imagine that she'd be out there waiting for you in twenty years. She wouldn't receive a serious punishment, since she's a minor and a female. She'd receive only a minimum sentence, she could claim that her father was a man who habitually abused all those around him. Retract your statement, Romua'. I can put in a request today to reopen the investigation."

Romualdo sat in silence for a while, steadily staring at Ricciardi. Then he replied, resolutely: "If all this were true, and if I were actually to retract, can you tell me what would become of her? A young woman carrying the infamy of having murdered her father. A ruined woman, without a chance at friendship, of any social life. Who has moreover tied herself to a rootless misfit, a man over his head in debt and so much older than her. Someone who chose to go to jail out of love, just think how crazy that is. They'd put her in prison, she who is as delicate as a butterfly, she, who is freer than the air itself. She, who is a smile made flesh, would never smile again as long as she lives. Having murdered only for the sake of my love, and because they wanted to lock her up in a nunnery. If all this were true, and if I were to accept your proposal, Atti', what kind of life would be left to me? Living with a woman I hate and who judges me in silence every instant of the day. Now that I have found love and I've also found the strength to renounce the lived experience of that love with the sole courageous act of a pointless life. If all this were true."

He stood up with a surprising burst of energy, gesturing to the guard at the far end of the room to come and retrieve him.

"But to the immense good fortune of one and all, first and foremost my beloved wife, who can now begin a new life without the burden of my debts, all this in fact is not true. I murdered Ludovico Piro, the infamous loan shark, and I am going to serve my sentence. And let me tell you one last thing, Commissario: I know perfectly well that she won't wait for me. I don't want her to. I want her to enjoy a life of freedom and happiness, because I love her."

He left the room, the guard steering him by the arm.

In some strange way, in the loose prison clothing that hung off his body, flapping as he walked, he seemed positively regal.

Once he was within a short distance of police headquarters, Ricciardi grew increasingly confused. Sacrifice and renunciation, those were the words that had been written on the walls of the visiting room. Could it be that in order to love, one had to be willing to suffer so greatly?

As he was mulling over these thoughts, he was reminded of Enrica, Livia, Bianca, and the tears they had all shed. And Rosa, too, how she had worried about him.

Who knows if any of this is worth the trouble, he thought.

Concentrating on his thoughts, he failed to notice the black car parked in the shadows at the corner of the street, nor the two men who, the moment he came into view, stepped out of it and walked over, flanking him.

The elder of the two said, in a low voice: "Commissario Luigi Alfredo Ricciardi, correct? I'm going to have to ask you to come with us."

L

They were only a short distance from police headquarters, and yet it never even occurred to Ricciardi to call out for help, to shout, or to try breaking and running, or putting up any kind of resistance. The courteous behavior of the two men, their confident voices, the urgency of their manner wrongfooted him. Once he realized that he might be in serious danger, the large black automobile was already moving.

The younger man was driving, calmly, at moderate speed. The older man was sitting next to him in the backseat. His expression was relaxed, but under his jacket was an unmistakable bulge.

A sidearm. That man was packing a pistol, and the position of his right hand made it clear that he was ready to use it. Ricciardi took all this in with a hollow in the pit of his stomach.

"Who are you? Where are we going?"

His voice had come out a little too squeaky. He had betrayed his fear. And he was sorry for that.

Smiling in a way that was anything but reassuring, the man sitting beside him replied in a tone that clashed with the context.

"Nothing but a little drive, Commissario. You have nothing to fear. Nothing but an excursion among friends."

Ricciardi let his eyes run down the car door beside him: there was no handle to open it, no crank to lower the window.

"Am I being kidnapped or am I under arrest?"

The question was ironical, meant to point out the absurdity of the situation, but the man beside him considered it seriously.

"Neither of the two," he replied. "We're just going to see some people who'd like to talk with you. I can't tell you anything more."

The automobile made its way through traffic, pushing past carts and wagons and public conveyances, moving steadily away from the center of town. Ricciardi locked eyes with a child who first waved his hand in greeting, then caught himself, as he read the despair in Ricciardi's eyes. He had nothing to fear, he kept saying to himself. He had done nothing wrong.

Even he, who wasn't accustomed to spending time conversing in the hallways of police headquarters, had heard of people who'd vanished from one evening to the following morning, people about whom the organs of the Ministry of the Interior had extended an unsettling veil of silence. But for the most part, these people were dissidents, individuals who were carrying on political activities, and who publicly expressed ideas that were openly in opposition to the Fascist regime, often publishing articles to that effect. Ricciardi was completely indifferent to certain matters, and he steered clear of any and all discussions on the subject.

His mind darted to Bruno Modo. He was the only person he knew and frequented who had openly expressed, speaking aloud, indeed often far too loud, his own thoughts which were anything but orthodox. More than once, Ricciardi had urged him to show more care, not to expose himself like that. A few months earlier he had even helped Modo out of a dangerous situation, and the people he had approached to do so had acknowledged Ricciardi's own clear position of political indifference.

So what could those people want from him now? Was it possible that this was a common criminal operation? That someone he'd arrested wanted to take revenge on him, or something of that sort?

No. There was nothing about the two men in the car that suggested they were common criminals. They were silent, nondescript, clean shaven, neatly brushed. They wore well-made suits and new hats. They could be a pair of businessmen, or two university professors, if it hadn't been for that bulge under the jacket.

They were heading toward the eastern outskirts of town. The broad dirt road was lined to the right by the high walls of the cargo port and to the left by the endless procession of hovels housing the families of workers employed at the factories that could be glimpsed in the distance.

"We're almost here," said the man.

The automobile turned off onto a side street, and then into another, plunging into a grid of streets that all looked alike. He was driving in circles, Ricciardi realized. He wanted to confuse him, make it harder for him ever to find the place again. At last, and rather suddenly, they swerved through a nondescript gate that led into the courtyard of what could easily be a small abandoned factory. There was no one in sight, nor did the dusty windowpanes seem to conceal offices of any kind.

The driver got out and opened the door from the outside for his colleague, who in his turn went around and opened the door on the opposite side for the commissario. Ricciardi stepped out into the dusty courtyard. The silence was absolute. His heart was pounding in his throat: if they shot him and abandoned his body there, no one would ever find out anything about it.

He thought of Enrica, and then Maione. Who knows what they would think, if he simply vanished. Who knows if they would get together and share their memories of him. The absurdity of the thought almost made him smile, but immediately thereafter he was filled with a cold rage: what did these men want with him? How dare they treat him like this?

The older man took him by the arm, as if about to lead him somewhere. Ricciardi reacted by pushing his hand away with a brusque gesture and making a show of brushing off his sleeve. The man replied with a sort of malignant grin and affectedly showed him to a door.

They entered a space where the air was cool, immersed in shade. Ricciardi caught a whiff of stale air and mold. They walked across a large room that, when the plant was in operation, must have been a manufacturing floor. They came to a flight of stairs, climbed it, and came to another door.

The younger man knocked discreetly.

A voice replied from within.

"Come in."

The room was moderately large, without windows or any other openings. The younger man remained outside the door, with a broad stance, arms folded. The other man led Ricciardi to a table at which four men sat, and took up a position to Ricciardi's right.

To the left was a little man with a truculent expression and a scar on his forehead; beside him was a fat man smoking a cigar that put out a pestilential stench; then there was a distinguished looking man with white hair, elegantly dressed; all the way to the right was a very young man, little more than a boy, in a black shirt. No, these weren't criminals. At first Ricciardi thought that he ought to feel reassured now, but instead he felt a wave of great anxiety wash over him.

He decided that he would be the first to speak.

"Gentlemen, I don't know who you are or what you want from me. But I should warn you that I'm a police officer and that my prolonged absence will surely be noticed by my colleagues, and therefore . . . "

The white-haired man interrupted.

"We've brought you here precisely because we know who you are. In every sense of the word."

The other three men all chuckled, as if they'd just heard a funny joke. Ricciardi felt a surge of irritation.

"Then would you care to explain to me, Signor . . . ?"

The man shook his head.

"No, Commissario. Our names should be of no interest to you."

Ricciardi refused to allow that matter to be dismissed so cavalierly.

"I believe I have the right to know with whom I'm speaking, don't you agree?"

The fat man with the cigar answered him. He had a strong northern accent that Ricciardi was unable to place.

"We are people who have the security of our nation at heart, my good man. And who are convinced that that security rests also upon common decorum and healthy habits."

Ricciardi looked at him, perplexed.

"I have no idea what you're driving at. I think there must be some mistake."

The young man with the black shirt suddenly spoke up, narrowing his eyes.

"There's been no mistake, Ricciardi. If anything, there's been a criminal act, a series of illegal behaviors that require our immediate intervention. Fascist cities are orderly places, full of manly Roman pride. Not places that will tolerate behavior that is aimed at undermining the general order, and I'm speaking in moral terms as well."

Ricciardi felt his head spin: this was starting to seem like a nightmare.

"And what am I supposed to have done? What behavior . . . "

The man with white hair snapped the fingers of his right hand in the direction of the man with the scar on his forehead, who then spoke up in a high-pitched voice, practically falsetto.

"Now then, we have here a number of surveillance reports. Let me first state that this surveillance activity became necessary as a result of a complaint filed with one of our functionaries. And from these reports there emerges an unmistakable picture of your personal inclination to pederasty."

The word dropped into the silence like a hand grenade. Ricciardi said: "What? Have you lost your minds?"

The man in the black shirt replied flatly.

"No. The deviant, the sick man, the one breaking the laws of nature is you. And as such, we'll have you surgically removed, as we would any ordinary abscess."

The man with the scar on his forehead went on, leafing through a stack of paper on the table in front of him.

"We see no indication that you've had any relationships with women over the past six years. No one has seen you frequent a brothel or receive prostitutes at your own place of residence. You aren't engaged to be married, nor do we see any evidence you ever have been."

"What does that have to do with anything?" asked Ricciardi.

The little man continued to speak in his squeaky voice.

"On the other hand, you spend a great deal of time with a man, a certain Bruno Modo, a physician at the Pellegrini hospital, who is already under our regular surveillance because he is suspected of political activity against the state. You've met with this man, without any other company, and no more than two evenings ago you were at his home, where the two of you remained alone."

Ricciardi shouted: "But he was drunk! I just helped him get into bed, he couldn't stand on his own two feet!"

The fat man with the cigar laughed raucously.

"Ah, so you admit it! You helped him get into bed, and how else did you help him out?"

The man with the snowy hair, who was clearly the highest-ranking man at the table, went on talking in a tone that actually seemed conciliatory.

"As you can imagine, Ricciardi, in cases like this, we proceed with extreme caution; if someone wishes to practice this horrible vice discreetly and silently and minding their own business, never kicking up a fuss and avoiding public display as you do, and I have to give you credit for it, then we tend to overlook it. But you're a representative of the state, in fact, you're a commissario of police. Men like you are supposed to set an example."

The young man in the black shirt completed the thought.

"Which is why we have no intention of allowing this abhorrent behavior to continue. Nor can we afford to resolve this through a public criminal trial, heaping ridicule upon the very institution that you, infamous faggot that you are, work for. So we're going to cart you off and dump you on a deserted beach where you can remain for all the years that it takes to turn you normal again, that is, if you ever were."

Ricciardi couldn't bring himself to believe it. He took a step toward the young man, and the man standing beside him grabbed him firmly by the arm.

"You can't do that, without any evidence! These are just conjectures, your diseased imagining and fantasies! Who . . . "

The little man with the scar on his forehead scanned the sheet of paper in his hands.

"We do possess the eyewitness testimony of a respected and prominent member of this city's better society, a woman who is, in fact, honored to call herself a personal friend of Il Duce's own family. This woman stated to one of our functionaries that she had attempted to have personal relations with you, but that you refused to do so. Is this true?"

Livia. Had it been Livia who said this about him? How could that be?

"I . . . well, yes, but that was a very particular situation; she had drunk quite a lot and . . . "

The young man in the black shirt spoke over him, contemptuously.

"I just screw the drunk ones all the better. Or was she ugly, the lady in question? Perhaps she wasn't attractive?"

The man with the white hair smiled.

"No, no. Quite the opposite. I would say that as of now, the lady in question is perhaps the most attractive woman in the whole city."

The man with the cigar sighed in exasperation.

"Gentlemen, what are we waiting for? Let's toss this degenerate onto the first outbound ship heading for you-know-where and just scratch this off the list. What's more, Commissario, where we're sending you, you'll find a bunch of people just like you. You'll be very happy there, I assure you."

Before Ricciardi could even retort, the door swung open. The man who had driven the car that brought him there entered the room, walked over, and leaned down to whisper something in the ear of the white-haired man, whose face took on an annoyed but also slightly uneasy expression. After taking a moment to reflect, he said: "All right. If it's really all that urgent, show them in."

The other three men looked at him curiously, but he said nothing more.

The door swung open once again and, hobbling on a cane, Carlo Maria Fossati Berti, Duke Marangolo, entered the room.

At his side was Bianca di Roccaspina.

LI

The sight of the new arrivals only sharpened in Ricciardi the sensation that he was in the throes of some nightmare or a weird, unpleasant delusion. What could Bianca and the duke be doing there? How could they have found out that he'd been dragged into that absurd excuse for a trial, without arguments or evidence, and with a prefabricated verdict ready to be handed down? Who had warned them, and why?

He tried to speak, but no words came out. The contessa's gaze was calm, as if running into each other in a place like that was the most normal thing in the world. Marangolo, on the other hand, didn't even seem to have noticed him. He had his eyes fixed on the man with white hair, who had stood up to greet him. The others remained seated at the table: the man with the scar on his forehead leaned toward the man with the cigar and whispered something to him.

The man with white hair said: "My dear friend, as you can see we're in the middle of something, but we've almost finished and . . . "

Marangolo raised a hand to interrupt him.

"But this is exactly why I'm here, Iaselli. You're about to make a terrible mistake, and I'm here to stop you."

The man with white hair turned beet red.

"No names, if you please! This is a confidential meeting, and . . . "

Marangolo burst into a small laugh.

"Oh, of course, your confidential meetings. I know very well how those work. Well, since you're not bothering to do it, I will. Allow me to introduce myself: I am Carlo Maria Marangolo. The Duke of Marangolo. The fact that I am here is a clear sign that someone very important authorized me to come, so I'm not going to waste your time and my own explaining my credentials; you can look into that matter after we've taken care of the matter at hand, perhaps by placing a call to that number in Rome that I feel sure you all know by heart."

The young man in the black shirt stood up, glowering, and addressed Iaselli.

"Could someone explain to me what's happening? If everyone knows where this meeting is happening, then we might as well have gone and held it at the police tribunal! I have no time to waste. Who are these people?"

Marangolo glared at him.

"Young man, I've already introduced myself. And believe me, I'm not someone who goes out and about much, especially not to come to places like this. But just to put matters in a very clear light, I think you should know that I *am* someone who can arrange for you to be dismissed immediately from the rank and position you have been given rather too hastily, Colonel Sansonetti."

Upon hearing himself addressed by name by that complete stranger, and in a low and menacing tone, to boot, the young man sits down again immediately, glowering.

Iaselli was uncertain.

"I beg of you, Marangolo, no names. And no one here is questioning your authority, but . . . "

Paying no mind to the interruption, the duke went on, in a more conciliatory tone.

"All right then. As I've told you, I'm here to make sure a terrible mistake isn't made. And with that aim in mind, I inform you that the charges of homosexuality that you are discussing with reference to the Baron Malomonte are . . . "

The man with the cigar asked Iaselli: "Who is this Baron Malomonte supposed to be? Aren't we talking about this guy, Ricciardi?"

Marangolo cracked a half smile.

"They're the same person, my sincere compliments for the thoroughness of the information you've collected, Your Excellency Rossini."

Iaselli was disconcerted.

"No names, if you please . . . "

The man with the scar turned red in the face and said: "The information is quite complete, Signore. It wasn't divulged in its entirety because that wasn't thought necessary."

Marangolo turned to look at him as if he'd only just become aware of his existence at that moment.

"I don't know who you are, but I can certainly guess. And I take note of the fact that you have redacted the name and the identity of this man who has been so absurdly accused, while the other conjectures—as I have been informed by a very authoritative source, the same source that allowed me to come here—were very carefully constructed. I wonder what the reason for that might be."

The little man slapped his hand down on the papers.

"It's all documented, Signore, all of it. We have a very reliable surveillance system, nothing can elude our notice . . . "

"I know all about your system. I was present when it was created; it's based on informants, not on surveillance. But let's drop that matter. Here is the way matters stand: If I give you my word of honor that Commissario Luigi Alfredo Ricciardi, Baron Malomonte, is innocent of homosexuality, will that be sufficient? Can you take it on trust?"

The little man with the scar protested.

"No, we most certainly don't trust you! Here we have proof: reports, movements, certifications!"

The young colonel, too, though remaining cautious, shook his head.

"It seems to me that the overall situation is quite clear. We cannot leave a pederast in that position of responsibility, as a representative of the state. We're responsible for these matters, after all."

The man with the cigar put in his two cents.

"No, it's not sufficient. I don't want to cast any doubt on your word, Duke, but . . . couldn't you be mistaken? We have . . . proceeded for much less solid evidence, with other subjects."

Iaselli, who had remained standing, seemed extremely uncomfortable.

"You see, Marangolo, here a great many . . . structures are represented. And I can assure you that we do serious, extremely serious work to keep the country clean."

Marangolo seemed unsurprised.

"I imagined that would be your reply. Too bad. Well, in that case, I'm going to have to ask the Contessa Bianca Palmieri di Roccaspina to tell you why she accompanied me here today."

Everyone's attention turned to Bianca, who took a step forward out of the shadows, entering into the cone of light from the lamp that hung from the ceiling.

Ricciardi, who had witnessed the exchange of remarks with growing hope and ever increasing attention, only to be disappointed at the end, noticed a new glow in the contessa's beautiful face. She no longer wore her usual black dress, but a sky-blue dress with buttons up the front and a belted waist that clung to her figure, giving her a profound and unfamiliar new sensuality, accentuated by the high-heeled shoes. The little cloche hat brought out the coppery highlights in her hair. She looked like another woman.

The real difference lay in her expression, thought Ricciardi. On her lightly made-up face there glowed a new confidence.

The commissario had never seen her so aware of her own beauty and the natural elegance that she wore like a crown.

She smiled at Marangolo, who gazed at her in adoration.

Then she said: "*Buongiorno*, Signori. I've come here today to give you a piece of information concerning myself, which I would never have expected to be called upon to make public, but to all appearances, it has now become necessary, unfortunately. Commissario Ricciardi and I have a relationship. A romantic relationship."

She had uttered those words with the utmost calm, as if she were telling them about the last equestrian competition she'd attended. Her tone of voice, warm and deep, betrayed no uncertainties or inner travails.

The first one to snap out of it was the little man with the scar, the only one still left without a name. He shuffled through the papers still in front of him and stammered: "That's not what I see here. Not according to my information. That's impossible, your meetings with Ricciardi only began in the past few days, and . . . "

Marangolo upbraided him.

"It's clear that your famous system, the perfect surveillance network that you boast about, has some defects."

Bianca smiled and turned to Ricciardi, who stood there openmouthed.

"You see, dearest? We were very good at going unnoticed."

The eyes of the little man with the scar narrowed to a pair of slits. He was oozing mistrust from every pore.

"And how long has it been going on, this alleged relationship?"

The woman retorted, unruffled.

"Two years. It's been two years, hasn't it, Luigi Alfredo? I confess that I was tired of all the subterfuge and chicanery, but we couldn't do any differently, until now."

Rossini, who had lit another cigar, seemed almost amused.

"What about the other woman, the one who filed the accusation of homosexuality? The one with whom he was unwilling to . . . "

Bianca gave him an indignant glare.

"I don't think the explanation is especially challenging. Luigi Alfredo knows perfectly well that if I were to learn he had cheated on me, I'd claw his eyes out of his head with both hands."

Ricciardi did his best to think quickly. What Bianca was doing for him constituted a sacrifice of unimaginable proportions. She was giving up the one thing that remained to her, and which was supposed to serve as the foundation for all her hopes of building a future for herself. Why would she be doing this? And most important of all: Could he allow her to do it?

"Bianca," he said, "there's really no need for you to do this. Leave it be."

The contessa turned to look at him, with a supremely sweet smile.

"Luigi Alfredo, thank you so much for worrying about me. But I cannot permit that, in order to protect me, you expose yourself to this terrible injustice."

The young colonel, who still couldn't resign himself to the idea that he'd been wasting his time, decided that this was the time to intervene.

"A contessa, no less. And unless I'm mistaken, a contessa with a husband in prison for murder, am I right? A fine example of the debauched aristocracy of this filthy mess of a city. In any case, the information that you're giving us makes you an adulteress, is that clear to you? Adultery is another shameful aberration we intend to sweep clean."

Marangolo turned pale, as if he'd just been slapped.

"You damned idiot, how dare you speak in these terms to a woman like the contessa? In the first place you ought to know that adultery, according to our legal code, can only be punished if there is a formal complaint on the husband's part, and we are quite certain that he has other matters on his mind at the moment. In any case, I won't allow a buffoon of your caliber to dare to spit out certain insults. Shall I remind you of the circumstances in which your father, no more than three years ago, was found among the other clients at a clandestine brothel during a police raid? As long as we're talking about vices and virtues."

The duke's tirade landed with considerable impact and was followed by the embarrassed silence of those present. The young colonel turned ashen, his eyes blazing with rage. Then he jerked to his feet, overturning his chair, and stormed out, slamming the door behind him.

Rossini giggled once again and spoke to the man with the scar.

"Well, I think we can go now, no? And it also strikes me that you may need to do some work on your intelligence network. I think I'll discuss that with Rome, someone is going to have to pay for the time we wasted today. Have a good day, Duke . . . "

One at a time, all the members of that improvised secret tribunal filed out of the room. The last one to leave was Iaselli, the man with the white hair, who extended his hand to bid Marangolo farewell. The duke declined to shake it.

Once they were alone again, Ricciardi addressed him.

"Marangolo, I don't know how to thank you. It's incredible to be the subject of an accusation and be unable to do anything to prove your innocence."

The man smiled, sadly.

"No, Commissario. It's incredible that anyone should consider something so private and personal to be a crime, something that hurts no one. Love, you know, is love. It doesn't need to find concrete form, any final achievement, to remain itself. It's love and nothing more."

Bianca caressed his arm.

"Carlo Maria, if it hadn't been for you . . . "

The duke waved his hand airily.

"Forget about it. They're a herd of imbeciles and don't deserve the power they've been given. Luckily there are people in Rome who have profound reasons for gratitude toward me, and they don't forget the fact. I need to go now, I think that Iaselli is waiting for me. I'll leave you my car to get back."

He bade them farewell with a smile and left, limping slightly.

LII

As he was riding back to the center of town in the duke's automobile, Ricciardi felt exhausted.

That day truly had been an overwhelming experience; the commissario's thoughts turned to all the people he'd charged with a crime, all the people he'd put behind bars on the basis of conjectures and deductions. He believed himself to be a conscientious policeman and he had never brought unfounded charges just to solve a case successfully; but now that he experienced the immense frustration of being unable to defend himself, he wondered whether he'd ever, albeit unconsciously, played the role of the insensitive jailer or the dull-witted accuser.

Sitting next to him, Bianca kept her eyes on the road, a half smile playing over the face in which there still glowed the light that had practically transfigured her just a short while before, in that dark room where his life had come so dangerously close to being destroyed. Ricciardi couldn't stop looking at her.

"Contessa, I hardly know what to say. You were just . . . Without your help I'd have had no way out and right now I'd be aboard a vessel heading who knows where, without even having had a chance to say goodbye to those who are dear to me. I'll always be grateful."

Bianca locked arms with him, with a faintly coquettish gesture.

"Now that we have a relationship, Baron, well known to those idiots, if no one else, we might also be on a first-name basis, don't you think?"

Ricciardi was bit intimidated.

"Certainly, and thank you for that as well. I don't know if you really understand what you did, or whether it was a momentary impulse. You accused yourself of a crime and endangered your good name and reputation for a stranger. Would you care to explain why?"

The contessa went back to looking out the car window, with a smile.

"As a girl I always wanted to be an actress. Sometimes, with a friend or two, we'd put on performances, just for fun. People like me, born into certain families, can't choose their own path, but I'd have gladly trod the boards. Once, a friend of my father's, a famous actor, begged him to let me try, perhaps under a different name. He told him he'd never seen such unmistakable promise. Today, you gave me a chance to dust off this old love of mine, and I had a rollicking good time. So really it's me who should be thanking you. But did you like me? Was I good?"

There were no more shadows in Ricciardi at this point. He flashed her a smile of pure admiration.

"Good? You were fantastic. I would have believed you myself, if I didn't know the truth. But I would have kept you from doing it. I'm amazed that Marangolo . . . "

Bianca interrupted him.

"Listen, it was Carlo Maria himself who warned me and asked me to take the exact steps that I did. He learned of what was happening from one of his many mysterious friends and came straight to me. He said that this was the only solution, and that there was no time to waste. Just think, he brought me the dress and the hat, as well as the shoes and the pocketbook. By the way: How do I look?"

She assumed a languid pose, like a diva, her gloved hand holding her hat in place. Ricciardi continued the game.

"Those gentlemen are no doubt still wondering why on earth such a lovely woman should be in a relationship with me."

"You're too gallant, Commissario."

"But let me ask you again, do you realize what you've done? Aren't you afraid that there will be consequences?"

Bianca turned serious and fell silent for a while. Then she said: "You know, I thought about Romualdo. About what he did. He confessed to something he'd never done, and in so doing, it's as if he'd changed the hand he'd been dealt; a metaphor that he might appreciate. I know that he's in prison, and that he may never walk out of there alive. But if this was his only chance at cultivating a dream, the dream of a new happiness with a person that he loves, then he did the right thing. I'd tell him myself, if I could, I'd tell him that I understand what he did. A chance at happiness, even if it's through suffering, is worth much more than the certainty of unhappiness. He did the right thing."

Ricciardi decided that what the contessa was saying had the ring of truth. It really was true.

The woman continued.

"And today I did the same thing. Out of gratitude to you, certainly: You chose, without payment and for no good reason, to investigate so that I could have a reason, a motivation for everything that happened. And this motivation became a handle that allowed me to reach out for my new life. That's no small thing. But I'd be a liar if I said I did it only for you. I also did it for myself."

"I don't think I understand."

Bianca turned to look at him. Once again, Ricciardi drowned in those twin lakes of such an impossible color, familiar and alien at the same time.

"You see, a good name, a reputation, a certain seriousness can all become a suffocating cage. But now that people find out I have a relationship—and people will find out, because even though the gentlemen present in that room won't be allowed to tell every detail of what happened, they'll still have the irresistible temptation to let the news get out—I'll no longer be a widow in mourning. And perhaps I'll be able to go back to living my life. A little."

They'd arrived in the area surrounding police headquarters and the chauffeur pulled over to let Ricciardi out.

The commissario took Bianca's hand and bent low to kiss it, without actually touching it.

"Then what can I tell you, Bianca? *Grazie*. From the bottom of my heart, *grazie*. I hope to see you again."

The woman seemed to light up from within.

"Why, of course, you'll see me again. We have a relationship, remember? We're practically engaged, illicitly speaking. You owe me a little attention, Baron Malomonte: perhaps we could even go out together, one of these evenings. Certainly, it would have to be your treat, you know that I'm not wealthy like your lovely Roman girlfriend."

Ricciardi felt a stab of sorrow. He hadn't thought about Livia since he'd made the sorrowful discovery of her accusation. He told himself that perhaps he should arrange to see her, to ask for an explanation. He couldn't bring himself to believe that she had willingly put him in this kind of trouble to avenge herself. And for what, after all? For his decision not to take advantage of her?

He smiled at Bianca and said to her: "It will be a real privilege, Contessa. I need a female friend, you know. Women are a genuine mystery to me, and perhaps you could help me understand a little something more about them."

She fluttered her fingers in farewell.

"Or maybe I could help to muddle your ideas even more. *Ciao*, Commissario. Remember that I expect an invitation from you."

She tapped on the glass separating the driver's compartment. Ricciardi watched as she drove off laughing.

LIII

Enrica returned from her walk at a slow pace, her head bowed, lost in her uncertainties.

She really hadn't needed to go out at all, but at least one advantage had come with Manfred's arrival: now, if she said she needed to go out to do some shopping or be on her own for a while, no one had the nerve to raise an objection. So she had got in the habit of going out in the afternoon and strolling down the main street, plunging herself into the crowd in a cocoon of welcome anonymity.

She didn't do anything special on her walks: she'd look in shopwindows, get an espresso, stop to listen to some street musician playing the violin, accordion, or mandolin. She breathed in the air of her city, observing the housewives hanging sheets from one building to another and calling across the space between; families joined by a clothesline and a pulley, as good a way as any to feel close.

She knew that her mother would be only too glad to go with her on those walks, to fantasize about ceremonies and gigantic additions to the elements of her dowry, but Enrica had become very good at dodging her invitations. She didn't want to engage in that kind of conversation.

She liked Manfred, of that much she was certain. He was handsome, athletic, and well read. The difference in age wasn't a problem at all, in fact, if anything it was a source of attraction, ensuring a bottomless store of stories and memories she could listen to with enjoyment; because the major knew how to cast a spell with his stories.

She felt gratified by the gazes of the other girls when she walked arm in arm with him; she, who had always been alone, who was accustomed to receiving the silent but unmistakable commiseration of her few girlfriends, her sister, and, above all, her mother for the fact that she was still, at her age, unmarried and unengaged, had become deeply envied even by people who met her out on the street.

There were times when she wondered what it was about her that attracted someone like Manfred. She knew that she was intelligent, well above the average of the women who were interested only in home economics; and that she wasn't bad to look at or devoid of elegance. But she wasn't an eye-catcher, at least not like the notorious lady with whom Ricciardi went out nights.

She thought for the umpteenth time about that absurd encounter down by the sea. But then, hadn't everything about her relationship with that man always been absurd? And wasn't the sentiment that she'd cultivated for no good reason, from a distance, in silence and in dreams, every bit as absurd?

Perhaps her thoughts of Ricciardi were the thoughts of a little girl, she told herself. Perhaps he was the dream and Manfred was the reality that waited upon awakening. And after all, he wasn't bad to wake up to, was he? Actually, to be objective, he was even better than the dream.

I just have to work at it a little, she thought as she walked toward the last corner before home. She was good at doing her homework, and she'd always been highly disciplined. If she made a decision, she would be able to stick to it. She just had to make up her mind, and then . . .

Just as she was thinking these thoughts, Ricciardi emerged from the shadows and came to a halt before her. His bangs were plastered to his forehead, as if he'd been sweating, and he was breathing hard. He was very pale, the collar of his shirt was unbuttoned beneath the loosened knot of his tie, his hands were in the pockets of his overcoat.

She stopped, stunned and a little frightened. It was almost dinnertime and there was no one out on the streets. She opened her mouth to talk, but he stopped her.

"No. No. This time, you listen to me. Every time I just stand there and don't know what to say, but now I want you to listen to me. Is that all right? Can I go ahead?"

Enrica didn't know what to say so she just nodded.

"All right, then: Sacrifice. Because if a person cares, or wants to care for someone, then he wants them to be happy, doesn't he? Otherwise, it makes no sense. And if he wants them to be happy, it might even be that he needs to choose to keep his distance. That's natural, isn't it? It's natural. But then a person shouldn't be unhappy, and if a person is unhappy then it stands to reason that the other person will be unhappy, too, so a person wonders: Is it worth it? And a soul might surely be made of glass, but sometimes it will shatter into a thousand pieces. And the hand gets burnt and the moth still won't stay away. Or you might miss the moth, after all."

Enrica looked at him, wide-eyed.

"And in that case, a person ought to resign themselves, and you ought to be relaxed at least. But a person, in fact a person just keeps feeling worse and worse. And it's as if one person in a room were two people, and one of them talks and has a point, and then the other one talks and he's right too. Which is why a person might start to seem crazy, and maybe a person really is. And a person can make all the decisions in this world, but then they're down by the sea and . . . "

His voice broke, as if he were out of breath.

She slowly shook her head, but he stopped her again.

"No. No. Because I don't know what all this sea is even good for. I don't know. But I can try and find out, you know? That's exactly the profession I practice: I find out things. And I'll be able to do it, I'll find out what the sea is good for. I'll do it."

He took a deep breath and, unexpectedly, he smiled. It was the first time Enrica had ever seen him smile, and she decided in a flash that Manfred, with his blond hair and his athletic physique, with his uniform and that exotic allure of his, could never ever be as beautiful, not even half as handsome, as that one smile under those eyes as green as the sea.

Ricciardi nodded at her one last time and said goodbye. Then he turned on his heel and headed for home.

Enrica stood there, wondering what had just happened and whether it had really happened at all, or if it had just been a dream.

Then she thought about the sea.

EPILOGUE

The young man wonders how long he ought to wait before standing up and leaving. The old man stopped playing more than ten minutes ago, leaving the incredible beauty of his music suspended in the air along with the heartbreaking sorrow of the story he has told.

Then the old man set down his instrument and without a word laid his head on the back of the sofa and shut his eyes.

The young man remained motionless, observing the profile as it was slowly swallowed up by the shadows. The aquiline nose, the haggard cheeks. The hairs of his eyebrows, the small, recent scar from a cut on his throat, the whiskers to be shaved by those shaky hands.

The young man wonders how it can be. How can it be that someone capable of transmitting such powerful emotions, splitting his listeners' hearts in two, should decide to stop playing in public. He had asked that same question of the person who'd acted as the intermediary for this meeting, and in reply he'd only received a shrug and a strange smile.

His heart has slowly resumed its normal beat, after the song. Now, yes. Now he understands.

In the minutes he's spent watching the old man breathing regularly, the young man has decided that he wants to learn. That he wants it with every ounce of will in his body, so that he can learn to play and sing like that, even if only just once. It's necessary, because that vague sense of incompleteness that he's felt till now is nothing compared to the certainty that now possesses him.

Just as he's about to get up and leave, the old man begins to speak as if in a dream.

The sacrifice, he says. The renunciation. What you want, and what you ought. But what you can't bring yourself to do. Luckily, you can't bring yourself to do it.

He opens his eyes and turns around.

The poet and the young woman, in the end, got together. Amidst jealousies, sufferings, and terrible quarrels that went down in history, they stayed together for eleven years as lovers and eighteen years as a married couple. Until he died, and she went insane with sorrow. The moth never managed to reach safety after all. The hand hadn't been able to shoo it away.

The young man murmurs: Maestro, thank you. Thank you for this story, thank you for this song.

The old man chuckles and says: It's not mine, the song. And neither is the story. I just told it to you.

He reclines against the backrest and shuts his eyes. The young man gets up and heads for the door. Just as he's about to open it, he hears the old man's voice coming to him out of the darkness, and it's little more than a whisper.

Next time we'll talk about jealousy. Of how it rends your flesh and plunges its fingers into your body.

Of the torment of an ancient love affair.

The old man closes his eyes.

And smiling he begins to dream.

Acknowledgments

Ricciardi's world has many creators; he himself, without the attention of Francesco Pinto and the affection of Aldo Putignano, could never have existed.

The city, the things, and the air around him are all reconstructed and arranged by the gentle and cunning hand of Annamaria Torroncelli. His family and the people that surround him are profoundly familiar to the eyes of Stefania Negro. His investigations, simple and contorted like life itself, spring from conversations with Antonio Formicola. The dead people that he sees in their macabre dance come from the words of Giulio Di Mizio. My infinite thanks go to these people, without whom I'd never be able to imagine my green-eyed commissario.

This story in particular has the aromas of the foods imagined by Sabrina Prisco of the Osteria Canali in Salerno and Giovanni Serritelli, the Cuoco Galante of Naples. It takes into account the criminal procedure reconstructed by Titti Perna. It pierces the victim's throat in accordance with the path defined by Roberto de Giovanni. It unrolls in the accommodating, magical fantasies of Severino Cesari and Francesco Colombo and in the delicate attention of Daniela La Rosa.

But it is born in my heart, it grows without encountering pauses, and ends without ending, accompanied by the sentiment and the smile of she who is its author much more than I am: my sweetest Paola.

NOTE

The verses on pages 18–19, 183–84, and 303–4 are taken from the song *"Palomma 'e notte"* by Salvatore Di Giacomo and Francesco Buongiovanni (1906).

ABOUT THE AUTHOR

Maurizio de Giovanni's Commissario Ricciardi series is a bestselling crime fiction series in Italy and abroad. De Giovanni is also the author of the contemporary Neapolitan thriller, *The Crocodile*, and the new contemporary Neapolitan noir *series, The Bastards of Pizzofalcone.* He lives in Naples with his family.